POPPA'S BOY

Coming of Age in the Great War

By

Stephen L. Harris

THE OAKLEA PRESS

This book is dedicated to my wife, Sue,
who always has my back.

PART ONE

Calliope and the River

Chapter One

Poppa gave me the idea. He was a famous newspaperman for the *Kansas City Times* and later for the *New York Morning Sentinel*, Luther "Rough" Riley, who'd saved Colonel Roosevelt's life down in Cuba during the last war and became a cripple doing it. He was strapping tall, thick through the shoulders—tough as a bull moose, that's for sure. He'd known Jesse James and had fought Geronimo out in the Wild West with General Leonard Wood, and he wore a scar on his cheek to prove it. Later, he was a daring Rough Rider charging up Kettle Hill in '98. That's how Poppa got the nickname "Rough." A Spaniard shot off his kneecap, sending him to the sidelines a bitter man.

He wanted a son tough as he was so he could relive those glory days. To make certain, he called me "Bucky" after his Rough Rider pal, the Arizona lawman Bucky O'Neill. What he got instead was a Momma's Boy. He told me so more than once. So much so, it got so that I believed him. He never liked it that Momma called me Luther, my Christian name—never Bucky like he wanted or even Lute. He'd shake his head every time he'd see me hanging around with Momma and my sisters, doing women's work. I'd catch him out of the corner of my eye, his jaw clenched tight as a vise, the muscles outlined like a taut rope, and his tomahawk scar a seething red, and I'd know right off he figured I ought to be out rough-housing with the boys. He'd shake his head and, thirsting for a shot of Irish whiskey, and using his gold-knobbed cane, given to him by Colonel Roosevelt himself, he'd hobble into his study—a sacred place that I hadn't been invited into since I turned thirteen and failed to become the man he wanted.

But that's not what drove him out of the house, his despair that I was a Momma's Boy. It was the war. Plain and simple. For two years he begged the *Morning Sentinel*, his beloved newspaper, to give him a chance to cover the fighting in Europe. But Bull Dog Turner, the managing editor, turned him down time and time again, heartlessly telling him that he was too crippled to be tramping around battlefields, that he'd never rehire him unless he settled for a desk job. Instead, ol' Bull Dog assigned a known horse's ass, so Poppa said, name of Henry Davis Waddell, to go to France as the paper's top war correspondent. Poppa stewed and stewed, and every time he read an account of the fighting in the *Morning Sentinel* by that horse's ass, Henry Davis Waddell, he'd clump around the house on his busted knee, ornery as a trapped hornet, cussing up a storm, making Momma and me and my sisters worry that he'd lost his mind. That was until America got into the fight and word reached him up here in Vermont that Roosevelt planned to raise his own volunteer army with himself as general so he could lead the first American troops into battle. It didn't take Poppa more than a second to light out for Oyster Bay and the Colonel's home on Sagamore Hill. Momma just sighed and wondered why it had taken him so long. I even think she was glad, in her way, that he'd be gone for a spell, get the damn war out of his system, and thereby bring peace back to our home.

That's when I got the idea. I'd light out, too. Join the army and fight the Hun—even if I was a few months shy of my sixteenth birthday.

We were living in Burlington then, a seaport on Lake Champlain, except the lake wasn't really a sea like the Mediterranean Sea or some other big body of water. Even so, it was big enough for me—a mile across with the Adirondacks poking up on the other side, vast and proud. The English writer, Rudyard Kipling, who'd lived in Vermont for a few years, described our sunsets as the most beautiful he'd ever seen—with the exception of some spot in India he liked better. In case you've never been there, Burlington slopes down from a long hill to the waterfront. It's a busy waterfront, handling all sorts of goods—mostly fresh-cut trees shipped down from the Canadian forests and stripped into lumber along with slabs of granite and marble chiseled from the quarries around Barre and Proctor. Much of the lumber, granite and marble are sent on barges and towboats through the Champlain Canal to the Hudson River and on to Albany and New York City, and then on to faraway places.

The waterfront drew me down there on sultry summer days to mingle amongst the barges and towboats, tugs and other vessels and to listen to the bargemen swear up a storm in their French and Irish accents. I'd gawk at their exotic tattoos and wonder where they'd gotten them. Maybe on an isle somewhere, far off and romantic, cavorting with cannibals and lush native women. Some of the tough city boys got day jobs as dock wallopers, loading and unloading the vessels or, best yet, daring to hire on as deckhands. They'd ride the barges and towboats down through the Champlain Canal, hop off at Fort Edward or Waterford and then work their way back on another barge, making a fistful of dollars and having the adventure of their lives. I never had the courage to do it. Besides, Momma'd have a fit.

A week after Poppa lit out for Sagamore Hill I tried to enlist in the National Guard. I was turned down because of my age. But I had one last chance. Another of Poppa's friends from the Spanish War, Colonel Joseph Dickman, commanded a cavalry regiment out at Fort Ethan Allen, a few miles outside of Burlington. Because he'd been to our house several times to reminisce with Poppa and gaze at Momma, I figured I had a chance to be a real soldier. So I hopped on the electric trolley and rode it out to the fort to see Colonel Dickman.

As the trolley rattled along, I played over in my mind the confrontation I'd had at dinner the night before with Momma and my sisters. My sisters are older and nag me as much as Momma does. We were sitting around the dining room table, all of us—except Poppa's place, empty as his church pew every Sunday morning.

"I'm going to enlist in the army," I proclaimed.

Louisa, who at sixteen is next to me in age, which made us close, like best friends and mortal enemies all at the same time, snorted a mouthful of peas across the table. One pea actually flew out her nose and landed in the sugar bowl. We all howled and that took some of the edge of my announcement. Louisa was the only one in the family, besides Poppa, who called me Bucky. Her hair's as dark as Poppa's and she wears it up in a bun most of the time. But I like it best when she lets it fall down past her shoulders in waves. For more than a year now boys have crowded the front porch, knocking on the door at all times, trying to get her out on a date. I wonder what they would've thought had they seen that pea pop out her nose like a green bee bee. I couldn't help but laugh again, and then we all laughed once more, and Louisa's face turned red. Even so, she was laughing as hard as the rest of us.

"You can't enlist, you're too young," said Clara. The eldest, she's twenty and engaged to Claude Foshay, a professor of agriculture up the hill at the University of Vermont. She's the practical one because she's so old. Claude is the right man for her, I think. He's twenty-seven and acts like an old man, as far as I can figure. Clara's got Momma's hair, like me, the shade of walnut. "Besides," she added, "you've never shot a rifle in your life. And if you ever did, the kick would knock you clear across the lake."

"I fired a shotgun once," I said, and puffed myself up. "With Poppa at Uncle Will's farm. I put a hundred holes in a pail of water and the water leaked all over the place."

"A pail of water is not a human being, Luther, and you should never shoot another human being," Momma said. "It's against God's will." She said that a lot. *Against God's will.* It was her way of putting the fear of God in me so I'd do right.

"But the Huns are monsters," I argued. "They cut off the hands of Belgium babies and lock up women in cages for later torture. I read that in the *Gazette.* I'd shoot them as easy as pie."

"They'll shoot back," said Anna, my third sister. She's between Louisa and Clara in age; eighteen and just as pretty as Louisa with the same dark hair, and with just the same number of boys banging on the door all hours of the day. "And then you'll find out quick enough that shooting them wouldn't be as easy as pie. And besides, I don't think you could ever shoot a German. Why, that'd be like shooting Old Man Hofmann, our grocer over on Pine Street. He's German. His wife is, too. You wouldn't want to make Mrs. Hofmann a widow now, would you?"

Old Man Hofmann was a kindly man if ever there was one. Anna's right. I couldn't imagine shooting him.

Momma said, "Luther, you get that silly notion out of your head. You're not joining the army, and that's final. One man gone from this house because of that damn war is enough."

That was a strong word from Momma. Not one God would've used, I think. Yet she never said I was too young. Just that I couldn't go. So I figured I'd go anyway.

The electric trolley had been specially built to connect Fort Ethan Allen, headquarters of the First Regiment, to Burlington. The fort had been around since 1894 and once had been home to the Tenth Cavalry, the colored Buffalo Soldiers who'd fought alongside Colonel Roosevelt's Rough Riders in Cuba. Now and then Poppa'd go out to the fort and see some of the Buffalo soldiers he'd gotten to know after suffering that terrible wound. He'd take me once in a blue moon. They were the only colored people I'd ever seen. Then they got transferred and Poppa never went near the fort again.

The fort was beautiful, with tall, airy brick houses for the officers and spacious barracks for the enlisted men. When I got there, I was startled to see tents pitched all over the place, wherein lived the latest recruits who were getting ready for war. Soldiers were marching around, already in training. From across the parade ground I could hear the drill sergeants barking out orders.

Colonel Dickman's office was close to the main gate, among a stretch of buildings known as "Officers Row." I presented myself to his clerk. I told him I was Rough Riley's son and wanted to see the Colonel, an old friend of my Poppa's. That bit of personal information got me right in to see the Colonel. Squatting behind a heavy wooden desk stacked with reports, Dickman didn't look to me like what an officer of his rank ought to look like in this desperate time of war. He was rather flabby—from his face to his potbelly and when he got to his feet, to his baggy thighs. He had jowly cheeks and a droopy old mustache and glasses. More of a bookworm than a fighting man. He smelled of fried bacon and coffee. He must have just finished breakfast. A tin cup sat on his desk, and I saw several papers stained with brown rings of coffee. An unlit cigar straddled the edge of an ashtray that'd been cut out of an artillery shell. On the wall behind him was a map of Europe, Russia, northern Africa and the Middle East. Pushpins dotted the map, each one showing the progress on all fronts of the Great War.

He nodded for me to take a seat. I knew he was being friendly only because of Poppa.

"How's your father?"

"He's off to join the army that President Roosevelt's raisin'. He left a few weeks ago for Oyster Bay, Long Island, New York." I said, trying to make it sound important.

"With that knee of his?" He seemed to ponder this fact for a moment. "How's your Mother then?"

"She's fine. I think she's relieved that Poppa's doing something besides moping around the house."

Dickman smiled knowingly. He sat down, took some time putting a match flame to the unlit cigar and, once it caught, blew smoke toward the tin-plated ceiling with a slight snap of his head and asked, "Now what can I do for you, Bucky Riley?"

"Let me enlist in your cavalry, Colonel Dickman, Sir!"

A second cloud of smoke swirled toward the ceiling. "Have you got your Mother's blessing?"

"Momma said she doesn't want me in the army. But I think that's true of every Momma, isn't it Colonel Dickman? They don't want their sons going off to war, but once the boys enlist they're proud as punch. I wanna fight the Hun like my Poppa and make him and Momma proud."

"I guess it'd make your parents proud, alright. But you're too young, not yet sixteen. Hell, I'm trying to discourage seventeen- and eighteen-year olds from joining because I know what it'll be like over in France. There's no glory for the dead, Bucky. None. And here at home there's going to be too many broken-hearted Mothers. I don't want to see your Mother broken hearted. I like her too much for that."

"I'm big for my age," I countered. "Strong, too, like Poppa. I know I can fight."

He sucked on his cigar and let the smoke out slowly between yellowed teeth. "I know you'd like to be like your old man, live a fairy-tale life of adventure and maybe save some future President's life. Yet you're still a boy and the answer's no!"

I needed to change the subject then, and so I asked, "Were you there when Poppa saved Roosevelt's life? I wonder sometimes if it really happened."

"I was there. Roosevelt was a foolhardy character, but his men loved him. He was riding his horse, Little Texas, the only Rough Rider who had a horse, as I recall. I remember his silly store-bought uniform, funny hat and blue neckerchief and how he rode Little Texas up the hill with bullets flying and his men storming behind him. Rough Riders were getting shot all around him like fish in a rain barrel, and when a slug tore through Bucky O'Neill's brain your father leaped up on Little Texas like a mad man. He tried like hell to protect Roosevelt by throwing him off that damned horse. That's when he got shot. If he hadn't been in front of Roosevelt the bullet that got him would've killed the President sure as I'm sitting here. Your Father stayed on the horse with Roosevelt screaming for him to get off. They rode on up Kettle

Hill until your Father slid from Little Texas to the ground, doubled over in dreadful pain, holding what was left of his bloody knee. Roosevelt continued up the hill and damned if he didn't charge right into history."

Colonel Dickman looked at me queerly. I guess to see if I believed him. Then he stubbed out his cigar, mashed it into the cut-down artillery shell and said, "That's the truth, Bucky. And my answer's still no. Go home to you Mother now and be a good boy."

It was a discouraging ride back to Burlington aboard the half-empty electric trolley, creaking and groaning along like some over-worked beast of burden. Any chance of enlisting in the army had been dashed. I stared out of the dirt-streaked window and off in the east I saw the long, crouching shape of Mount Mansfield, a thick forest covering her steep slopes with a lacy canopy of green. For some reason, maybe it was while I was looking up at Mount Mansfield in all her springtime glory, but at that moment I knew I still had a chance to go to war. I'd run off like Poppa. I'd go down to Oyster Bay and be a soldier in Colonel Roosevelt's army. He'd have to take me. I felt it in my heart of hearts. I'd be fighting right next to Poppa. We'd be Rough Riders together. I smiled as high and wide as that grand old mountain.

Chapter Two

The best time to run away is in the middle of the night. Nobody knows you're gone until breakfast when you don't show up, and by then you've got a good head start. I'd slip away at two in the morning—that's what I decided. But first I needed to figure out how I would get from Burlington to Oyster Bay without Momma knowing. Heck, I didn't even know where Oyster Bay was except on Long Island somewhere and I hardly knew where that was. I had to rummage through an old atlas to find the exact location. I found it easy, a tiny inlet on Long island's north shore. Then I struck upon an idea. I'd take a towboat or a barge all the way to New York City. I'd work my way down as a deckhand. So for the next few weeks I hung around the pier at the end of Main Street like a water rat, making it known I was looking for a deckhand's job. I watched how the deckhands worked and picked up a few tricks of the trade. I worked as a dock walloper for the first time, unloading canal boats, barges and towboats down from Canada—anything afloat. Although it was hard work, I kept an eagle eye out for a vessel bound for Manhattan. Then I found *The Frank White.*

She was a steam-driven, wooden towboat that'd seen better days. She pulled all kinds of goods, from apples to lumber to slabs of marble and granite. Now and then she carried a passenger or two for the long haul down the Hudson. There was a small pilothouse and a snug cabin next to it where the captain slept and below there was a cramped engine room, an equally cramped galley—even though the towboat didn't have a cook because everyone had KP duty—and three tight cabins with narrow bunks. A one-armed captain owned her. For a crew he had an engineer and fireman and, when he could afford it, a deckhand to handle odd jobs, tie up the towboat at each stop and keep her scrubbed at all times. *The Frank White* was being loaded when I got enough nerve to approach the captain.

Captain Chauncey Cobb, missing his left arm, had a gob of tobacco ready to spit on the ground when I closed in on him during the middle of the day. Poppa thought tobacco chewers to be men of mean spirit, yet he tolerated them. So I took my chance. Captain Cobb was watching the barge he'd be towing down the river as it filled up. He was a man of about fifty, I reckoned, of slight build and taller by a couple of inches than myself with thin, gray hair parted down the middle. He was dressed in dungarees and had on a red and blue flannel shirt with the right sleeve rolled up to a bony elbow while the empty sleeve had been folded once, the cuff pinned to the shoulder. He had a hard face. His discolored nose had a purplish hue to it and obviously it'd been broken at one time for it slanted to the left and gave his face a lopsided look. A crooked scar ran between his eyes up to his hairline. The eyes, gray as they were, seemed filled with good-natured mischief. Working his tongue around another gob of tobacco, I heard him humming some sea chantey like a pirate. When I stopped in front of him, he let go with a stream of tobacco juice that splattered on the planks of the dock between my feet. Poppa would've knocked him off the dock for such rudeness.

"In the way, Boy," Captain Cobb said, his voice gruff.

I stepped back a few paces. With my heart pounding, I said, "Captain Cobb I know you're looking to hire a deckhand and I want the job."

"Want the job? Or need the job?" He didn't look at me. Instead he shouted at someone on the barge. "Be careful with that, Stubby!"

I looked over and there was a stub of man, about five feet tall, if that, deftly guiding sheets of granite, wrapped in rope netting, onto the barge. The barge was lashed to the stern of *The Frank White* by three thick wire cables. He made sure the granite landed gently, slipped off the rope netting and waved it away.

"Well?" Captain Cobb said. "Wanna job? Need a job. How far ya goin'? Whitehall? Fort Edward? Waterford?" He still hadn't cast an eye my way.

"New York City, Sir."

Now he looked at me. "Long haul, by gum. You think bein' a deckhand you kin beat outa payin' me what I charge my regular passengers for such a trip?"

"No Sir. It's just I don't have much money and I gotta get to New York."

"What's so important that you gotta get down to Gotham?"

"Gotham?"

"New York City, by gum."

"I'm joining President Roosevelt's army."

"Roosevelt's army?" He eyed me more thoroughly, spat and said, "The old coot's got an army?"

"Yes Sir. Well, I think he's trying to raise one."

"Kinda young, ain't you, to go trottin' off to fight the Germans?" Then he laughed. "Whattaya gonna do? Walk up to Roosevelt hisself and offer yer services? He ain't easy to see."

"I know, Sir. But he and my Poppa are friends. Poppa's down there right now with Mr. Roosevelt, becoming a part of his army."

"Yer sayin' yer old man knows the President?"

"Poppa saved his life in the last war."

"That a fact?" he turned toward the barge. "Hey, Stubby, git up here. I wantcha to hear this."

Stubby came limping up and stood by us. He was shorter than any man I'd ever seen, except for midgets in the Sells-Floto Circus that came to Burlington once a year. He was no midget, though. He looked the same age as the Captain, about fifty. Like the Captain, he wore dungarees, but they were blotchy with coal dust. He had on a ragged, soot-stained sleeveless shirt. It showed off the sharp muscles and fancy tattoos on both forearms—one of them with the words "Remember the Maine." Stubby had a handsome, but leathery face of cracked skin, like one of Poppa's old cowboy boots, and he had a ready smile.

"Tell us how yer old man saved President Roosevelt's life," Captain Cobb ordered. He winked at Stubby. Stubby glanced up at me.

"I don't rightly know, except what I've been told," I said, the words stumbling out of my mouth. "It happened when the President charged up a hill in Cuba with his Rough Riders. Poppa was a Rough Rider. He jumped in front of the President and got shot. The bullet was meant for Mr. Roosevelt. That's what saved him, my Poppa getting in the way."

"What's yer Poppa's name?" Captain Cobb asked.

"Luther Riley, same as mine," I said. "But he's called Rough Riley, I guess because he was a Rough Rider.

"Stubby was in that war, down in Havana aboard the Maine when she blew," the Captain said. "He fell fifty feet onto a steel deck and his legs got all scrunched up like an accordion. That's what made him so short. Stubby, you ever hear of a Rough Rider name of Rough Riley?"

"I recollect hearin' about some cowboy savin' Roosevelt's hide," Stubby said.

"So this Riley character's yer old man, by gum?" said the Captain.

"He is, Sir," I said.

More tobacco juice sailed out of Captain Cobb's mouth. He wiped his lips with the back of his gnarly hand and studied me awhile, gray eyes squinting.

"Any opinion, Stubby?" he said at last.

"Well, he looks strong enough." Stubby pointed to his mouth with a finger missing its nail, just a round knob, and then turned and limped back to loading the barge cabled to *The Frank White*.

"Can you carry a tune?" the Captain asked me.

"I guess so," I said, wondering why a deckhand had to carry a tune.

"Then Stubby and me'll take you down river. Stubby's my engineer, been with me close to twenty years, in the Navy, on the high seas and such. It's like we're partners. We're the last of a dying breed, by gum. The damn railroads are killing off our way of life. Look yonder at all them canal boats and barges abandoned in this two-bit harbor. It's like that all the way to New York. Nuthin' but rotting boats." He spat for emphasis. For the first time I noticed the empty vessels like strange sea creatures half-submerged in the water. The Captain tapped me on the arm. "We'll pay you a dollar a day and feed you, too. Yer job'll be an easy one. Tie up our towboat at all docks and locks we come to and untie us when we cast off. Give us a hand loadin' and unloadin'. Fill the coal bunkers. Dump coal ash in the water. Swab out the galley. And they'll be some other errands to run. Like feed my three-legged cat, Tripod. A rat had chewed off the front leg a few years back. Me and Tripod are not jest shipmates," he said, tapping the empty sleeve where his arm ought to have been. "We're soul mates, see. We'll be leavin' at about six in the mornin', at first light. Now you better get yer gear, Rough Riley Junior, including dungarees, if you got 'em. Don't forgit to kiss yer old lady good-bye and git back here no later than five. We gotta tow this barge down to Waterford and then head to Gotham for another load to bring back here."

"Yes, Sir." My legs trembled with excitement.

"Call me Cap'n, you hear. Never Sir. And never Chauncey. Yes, Sir. I mean, Cap'n."

"Now how are you to be called?"

"Bucky, Cap'n!" And then I dashed for home!

I was so excited I started to pack everything. After shutting and locking my bedroom door, I spread all my underwear and socks and shoes on my bed, shirts and pants, toothbrush, hairbrush, soap and towels. Soon I had too much stuff. I couldn't carry it all. Not even half of it. Then I figured as a soldier I'd get a uniform and all sorts of army gear and so that meant I wouldn't need much of my own stuff. I became prudent and packed a couple of changes of clothes, a toothbrush and an extra pair of shoes. And that was it. Because I didn't have a suitcase, I rolled them up in a pillowcase. I shoved the pillowcase under my bed, opened the door and there was Louisa, hands on her hips.

"You're up to no good," she declared, scaring me half to death. "I can tell."

"Am not," I said.

I glanced toward my bed, praying she'd not see the pillowcase sticking part way out.

"You're hiding something," Louisa said. "What are you hiding?"

"Nuthin'."

"*Nuthin'*, my eye."

Before I knew it she'd brushed past me, knelt down and looked under the bed. She pulled out the stuffed pillowcase. Her dark eyes flashed in triumph. "See, you are up to no good."

"No I am not! Now get outta my room!"

"Not 'til I see what you're hiding." She turned the pillowcase upside down and my clothes, shoes and toothbrush tumbled out. Louisa stared at the stuff. "You're running away, aren't you?"

"No, I am not."

"Why, you're going after Poppa! I knew you'd try it the other night at dinner when you said you wanted to enlist in the army and shoot Germans. That's why I laughed so hard—the notion of you in a soldier's uniform is darn right silly."

The words froze me like a block of ice. If she told Momma, I'd be sunk. There'd be no running away, no adventuring with President Roosevelt and his army of Rough Riders—and no fighting alongside Poppa.

"You aren't gonna tell Momma, are you? You just can't!"

"Maybe I will. Maybe I won't."

"I just gotta go! I'll die if I stay here with Poppa gone. He'll take care of me once I find him. You know he will."

Louisa put my stuff back in the pillowcase. First the shoes, then the clothes and last the toothbrush. "Don't you think you'll need a hairbrush?" she said. "How are you going to comb your hair? And what about a sweater? It gets cold on the lake."

"You won't tell Momma then?

I saw her eyes sparkle again, as always when she had the upper hand, and I knew then that she wouldn't say a word. "But how are you getting to Oyster Bay?"

"I've been hired to work on a towboat going down the Hudson River. It's leavin' at six in the morning. First light, the Cap'n said. He's got only one arm."

"Oh," she said. That bit of information stopped her for a moment.

"I must be there by five."

She reached her hands toward mine, squeezing them gently. "Oh, Bucky, it'll be so dull around here if you go."

"Aw, you got them boys hanging around like puppies wagging their tails," I answered. "They can't all be dull."

She laughed. "I'm afraid for you. It's such a long way to New York City and anything can happen."

"I said I have a job," I reassured her. "I'm to be a deckhand with a captain and mate and fireman on board. My trip will be as easy as pie."

"As easy as shooting Germans, huh?"

"I'll be okay. I promise."

She squeezed my hands again. "Come with me to Poppa's study. I must show you something there."

"But we aren't supposed to go in there unless he invites us!"

"I've been in there plenty of times. Poppa never found out. He's got lots of fabulous things. One of them is an autobiography or something. That's what I want to show you."

Louisa led me down the hall, down the stairs on our tiptoes, through the living room and past the kitchen where Momma was making dinner to the door of Poppa's study. I could count the number of times I'd been inside on one hand, mostly to be scolded. We opened the door and stole in. A dark place it was—mahogany paneled, smelling of cigar and pipe smoke, shelves crammed with books and things, two rifles and a pistol on the wall behind Poppa's desk—mementoes of times past. Louisa turned on a lamp and then motioned for me to close the door. In the dim light I saw dozens of photographs that hung aslant on the walls. I'd seen them all before, but when I looked at them this time they were different. Maybe because I was about to head off on my own great adventure, I now felt part of each photograph. That was *me* in those photographs, not Poppa. One showed the Rough Riders bunched atop a hill with the Colonel standing in the middle, hands on his hips and Old Glory waving in the background. Every Rough Rider had on a wide-brimmed campaign hat. Missing from the photograph was Bucky O'Neill, shot dead only minutes earlier. I looked for Poppa. He was stretched out on a litter in front of the group, his right leg completely bandaged. At that moment it was *my* face shaded under the campaign hat, not his. There was a portrait of Roosevelt in his uniform wearing the hat that Colonel Dickman had called silly, cross sabers pinned on its upturned brim. Pince-nez glasses were balanced on the bridge of his nose. For the first time I saw that he'd autographed the portrait. I got up close to read it. "With grateful thanks to Luther Riley, Theodore Roosevelt." There were photographs of other famous people and Indians, too, and even though I'd seen them all before I had no idea who they were. But one of the Indians had the coldest eyes I'd ever seen. I lingered over his photograph. I'd seen the photograph before in magazines, and knew it was Geronimo.

Louisa, meanwhile, opened a drawer in Poppa's desk. She lifted out a bundle of bound papers. "Here it is," she said, her voice barely above a whisper. "Poppa's story. She placed it in my hands. The first page just had the title typed on it.

INK-STAINED WRETCH
MY LIFE AND TIMES AMONG AMERICA'S
GREAT HEROES, GOOD AND BAD
THE AUTOBIOGRAPHY OF LUTHER "ROUGH" RILEY

"When you come back from the war you have to read this. I have. It's dynamite."

I glanced at the first page.

CHAPTER ONE: I MEET JESSE JAMES

I was born on a hill farm in southwest Missouri in 1863, the youngest of four children and the only one to survive. The others all died before their fifth year, two sisters and a brother. After their deaths, my broken-hearted parents, Jacob and Rebecca Riley, traveled by wagon from the mountains of North Carolina to the tail end of the Ozarks. It was 1856, the year the abolitionist John Brown was riling up Kansas and neighboring Missouri by killing anyone who favored slavery.

Jesse James? Poppa never told me he'd met Jesse James. Before I could read more, Louisa placed it back in the desk drawer. "You can read it when you come home from the war," she said." We then slipped out of the study. She sashayed into the kitchen to help out.

Later, throughout our dinner, Louisa and I exchanged secretive glances. We were so quiet that Momma and the others probably wondered if we were up to no good. We were, of course, but if they'd only known.

I went to my room early and knelt by the open window, my arms folded on the sill, my chin on my arms and my gaze toward the lights of downtown Burlington. I trembled thinking of what I was about to do. The hours dragged on. A slight breeze brushed against my face. Every hour church bells tolled and now and then a horn sounded somewhere out on the lake, lonesome and forlorn. Night crept in and sometime past midnight I fell asleep against the windowsill.

A little after four I felt a tug on my arm. Louisa had come to see me off. If she hadn't I'd have slept straight through until daylight and missed my boat ride down the Hudson.

"You're asleep," she whispered.

I awoke with a start, cracking my head against the open window. Before I could yelp "ouch!" she pushed her hand against my mouth, shushing me.

"It's time," she said. She kissed my cheek. "Oh, Bucky, be safe and write often. And take care of Poppa."

She handed me the pillowcase. I climbed out the window onto the roof of our back porch. I poked my head back inside and Louisa threw her arms around my neck.

"When you find Poppa, tell him I love him and miss him," she whispered. "But you take care of him, too. He's not as robust as he thinks. Oh, Bucky, good-bye. Good-bye!"

"Good-bye," I whispered back, and felt my eyes watering.

We didn't want to let go, but we did. Her fingers slid down my arm and then she gave my hand one last squeeze. With a shudder of sadness, she watched me crawl across the roof and swing down to the backyard. There was no moon, just the big, old starry sky. On the ground it was pitch black and cold. I turned up the collar of my jacket and slung the pillowcase over my shoulder and loped downtown like a fugitive on the run. I looked up once and saw Louisa still at the window. I wondered if I'd ever see her again. And then my feet struck the concrete of the city sidewalk and I was on my way to the waterfront and the unknown.

Chapter Three

In the wee hours of the morning, Burlington's waterfront seemed bathed in secrecy. Maybe it was because I came down the hill through a city fast asleep and saw the arc lights for the first time casting an orange glow, like a huge halo, through the darkness to illuminate the vessels moored along the docks. The arc lights created spooky shadows and made the men at work look furtive in their movements—like pirates preparing to sail off into the utter blackness of the lake. I found *The Frank White* and the wooden barge it was to tow loaded with lumber and granite. I didn't see Cap'n Cobb and his crew. Except for a tall man with a derby hat and black cloak draped over his shoulders, pacing up and down the pier in a way that made my back crawl, there was no one paying attention to *The Frank White*. Shadows flickering inside the pilothouse told me the crew was there. I hurried past the pacing man and, feeling like an old sea dog and my heart racing, jumped onto the deck. I rapped on the pilothouse door. Stubby thrust his head out. A blackened pipe jutted from his mouth. Smoke drifted about his face.

"Ah, the Rough Rider's son," he said. "Come on in."

Stubby stepped aside and I entered, immediately shedding my sea-dog persona. The Cap'n leaned against the wheel, a crooked smile on his face, his busted nose purple in the muted light of a kerosene lamp and his empty sleeve pinned to his shoulder. Standing next to him was a giant of man, black as the night outside. The only colored men I'd ever seen were the Buffalo soldiers of the Tenth Cavalry before they rode out of Fort Ethan Allen. His presence there in the pilothouse startled me. I couldn't see well enough in the dark, but I could make out a bulging neck and shoulders as big as a Vermont ox. Like Stubby he chewed on a pipe. Curled up on the floor, washing its face with its only front paw was a three-legged calico cat.

"The first thing you need to know, Bucky," said the Cap'n without introducing me to the big man, "don't go jumpin' onto a ship without askin' the Cap'n for permission to come aboard." He beckoned toward the window. "See that fella out there? He's a payin' passenger, goin' all the way to West Point. He ain't asked permission yet, and he ain't getting' on board 'till I'm good and ready." With one hand he deftly cut off a plug of tobacco with a folding knife. Before sticking the plug into his mouth he said, "This here is Thornwhistle, our fireman for many a year. He goes by Thorny. He'll be down in the engine room with Stubby most times. He'll need you to lower coal down to him and haul up the ashes." He worked the plug around inside his mouth. "Now, did you kiss yer old lady good-bye like I asked you? Or did you run off in the still of the night?"

"I run off, Cap'n," I confessed.

"All sailors worth their salt run off to sea," he shot back. "Tis a shame this lake ain't the sea. But it's the best bucket of water we got. Let's drop below and fry up some eggs and feed old Tripod." His gray eyes took in my pillowcase and he smiled. "After we eat, Stubby I'll show you where to stow yer gear."

Outside, the man in the derby hat and cloak continued to pace. The Cap'n cast an odd look his way before leading us down a narrow, dark, unlit stairway to the galley. Stubby and Thorny bounced down behind me, with Stubby whistling some Irish tune.

I felt caught up in some wonderful adventure—afraid maybe it was only a dream and soon enough I'd awake back at the house and my tedious life there.

The galley wasn't much with four of us packed inside. A single lamp was its only light, although it had two windows like gun slits in a wilderness cabin. I saw a long bench with six wooden chairs around it, a wood sink with a water pump, an icebox with its top used as a cutting board, and a coal-fired stove, already lit, that generated plenty of warmth and next to it a bin full of coal. Several shelves had been hitched to the wall. Lined up on each shelf were tins filled with salt, pepper, sugar and other spices. A sack of potatoes and a sack of flour were on the floor next to the stove. Over the stove, cooking utensils hung from a low beam. A skillet, three pots of different sizes and some large knives, forks and spoons. On one of the stove's burners sat a dented coffee pot. The Cap'n reached for the coffee pot.

"You said you could sing," he said. "Can you cook? Stubby and Thorny usually do the cookin' fer us, but I'm durn tired of their recipes."

"I can," I said, glad now that I'd spent time in Momma's kitchen and could be useful.

"By gum, then, fry us a passel of eggs." He poured himself a mug of coffee and handed the pot to Thorny. Nodding toward the icebox, he said, "There's a dozen eggs in there. Fry every one of 'em. I believe we're all starving."

While fishing out the eggs, I made a mental note of what else was in the icebox. Mostly bacon and dozens of more eggs, steak, salt pork and some chicken parts and a wheel of cheddar cheese, all crammed in among blocks of ice. I got out twelve eggs on top of the icebox and some bacon and reached for the skillet. Cap'n Cobb, Stubby, Thorny and Tripod, who'd jumped up on the bench, watched my every move like a panel of judges. I cracked open the eggs and fried the whole lot along with slabs of bacon, and afterward knew I'd passed my first test.

The Cap'n poured a second mug of coffee and set it by my plate. "I don't know if you drink this bilge, but it's time you started." He saw me wince at my first sip, the taste too bitter for me. "You'll be likin' it by the time we git to New York harbor."

When we'd finished, he ordered me to feed some chicken parts to Tripod and then clean up, stoke the stove, stow my pillowcase, and he'd see me in the pilothouse. Turning to Stubby and Thorny, he said, "Looks like we finally got us a cook—if all we'll be eatin' is bacon and eggs." He snapped open a gold pocket watch. "Five-thirty. I better check on Mr. Van Pelt. He's been waitin' to git on board long enough. Stubby, show our new deckhand his posh quarters."

Beyond the galley was a passageway, I guess you'd call it that, unlit and hardly wide enough to get through. Off the passageway were three cabins, closets more like it, each big enough to turn around in. While he took me to the furthermost cabin, Stubby said that the first was his, the second Thorny's and that the Cap'n slept in the cabin off the wheelhouse. Tripod slept wherever she had a mind to. The last cabin had two bunks wedged into it, one atop the other. A darkened lamp dangled from a beam.

"Mind your noggin," Stubby warned, "the overhead's mighty low."

I looked up. My head barely cleared the ceiling. The beams were the real obstacles and if I weren't careful I'd crack my head on them.

"You'll be taking the upper bank. Van Pelt's paying for the lower one. I guess you and he'll become good friends on this voyage or git to where you'd like to kill each other. One or the other, that's for sure. Toss your gear up on the bunk and let's get to work."

Mr. Van pelt had entered the pilothouse by the time we got there. He and the Cap'n were jawing at each other.

"Let's go in and meet this Mister Van Pelt," Stubby said, with emphasis on the Mister. I didn't think we ought to interrupt their conversation, but we went in anyway, first Stubby, then me. Mr. Van Pelt turned around. Because of his height and the pilothouse's low ceiling, he had taken off his derby hat. I took him to be about forty, a man of light-colored hair, parted in the middle and slicked down. He had watery blue eyes that gave off an aura of boredom. A magnificent mustache covered his upper lip, drooping down on each side ever so slightly before its tapered waxed ends twirled upward in grandiloquent flourishes. I'd never seen such an elegant face in my life. It had a cold look, though, like those villains in the Saturday matinee flickers. He shot us an amused smile. There was not a glint of welcome to it. I felt my back crawling again.

"Mr. Van Pelt," said the Cap'n. "This is our engineer, Stubby O'Hara, formerly of the U.S.S. Maine and, along with yours truly, late of President Roosevelt's Great White Fleet that sailed around the globe in Aught Eight." Stubby stuck out his hand. Mr. Van Pelt recast his cold, high-handed look and waited a moment too long before he clasped Stubby's hand. "Stubby, this is Mr. Dalton Van Pelt, a Wall Street banker and a director of the Edison Electric Company. He's on his way home to Garrison. We'll drop him off at West Point. Now when we git to Whitehall we'll be pickin' up his daughter, Calliope, who's waitin' there with a sheriff name of Roscoe Lynch." There was an edge to the Cap'n's voice when he said Lynch's name.

Mr. Van Pelt and Stubby finished shaking hands, although it seemed to me neither got satisfaction from the ordeal. Stubby kept on smiling, though.

"And this young chap," the Cap'n continued, "is our new deckhand, Luther Riley Junior. We call him Bucky. He's runnin' away to fight the Hun with Teddy Roosevelt." Mr. Van Pelt didn't bother to shake my hand. "Quarters is crowded aboard the Frank White, Mr. Van Pelt. Nuthin' we kin do about that. So you'll be sharin' a cabin with young Bucky here 'til we git to where we're pickin' up yer daughter, then we'll make other arrangements.

"I shall stay on deck until my daughter comes aboard," Mr. Van Pelt said. "We should be getting there about dark, I surmise."

"You surmise right," the Cap'n said.

Stubby touched my shoulder. "Come, Rough Rider's son. We got work to do before this old tub sets sail." He eased me out the door. When we got some distance from the pilothouse, he re-lit his pipe. "Can't figure why a man as wealthy as Mister Dalton Van Pelt and his little Calliope are going down the river on a smoky towboat. Why not the train? Or one of them new-fangled automobiles? I'm sure he can afford either. Maybe it's got something to with that Sheriff Roscoe Lynch. The Cap'n and me know him well. He's a hard man, that one."

I looked back at the pilothouse. Through the window I saw the Cap'n and Mr. Van Pelt still in earnest conversation when all of a sudden Mr. Van Pelt handed over a wad of money. They shook hands as if they'd closed a secret deal. Mr. Van Pelt came out onto the deck and began to pace again.

First light came soon enough. I stood on the deck, holding a thick line of rope that looped around a cleat. The cleat reminded me of a blacksmith's anvil bolted fast to the dock. Stubby had taught me how to tie a cleat hitch knot. I was ready. When the Cap'n came out of the pilothouse, Tripod draped over his good arm, we all awaited his orders. Even Mr. Van Pelt stopped his pacing and clasped his hands behind his back. Several of the wallopers held off on their dockside work to stand by *The Frank White*. The Cap'n spat some tobacco over the side, watching it plop into the harbor.

"Mr. O'Hara," he barked, all formal like. "Are we ready to cast off?"

From down below in the engine room, Stubby barked back. "Aye, aye, Cap'n Cobb!"

"Are you ready, Deckhand Apprentice Luther Riley Junior?"

I heard Stubby yell up at me. "Say, 'aye, aye, Cap'n Cobb. 'Tis a game we've been playing ever since we bought this tub. Makes us think we're in the Navy still."

I looked at the Cap'n. "Aye, aye, Cap'n Cobb!"

"Then by gum, we're New York bound!"

The wallopers ashore cheered, like they'd been watching a show. And sure enough they were. With just a twitch of a grin, the Cap'n turned sharply about and stepped back into the pilothouse and set Tripod down. Then the towboat horn tooted three times.

The sun had not yet cleared Burlington's hillside and so the city was still awash in the grayness of dawn. The eastern sky was pink, with nary a cloud. On the western side of Lake Champlain the sun's rays were just striking the upper reaches of the Adirondacks. The air on the black water was cold and crisp, and it chilled me to the bone even though I'd pulled on my sweater, thanking Louisa that I had it. *The Frank White* shook as its steam engine growled to life and dark smoke belched from the smokestack. My whole body, blood racing through it, shook, too. Casting off the lines, I never felt so happy, so alive. I couldn't help myself, but I waved to the wallopers. Heck, if they didn't wave back. The feeling that I was an old sea dog again flooded my imagination. The towboat eased away from the dock, pulling the loaded-down barge with it, and we were on our way.

Chapter Four

The Cap'n took the towboat out into the broad lake, and we plowed south toward Shelburne Point. Beyond that was all new to me. We passed the Lake Champlain Steamboat Company at the very end of the point. Several steamboats were in various stages of construction, one with its frame much like the rib cage of a great whale. We then pushed on between the mainland and the big island of Queneska and soon after for the first time I saw the legendary Webb estate. The Webbs were related to the Vanderbilts. I remember Poppa reading aloud one morning from the newspaper that Vanderbilt Webb had enlisted in the National Guard and had been made sergeant major.

I'd never seen such a palatial estate, built high on a knoll, even though at the moment it was shrouded in shadow—the morning sun hadn't yet risen high enough to shine down on such a splendid place. The lawn and flower gardens blended with beautiful stately trees; all planted in perfect harmony with the rolling landscape. Further on I could see fertile farmland that dipped and rose majestically—the Garden of Eden itself.

Stubby came up on deck then. "I always take a gander at the Webb estate," he said. "The gent who designed this place designed New York's Central Park."

The Cap'n stuck his head out of the pilothouse and shouted down to Mr. Van Pelt, standing up front like a sentinel, the wind in his face.

"Mr. Van Pelt, since you stayed there the last few days I'm bettin' that mansion is as grand on the inside as it is on the outside."

Mr. Van Pelt stood stone quiet and erect, his cloak billowing because of the wind and did not answer the Cap'n.

We slipped on past the estate and soon there were no houses at all. The rolling farmland was now covered over by a forest of maples and oaks and sycamores and other hardwoods I was unfamiliar with. Scrub pine grew right up to the shore, some hanging on for dear life where the water had carved the land's end into jagged cliffs ten to twenty feet high. Roots and red rocks all a-tangle. Rough land, it was.

Stubby patted me on the shoulder. He had to reach up to it. He pushed me toward the pilothouse, saying, "We got little work to do for a spell except keep watch on the lake, so let's do some singing. It's the only bit of pastime we got on this old tub to while away the hours. Thorny can handle the engine easily enough. And besides, he don't like to sing much."

Mr. Van Pelt, long finished with his pacing, never moved from his position on the prow of *The Frank White*, his hands on the rail, his sharp gaze dead ahead.

Inside the pilothouse, the Cap'n plucked a harmonica from his shirt pocket. He ran it across his lips once or twice while using his stump to keep *The Frank White* on her steady course. A fiddle and bow leaned in a corner—Stubby picked them up. "The Cap'n blew a few notes then nodded yonder to Mr. Van Pelt.

"He ain't gonna join us, that's fer sure," he said. "I reckon he'll ride all the way to Whitehall like that. He ain't seen his daughter in four years, poor man. Lost her durin' a messy divorce. Wife was Irish and that didn't hold well with the Van Pelt people, old New York Dutchmen, members of the snooty '400' only those that could fit into Mrs. Astor's ballroom. His old man disinherited him. Sheriff Lynch's bringing the daughter from Lake George down to the locks. By gum, about as mean an hombre as Stubby and me ever laid eyes on. Mr. Van Pelt's payin' a goodly sum for her passage down the river."

I looked out the pilothouse window. Mr. Van Pelt was staring straight ahead as we plowed southward on our course to White-hall.

"Start us off with Shenandoah, Stubby," the Cap'n said. "Me and Tripod's favorite song and a fittin' tune for the voyage we're on."

I looked at Tripod, curled up at her spot on the floor close to the Cap'n's feet.

Stubby tucked the fiddle under his chin and drew back the bow. While his foot began tapping on the floor he winked at me. Then he and the Cap'n, blowing on the harmonica, played that sorrowful tune about love and separation. The first swipes of the bow across the strings touched my heart so strongly as a tune I'd ever heard. Then the beauty of Stubby's voice, deep and melancholy, filled the pilothouse. He sang with his eyes closed, and as he sang I couldn't stop looking at him.

Oh, Shenandoah I love your daughter
Far away, you rollin' river
Oh Shenandoah, I long to hear you.
Away, I'm bound away
Cross the wide Missouri

My eyes fell again on Mr. Van Pelt. He was now listening to the song, his head bent against his chest.

For seven years I courted Sally
Far away you rollin' river
For seven more I long to love her.
Away, I'm bound away across the wide Missouri.

The Cap'n saw Mr. Van Pelt, too, with his head hanging low, and stopped blowing on the harmonica. With Cap'n not playing Stubby's voice trailed off.

"We best sing sumthin' else, sumthin' more lively," the Cap'n said. "Mr. Van Pelt's thinkin' sad thoughts, I figger. How about the Good Ship Venus?" He thumped the harmonic against his thigh and started singing and laughing all at once.

On the good ship Venus, By Christ you shoulda seen us
The figurehead was a whore in bed and . . .

"Don't you think Bucky's too young a pup for this one?" Stubby said.

The Cap'n stopped singing and there was mischief in his gray eyes and his scarred nose a brighter purple. "He'll be hearin' worse songs when he joins the dang army, but maybe yer right. Then how's about Sally Brown? It's a bit tamer."

Stubby nodded and they were playing again. And it was more lively. Even my foot got to tapping. I don't recall all the words, but some of them I liked.

Sally Brown she's a nice young girl
Way Hey, we roll all night and we roll day
Spend our money on Sally Brown.

She once got married to a one-armed captain,
Way Hey, we roll all night and we roll day.
Spend our money on Sally Brown.
She drinks dark rum and she chews tobacky
Way Hey, we roll all night and we roll day.
Spend our money on Sally Brown.

When they'd finished the Cap'n said, "Bucky, you promised us you could sing. So now we'll teach you an old sea chantey and see if you can."

They picked out "What Do You Do With a Drunken Sailor" and taught me just the chorus. I felt nervous singing, but knew I had to do it. It was the only way I'd feel a true part of the crew. Most of the words I had to sing were Way Hey. I guess all singing sailors like those words. Stubby started off because the Cap'n couldn't sing and play the harmonica at the same time.

What do you do with a drunken sailor?
What do you do with a drunken sailor?
What do you do with a drunken sailor early in the mornin'?

Then it was my turn, singing the chorus along with Stubby.

Way Hey, up she's risin'
Way Hey up she's risin'
Way Hey up she's risin' early in the mornin'.

Then Stubby by himself.

Shave his belly with a rusty razor
Shave his belly with a rusty razor
Shave his belly with a rusty razor early in the mornin'.

Then the two of us.

Way Hey, up she's risin'
Way Hey up she's risin'
Way Hey up she's risin' early in the mornin'.
Then again Stubby's solo.
Put him in the hold with the captain's daughter
Put him in the hold with the captain's daughter
Put him in the hold with captain's daughter early in the mornin'.

I was now belting out the chorus, loving every moment.

Way Hey, up she's risin'
Way Hey up she's risin'
Way Hey up she's risin' early in the mornin'.

We sang a few more chanteys and then the Cap'n said, "Back to yer posts, gentlemen. The lake'll be narrowin' soon so we best be lookin' for submerged logs and such. You take the portside of the bow. Thorny'll be on the starboard." Then, while he poked a fresh plug of tobacco into his mouth, said to me, "I bet you'll never be a landlubber again. Maybe you ought to be joinin' the navy instead of Roosevelt's dang army."

As we left the pilothouse, I heard the Cap'n softly singing, *"On the good ship Venus, by Christ you shoulda seen us. The figurehead was a whore in bed . . ."*

My next task seemed easy enough. Stand on the portside while Thorny tended the starboard and watch for big jagged logs beneath the dark surface of the lake and for broken-up wood shanties, too, that'd been left behind by fishermen when the ice went out and even for sunken ships or abandoned barges that had gone down years ago, but now lurked close to the surface. *The Frank White* steamed on against a strong headwind and the land on the New York side rose up in steep granite cliffs covered along the ridgeline with pine trees and scraggly bushes. A bald eagle perched atop one of the taller pines sharply observed us as we passed by. I thought myself the great raptor then searching the water with my eagle eyes for any sign of danger as the wind ruffled my black feathers.

Then dead ahead like a sea serpent, a mighty log rose up with its thick, twisted roots clawing the water. It was fifty feet off to port and I tried calling to Thorny, but in the excitement my voice caught in my throat. All that came out was a hoarse whisper. *"Thorny!"*

Mr. Van Pelt saw the log. He turned toward the pilothouse and yelled quickly up to the Cap'n. The towboat slowed and made a wide pass of the log with its roots like talons and then picked up speed again. I swallowed hard, trying to clear my throat, ashamed I'd not come through for the Cap'n. I was grateful for Mr. Van Pelt and wanted to thank him. But he turned and resumed his lonely vigil on the lake.

All morning and into the early afternoon we churned south, going *up* the lake, not down. The Cap'n had explained that Champlain's waters flowed north to Canada, not south like you'd think. So while we headed up the lake, we passed several working boats making their way down the lake to Burlington. Each time the Cap'n sounded our horn they answered us with their own high-pitched blasts. We entered Button Bay and Champlain widened up, but then began to narrow again and with each passing mile looked more and more like a river than a lake. On both sides the land kept changing, too, from woods to farmland to woods again and back to farmland. Cows munched in the meadows, paying us no mind. We moved past Crown Point and the remnants of the old fort where Roberts' Rangers had been stationed in the French and Indian War before traveling to Canada to burn the village of the Abenakis. We came to Fort Ticonderoga, America's Rock of Gibraltar. In the Revolutionary War, Ethan Allen and his band of Green Mountain boys, along with Benedict Arnold, had captured Fort Ti without firing a shot. Vermonters are proud of their Ethan Allen. When he died they buried him on Burlington's highest point of land.

By now it was well past noon and we were a hungry bunch. The moment my stomach growled I sensed I had a new task to perform.

"Go down to the galley, Bucky," the Cap'n hollered, "and whip us up two hearty sandwiches each. Look around and you'll find all the fixin's."

Down in the galley I lit the oil lamp and looked around. I found a loaf of dark bread, the crust about as hard as a turtle shell. Using the top of the icebox as a cutting board I sliced it up, enough for ten sandwiches, two each, for I counted on Mr. Van Pelt to join us for lunch. From the icebox I took out a chicken breast and sliced plenty of meat for sandwiches. I cut up thick slabs of cheddar cheese and sprinkled on salt and pepper, and when I was almost done Mr. Van Pelt stepped into the galley.

"I'll eat here," he said. He pulled out one of the chairs from around the bench, sat and watched me finish making the sandwiches. I noticed how smooth his hands looked, two fingers adorned with glittery rings, but no wedding band.

"Your little daughter'll be with us soon," I ventured.

"Mind your business," he said.

I put his sandwiches in front of him and took the rest topside, leaving him to eat alone. I was glad to be out of the galley with him sitting there surly as a snake. Stubby was at the helm when I brought up the sandwiches. Thorny was next to him. The Cap'n was outside the pilothouse, peeing over the side.

"How's his lordship?" Stubby asked.

"Not very pleasant," I said. "I thought he'd be happy to be seeing his daughter again."

"There's more there than we know, and my old seaman's sense tells me none of it's good."

The Cap'n came in, buttoning up his fly. He picked up a sandwich, looked it over and grunted. He picked out a piece of cheese and tossed it on the floor in front of Tripod. She sniffed the cheese and then ate it.

It was dusk when we reached the end of Lake Champlain at Whitehall. Here you could almost spit across the lake, it was so narrow. Mr. Van Pelt had taken up his post in front of *The Frank White*. He was now near the long-awaited reunion with his daughter. He began to pace, hands once again clasped behind his back.

I pictured his daughter, six or seven years old, on the wharf, pacing, too, longing to see her father. Maybe when they saw each other after four years and embraced, he'd lose his surliness. If I had to bunk with him all the way to West Point I hoped we'd be on better terms. Then I wondered where his daughter would bunk. Maybe I'd have to move out, sleep on the deck. I wouldn't mind that, bunking under the stars like a soldier on the march.

Chapter Five

As we neared the lock that would lift us up into the ancient Champlain Canal, Whitehall closed in on both sides of the waterway, a weary village of old rust-colored brick buildings hanging on for dear life while black water churned below them. Lights had just flicked on, and in the early evening, more lights began to dot a huge hill on our portside. At the top of the hill stood a castle that Stubby later told me was Lowen's Castle. It had been built fifty years earlier by some old-time judge, he said, and the name of the hill was "Skene Mountain." The walls of the lock were built of thick blocks of concrete. When we eased into the lock, the water was low and the chamber's slimy sides rose upward fifty feet. It seemed we'd entered a long tunnel, and *The Frank White* became cloaked in darkness. Now the only lights I could see glowed feebly—one inside the pilothouse, where the Cap'n gingerly steered his towboat with one hand, and the others atop the lock itself where they did no good as far as we were concerned.

On both sides of the lock's wall, men tossed down their thick, damp mooring lines. In the dank gloom, I looped them securely around a cleat and held them taut to keep our vessel from banging hard against the concrete walls. Behind us, a foot-thick iron and timbered gate cranked shut with a hard grinding noise. It sealed us in—towboat, barge and all. Water flowing in from the bottom of the lock, lifted us slowly up. My job, Stubby had shown me, was to keep the lanyard taut all the way and not let there be any slack.

As water filled the lock's chamber and we made our ascent, I saw Mr. Van Pelt in his black derby and cape. His head, craned upward, swayed back and forth like a cobra to catch sight of his dear daughter in case she might be peering down at him from the top of the wall.

Gripping the mooring line tight as I could I searched for her, too.

With water gushing in, the higher up we got the more light there was. Men stood on the edge of the wall, half in light, half in shadow. At first, I saw their heads and then their entire bodies. Two of the men were soldiers with rifles on guard duty against possible German saboteurs. I saw no girl. They greeted us in grunts of "hallo" as we came even with the top of the wall. When the Cap'n stuck his head out of the pilothouse one of them called to him, "Welcome to Whitehall, Cap'n Cobb!"

At that moment Mr. Van Pelt vaulted onto the wall, calling "Calliope! Calliope!" His derby flipped off his head and went floating down into the water.

I held the mooring line and my breath tight at the same time. And then I saw her. She was in front of some large barrel, a thickset man next to her. She was no tyke, but a teenager. She had a tumble of long red hair, from what I could make out, and her eyes were wide with fright. I was sure of it. She looked about my age. Fifteen. She wore a blue dress that came down past the tops of her high-button walking boots. In one hand she clutched a pathetic suitcase, hardly big enough to carry much at all. The man by her side held her arm in a grip so hard she couldn't run off. There wasn't a flicker of expression on his face. His eyes were hard and piercing, though, like that picture I'd seen in Poppa's study of Geronimo. I took him to be Sheriff Lynch. I remembered the Cap'n saying he was the meanest hombre he'd ever laid eyes on. Seeing him there next to Calliope, holding her against her will, I felt that meanness.

Then someone on the wall yelled at me. "Hey, wake up, you fool! Tighten yer goddamn line!"

I looked down at the line and saw a yard of slack. I yanked it taut, thankful that Stubby was down in the engine room.

"Now hold her fast!"

I coiled the line twice around the cleat. The man yelled at me again over the sound of our throbbing engine and roiling water. "Once yer passengers get aboard cast off the line so you can be on yer way. A canal boat's waitin' at the other end."

I looked for Mr. Van Pelt and his daughter and Sheriff Lynch. I expected them to be ready to jump aboard. They were gone.

The Cap'n stepped from the pilothouse. "What the hell's goin' on," he shouted to the men on the wall. He eyed me. "Hold her tight, Bucky!"

"The girl got away! Run off!" someone shouted back.

"How the hell did that happen?" the Cap'n asked.

"The girl's father ordered Lynch to let her go. Held out his arms to her. Stead of runnin' to him she bolted 'twixt them buildings yonder, scared to death. I told 'em that's where she run to. She can't git far. That's a dead-end alley."

"Well, we ain't got time to dally. If they ain't on board in the next minute we're leavin' 'em high and dry. Bucky, when you hear my whistle cast off!" The Cap'n thumped back into the pilothouse.

Beyond the landing it was dark enough, but the alley between the buildings was darker yet. If it was a deadend there was no escape for Calliope. I wondered why she feared her own Poppa, and why the Sheriff had dragged her down to the canal. At that moment, Mr. Van Pelt and Sheriff Lynch ran out of the alley empty-handed, unsure which way to go next.

When the whistle sounded, startling loud, I almost jumped out of my skin.

I uncoiled the line and let it slip through my hands. *The Frank White* pitched forward, water sloshing her sides. Mr. Van Pelt sprinted alongside us.

"You sons of bitches! You wait!"

Stubby bounded up from the engine room. He cupped his hands to his mouth. "You're the son of a bitch. Me and the Cap'n ain't going to be no accomplices to a kidnappin'!"

Mr. Van Pelt screamed back. "I'll get you. By God I promise you that!"

"Go find your poor daughter!" Stubby hollered.

"I'll get you! Somewhere along the river or in New York harbor, I'll get you!"

Even in the dim lights his face showed scarlet. He slowed down and stopped altogether. He shook a fist at us and spun around and went back to search for his daughter among the barrels and boxes and crates and worn-down buildings along the lock while Sheriff Lynch hurriedly returned to the alley for a second look. The two soldiers on guard did nothing.

"Don't worry none, Bucky," Stubby said. "He sure ain't gonna come after us once he gets that daughter of his. If he can find her." Stubby laughed then and winked. "Anyways, that arrogant stuffed shirt'll hafta to come up with another way down the river."

I was now all out of breath, my face damp with sweat, and I hadn't done hardly a thing. The towboat passed under a bridge.

Whitehall was all lit up, a small, drab city, and sadder yet by what had just happened. The poor girl running away from her Poppa, and me running toward mine.

"Well then it's close to suppertime," Stubby said, sensing my melancholy. "There's some steaks in the icebox. Pick out good-sized ones and plenty of potatoes for the four us since Mr. Van Pelt and his daughter won't be joinin' us. Grill 'em up nice and juicy and bring our supper up to the pilothouse along with some bottles of beer. And don't make it fancy. We're all pretty hungry."

After we passed through the lock and had tied up on the other side of Whitehall for the night, we ate our dinner. I felt better as we talked about our adventure and how there was no way we'd be a party to a kidnapping. Then the Cap'n said that he was exhausted and would turn in for the night. He told me to turn in, too, bed down in my stateroom. *Stateroom!* Two bunks and not much space to move about. Tight as a closet, like the one in my room back in Burlington. I then wondered if Momma missed me and how she might be doing, and if Louisa had told her that I was off to join Colonel Roosevelt's army. I put out the lamp and slumped down in the lower bunk. I listened to the engine throb hard enough to rattle the walls. Then I thought about our trip through the lock, not quite up there with Poppa's adventures I'd heard about, but plenty of excitement. Closing my eyes, I saw in my mind the red-haired girl in her blue dress and button boots and small suitcase, and how frightened she seemed, and how Sheriff Lynch held her like some criminal. I felt a new sadness and hoped she'd gotten away. But where could she go? Then I must have dozed off. Maybe it was the sudden quiet. The engine had

been shut down for the night. Or maybe it was something else—
for I knew I wasn't alone.

"Who's there?" I whispered and fumbled in the dark for a
match. I lit the lamp and turned up the wick for more light. I got
off my bunk and stood. Scrunched up in the corner of the top
bunk was Calliope Van Pelt! We looked at each other for a long
while, neither of us knowing what to say. Her knees were drawn
up under her chin, her dark eyes wide, her hair a tangle, a gold
crucifix at her throat. She'd tried to pull the blanket over her and
I think that's what woke me.

After a spell she whispered, "Please don't tell!"

I didn't answer because I didn't know what to say.

"You can't tell!" she whispered again. "You just can't!"

"The Cap'n has to know," I said.

"He'll send me back to that sheriff. He hurt my arm. He hurt
my Mother, too."

"Hurt your Momma?"

"Mother cried for him not to take me away. He slapped her
and shoved her into a chair and yelled that he was bringing me to
my father and that he was the law and if she said anything he'd
have her arrested! Mother got down on her knees and begged. It
didn't matter. He slapped her again and made me pack my suitcase. He pulled me out of the house. He and two other men drove
me to Whitehall. The whole time he wouldn't let go of my arm.
It's all bruised."

"How'd you get away?"

"As soon as my arm was free I ducked behind a barrel and
some man who was holding a rope said I'd run into an alley. I
watched them go in there, Father and the sheriff. I snuck close

to the boat and two men swung me aboard. I hid for a bit and then crept down here where it's dark and nobody'd find me."

"I won't tell, I promise." At once I regretted the promise because of how the Cap'n and Stubby took me under their wings, and it meant I'd be betraying them and Thorny, too. She saw that regret in my face. A blush of heat passed through me. "What's your name?" I asked, although I already knew.

"Calliope Van Pelt. What's yours?"

"Bucky Riley."

"You won't tell then, Bucky Riley."

"The Cap'n's gonna find out sooner or later. You can't hide here forever."

"I can stay here with you. He won't find out if you don't say a word."

"Well, there's Stubby. I can't lie to him—or the Cap'n."

"They'll throw me off for sure and the sheriff will come get me and give me to father and I'll have to live with him and my brother in their big house, where the rooms are cold and the chauffeur has more hands than an octopus."

As my eyes got used to the lamplight I saw Calliope's face more clearly. Her mass of hair was the color of bright copper and ran wild over her head and down the sides of her face. Her keen eyes were dark as pitch against her white skin. I took a deep breath and asked why she didn't want to be with her father. She refused to answer. So I asked how old she was.

"Sixteen. Well, almost sixteen."

"I'm gonna be sixteen in a couple of months."

We heard Stubby in the narrow hallway, coming down to wake me. Calliope squeezed my arm. I put out the lamp. As he clumped down the passageway, Stubby barked, "Rise and shine!"

I walked out of the cabin, faking a yawn.

"You look like you ain't slept a wink," he said.

"The pounding of the engine," I stammered.

"Aye, that happens, but only when the engine is actually pounding. That's why you've been talking to yourself?" He turned away, saying, "Bring the Cap'n his morning coffee and something for Tripod's breakfast."

The Cap'n had a cigar crammed into the corner of his mouth. I didn't know he not only chewed tobacco, but smoked cigars, too. His head was wreathed in smoke. The heavy aroma put me in mind of Poppa when he smoked his evening cigar. The Cap'n told me to put the mug of coffee and chicken scraps on the ledge next to Tripod.

"I can't do two things at once 'cause I only got one arm," he said. He had a hard scowl on his face. "You got anything you wanna say."

"No, Sir."

"It's Cap'n."

I had to tell him about Calliope, but I didn't have the nerve. He grunted. I betrayed him, and he knew it. I could tell by the scowl. Had I also betrayed Stubby? The Cap'n blew several smoke rings and we watched them float through the air until they lost their shapes. He eyed me over the rim of the mug while drinking his coffee." "You sure you got nuthin' to say, eh?"

I stood there as dumb as a doorknob.

"Why don't you sneak back to yer cabin and bring up Van Pelt's daughter. We'd all like to meet her."

"She's afraid you'll turn her back over to the sheriff," I mumbled.

"Git her, Bucky!" The Cap'n blew another set of perfect smoke rings.

I slunk out of the pilothouse like a boy told to go to his room, feeling so rotten that my stomach was as unsteady as if I'd swallowed a sack of rocks. My days as a deckhand were over. Now I'd never get to Oyster Bay to join Colonel Roosevelt's army. Or see Poppa. I again thought of the irony that here I am trying to get to my Poppa while Calliope's trying to get away from hers.

Calliope was still scrunched up in the top bunk, knees folded under her chin, the blanket tight around her.

I said, "I got to take you topside to meet the Cap'n."

"I knew you'd tell!" She pulled the blanket tighter around her.

"The Cap'n knew. He just knew." It hurt me to see such disappointment in her eyes. "We've got to go." I felt awful saying it.

"I'll jump overboard before I go back. I'll swim away!"

Calliope slid off the bunk and followed me along the darkly lit passageway to the stairs leading to the deck. I heard her take a deep breath as we started up. We went inside the pilothouse. Stubby sat at the wheel. The Cap'n was up, pacing, still smoking his cigar.

"Aye, Calliope Van Pelt," he said. He extended his hand. "I'm the captain of this rickety old bucket, Chauncey Cobb, by gum."

Calliope almost pulled away from the Cap'n, but then gingerly held out her hand.

"Don't be frightened, Miss," His voice was so gentle that it didn't sound like him at all. "Me and Stubby and several of the fellas back there at the lock hatched this plot to get you away from your old man." The Cap'n looked at me with that twinkle back in his eyes. "All it took fer our plot to work was fer you to run off when you had the chance, and you did, by gum. You probably thought the fellas on the landing were helpin' you on their own without us knowin' about it, swingin' you onboard and such. Well, t'was us told 'em what to do if they got the chance. We'd called ahead when we was back in Burlington and had a notion of somethin' foul was afoot."

Calliope's mouth curled into a smile of uncertainty.

"And you can bank on the fact that we're not gonna throw you off. Yer with us all the way down the Hudson to New York harbor. You can work as a deckhand, too, because Stubby and me are thinkin' we might be needin' a new deckhand, seeing we might be losin' one pretty soon." He shot me a look that sent a chill down my spine. The Cap'n sent a smoke ring spiraling straight toward my face. They were throwing me off at the next lock, I feared.

"Now, Bucky," he said as the smoke ring struck my eyes. "Me and Stubby had a powwow about what to do with you. 'Throw him in the brig,' I said. 'Make him walk the plank,' Stubby said, like we were pirates."

"You can't do any of those things," Calliope said. She faced the Cap'n with her dark eyes blazing.

We stared at her. Then the Cap'n laughed. "Miss Calliope, yer right. There's no brig on this tub, and we ain't no pirates. We agreed among ourselves that if we'd have been in Bucky's shoes we'd have done the same thing for such a pretty lassie as yerself." The Cap'n nudged me. "We just figured you'd have trusted us some. Now, Bucky, whyn't you take Miss Calliope here and show her some of the chores of a deckhand. Show her what you've learned, if anything. Stubby, Thorny and me will worry about Sheriff Lynch. I don't think we've heard the last of him. Not by a long shot, by gum."

Chapter Six

The Frank White was moored to two heavy cleats, fore and aft, when we went out on deck. I led Calliope to the bow to show her what to do. While clutching the thick line, stretched rigid as an iron bar by the pull of the towboat against the canal's current, I observed a single tear slipping down her cheek. She wiped it away with her thumb, hoping I hadn't noticed. I stood still as a tin soldier, the rope's fibers rough in my hand. Calliope put her hand around the rope and for a moment our fingers touched. The sun had just come up and the wind with it. Her hair blew around her face. My heart was heavy, the way it was whenever Poppa gave me that "Momma's Boy" look. I was a fool, and knew it.

"If I go back to my Mother, Father will come there," she said. She let go of the rope so our fingers wouldn't touch. "He'll have that sheriff with him. The sheriff will hurt Mother like he did before."

"I'm on my way to President Roosevelt's home on Sagamore Hill. Come with me. He'll know what to do."

She said, "That old man wouldn't be bothered with the likes of me."

"But he and my Poppa are friends from the Spanish War. That's where Poppa is now, with Roosevelt. He'll know what to do, Poppa will."

I could tell Calliope didn't believe a word I'd said.

The sun had risen high enough now so we could clearly see the canal. Stubby appeared outside the pilothouse. He yawned and then hollered down to us. "Empty the coal ashes and when you're done prepare to cast off." He then went down to the engine room.

"You really think they might help—I mean the President and your Father?" There was a trace of hope in Calliope's voice.

"I do." I smiled and she managed a slight smile in return.

Feeling good at last, I taught her how to slip the rope off the cleat, to hold it tight until the towboat started to pull away, how to toss it back on deck and jump aboard. After I'd shown her all that, I hauled up several buckets of coal ash that Thorny had filled and dumped the ashes into the canal. Finished, now, I ran to the tow boat's stern where the other mooring line had been secured. Calliope and I stood there waiting for the command to cast off. The engines throbbed and water roiled. The Cap'n gave three blasts of the horn, the signal for us to free *The Frank White*. Following my lead, Calliope slipped her line off the cleat and with a lot of effort threw the heavy rope on deck and jumped on. I leaped on after her.

We were off again.

Throughout the sixty-mile length of the Champlain Canal, we had to negotiate a number of locks, each going up like steps until we reached the high point and then we'd descend step-by-step, lock-by-lock, until we reached the final lock at Waterford, just north of Troy, where the Mohawk River flows into the Hudson.

The locks are all numbered. The Whitehall Lock is Number 12, the last of the locks if you're coming up from Waterford. About seven miles south of Whitehall at Fort Ann, which was the scene of a big Indian massacre back in the seventeenth century, is Lock 11. Because the Cap'n feared that Sheriff Lynch might make a beeline to Fort Ann to be sure that Calliope hadn't sneaked on the barge, he ordered her below deck. She was to keep out of sight, and if need be, to hide in the engine room. The Cap'n said his crew, which included me, wouldn't let any man aboard—we'd fight them off if we had to.

Fort Ann's a typical canal town. Lock 11 is a lot like Lock 12. The entrance has a thick iron and oaken gate and high concrete walls. The landing is fifty feet up. Men there held ropes, which they dropped down to us.

It turned out, the sheriff was not there, and so we passed through the lock and were again on our way—this time to Lock 9 because there's no Lock 10. Lock 9 is between Fort Ann and Fort Edward. It's the high point of the canal and once past it, we'd drop down all the way to the Hudson.

The Cap'n didn't think the sheriff would show up at this lock. But even so he didn't take any chances. He figured it best if Calliope wore a disguise instead of hiding below. She'd dress up as a boy, like me. Outfitting her was no problem, the Cap'n explained. She'd wear some of Stubby's clothes. They were the only clothes that'd come close to fitting her. I thought Stubby was taken aback after he handed her a pair of his britches because the cuffs barely touched her ankles. The clothes, among them a well-worn flannel shirt with half its buttons missing, hung on her like a tent. Stubby said he'd fix the back of the shirt so it'd fit better. And he did, another marvel—him so skillful with needle and thread. He found a slouch hat, too. He cut a slit in the back, overlapped the two ends and sewed them up so that the hat'd be snug when Calliope's wild hair was bunched up inside. Of course she had to stash her high-button canvas walking boots and go barefoot. The boots would be a dead give away Calliope was onboard. The *coup de grace* was Stubby's old chewed-up pipe. The Cap'n directed her to keep it in her mouth at all times when topside. She made a face at the pipe and Stubby promised to wash it clean as a whistle.

When she was all decked out, barefoot and sucking on the black pipe like it was a lollipop, Calliope did resemble a boy, somewhat. Yet in my heart I didn't believe anybody'd be fooled by her Huck Finn outfit—not Sheriff Lynch, that's for certain. I reckoned he was too shrewd, and besides, if he knew she was on *The Frank White* he'd never quit until he got her back and handed her over to her Poppa.

After looking Calliope over, and approving her getup, the Cap'n said that she and me had to bunk together in the same cabin, unless I was willing to sleep out-of-doors on the deck in all weathers. He gave me a stern look and snorted, "And by gum there better not be any hanky-panky. Not at your ages."

Standing aslant with her hands on her hips and the slouch hat drooping over her forehead, she pushed up the brim with a twinkle in her dark eyes at the Cap'n's sleeping arrangement and, taking the pipe from her mouth and tapping it twice against my chest, said, "Bottom bunk!" Then she bolted from the pilothouse.

Before I took off after her, the Cap'n said, "Keep a stalwart eye on her, Bucky. It's a ways to Gotham and anything can happen. While I figger out what to do with her, just watch her."

Following Calliope down to the cabin, I found her on the edge of the lower bunk, head cupped in her hands, bare feet dangling just above the floor. The hat was off and her hair fell against her cheeks. The pipe was in her lap. In the corner of the bunk she had rolled up her dress. She looked up at me.

"No hanky-panky," she said.

I didn't dare sit next to her or climb onto the top bunk. I stood there in the cramped cabin's doorway, feeling in my mind the moment her hand had touched mine.

She said, "How will we get to Roosevelt's house once we're in New York?"

I hadn't thought that far ahead and had no idea. Maybe the Cap'n would come up with something.

"How come your Poppa had you kidnapped?"

"He wants me back." Her eyes fell away from mine. "I lived with him until I was ten and a judge ruled that I had to live with my Mother at our summer house on Lake George, which Mother got in the divorce. When I moved in with her, I felt sorry for Schuyler, my brother, because he had to live with my Father. He's at Harvard College now. I miss him, but I don't miss him all that much."

"Why?"

"None of your business." She grabbed the pipe, slipped off the bunk and went up on deck. I was dead tired and climbed up on the top bunk. A moment later, I was out.

I didn't sleep long. We finally came up to Lock 9, the canal's highest section. Calliope shook me awake and said we needed to go to work. But the Cap'n didn't want her roping the cleats in case Sheriff Lynch lurked about. Instead, he kept her in the pilothouse with him and Tripod. He didn't have her duck down out of sight, or anything. But at Lock 9 there was no sheriff. And down we went, descending to Fort Edward where for the first time we saw the Hudson River flowing along the west side of the canal. While I pondered the Hudson, the Cap'n and Stubby pondered where Sheriff Lynch might hit us. The Cap'n figured he'd be waiting at Waterford because that's where the Champlain Canal meets the Erie Canal, making it a busy place. Stubby reckoned he'd be at West Point because Calliope's Poppa lived across the river. It made the most sense, he argued. He wouldn't have far to take her.

In the meantime, we stayed alert and soon enough reached Fort Edward and the great Hudson itself.

Fort Edward's another of those towns along the canal whose history is caught up in either the French and Indian War or the American Revolution. Before we entered the lock, I saw the Hudson River off our starboard side. It was a black body of water with an island in it that was a stone's throw from the canal. Stubby said it was Roger's Island, named after that intrepid ranger who now seemed to me to have roamed all over New York during those far off frontier days.

Fort Edward was also home to another character of legend, Jane McCrea. The way Stubby told it, she had beautiful red hair, like Calliope's, he said, that was so long it touched her cabin floor. When General Johnny Burgoyne led his British army south from Canada, the Indians with him captured her, and in a moment of rage, scalped her and mutilated her body. Word of her murder spread throughout the valley and her death turned into a rallying point for the rebels at the Battle of Saratoga.

On the lock's portside, the ground sloped up, and to my surprise, I saw a military barracks and a number of soldiers encamped there—many more than at Whitehall. New York's National Guard had been posted at all the waterways serving the Empire State in case German spies were plotting to blow them up. The moment we were in the lock and had been lifted level with the wall, I got a better view of the Hudson. But my eyes didn't stay on the Hudson very long. Instead, they locked on Sheriff Lynch, black suit, derby hat and all. He had two hefty deputies similarly clad. Calliope saw the sheriff and scrambled into the pilothouse. The sheriff pointed a threatening finger at the pilothouse window where the Cap'n had stuck his head out. Flashing his badge, he bellowed like an angry bull, "We're coming aboard!"

"You ain't doin' no such thing!" the Cap'n coolly replied. "I'm the captain here and that makes me the law aboard this vessel. So keep yer lard arse off!"

"The hell with you," growled the sheriff. He started to get on *The Frank White* with his deputies right behind him.

Leveling a shotgun at the sheriff, the Cap'n snapped back. "I may have only one arm, but by gum, I'll blow you to smithereens if you and yer hooligans take another step forward!" His voice and the dark look in his eyes made it clear there was no doubt he'd shoot them all—the sheriff first. The National Guardsmen, patrolling the lock, halted. They unslung their rifles. I took a big swallow.

By then Stubby, up from his engine room, had taken a position close to the landing. He wore a holster with a silver-plated pistol in it shining clear as the morning sun, his right hand resting on the grip of that pistol. Behind him loomed Thorny, a heavy coal shovel in his thick ebony hands.

Sheriff Lynch stopped. He looked at the shotgun, then at Stubby and finally at Thorny. "I'm a duly appointed sheriff. I've the right—"

"You got no rights on my vessel!"

"Damn your rights. I'm here looking for a runaway girl and I've reason to believe she's on board against her will!"

"There ain't no runaway girl aboard my vessel who's bein' held against her will. No sirree!"

"You and that sawed off punk with the holstered pistol, don't you dare shoot us!" The sheriff moved closer to the towboat. The deputies, now unsure of themselves, stayed put.

"Try us, you son of a bitch!" It was Stubby barking now and he moved directly in front of the sheriff, his hand still on the pistol grip.

"I'll have you all arrested and thrown in jail. You, too, kid!" Sheriff Lynch looked right at me, and I thought "Geronimo!" He pulled back his black coat. A pistol was strapped to his waist. "And the kid in the pilothouse!"

The canal workers backed away. The National Guardsmen, not sure what to do, also backed away.

"Touch that sidearm and I'll blast you where you stand, Lynch." The Cap'n cocked the dual hammers of his shotgun. Stubby drew his pistol and pointed it at the sheriff. Thorny cocked the coal shovel over his shoulder. If only I had a club.

We were at that moment where if no one backed down there'd be blood everywhere. I wanted to duck out of sight. But I stood there instead, anchored fast by a weird fascination to see who'd blink first. I'd never seen a fight between men, just kids swinging wildly at each other on the school playground. A cut, a bloody nose.

Then I got mad.

"You damn kidnapper," I shouted. "What kind of a sheriff are you? You beat women, steal girls from their homes." I walked across the deck, startling even myself. I held the lanyard tight in my fist, my body trembling with anger. I jumped up on the wall, close enough to Sheriff Lynch to smell his foul breath, see the stubble on his chin and the color of his eyes. "I'm telling my Poppa. He's a Roosevelt Rough Rider and he'll come here and box your damn ears!" I turned my fury at the deputies. "Box all your ears, damn it!"

The sheriff stared at me in disbelief. Slowly, he took his hand away from his hip. His coat closed over the pistol. The Cap'n and Stubby and Thorny didn't move, and kept their weapons at the ready.

"You may have this round, Cobb," he snarled. "But it ain't over yet. I know the girl's on your boat because of what that snot-nosed kid just said. So I'll be seeing you folks somewhere along the river and you can bet this time I'll be ready."

I choked on my words.

Lynch looked once more at Calliope, still not sure it was her. "I'll be seeing you, too, kid!" Then he signaled his deputies to back off. They got into their automobiles, the sheriff had a sleek Saxon Roadster all to himself, and drove away.

I didn't stop shaking 'til they'd all gone. The Cap'n put up his shotgun and went back to work as if nothing had happened. Stubby holstered his pistol in the same cool manner. Thorny swung his coal shovel to the ground with a loud metallic whap. When I hopped back on *The Frank White*, Stubby walked by and muttered under his breath, but loud enough for me to hear, "Box your ears?"

Chapter Seven

To cool down and get our minds off the showdown between us, Sheriff Lynch and his hooligans, the Cap'n thought it best if we did some singing. We were puttering down the Champlain Canal toward a place called Moses Kill. With Calliope now part of our group, the Cap'n promised he'd keep the lyrics clean. He got out his harmonica while Stubby, up from the engine room, had his fiddle and bow. But Calliope wasn't in the mood for singing just yet. She went on the deck and sat there staring at the passing farmland, her knees folded up under her chin, her arms hooked around her knees—like the first time I saw her up in the corner of the bunk. She had that slouch hat pulled across her eyes and Stubby's old black pipe stuck in her mouth.

Looking at her, too, the Cap'n said, "Go out there, Bucky, and keep the lassie company. Me and Stubby can sing amongst ourselves fer a bit."

The Cap'n's hunch was right. Calliope needed company. I sat down next to her and said, "Hi."

We drifted along in silence, the running of the engine belching black smoke so you couldn't hear the water rushing against the towboat. Now and then we'd pass another canal boat cruising north. The Cap'n would toot his horn and the pilot in the vessel opposite would answer with his own blast.

There weren't many farmhouses along this stretch of the canal, but a lot of open land broken up by stands of sycamore trees. Once in a while we'd pass a sprawling sycamore, its silvery-gray trunk big and round as a silo, its thick branches spreading out on the water's edge as if the tree itself was beckoning us to come ashore. The great sycamore made me think of Joyce Kilmer's *Trees*, which was Momma's favorite poem. I tried to remember it, but couldn't, even though Momma recited it often enough. Only the last two lines came to mind. "Poems are made by fools like me, but only God can make a tree."

Calliope took Stubby's pipe from her mouth. "Do you miss your Mother?"

I hungered to know all about Calliope then, why her Momma and Poppa fell out of love and why her Poppa wanted her back so much that he'd dare kidnap her. As we sat there on the deck, we heard the Cap'n and Stubby singing their sea chanteys. The harmonica and fiddle and Stubby's sweet voice.

"My Mother must be frantic," she said. "Not knowing what's become of me."

I sat there quiet as a church mouse.

"Mother wanted to take back her maiden name after the divorce. She wanted to be Miss Caithleen O'Malley all over again with a clean slate. Not Mrs. Dalton Van Pelt, the rich lady with no proper upbringing. She wanted to go back to her own people, back to before she took the position as scullery maid in the Van Pelt houses."

I kept quiet.

"Mother's people were from County Cavan and came over during the potato famine, so I'm told. They lived in lower Manhattan somewhere. Mother's first job was at the home of Grandfather Van Pelt, working in his kitchen on Fifth Avenue and later at his big house in Garrison. The Van Pelt people are Dutch and

English—old families descended from the Schuylers. They're all bankers. Father, too. He was supposed to marry one of his own kind, a Van Rensselaer or a Rhinelander or a Hamilton Fish, but fell in love with his Irish maid. They ran off and got married. That was improper. It was in all the newspapers. Father was disinherited and they wrote that up, as bold and hateful as anything. But he still had a lot of money. After the marriage, he and Mother moved to Garrison into a new place near Grandfather Van Pelt, hoping things would work out, and that's where Schuyler and I were born."

"Is your grandfather still alive?"

"He died before the divorce. He had nothing to do with Schuyler and me, his only grandchildren. Because we're half-Irish, he thought we were tainted."

"Why did your folks divorce?"

She hugged her knees tighter, and we listened to Stubby singing.

"Let's go up and join them," she said.

The Cap'n nodded when we entered the pilothouse. He and Stubby were just finishing up a tune. The moment they were done, the Cap'n bowed.

"Would you like to join us, Calliope?"

"I don't know any sea songs," she admitted. She picked up Tripod, hugged her and stroked the top of her head.

"Pet the left side of her head," the Cap'n said. "'Cause of her missing her paw she can't get to the left side. She loves it when you pet her there."

Calliope stroked Tripod's left side, behind the ear, and the cat purred. She then put her cheek against Tripod's cheek and whispered, "I love you, Tripod."

Stubby cut in. "Any Celtic tunes, you know of."

"Wild Mountain Thyme," she said and looked at Stubby. "Do you know it? It was Mother's favorite."

"Me last name's O'Hara," he said in a feigned Irish brogue. "I know that song well."

Before Calliope could say anything, he started sawing on his fiddle, Wild Mountain Thyme. I'd never heard it, but Stubby got my foot to tapping. The Cap'n joined in with his harmonica.

"Anytime, Calliope," Stubby said. "We'll sing the chorus together."

Calliope put Tripod down, removed the slouch hat and, holding it in one hand and the pipe in the other, started to sing. I thought right away of Louisa and how she'd sing around the old family piano, how we'd all sing around the piano, even Poppa, his booming voice filling the downstairs. Calliope's voice made me homesick, and that feeling of lonesomeness took me by surprise. At that moment, fleeting as it was, I wondered if running away had been a mistake. But Calliope's voice and her wild hair soon lifted my spirits.

Oh, the summertime is comin'
And the trees are sweetly bloomin'
And the wild mountain thyme
Grows around the bloomin' heather. Will ye go laddie go?
Stubby joined her in the chorus with that sweet voice of his.
And we'll all go together
To pluck wild mountain thyme

All around the bloomin' heather.
Will ye go laddie go?
Now Calliope was on her own, looking me straight in the eye.
I will build my love a bower
By yon clear crystal fountain
And on it I will pile all the flowers of the mountain.
Will ye go laddie go?
When the chorus came around again I found myself singing
right along.

And we'll all go together
To pluck wild mountain thyme
All around the bloomin heather.
Will ye go laddie go?

If my true love should ever leave
I will surely find another
To pluck wild mountain thyme
All around the bloomin' heather.
Will ye go laddie go.

And we'll all go together
To pluck wild mountain thyme
All around the bloomin' heather.
Will ye go laddie go?

"Aye there," said the Cap'n when we'd finished. "You've got a
beautiful voice there, Calliope."

We sang several other tunes. Then we were done. Stubby said
he'd best go below and keep Thorny company. Once we got south

of Schuylerville, the Cap'n said he planned to tie up for the night. He said that in the morning we'd pass through the locks south of Waterford and with the Mohawk River rushing into the Hudson we'd be on the real river at last.

When it got toward dusk we stopped at a mooring place on the east side of the canal. There were several canal boats already tied up for the night and you could see their lights below decks, meaning the crews were settled in. When we were moored fast, Stubby shut down the engine and Thorny came up for air, his black face smeared darker with coal dust and sweat. He pulled off his shirt and pants. Then like a crazy bear he jumped overboard. He was gone. It was still light enough and we looked for him. He soon bobbed up, spouting water from his mouth like a whale's blowhole and laughing. He had a bar of soap and started scrubbing off the coal dust.

"Brrr," he said, looking up at us with merriment. "It's chilly, but it sure feels good to be getting clean again."

Behind us, Stubby said, "I think I'll join Thorny." To Calliope, he added, "Please look the other way, Ma'am." When she had turned away, he stripped down to his skivvies, as he called his underwear, and dove in next to Thorny.

"Don't dunk me you big black bastard," he warned Thorny.

Thorny dunked him anyway.

The Cap'n came out of the pilothouse. "I'd jump in, too, by gum, but I can't swim a lick. Never could—even with two good arms."

After the swim and bath, Stubby went down to his cabin to put on clean clothes. Thorny stayed in the canal thoroughly enjoying himself. I wanted to swim, but was too shy.

"Go ahead in." Calliope smiled. "I won't look. I might go in myself."

Calliope went behind a line of barrels lashed along the stern of the towboat. A moment later I heard a splash and shout. A few seconds later she came around the starboard side, just her head above water. "I dare you," she hollered.

I shot a look at the Cap'n. Cradled in his arm was a shotgun. "Lynch might know about this place and Calliope sure don't look like a boy now. And besides there might be a wolf or two amongst the other vessels tied up here, and they might be sneaking about."

I went to the bow, took off most of my clothes and jumped in. The water was cold, and after days of hard work it soothed my skin.

Thorny splashed nearby and then roared. "By jiggers, I should've been a river otter." He swam out to the middle of the canal and back. Happily finished, he hauled himself out of the water by a rope, picked up his clothes and headed for his cabin.

Calliope came paddling toward me. Although the light was fading, I saw her hair plastered wet against her head. I back-stroked away, keeping a decent distance.

"Our house is right on Lake George," she said. Her voice came across the water like a skipped stone. "In the summertime I swim every day. I even know how to fish." Seeing that I kept backing away, she stopped her paddle. "I won't get close. And you better not either."

Then the Cap'n barked down to us that swimming time was over. "Gittin' too dark," he said. Calliope swam to the stern and I headed for the bow. After I threw on my clothes and Calliope had done the same a bit later, the Cap'n ordered us to the galley to prepare supper. And off we went. Calliope did most of the cooking. I peeled potatoes and when they'd been boiled I mashed them up with gobs of butter. She fried pork chops for us all. When she was done she said to tell everyone our meal was ready. By the time we'd all crowded into the galley, she had the table set, coffee poured, platters heaped with food and, setting in the middle, a single glass holding a bouquet of dandelions. Calliope sat between the Cap'n and Stubby and I squeezed in next to Thorny. The Cap'n surveyed the table, impressed.

"This calls for something special," he said. "I'll say grace."

"Grace!" Stubby snickered. "You're gonna say grace?"

"I am, by gum."

We bowed our heads.

"Us poor sea-farin' folk, far from the seas we love, humbly thank you O' Lord for a handsome supper such as this. It's been a long time since we dined in the midst of a pretty young maiden, a stout lad and a lovely bunch of dandelions. Amen."

There wasn't much talking, just lots of satisfied grunts from the men. As the Cap'n forked his last bite of pork chop into his mouth, he and Stubby abruptly cocked their heads.

"Quiet!" the Cap'n said.

We stopped eating at once. We heard the scrape of someone shuffling across our deck. Calliope jumped up, knocking her chair over. The Cap'n reached out with his good arm. "Hold steady," he said.

Stubby was out of his chair like a cat and down the passageway. The Cap'n told Calliope and me to stay put.

"Grab something sturdy, Thorny, and follow me!"

Thorny pulled the iron skillet from the sink, coated in coagulated pork-chop juice. He hefted it a few times and nodded to himself. He hurried after the Cap'n, who was already halfway up the stairs. Stubby slipped out of the shadows of the passageway, holding his pistol. Calliope tried to hide between the icebox and the stove. I looked around for some kind of weapon. Picking up a carving knife from the sink, I held it in front of my chest to fend off any attack. I stepped between Calliope and the galley door and waited with my heart racing so hard I could feel the vibration in my temples. Overhead there was shouting and footfalls on the deck. Then it grew strangely quiet. My grip on the knife's handle tightened. I could hear Calliope panting. Someone was in the passageway, heading toward us. Calliope hunched herself into a ball. We dared not breathe.

A shadow darkened the doorway. The Cap'n walked in. He wore a mean and nasty look and his scarred nose glowed purple. He looked at me with the knife in my hand and at Calliope huddled between the icebox and the stove. The hard features of his face then softened.

"Damn soldiers," he said. He ran his hand across the top of his head. "Two of 'em on guard duty thought it perfectly alright to come aboard without asking my permission. Jest checkin' to make sure we weren't German saboteurs."

When Calliope straightened up she was shivering, her face white, her eyes wide.

"Now tell me, Calliope," the Cap'n said ever so softly, "where'd you pick them dandelions that turned our supper into somethin' special?"

"I saw them growing on the bank while I was swimming. I swam over, climbed up on the bank, but not too far, and picked a handful."

"Yer a daring lassie." The Cap'n laughed and sat down at the table, picked up the dandelions, brought them to his nose, glanced at Calliope, and sniffed them. "A woman's touch. How I miss it, so."

Chapter Eight

That night Calliope and I didn't bunk together. The wise Cap'n sensed we were getting along in such a way that he changed his mind. He had Calliope and Thorny switch cabins. The move didn't thrill Thorny, but he went about it without a complaint. The top bunk was still mine, not that I wanted it. Thorny slid into the lower bunk, hollered up, "My snoring is bothersome and if it bothers you then go up on deck and sleep."

He nodded off as soon as he rolled himself into his blanket and snored like a lumberjack felling a forest. I doubt I'd have fallen asleep even with the ruckus below me. Too much was going on. Calliope was mired in a nightmare, pursued by her Poppa and Sheriff Lynch. She had no place to go. Me? I was off on a lark, running away from home. I could quit anytime I wanted, anytime I got homesick, and be welcomed back. I stared through the dark, barely making out the overhead. For at least an hour I didn't move while Thorny sawed down one tree after another. Unable to stand it anymore, I slipped up on deck.

There was no moon and so the infinite black sky was aglitter with stars. The air was cool with enough breeze to tousle my hair. The only noise came from the lapping of water against the hull of *The Frank White*. All the boats moored in a row along the edge of the Hudson had their running lights on, glowing like jack-o'-lanterns. If there were soldiers guarding the landing I couldn't see them. We had one lamp lit, spreading a weak beam of light across the deck. It was still dark enough in places that I had to feel my way to the side of the towboat facing the water. I sat down Indian style and leaned my back against a rough barrel. Looking at the sky, I easily made out in the north the Big Dipper pointing to Polaris, the North Star. I took in all the stars that outlined Ursa Major, the Great Bear. Poppa had taught me to read the stars. He said it had come in handy for him when he was down in the Arizona Territory with Captain Leonard Wood hunting Geronimo. He said he always longed to see the Southern Cross, but his adventures never took him to the part of the world where he could see it. He promised that once I became a man like him, the two of us would someday head down to the Andes and see the Southern Cross together.

After a bit I was able to see across the river. In the deep shadows along the bank a big tree had fallen in, its dead branches half-submerged. Far from the bank there was a lonely light probably from a farmhouse. Otherwise, the night was as black and as still as a tomb. Something off to my left caught my eye. Calliope stood about ten feet from me, looking out across the Hudson. She must have just come up. She had on Stubby's plaid shirt, its edges ruffling in the slight breeze. Even in the dimness of the lamplight I could see where the back of the shirt had been gathered up and stitched to fit her. I could see how the shirt fluttered a few inches below her waist and below that I could see that she wore nothing but a pair of frilly drawers that reached a short way down her thighs. The rest of her legs had not a stitch on them. A strange feeling I'd never known swept through me. I looked at her graceful legs in the lamplight longer than I ought and was soon afraid she'd catch me spying on her. I turned my head away, but that slight movement was enough. She spun around, her hand to her throat and gasped.

"It's me! Bucky," I told her.

"Bucky?"

I said, "I couldn't sleep."

Her hand was still pressed to her throat. "Me either."

She came toward me, seemingly unabashed that she was in her drawers. I couldn't help but look at her—at her bare legs. She sat down and curled her legs under her and pushed her back against the rough barrel, the scent of the river still in her hair.

I said, "Thorny snores so loud there's no way I could sleep."

"I heard him even with my door shut," she said.

We sat silently. In the pilothouse a match flamed to life, taking us by surprise. It was the Cap'n lighting his cigar. In that twinkle of firelight I saw the barrel of his shotgun. He held the match to the end of his cigar until it glowed red. Then it was dark again in the pilothouse, except that each time he took a drag from the cigar, it glowed like a beacon.

I whispered, "You think the Cap'n knows we're here?"

"Maybe, but that's all right," she whispered back. "He's watching over me."

I said, "I know."

"You are, too."

Her shoulder touched mine. Warmth spread through my entire body. I dreaded being tongue-tied. "I could stay here all night," I said.

"Me, too," and she nestled into me. "You smell of the river," she said. "From our swim."

"So do you."

"As well as fried pork chops, I bet."

I sniffed her hair, the soft touch of it on my nose. "No, just the river."

Because it felt natural to do, I wrapped my arms around Calliope to keep her warm. There was no need to talk. We just huddled there, the heat from our bodies keeping us warm. After a while I was aware of the steady rise and fall of her chest in that deep rhythm of peaceful sleep. I looked up at the North Star, that wonderful guiding light. Now and then I heard a fish jump and the sound of its quick splash was here and gone. Low voices from a nearby canal boat drifted over the water, mysterious as the night and incomprehensible. I was in a strange place—Momma's Boy watching over a fifteen-year-old girl.

In the early morning when it was still dark, my body chilly and damp with dew, the Cap'n nudged me awake with his foot. He was chewing his tobacco and spit a stringy stream over the towboat's gunnels.

"Breakfast's bein' served in the dining room, courtesy of Stubby and Calliope. Fried eggs, bacon, toast and coffee. The usual." He saw that I was surprised to be found sleeping on deck. "So, Thorny's snorin' got to you?"

"It did," I said. Remembering last night, I twisted around to look for Calliope. She was gone. The Cap'n watched me look for her, and I think he knew we'd been together most of the night. As I got up, my body hurt from the hardness of my makeshift sleeping place.

"Stretch out the kinks and go eat," the Cap'n ordered. "There's work to be done. We gotta drop the barge off in Troy."

In the galley, Thorny and Stubby were at the table, full plates before them. Calliope was piling breakfast onto another plate.

"Pour your own coffee, Bucky," she said. For a moment our eyes met and I saw into hers, as dark and blue as they were, a radiant, but secret look that meant we'd shared a special thing in our lives and no matter what else might happen, it would be ours forever. She put the plate on the table and went back to the stove.

"What's put you in a chipper mood?" Stubby asked as he watched her fix another plate.

"I had a beautiful dream last night." She sat down next to me. "The Cap'n's already eaten," she said.

"Up early he was," said Thorny. He mopped up the last of the yolk with a crust of toast. "When you're finished, Bucky, empty the ashes. You need to do it before we can start down river."

I wolfed down my meal and before leaving the galley shared one last look with Calliope. I wondered then about the coming night.

The ash buckets were heavier than usual and it was a strain to pull them up. Lugging them to the edge of the towboat proved just as hard. I dumped the ashes into the river and dropped the empty buckets down to Thorny. I was glad the chore was done. Stubby had the engine rattling away by then. By six-thirty the Cap'n blew his horn three times and we were under way. Some of the crew from the other canal boats were outside and waved. We steamed by with our black smoke billowing behind us.

The Cap'n made good time down the river and we passed through several locks. At each lock we kept a close watch for Sheriff Lynch. He never showed, not even when we cleared Lock 1 at Waterford and reached the busy federal locks at Troy where the Erie and Champlain Canals came together. Here the Mohawk River flowed into the Hudson, and the Cap'n was right. The Hudson took on a mighty life of its own, dark and wide and filled with traffic. Ferries crisscrossed the river, coal and lumber barges, tugboats, camouflaged gunboats and a yacht or two. We dropped off the barge we'd been towing at a huge terminal in Troy. It took us most of the day, all of us working hard.

When we were done, the Cap'n said to Calliope and me, "We'll be in Gotham tomorrow."

Calliope, sucking on Stubby's pipe, touched the brim of her slouch hat like an old-timer. "He's waiting somewhere down the river," she said. "Maybe he's watching us right now."

"Sheriff Lynch?"

"No," she said. "Father."

On the eastern side of the Hudson, a freight train rolled toward Manhattan. It outpaced the speed of *The Frank White*, an omen that the commerce of the river was threatened and men like Cap'n and Stubby and Thorny would soon be gone.

After so much peaceful farmland, the landscape changed. Between Troy and Albany it was more industrialized, and once past Albany more and more villages clung to the banks of the Hudson. But the terrain rose up, steeper, wilder—like that of Lake Champlain—the number of villages were fewer. Now the Hudson was truly beautiful. Someone, according to the Cap'n, had once compared it to Germany's Rhine River because of its high forested hills and mansions like castles. Maybe, when I got overseas to fight the Hun with Colonel Roosevelt, I'd see the Rhine for myself, with Poppa by my side, and make the same comparison. The thought thrilled me.

The Cap'n ordered me to swab the deck and polish all the brass. He gave Calliope the chore of cleaning the galley, top to bottom.

"There'll be no freeloaders," he barked.

And on we plunged, down the Hudson. We steamed along the east side of Houghtaling Island, an ancient place where the folks there hadn't changed in two hundred years. Then we passed by Kinderhook, President Martin Van Buren's hometown.

The Cap'n usually moored at West Point close to the Thayer Hotel, he said, but this night we tied up north of the village. He wasn't taking any chances that Calliope's father was somewhere about, since he lived across the river in Garrison. I wanted to see the military academy, but that had to wait until morning. After dinner of fried chicken and fried potatoes, we turned in without a swim. Stubby went up to the pilothouse to stand watch while the Cap'n went to bed. I climbed into my bunk and Thorny in his. All I thought about was Calliope in the next cabin. I was impatient for Thorny to start snoring. Instead, he tossed and turned. Minute upon precious minute piled up. Fifteen minutes, a half hour. I don't know how long before he started sawing away. But once he began the racket would've driven away any rat onboard.

I got down off my bunk without disturbing him. I went softly on deck and groped my way to the barrel where the night before Calliope and I had huddled together. She wasn't there. I sat down to wait. She didn't come. After about an hour I reluctantly headed back to my cabin. Coming down the steps to the narrow, gloomy passageway, I heard Thorny's rattling snore. Passing Stubby's cabin I made out a dull light from Calliope's cabin. It spread a soft glow across part of the passageway. Her door was open just a crack. I quietly walked by, not daring to peek in.

"Bucky?" Her voice hushed. "Bucky?"

The door opened wider and Calliope stood in the light, her

hair pulled back, her dark eyes glistening. She wore Stubby's complete makeshift outfit. No bare legs this time. She backed away from the door as if beckoning me to enter. I went in. Like my cabin it was as tight as a closet. She perched herself on the edge of the bunk.

"I'm frightened," she said. "Tomorrow we'll be at West Point." She held her arms across her chest and rocked back and forth. "I can't go back to my Father."

"The Cap'n will do something," I said. "You know he's watching over you."

"What can he do? Turn me over to the police? Father's got too much influence in New York, you don't know."

"Then we'll make a dash to Colonel Roosevelt's home. Your Poppa can't have more influence than the former president of the United States."

Calliope leaned against me, like she'd done the night before.

"When we were a family—Mother and Father, Schuyler and me—I was happy. We had everything, it seemed. Servants and candlelit parties. I'd stay up late to watch the grown-ups dance round and round to an orchestra. Sometimes they'd let me dance, try to learn the new steps. I 'd dance with a big kid from next door, much older than me, Ham Fish. I'll never forget the big colored man who conducted the ragtime band with a baton and how Vernon and Irene Castle taught everyone new dance steps. It was so exciting I couldn't wait to grow up and dance like Mrs. Castle. She was so beautiful with her bobbed hair all the rage.

"But it wasn't all candlelit parties. Father would take me for drives in his automobile. We had a chauffeur named Walker, who was Father's bodyguard. He would drive us into the city, to some apartment, and Father would be gone for an hour. I would wait in the backseat. Walker would turn around, one hand on the steering wheel and the other along the top of the front seat. He had bear-like hands, thick and hairy and wore a diamond ring Father had given him. He would talk to me, using crude language and rub my cheek from time to time and then stroke my neck. I was paralyzed with fear. He would say if I ever told Father he would break my neck.

"Then Father started going to another apartment. Only this time I had to go in with him and sit in the front room on the couch while he went into a back room and closed the door. I could hear him talking low to a lady. One day I asked why he had to see that lady, and did Mother know? He cuffed me so hard my ears rang all day. He told me Mother was not to know, or he would give me the licking of my life. Between father and Walter I was either going to get the licking of my life or end up with a broken neck.

"But Mother knew. They argued bitterly, he'd yell at her and say she was nothing but a scullery maid when he found her, and she would always be a scullery maid. Schuyler did nothing. He let Father yell those horrible things at Mother. When Walker saw how the marriage was he tried to get fresh with Mother. He would trap her in some room when Father was out and paw at her while she fought him off, even while I was there. I would flail at Walker with my fists. He would laugh at me and say I was next. Mother divorced Father, a huge story in all the newspapers, and when it got out that Walker had been fresh with me, the judge took me away from Father, and I went to live with Mother at our summer house on Lake George. Schuyler stayed with father.

"I always knew that someday Father would want me back. He has to own everything, especially people he thinks he loves. He wants me back now because I'll be sixteen soon and a young lady that he can proudly introduce into high society. But I won't go back."

Calliope put her arms tightly around me, her body trembling. Then she said, "Do you believe in happy endings?"

When she tilted her head up, and I saw tears glisten in the light.

"I do believe in happy endings," I said. I kissed her damp eyes. My left hand touched Calliope's cheek and the image of Walker in the automobile jabbed at my mind like an assassin's dagger. I pulled my hand away.

"What's the matter?"

I said, "I don't want you to think I'm like your Poppa's chauffeur."

"I'd never think that." She kissed me on the chin. "You just hold me." She pushed me down on the cramped bunk so that she was on top of me. Oh, Lord, how my heart jumped. She kissed me then with her lips slightly parted and a rush of warm breath in my mouth. Wild copper hair covered my face. My fingers entwined with her hair and I eased Calliope's head up for a moment to look into her eyes. Our faces were inches apart and we studied each other's eyes, as if trying to look through them, into our very souls. We were like that for sometime—our eyes locked.

"Hold me all night, Bucky."

She brought her face down on mine and hugged me hard, the sweet smell of the Hudson in her hair. For the longest time she held me until sweat dampened our hair and mingled against our cheeks, warm and honey-sweet. It was my turn to tremble. She felt it. She pushed herself up on her elbows and our eyes locked once again. She smiled and I smiled back. Her shirt had fallen open and I glimpsed the shadowy roundness of her breasts, the vague outline of her nipples. She caught me and without trying to cover them up, held her body for a beat so I'd see them more clearly, then lowered herself down on my chest again. Feeling me tremble, she laughed in my ear. "Hold me tight, Bucky, but no hanky-panky."

Chapter Nine

I left her before first light and went up on deck. I watched the sun come up, heart still jumping, mind racing—every detail so clear. I savored each one, over and over again. The weight of her body, the heat from it, her breasts pressing against my chest, the quiver of her heart, the smell of her hair, each bead of sweat on her temple, her breath on my face. My mind raced for other reasons, too. Today could turn out to be the most threatening for Calliope.

The Cap'n came out of the pilothouse, breaking my reverie.

"Where's our damsel in distress?" he shouted down to me.

"In her cabin, I suppose."

He unbuttoned his dungarees and peed over the side.

When he'd finished he hollered, "I want to cast off in a few minutes so we can make New York harbor by lunchtime. Go roust everyone. I'll start the coffee going."

Turning to go below, I saw a soldier sitting on one of the bollards near our towboat. I'd seen a number of soldiers guarding the locks since we'd started out, but this one was different. There was something familiar about him. Had I seen him before? The chevrons on his sleeves and the insignia on his collar indicated he was a corporal in the Seventh New York National Guard Regiment. He nodded. I nodded back.

"Looks like another nice day," he said.

"Yep," I said.

"You come down from Lake Champlain?"

"Yes, Sir," I said. "But you gotta excuse me. I've been ordered by the Cap'n to wake up the crew so we can get under way,"

"Many in the crew?" the soldier asked. He rolled a cigarette.

Behind me the Cap'n growled, "Four, if it's any of yer business."

I hurried below. The Cap'n followed and went into the galley. The soldier didn't seem to worry him much. Stubby was up. Thorny was still snoring. I shook him until he awoke. I then bumped into Calliope in the passageway.

I said, "There's a nosy soldier sitting on the landing."

She backed into her cabin, but came right back out again, putting on the slouch hat and pulling it down over her long hair. She clamped Stubby's old pipe between her teeth. "I want to see what he looks like."

"Don't go on deck," I warned.

She ignored me and started up. I went after her.

"Let me go first," I said.

The soldier was still there, sitting with one leg crossed over the other, casually puffing on his cigarette. Calliope came up partway. Clutching the calf of my left leg, she peeked from around my knee.

A wisp of smoke curled from the soldier's mouth.

"Everybody up?" the soldier asked.

"Just about," I said.

"That must be Chauncey Cobb I just seen. The one-armed captain's pretty famous up and down the river. I've heard a lot about him. That him?"

"Yes," I answered.

"I hear you're carrying a special load to New York."

"We dropped it off at Troy. We're picking up another load in New York."

"What kind of cargo you drop off?"

"Just slate and some lumber."

"It's human cargo I'm thinking of.

Calliope's nails dug into my calf.

"Only human cargo is the crew. The Cap'n, engineer, fireman and me."

The soldier flipped his cigarette into the river. "It's a young girl I'm thinking of. Your damsel in distress, as Captain Cobb calls her. She's Calliope Van Pelt, my sister. I'd like to see her."

Calliope's hand went limp and slid down my calf. Her fingers then dug sharply into my bare foot. "Schuyler?" she said, like she wasn't certain it was him. She came all the way up and stood next to me.

Schuyler kept his smile. "After all these years, and here you are," he said, "looking like Huckleberry Finn. Even so, it's wonderful to see you, Cal." He got up.

I said, "You can't come aboard without the Cap'n's permission."

"That's right," The Cap'n had come up.

"There's no reason to," Schuyler said. "I wanted to be sure my sister was on your boat. Talk to her. I presume I can do that without your permission."

I said, "You'll need hers."

"It's fine," Calliope said and stepped away from me. "When did you join the army?"

"Last month. Oak Rhinelander, and I quit Harvard to enlist in the Seventh Regiment. We're both in K Company. Father wants you to come home."

"I *was* home until Father had me kidnapped!"

"That was a mistake, and he's sorry for it. He wants you to know that."

"Is he sorry the sheriff slapped Mother and threatened to throw her in jail? Is he sorry for that?"

Schuyler seemed taken aback. I saw it in his eyes, and the quick way the line of his mouth straightened.

"I didn't know," he said. "I don't think Father knows either."

"He knows. And you know, too. How come you never came to Lake George to see Mother?"

"I couldn't," he said. "That was part of the divorce settlement. You knew the judge split us up. I was to stay away from Mother and you were to stay away from Father." Schuyler looked around at Cap'n and me. "I'd sure like to talk to my sister alone. I don't want you fellers hearing family secrets."

Calliope said, "Bucky knows most of them."

"Bucky?"

Calliope put her hand in mine. Schuyler noticed.

Then the Cap'n spoke. "I'm allowin' you on my towboat, Corporal Van Pelt," he said. "So you and Calliope here can have yer chat in private. You'll have it in her cabin. When it's over yer to leave. Calliope's stayin' with us."

Calliope shot me a worrisome look and let go of my hand. In a faltering way she led her brother down the stairs to her cabin. The moment they were gone, Thorny appeared on deck. "What's goin' on?"

"A family pow-wow," said the Cap'n. He rattled into the pilot-house.

Looking at me, Thorny said, "I'm starving."

"Make your own breakfast," I said. "I'm not moving from this deck until that soldier's gone."

Thorny was none too pleased because he was the fireman and I the deckhand. But he went off to make his own breakfast, grousing all the way. I took up a position on the gunnels close to the bollard where Schuyler'd been sitting when I first saw him. If he came up with Calliope in tow there was no way he'd get past me. He might be a college man and a soldier, but I was about his size. I waited, all tensed up, eager for it to be over. I knew the Cap'n felt the same way. And where was Stubby the whole time?

The Cap'n stuck his head outside the pilothouse. "Bucky, I want you to go ashore and look around to make sure Sheriff Lynch and Calliope's old man ain't hidin' about. I'd surely hate to be taken by surprise."

"Yes, Cap'n." I didn't want to give up my post. But I obeyed his order. I jumped on to the landing. I walked the length of the landing, went inland a few hundred feet, poked behind bushes and several small buildings and finally circled back to *The Frank White*. I'd been gone maybe twenty minutes. I got back onboard, surprised to hear the engine banging away.

"It's all clear," I called up to the Cap'n.

"Okay, then. Git ready to cast off."

"Cast off?" I was alarmed. "Where's Schuyler and Calliope?"

"Gone."

"Gone?!"

"Schuyler's gone. Calliope's in her cabin. Now let's git the hell out of here."

I wanted to go to Calliope. The Cap'n read my mind. "Let her be, Bucky. Jest let her be."

Once more we were steaming down the Hudson. The United States Military Academy stood on a high plain surrounded on both sides of the river by mountains with great names. Brackanack and Bear, Anthony's Nose and Storm King. Impressive granite edifices were clustered about like medieval cities to me. The stark monuments and statues to West Point's past heroes added to the glory of the place. But I didn't gawk at West Point for long. My heart wasn't in it.

Calliope came up. She went to the portside of our towboat and looked across the Hudson to the east bank, to the village there.

Garrison!

Along the hillside behind the village and to either side spread the mansions of some of New York's wealthiest families. She looked, it seemed, with all her might, at one of the mansions. It was a three-story affair of red brick, with a long green lawn sweeping elegantly down to the river. It had tall, wide windows and an upstairs porch with thick columns and a wrought iron railing in front. Although the distance was considerable, I was able to make out a man on the porch, both hands on the railing, and knew by his stance that it was her Poppa. It was the same pose he'd held when *The Frank White* had first entered the locks at Whitehall. Calliope saw him as well. She pulled off the slouch hat that hid her face and shook her red hair so it flew about.

My Lord, I thought, *She's taunting her Poppa!*

I looked back at the porch in time to see him turn and leave. When he'd gone, Calliope remained motionless until the mansion was no longer in sight—only the edge of the vast lawn was still visible where it touched the Hudson. Then it, too, was gone.

Calliope turned and looked at me defiantly with those dark eyes of hers and crushed the hat back on her head. She didn't bother hiding her hair. What was the point now that her Poppa knew she was on board.

"I suppose I can give Stubby back his pipe," she said and headed for the engine room. I started after her.

"Bucky!" the Cap'n snapped. "I told you to leave her be. Now come in here and git yer first lesson in pilotin' a towboat."

I knew he was doing this so I'd get my mind off Calliope. He got up from his chair and told me to take a load off and sit. He went outside for a second and threw his wad of tobacco overboard. He deftly lit a cigar, puffed on it a few times to get it going and came back in.

He said, "I'll be a son of a bitch if that gal ain't full of piss and vinegar."

Calliope was back on deck. She'd shed Stubby's clothes and had put her own back on. She looked just the way she'd looked when I first saw her standing on the landing at Whitehall in her blue dress and high-button shoes, except she wasn't holding the suitcase this time and her eyes weren't so full of fright. Her tumble of hair was there for all to see.

She regarded us only for a moment, smiled and turned away. Had I lost, well, the love I felt she held for me? My spirits sank.

"When we get to New York," the Cap'n said, looking down at Calliope as she crossed the deck, "God help us."

Chapter Ten

The Palisades loomed up on our starboard side, forested cliffs that were wondrous, but overshadowed on our portside by New York City itself. Gotham, as the Cap'n called New York, was unlike anything I'd ever seen. Nothing but buildings—and billows of great gray smoke that smudged over the city like a dirty halo. I beheld every kind of building. Tall ones, short ones, fat ugly ones, brown and black ones, red ones of every shade. Even buildings as white as snow. And all that smoke. The Cap'n singled out the Woolworth Building and said it was the tallest in the world. He said I ought to take a ride to the top in the elevator. He'd done it and his ears popped on the way up and on the way down his insides felt as if they were being ripped out like riding on the old Coney Island loop-the-loop roller coaster.

Boat traffic on the Hudson was as astonishing as the city, thick as honeybees around their hive and that hive was New York harbor. Every kind of vessel was afloat: freighters, liners, tankers, barges, fishing trawlers, even sailboats and ships with masts. There was a steady sound of horns and whistles. Tugs pushed and nosed huge ships into and out of the finger piers that jutted out into the river hundreds of yards. The Cap'n said the harbor was the largest and busiest in the world. He said there was almost eight hundred miles of waterfront. On the New Jersey side, at Hoboken, I saw rows of battleships, troopships with American flags fluttering on masts and navy crewmen dangling off the sides, painting them all a sea-colored brown, getting them ready for war.

Even Tripod felt the excitement, pacing along the ledge of the pilothouse window.

The Cap'n piloted *The Frank White* through—well, an armada—with one hand. I'd no idea where he was going, but he certainly did. For an hour we plowed on, dodging one boat after another. Then I saw the Statue of Liberty off in the distance in the Upper Bay. She looked unreal to me I guess because she *was* real and not one of those photographs from the rotogravure section of the *Sunday New York Sentinel*. She was coated in a haunting aquamarine. I knew then why Poppa felt so trapped in Burlington, banged around the house, drank, was often irritable, and called me Momma's Boy for spite. He missed this. He missed Gotham's excitement.

While I stared out of the pilothouse window, the Cap'n, chewing on an unlit cigar, wiggled his back and ordered me to scratch it, saying there was an awful itch under his right shoulder blade that he couldn't get at and he'd be grateful if I'd get it for him. I readily obliged, digging my fingernails into his skin.

"How's that?" I asked.

"Aw," he sighed, wiggling his back once more. "Now we gotta decide on Calliope. After that stunt she pulled up at West Point this mornin', I know her old man's gonna be waiting at our slip along with Lynch and his cronies. Once she's off the towboat there's nuthin' I can do. She'll be fair game. What about yer plan to take her out to Oyster Bay? Can ye do it?"

"I don't know, Cap'n," I said. "I don't know how to get there. It's too far to walk, isn't it?"

"Bucky, my boy, you'll never get there on foot. What I must know is, will Teddy Roosevelt welcome her along with you. Does yer old man have that much pull with the old President?"

"He saved his life, didn't he?"

"I figger it's our only chance, by gum."

"But how do we get to Oyster Bay?"

"By boat," the Cap'n said, steering ours easily among the other craft on the river. "You and Calliope need to make yer way across the Island of Manhattan to the East River to where Fulton Street meets South Street. It's a busy place at all hours and smells to high heaven. I've a friend there who owns a fast tug. He owes me plenty since the war when we were in the Pacific with Dewey. That's where I lost my arm. He'll take you and Calliope out to Oyster Bay. From there I think you can get to the Roosevelt home on foot." The Cap'n handed me a sealed envelope addressed to Captain John Bingham. "Yer to go to the New London Line. They run passenger boats and tugs up the Long Island Sound. Find that man, Cap'n Bingham, give him this, and he'll do what I ask. That I promise."

"Yes, Sir," I said. The Cap'n gave me a growly look for calling him Sir.

"Our biggest task is to set you and the girl free. Sneak you both off *The Frank White* without anyone knowin'. I'm sure they'll be watchin' us hard. You'll hafta make a helluva dash to the other side of Manhattan because if they spot you they'll be on you faster than a starvin' fox on a plump chicken." Then the Cap'n said, "We're comin' up to our dockin' place just off Canal Street. Git ready to tie up.

I went out on deck to where Calliope was standing.

I said, "I've never seen a deckhand in a dress before," She laughed, which made me feel better. "We're coming up to our dock. I'll take the bow. You stay and handle the backside. Watch for your Poppa and Sheriff Lynch. The Cap'n believes they'll be waiting for us."

I left Calliope there, worried they might be close enough to grab her.

With a dozen towboats already moored along the finger pier, some with laundry hanging on makeshift clotheslines, children darting about on the decks playing games, *The Frank White* eased into her slip and we tied up without any trouble. If anyone suspicious was lurking about the pier we didn't see him, only friendly boat people who bid us welcome to New York. The engine was shut down, and a few minutes later Stubby appeared on deck, wiping his sweaty face with a rag. Stubby nodded to a young lady with a bundle of wash in her arms. Thorny showed up next. He hadn't bothered to wipe the sweat from his face. It dripped off in buckets, and he didn't seem to mind.

"You got one last chore," he said to me. "Empty the coal ash into the Hudson."

By then we'd all gathered in the pilothouse. The Cap'n sat in his swivel chair and relit the cigar he'd been chewing on. He waved the match back and forth until the flame went out. He flipped the match out the window. He then picked up Tripod and stroked the side of her face she couldn't get at with her one front paw.

"Well," he said under a cloud of smoke, "we had us quite a trip this time 'round."

"Amen," Stubby said. He planted his old blackened pipe between his teeth and grinned at Calliope now that he had it back.

"You turned out to be a tolerable good deckhand, Bucky," the Cap'n went on. He winked at Stubby, who was now filling his pipe with tobacco. "But you need to trust in folks more. Folks who trusted you from the start and gave you the job of a lifetime."

"Yes, Cap'n."

"But don't trust folks overly much. They'll only break your heart."

I looked at Calliope who was looking at the Cap'n—not at me. The Cap'n then slipped me five dollars. "Where you're goin' you'll need all of this."

I thanked him.

"Calliope," the Cap'n said, "I'm returning this. It was for your safe voyage down the river, but you worked hard and proved to be a good deckhand, even in a dress." He handed her a wad of bills, the same wad, I was willing to bet, that I'd seen her Poppa give the Cap'n in Burlington. "Keep it well hid," warned the Cap'n. "Gotham's a dangerous city."

The Cap'n took the cigar from his mouth and with the back of his hand, touched the end of his lopsided purple nose and sighed.

"Well, then," he said.

It seemed to dawn on Calliope that she and I were really leaving. She looked at the Cap'n and then me and back to Stubby and Thorny. Uncertainty clouded her eyes. Her mouth opened part way. She looked at all of us again.

"Are we going to Oyster Bay?"

"Yep," said the Cap'n.

"How?"

"By tugboat. Only thing is, we gotta figger a way to git you across the tip of Manhattan without certain people knowin'. Once off our towboat there's nuthin' I can do with the law on your Daddy's side. There'll be the sheriff and his deputies and I'm bettin' a few policemen have been recruited to help out. They're keepin' out of sight, makin' us think they ain't around. But they're around alright."

"Let's go in," argued Thorny. "You know, like blockers in a football contest. I'll lead the way." He flexed his meaty arms.

Stubby said, "All the way across the island?"

"Well, sure. It ain't far."

"It's far enough."

"What we're gonna do is create a diversion," the Cap'n said. "Tonight me and Thorny will be escortin' a young gal off this vessel and they'll be certain to follow us. We'll go to Delahanty's Saloon a couple of blocks from here up on Hudson Street and have some beer and beefsteaks. Whilst they're peerin' in the window, Calliope and Bucky will take off a-runnin'. By the time Lynch figgers it all out you two will be gone, lost in a maze of streets."

Stubby said, "Where we getting' a gal?"

"My friend, you're gonna make us a durn pretty lassie. Calliope'll put on that Huckleberry Finn outfit again and you can put on the dress she's been wearin' now."

We looked at the dress.

"Kinda tight, even for me," Stubby said. "And I sure as blue blazes ain't wearing it into Delahanty's. I'd be laughed out of Gotham."

"It's only fer tonight. And you can enlarge it so it'll fit around your middle."

"Thanks!" Calliope said, and threw her arms around Stubby and planted a big kiss on his cheek.

His face reddened. "That means I gotta give up my favorite pipe," he said, embarrassed but enjoying the attention all the same.

"She won't need the pipe this time," the Cap'n said. "But you better not be smokin' it when we git ashore. Now change your clothes Calliope and hand over your dress to Miss O'Hara. Bucky, you can empty the coal ash now."

"Aye, aye, Cap'n."

I worried if his plan would work and, worse, if I could carry it out. Gotham loomed over me, a city so enormous and threatening that it got me to feeling like the Momma's Boy that Poppa said I was—a Momma's Boy from the hick town of Burlington—a Momma's Boy who'd never seen anything or done anything. I shuddered while hauling up the buckets of ashes, my eyes taking in the immensity of the city that I knew could swallow Calliope and me up like Jonah's whale.

We waited until dark. The lights along the busy waterfront flicked on. There were running lights on the boats alongside the pier. Deep into the city more lights began to show in windows and signs over doors and on the streets stretching away from the pier in long straight lines. I had my silly pillowcase packed and met Calliope in the passageway. She was sitting on her little suitcase. The Cap'n had told us to stay below until they left. He'd bang on the railing at the top of the stairs, to let us know they were going ashore. Stubby looked fine in Calliope's dress, but for one thing. He was too thick through the middle. Maybe in the gathering dark that wouldn't be noticed. We could tell he was not pleased to be wearing so feminine a getup

We'd said our good-byes around the galley table, our last meal together. The Cap'n, Stubby and Thorny ate very little because they were dining later at Delahanty's. But Stubby had made a fine feast for us—steak and fried eggs, all we could eat. The Cap'n toasted everyone. He said there wasn't a finer crew anywhere on the Hudson. And if he ever had the chance to hire a deckhand of the opposite sex he'd do it in a minute—if she worked as hard as Calliope and was just as pretty.

After the meal, when nobody was near, he grabbed me by the arm. He nearly crushed my bicep.

"You watch over that little girl, hear me?"

"Yes, Cap'n," I said.

"You just point yourself east. Foller Canal Street til you run into Water Street. Turn right, that's south, and go all the way to Fulton Street and then go east til you're smack against the East River. Ask fer the New London Line and or Cap'n John Bingham. He'll do the rest, by gum."

"Yes, Cap'n."

"And fer God's sake don't stop to talk to nobody. There's a lotta confidence men out there that'll take everything you got. Your money, your clothes and even your life. And you won't ever know it. You'll be passin' through some mean neighborhoods like the Five Points. Be very watchful, Bucky."

"I will, Cap'n."

"You got that envelope for Bingham."

"I do."

"Here's another five bucks. When you get to Oyster Bay give the Colonel my regards." The Cap'n let go of my arm. He extended his hand and we shook. "You're a fine lad, Bucky. I know you'll take good care of Calliope. Your Daddy'd be proud."

He turned away quickly and went down the dimly lit passageway and mounted the stairs. I never saw him again. I heard after the war that he'd gotten a job on a merchant ship carrying American troops to the Western Front that was torpedoed off the Irish coast. With one arm he couldn't swim and was drowned.

Chapter Eleven

It was past eight when Calliope and I heard the thump at the top of the stairs. The Cap'n, Stubby and Thorny were on their way to Delahanty's. We were alone. We weren't to leave for ten minutes. Calliope held my hand the whole time. Neither of us said a word. The only sound was the pounding of our hearts.

We went up to the pilothouse so Calliope could give Tripod a final hug. Then we were off. The deck was in total darkness. The Cap'n had blackened every light on board. We crept to the gunnels. Except for the four or five boats moored along the pier, as far as the eye could see, there was not a soul in sight. Down at the far end of the pier, maybe fifty yards away, a single light glowed. We had to walk that distance. There was no place to hide. If they were waiting for us in the shadows it was there they'd grab us. The Cap'n's words still rang in my ears. "You watch over that little girl, ya hear me?"

"Aye, aye, Cap'n," I said to myself, and Calliope and I slipped down from *The Frank White* for the last time. Feeling like an old salt, I patted the old towboat, a friend.

We didn't run down the pier. We walked as carefree as we could. Two pals out on the town. Except one looked like a tramp in baggy clothes and carried a suitcase and the other swung a pillowcase. When we reached West Street at the end of the pier, we came upon people hustling along the sidewalks, trolley cars clanging by, motorcars honking here and there and horse-drawn wagons with the rhythmic clip-clop of hooves on the cobblestones.

"Hey, Mac, look where the hell yer goin'," a man yelled at me. I stepped out of his way too late. He smacked into me, but continued on by. Another man brushed by us then snarled, "Watch it!"

Calliope instinctively clutched my arm.

We dashed across West Street to Canal Street. "We're to follow Canal Street to Water Street," I said. "I don't know how far that is, but we best move fast. The faster the better."

We ran this time. In and out among the hurrying pedestrians. A few blocks into Canal Street, we crossed Hudson. Our eyes searched for any signs of Delahanty's. There weren't any. We ran on. I stopped once, now sweating. I looked back to see if we were being followed. Too many people. I couldn't know for sure. We slowed down some, walking briskly, ever vigilant. We both glanced back now and then, searching the faces of everyone. There was no Sheriff Lynch, although I tried to recall the faces of his two deputies.

Up ahead a policeman stood on the corner where West Broadway crossed Canal Street. I didn't know it was Broadway until we got up close enough to read the street sign. He saw us coming.

"The Cap'n told us not to trust anyone, even a policeman," I whispered. "He might be working for your Poppa."

We hastened past the policeman, who kept an eye on us the whole time. Neither of us dared look back to see if he started in our direction. At the next corner, I dared chance a look-see. He was walking our way, a good fifty feet behind us.

"He's not walking fast enough to be after us," Calliope said. "But let's hurry."

We began to run again, holding hands, our strange luggage bouncing off our sides, our feet slapping on the pavement. On we went. I don't know how many blocks we traveled. Another look-back and the policeman was gone. We slowed then and finally stopped altogether. Calliope put down her suitcase to catch her breath. We'd no way of knowing if someone was on our trail. We scanned the sidewalk we'd just trod for any telltale sign. But what could that be?

Calliope reached for her suitcase. "Bucky!" she cried. "My suitcase! It's been stolen. All my clothes and things."

I shot a look all around us. No suitcase. The thief had been quick. A pang of hopelessness wracked my body. Calliope had to feel the same way. The Cap'n wanted me to watch over her and I was doing a lousy job of it.

"I'm sorry, but we must keep going," I said, still searching for it among the men, women and children crowding the sidewalk. Several hard-looking men lounged on a stoop in front of an apartment building. Maybe one of them had taken it. There wasn't time to ask. And if I did they'd probably beat me up.

For some reason I glanced across Canal Street to the sidewalk on the other side. It wasn't as packed with people. Leaning against a lamppost, drawing on a cigarette, black derby hat tilted back on his head, a contemptuous smile curled on his thin lips was Sheriff Lynch. He tossed the cigarette into the gutter running with filthy water. He looked both ways for traffic, stepped into the street and headed straight for us.

"Lynch!" I gulped.

We took off again, sprinting as hard as we could. Lynch dodged between a trolley and a wagon, jumped onto the curb on our side of the street and bounded after us. He quickly closed the gap. We weaved among the crowd. He still gained on us. Soon I picked up the sound of his footfalls as he pounded closer, then his panting—deep and loud.

He yelled, "Stop you sons of bitches!"

I stopped short and swung my pillowcase with all my might. It caught him in the face, surprising him more than hurting him. He stumbled forward. I'd never hit a man before, but his chin was right in front of me. The stunned look in his eyes told me that he knew at that moment he was vulnerable. I socked him in the jaw. A hard, driving punch that knocked him to his knees. I hit him again on the cheek. The force of the blow dazed him. He slipped sideways. His face cracked down on the concrete. A front tooth popped out along with a droplet of blood. I turned, grabbed Calliope's hand and we took off again through the startled crowd.

"Don't look back! Just keep running! We got to hide! Lose him somehow!"

I hustled her down a bunch of stone steps that led into a dark, unlit nook beneath a stoop, more like a cave. Inside the nook was a door that I figured opened into a basement apartment. I was sure it was bolted tight. We ducked down, listening for Sheriff Lynch's footfalls. Instead, we heard his angry voice.

"I saw 'em here somewhere," he snarled. "They can't be far. Look at me feckin' mouth. When I get ahold of that kid I'll stomp his guts into mush."

Through the dark, Calliope and I looked at each other. Sheriff Lynch wasn't alone. His hooligans were with him—or a police officer.

"Maybe they crawled down one of these rat holes," one of them said. "Maybe they're hidin' under a stoop."

"Yeah, maybe. I'll take a look" The sheriff spat. "Van Pelt's payin' me too much money to let his brat get away now that he owes me more for my missin' tooth."

If they came down we were goners. I frantically tried the door. A twist of the knob and it opened. So it wasn't bolted. We crawled into an inky-black room that smelled strongly of fried onions and garlic. I slid the door shut and locked it. "Not a sound," I breathed into Calliope's ear.

We couldn't hear the sheriff when he came down the stone steps, but we sensed his closeness. Right then he lit a match to see in the dark. His shadow flared up for a moment against the wall. He tried the door. It rattled, but refused to open. He swore and the match went out.

"They ain't here," he called out. He ran up the steps. "They're somewhere nearby. Gotta be, goddamnit."

Calliope and I kept holding our breath, daring not to flinch a muscle. While I fretted over our next move, in the room in which we hid a dull light popped on. A voice in a shaky, thick Italian accent yelped, startling us almost to death.

"I have gun! You no rob me!"

An old man sat on the edge of a rumpled bed. Behind him was an old woman who had to be his wife. She had a blanket pulled up to her throat, crying "Dio ci salvi!" The old man held a gun in his thin, trembling hand. A small black pistol. They were as terrified as we were.

"I shoot!"

"We mean no harm," I said, my voice flying at him. "We're not thieves. We're running from a bad man who wants to harm us."

"Bad man? My son be home soon. He a bad man."

That was why the door wasn't locked. I spotted another bed, noticed a table and chairs, a sink and a stove and icebox. One room.

"Please don't fire. Look, we're kids."

"I see plenty bad kids in neighborhood. Steal from my store all de time. You steal from me," he said, his accent thick with alarm. "Bum's clothes you wear."

"We're frightened," Calliope cut in. "We've been chased by someone who's trying to kidnap me."

"Kidnap. Is like stealing, only steal people. No good this man."

"Please can we stay here for a bit?" I asked. "Until he goes away."

The man slipped out of bed, still holding the pistol on us. He had on long white underwear. His wife crossed herself on the forehead and kissed her thumb. Her husband went to the door, opened it and looked out.

"No man here," he said.

I said, "He's on the sidewalk."

The man went out and up the steps to the sidewalk in his long underwear. "You try to break ina my home?" we heard him say. "My son bad man." He came back into the apartment, standing a little taller, a flicker of a smile on his face. He closed the door and locked it. "I chase him away. You safe now. No kidnapping. You want coffee?"

"Where's your son?" I said. I expected to see a giant of a man burst through the door, red-faced, swearing a blue streak and fists doubled up.

"He in the army. He not Irish but he in the Fighting Sixth-Ninth. Private Tony Margiotta. He just join up."

"*Anthony*," his wife said in a raspy voice. "Private *Anthony* Margiotta." She got up. "I make coffee. You sit."

Calliope and I moved to the table and sat as ordered. The man sat, too, while his wife went in her nightgown to make coffee. He laid the pistol down and patted it to show he could grab it at any time. "Kidnapping not good. Why he want to kidnap you?"

Calliope answered. "It's my Father who wants to kidnap me. My parents are divorced and he's trying to take me away from my Mother for good."

"Where you go now? Back to your Mother?"

Calliope shrugged and turned toward me. The wife placed cups of coffee around the table. She sat down. She put her hand on Calliope's hand. "You a pretty girl. You stay til it's safe." Then she looked my way, pushing cream and sugar at me.

"You her brother?"

"I'm a friend," I said.

"Why you in no army? A big boy like you?"

"I'm only fifteen years old."

"My Anthony is seventeen."

"I'm going to fight with President Roosevelt."

"Bah on him. Mr. Roosevelt too old to fight."

We sipped our coffee all at once. I kept an eye on the door.

The man said, "Where you go now?"

"The East River at Fulton and South Streets," I said.

"Finish your coffee," he said. "I take you to my store and let you out on Walker Street. Kidnap man not find you then."

We downed our coffee and the man took us to a door at the back of the one-room apartment where we entered what I figured was a store's supply room. He lit a lamp and then went through another door and led us into the store itself. It was a variety store and not much bigger than their apartment on the lower level. But the shelves were stocked. Nothing expensive, though, simply a neighborhood store filled with miscellaneous stuff, from tobacco to candy, canned goods, newspapers and magazines. A place you'd go to if you needed something in a hurry. He unlocked the front door, poked his head out and shooed us up the steps and onto Walker Street—a dark, narrow street, almost empty of life. He pointed east.

"This street take you back to Canal," he said in a comforting way. "You safe now, but you be careful. City not nice."

We thanked him profusely, shaking his hand the whole time. As we started down Walker he called out, "You meet Tony you tell him I miss him. He not a bad man like I say."

"We'll tell him," Calliope said.

"Ciao!" he shouted back.

We hurried east on Walker until it ran into Canal—both grateful for our good fortune, which for the moment had taken us out of harm's way.

The human traffic on Canal Street had thinned out. I figured it was about ten, maybe a little later. With fewer people we were easier to spot. If Sheriff Lynch was back where we'd dodged into the Margiotta's apartment then we'd be in the clear. If he was up ahead it was a different story. Instead of walking on the south side of Canal Street, we crossed over. Keeping close to the buildings in case we had to duck behind a stoop again, we pressed on toward Water Street.

The city turned dingier the farther east we went, the buildings more rundown, the men and women shabbier. Lights seemed dimmer, the street darker. At the Bowery, a train banged and hissed along on an elevated track two stories high. Oil drippings and hot coals showered down on the pedestrians below. Trolleys plied the center of the street. Calliope was used to such commotion because she'd lived in New York for a few years. For me, a rustic from Vermont, it was a thrill. Yet, at any moment, among the commotion, I truly expected Sheriff Lynch or his hooligans to jump out of the shadows. We still had a long way to go.

Passing a saloon, a grizzled man in a frock coat staggered out. He stepped in front of us, blocking our way. He reeked of beer. He hadn't shaved in days. "How much for the girl," he said in a gruff, threatening voice.

We tried to slip by him, but he wouldn't let us pass.

"How much!"

"How much you got," Calliope said, stunning me.

His eyes lit up, as much surprised at what she said as I was. "I got enough," he said. He fumbled inside his pants pocket. I grabbed him by the coat and hurled him against the side of the saloon. He slunk to the ground and we darted past.

"How much?" he yelled after us. But he didn't chase us. He stayed on the ground, mumbling.

We reached Water Street and went south—every shadow still a threat.

"I don't think Sheriff Lynch'd expect us to be on this street," I said. "I think he'd look for us on Canal Street. Don't you?"

"He's here somewhere!" she said. "I can feel him."

But no Sheriff Lynch or any of his hooligans showed themselves along Water Street. We made it to Fulton Street and a few blocks ahead was the East River. Nearing the end of our journey,

Calliope held me tighter. With a free hand I fingered the envelope addressed to Captain John Bingham. Would he really take us to Oyster Bay, like the Cap'n said he would? How trustworthy would he be?

South Street reeked of fish. The stink hit my nostrils a block away. Before we reached it, I saw lights and wagons and gangs of haggling fishmongers, and then we were being jostled by men in rubber coats and rubber boots and blood-soaked leather aprons as they hauled crates of fish up from the river to a line of open, wooden sheds that stretched along both sides of the street. Fish of every kind were heaped on long tables or on wagons with flat beds, gutted, fileted, heads lopped off. Blood splashed down on the pavement and mixed with river water and shone pink in the moonlight. Men yelled back and forth to each other, cursed and laughed and bellowed out names. The entire length of South Street was a spirited madhouse.

"Look, Calliope," I said, hardly containing myself. Not because of the madhouse, but because I was staring up at a glorious bridge aglow in the night sky. "Look at that big bridge!"

"The Brooklyn Bridge," Calliope said. "I've walked across it." Calliope nudged me, drawing my attention away from the bridge. "We'd better find the New London Line."

I stopped a man who was wiping a bloody hand on a greasy leather apron. In his other hand he held a butcher's knife, its blade dripping with gore. I asked him if he knew where we could find the New London Line. He pointed the butcher's knife north. "Two, three blocks that way," he said. We thanked him and moved on.

The New London Line was just beyond the fish market. Its office was in a row of three and four-story brick buildings. A light was on inside. A middle-aged, heavy-set man with not much hair spread across the top of his head sat behind a desk. He had a newspaper opened. In the middle of the newspaper was a bowl of soup. The man spooned the broth into his mouth absent-mindedly. Behind him were several filing cabinets and shelves messed with papers, and high up, a supply of blankets. Calliope pushed open the door as the man was about to take another spoonful of soup. He looked up, surprised that two kids were coming into his office, one dressed like a tramp. He held the spoon in front of his partly opened mouth for a second or so and then put it back into the bowl. His eyes went up and down Calliope, not in a leering way. It was her outfit that drew his attention.

"Can I be of assistance?" He had a low, raspy voice. "I'm the night manager."

I said, "We need to see Captain John Bingham. Is he here?"

"I'm afraid Old John isn't here," the night manager said. "He don't come to work before five. Why do you want to see Old John?"

"I have a letter for him from Captain Chauncey Cobb of *The Frank White*. He says that Captain Bingham can help us."

"Never heard of this Captain Chauncey Cobb."

"He commands a towboat up and down the Hudson River."

The man picked up his soup bowl. "Commands, huh? You're welcome to wait here." He nodded toward the wall behind us. "There're some chairs there you can sit in. It'll be a long wait. It's not yet midnight."

"Thank you," I said. "We just walked over from the Hudson River."

Again the spoon stopped in front of the man's partly opened

mouth. He put it back into the bowl. "You walked?" he rasped. "Must've been a trek."

"It was," said Calliope, and she fell into the chair. "My feet hurt."

The night manager said, "I suspect they might."

I dropped into the chair next to her. The man got up and pulled two blankets off a top shelf. He tossed them to me. "Keep yourselves warm. Now let me finish my chowder."

He went back to his desk.

We covered ourselves with the blankets. Calliope rested her head against my shoulder and in no time had fallen asleep. I watched the man eat his chowder and read his newspaper—then I was out, too.

Chapter Twelve

The banging of a door woke us both up. An enormous man, over six feet tall and at least two hundred and fifty pounds, clad in an unbuttoned, billowing navy blue pea jacket and a tan captain's hat with a black bill and above the bill the words "New London Line" stitched on scowled at us. He had unkempt white hair and under a big red nose sported a walrus of a mustache that spilled over his lips so thick it completely hid his mouth. He had colossal, fleshy hands and a set of sad eyes that softened his behemoth build.

"What's this, Samuel?" he said, meaning us.

"They want to see you, Old John," the night manager said, chowder and newspaper gone from his desk. In their place was a dime novel.

"What fer?"

Samuel shrugged. "Beats me. They've been here all night."

"All night, huh?" He looked us over. "Well," he said.

I got up, body stiff, and handed him the Cap'n's envelope. Calliope remained in the chair, hair a tangled knot of copper.

I said, "It's from Captain Chauncey Cobb."

A surprised look on his face, Captain Bingham snatched the envelope from my hand. "What's the one-armed fart up to these days?" Then to Calliope, he added, "Excuse my French."

"He *commands* a towboat on the Hudson," Samuel remarked, stressing the word "commands."

"Nuthin' wrong with that, Samuel," Captain Bingham said. He tore open the envelope. "I mean how's he doin'?"

"He's fine," I said. "But I think he's wishing he was back in the Navy so he can help lick the Germans."

Captain Bingham grunted and then read the Cap'n's note. When he'd finished he took a long gander at Calliope, paying me no mind. Calliope looked right back at him with her dark eyes never wavering.

"Christ," he said. "Don't you kids move."

He left the office, the door thumping behind him.

"Must have been some letter," Samuel said. "Old John don't get riled easy. He's got a gruff way about him, but keeps a steady hand at all times." He closed the dime novel. "He used to be in the Navy. Won some medal back in the Spanish War when Dewey's fleet captured Manila. He's a talker, really loves to gab, but never utters a single word about that medal. Old John's the best tugboat man on the East River and all the way up to New London. He knows every inch of the waterway."

The door banged open and three men clomped in. Each one appeared to be as big as Captain Bingham——who followed them into the office.

"Samuel, me and the fellers have to make a quick trip up to Oyster Bay," he said. "We'll be gone all mornin', I expect. You'll need to get another tug crew ready. I'll be takin' *The Good Sally.* Jimmy's getting her ready now. You can have the owner dock my pay, if you want. Jus' don't ask no questions."

One of the men, with a prizefighter's flattened nose, stood vigilant by the window, looking out.

Samuel said, "Okay, Old John, no questions asked."

"You're a good man, Samuel." Captain Bingham came over to us. "Let's get goin'. You kids stay behind me and Jake." Jake was the man by the window with the prizefighter's nose. "Moe and Billy will be on either side of you."

Calliope and I fell in behind Captain Bingham and Jake. We walked outside in the early morning darkness. Across the street were lights from the tugboat, *The Good Sally*. We marched toward her like two prisoners herded off to jail.

"Stop right there!" The sharp, angry sound of Sheriff Lynch's voice sent shivers through me, and no doubt more so through Calliope.

Captain Bingham kept us moving ahead.

"Stop, damn it!" Sheriff Lynch stepped in front of us. He wasn't alone. With him were two of his deputies I recognized from back on the Champlain Canal plus three New York City police officers in their blue uniforms with billy clubs held in front of their chests at the ready. Off to the right of us, away from the lights, stood Calliope's Poppa and her brother, Schuyler. Their presence unsettled her, and for a split second she faltered. But Captain Bingham urged her to keep moving. She did by clutching tightly to the bottom edge of his pea jacket so she'd be pulled along.

"I ain't asking again!" Lynch threw open his coat so we'd see his pistol and badge. "You stop now or pay the consequences!"

"We aren't stopping for no two-bit sheriff," Captain Bingham said. He walked up to Sheriff Lynch and shoved him so hard that he stumbled backward four of five feet. The Captain wheeled around to face the police officers while Moe and Billy boxed out the two deputies. "Don't do something you fellers will regret," the Captain said to everyone. "Like aiding and abetting a kidnap!"

For a moment there was silence, and then to our right, Mr. Van Pelt spoke loud and clear to his daughter. "It doesn't have to be this way, Calliope. We'll work it out. I promise we will. Just come home."

"Please!" her brother said. "I've missed you all these years."

I heard a catch in Calliope's throat.

Schuyler came up to her. Captain Bingham was ready to stop him until he saw how they looked at each other. Schuyler opened his arms. Letting go of the pea jacket, Calliope took a hesitant step toward him. For a moment they embraced there on the cobbled street amongst the stink of fish and the rumble of a tugboat engine and in the distance the outline of the Brooklyn Bridge.

After a bit she pushed Schuyler away. "It's too late," she said. "I want to go home to Mother. That's where I belong."

Sheriff Lynch by now had regained his footing. His face was wrenched in a fit of rage. His lips were pulled tight across his Geronimo-like face and I saw the gap where a tooth had been. It made me feel good. He swung his hand down to his side and drew his pistol. Leveling it at Captain Bingham, he snarled like the cur he was. "I'll shoot you where you stand!"

Everyone froze. The sheriff held the pistol steady and advanced toward us. I feared he'd shoot us all, he was in such a fury.

"Put that gun away, you ass," Calliope's Poppa yelled. "Can't you see it's over. I've lost my daughter."

"The hell with your daughter," the sheriff shot back. "It's the boy I want! Last night he assaulted an officer of the law." His tongue traced the place where his tooth had been. "And I'm arrestin' the bastard for it."

"You're not arresting nobody," Captain Bingham said. "You've got no jurisdiction in New York City. Christ, you're just an upstate rube."

"I ain't no rube from upstate," Lynch spat back. "I'm from Brooklyn."

"Still no jurisdiction here in Manhattan. You best go back across the river, rube, where you belong."

One of the police officers snickered. That drained the fight out of Sheriff Lynch, but not the rage. He stared at me in a way I'll never forget.

As he stalked away he hissed, "You ain't seen the last of me!" Then passing Mr. Van Pelt he said loud enough for all to hear, "I'll be in touch. You owe five hundred bucks."

We began walking again toward the tugboat while Van Pelt's men hung back, none of them knowing what to do. Holding on again to the hem of the Captain's pea jacket, Calliope stole a last look back at her Poppa and brother.

"Oh, Calliope," her brother cried out. "Oh, Calliope."

Her eyes filled and when she turned away to board *The Good Sally* tears were splashing down her cheeks.

Chapter Thirteen

Morning light had spread across the East River by the time *The Good Sally*, running with the incoming tide, plowed northward toward Hell Gate and Long island Sound. We were in the pilothouse with Captain Bingham. Jake at the steering wheel while Moe and Billy were somewhere aft and Jimmy was on deck coiling a length of rope. New York seemed to glide by. The Captain handed Calliope his handkerchief.

"Here, I've not used it yet," he said gently.

Calliope wiped her swollen eyes with it.

"Families are funny sometimes, and there's nothing you can do about it," he said. He watched her with his own sad eyes. "Just pick yourself up and move on, that's been my way. Hard to do, I know, but I see that you can do it."

Calliope tried to smile.

"That sheriff's a hothead and he's going to get himself in a ton of trouble someday. Waving a gun about like that." Captain Bingham stroked his thick mustache. "So, tell me about Cobb. I haven't seen him in years."

We told him all about the Cap'n and Stubby and Thorny, too, and our adventure down the Hudson. I asked Captain Bingham how the Cap'n had lost his arm.

"Saved my life, he did. We were in Commodore Dewey's Asiatic Squadron having a grand time in Hong Kong when we got ordered to the Philippines. The Spaniards were waiting for us, but we outclassed them. We've nine ships in all, six of them the most modern warships afloat with the biggest guns. Me and Chauncey were mates on Dewey's flagship, the Olympia. We simply sailed right into Manila Bay and blew up the entire Spanish fleet. Everyone starts dancing on deck and singing 'There'll be a hot time in the old town tonight!' Not a single sailor or marine was killed." Captain Bingham stroked his mustache again. "But I come pretty close.

"Dewey wants a landing party, see, to reconnoiter the harbor that's ablaze what with Spanish ships burning and exploding and listing port to starboard, most about to go under and gun emplacements on shore blown to bits. Me and Chauncey, young fools we were then, volunteer, along with a couple of other sailors and a young lieutenant and two marines. In we go on a landing craft no bigger than a wash tub. When we reached the shore we come under heavy rifle fire even though the Spaniards had already surrendered. We jump for cover behind a stone monument of some kind. One of the marines runs ahead of us and gets himself wounded. He's stretched out on the sand, moaning. Without thinking I go after him. Being a big fella, I easily hoist him on my shoulder and start back. That's when I see the sand under foot kicking up like little tornados. I'm being shot at, see. Then Chauncey is yelling, 'Bingham, you're a goddamn fool!' Next thing I know he's leaping over the stone abutment, pistol in hand, firing away. He kills two Spaniards who are shooting at me. Two others he hasn't shot turn their rifles on him. He's hit once in the chest and twice in the arm. I get back safely and see I've a bunch of bullet holes in my uniform, but nary a bullet touched my body. The surviving ambushers then run off and I go back for Chauncey and carry him out of harm's way. I sez to him, 'Jesus, Cobb, you're leaking all over the place.' Blood's everywhere. He stares up at me all glassy-eyed, blood bubbling out of his mouth and he sez, "By gum, that was fun." I get a medal for that skirmish, don't mean a thing to me, and Chauncey gets a purple heart and later a navy surgeon amputates his arm at the elbow and deep sixes it somewhere at the bottom of Manila Bay. See, if he hadn't plugged them two Spaniards I wouldn't be here today to tell the story. He saved my life."

The whole time Captain Bingham was telling the story, I could see clear as day the Cap'n fighting on the shore with one arm. I just couldn't imagine him with two of them.

I said, "That's why you're taking us to Oyster Bay—because of the Cap'n?"

"I'd do anything for that one-armed geezer." Captain Bingham pointed out the window to let us know he was finished talking over old war stories. "We're coming up to Hell Gate. There's a lot to see here. Look to the portside. There's Gracie Mansion, where Mayor Mitchel lives. See the new bridge up ahead. Work on it's almost done. Naturally, it'll be called Hell Gate Bridge. It connects Manhattan to the mainland so trains can come into the city from New England. Trains aren't using it now. Hell Gate used to be a treacherous place because of all the rocks and the fact the second strongest tidal current in the world is here. Back in the old days, more than one hundred boats of all kinds got shipwrecked on the rocks every year. Some folks tell of a British frigate loaded down with gold and silver that sank during the Revolutionary War. They claim the treasure's still there. About thirty years ago the state had the rocks blown up. Now Hell Gate isn't so treacherous. We'll slip right through it, between Ward's and

Randall's Islands and be in the Sound and in no time we'll be coming into Oyster Bay."

The Good Sally cut through the passage under the Hell Gate railroad bridge and into the wider expanse of the East River where we came to another island.

"That's Riker's Island. There's a prison farm on it. Not much good for anything else, I suppose."

Once in the Sound, he pointed out smaller islands, inlets and bays and coves, and mansions grander than those along the Hudson, and told us little stories about each one. He never asked about us—why Calliope'd run away, and why I was off to fight with President Roosevelt's army with my Poppa. Not one word. The time passed quickly. I saw how the shore flattened out when compared to the banks of the Hudson or Lake Champlain—hardly a wrinkle.

The captain pointed southeast. "Oyster Bay," he said. "If you like oysters this is the place that's got the best in the world. Something to do with all the freshwater streams that empty into the Sound. Gives the oysters here a special flavor."

We strained to see the little village, but it was hard to make out from afar because the shore had turned hilly just then and jutted into the water to form a bay. In the bay was an island with the name Centre Island. Beyond Centre Island a high piece of land poked out like a thumb. The captain said it was called Cove Neck. It wasn't until we rounded the island that we saw on Cove Neck's highest point a large, sprawling house with a great grand porch.

"Sagamore Hill," the captain said. "Teddy Roosevelt's place. I used to have the pleasure of ferrying him up here when he wasn't in the mood for a train ride. That goes back almost twenty years when he was president and the newspaper men got to calling Sagamore Hill the Summer White House."

Calliope touched my arm. We were here at last.

The captain laughed. "Maybe he isn't home. Maybe he's already off fighting the Hun."

If he wasn't there I wondered what we'd do. Where would I go? Back to Vermont? And Calliope? Where would she go? At that moment I had the worst doubts about myself. I was nothing more than an oversized kid who didn't think things through to the end. A big kid who believed in luck. A knot of foreboding twisted in my gut. I thought this had better be my lucky day.

"Well, there's smoke rising from one of the chimneys," Captain Bingham said. "That's a good sign someone's there."

Jake brought *The Good Sally* into a small harbor and Moe and Billy tied her up. On the wooden slats of the dock, an old man, puffing away on a calabash pipe, walked slowly toward the tugboat. He eyed it suspiciously through pince-nez glasses. Behind him four men lounged on benches, smoking. Two of them were dressed in black suits, like hooligans. I wondered if Sheriff Lynch had hired them for one last try at kidnapping Calliope. The old man studied Moe and Billy and then saw Captain Bingham and us.

"Old John," he said between puffs. "Well, I'll be a coon's uncle, it is you."

"Hello, there, Morley," the captain said. "Long time no see. Glad to know you're still harbormaster here at Cove Neck."

"Long time's right," Morley said. "Maybe as far back as when Taft was making a presidential fool of himself. What brings you to Cove Neck?"

"Dropping off some passengers."

"They must be important if you brought them here."

When the two men I took for Lynch's hooligans heard passengers were to be dropped off they got up and ambled toward *The Good Sally*. My muscles tightened.

"To tell the truth, I don't know how important they are. But I'd lay down my life for the fella who asked me to bring them here. The gal's' Calliope Van Pelt. She's running away from some bad folks that've been chasing her down the Hudson River and across Manhattan. The boy is Rough Riley's son, Bucky."

Morley yanked the calabash from his mouth. "Rough's boy, you say?"

"That's correct."

Morley trained his eyes on me. He squinted through his pince-nez. "You really Rough's little tadpole?"

"He's my Poppa," I said. "Is he here?"

"No more, he ain't. He left a week ago."

I closed my eyes. Poppa's gone!

The two men took up positions behind Morley. "I'm sorry, boy. If you want to see the Colonel before you leave, one of these gentlemen will take you up to the big house. They're with the Secret Service. The other gents are ne'er-do-well newspapering men. The Colonel always got something to say now we're at war and they get to hear his every word so they hang out here like vultures. The Colonel's got company now, a delegation of National Guard officers. I understand they're asking to be part of his all-volunteer division. But I reckon he'd like to meet the son of the man who saved his life."

"Before you take him to the big house," Captain Bingham said, "give this letter to the Colonel. It's from an old shipmate of mine. The Colonel needs to read it." He handed Morley the envelope that I'd carried across the tip of Manhattan. Morley took it and turned it over to one of the secret service men.

"He'll get it, Old John." Then Morley signaled for me to get off *The Good Sally*. "Come along, son," he said.

I said, "Calliope must come, too."

Morley spoke to the man holding the envelope. He nodded.

"It's fine with him. Come down then." Calliope started to get off the tugboat. As Morley reached out a hand to help she turned back and gave Captain Bingham a hug. I shook his hand. He smiled with those sad eyes of his. Another parting. That wasn't what I had in my mind when I ran off from home. Soon Calliope and I'd be parting.

The hike up Sagamore Hill took a half hour along a winding gravel road. The secret serviceman led us up without speaking one word while one of the newspapermen tagged along. He said he was Putt Bigelow from the *Herald* and knew Poppa during the Spanish War. He asked questions about Poppa and why I'd come all the way from Vermont to see the ex-President. I answered his questions reluctantly. When we reached the summit we still had to walk past overgrown fields, an apple orchard with trees in need of trimming and a barn before we reached the house. To me it looked like a big hunting lodge, something you'd see in a private forest preserve owned by wealthy men.

The secret serviceman took us to the front of the house where three or four automobiles were parked in a circular driveway. Under the portico was another car, a black flivver. From the portico we followed the secret serviceman up several stone steps and into the house. He spoke quietly to an associate guarding the entryway, gave him the envelope and along with Putt Bigelow left.

"I'll tell President Roosevelt you're here," the associate said. "He's in a meeting and so you might have to wait a bit."

After he went away, Calliope and I, not sure whether to speak to each other in the home of a former President, looked uneasily around. Even inside, it was like a great hunting lodge. A gloomy place it was—not so much because of the dark paneling, but because of the remains of wild animals crammed into every nook and cranny and every inch of wall space. Heads of buffalo, antelope and deer stared down with their empty glass eyes. Elephant tusks were scattered about. We dared not touch a thing.

We didn't hear when the President came into the room. Calliope nudged me and I turned and there he was, smaller and older than I'd pictured him in my mind. Pudgier, too, in his dark frock suit. But I would've recognized him anywhere, with his pince-nez, shaggy mustache and famous teeth. He smiled, his teeth taking up most of the smile, and held out a hand. In his other hand was a letter that I was positive was the one from the Cap'n.

"Luther Riley, Junior! Delighted!" And there I was shaking hands with the President. "Sorry you missed your Father, but he's off to Paris. *The Evening Sentinel* took him back, and about time, I say. He's the paper's new war correspondent." He then reached out to Calliope, his eyes running over her outlandish get-up. "Ah, you are the runaway, Miss Calliope Van Pelt. If your grandfather was Schuyler Van Pelt I knew him well. A great supporter of mine. I miss him. Now who are you running away from?"

Calliope curtsied then and the Colonel roared out a laugh. "This isn't the royal palace. We'll have no bowing or kowtowing here. Now tell me why you've run off."

"I didn't run off, Mr. Roosevelt. My father took me from my mother, had me kidnapped in the middle of the night. They're divorced."

"Indeed."

"I got away from him and a sheriff and found a safe place on a towboat and we—Bucky and me—came here. Bucky wants to join your army."

"Bucky?" The Colonel turned to me. "I take it, Luther, that you're Bucky."

"Yes, sir. That's what Poppa calls me in honor of Bucky O'Neill."

"Ah, Bucky O'Neill, the Arizona sheriff. A stouthearted chap. It is quite an honor to have your Father call you Bucky. Indeed it is." The Colonel clasped his hands behind his back. "I've disappointing news for you, Bucky." A black cloud seemed to cross his face. "That little dilettante of a President, Woodrow Wilson, won't allow me to raise my all-volunteer division, so I've got to sit this war out. Your Father was disappointed when I had to tell him that, along with several other Rough Riders. Some of them came as far away as California. There was a seventy-year-old cowboy from Deadwood who said he'd been a boon companion of Wild Bill Hickok. The boxing champ John L. Sullivan was here the other day to volunteer." The Colonel laughed. "The famous evangelist Billy Sunday actually showed up, and with that booming voice of his, assured me that because all the biblical prophets had carried big sticks, and that I carried a big stick, there was no one better qualified than me to raise an army. He begged to join up just to black my boots." The Colonel shook his head. "Now there's a new batch of disappointed soldiers in the other room.

They all want to volunteer. But I've no division to lead. Wilson won't let me."

The Colonel squinted at me then. "You appear kind of young to be a soldier."

I said, "I'm going to be sixteen soon and I'm strong for my age."

"Why don't you two get cleaned up and then we'll have something to eat, if you don't mind dining with an old soldier like me and some officers from the Fighting Sixty-ninth and their chaplain." He signaled to a rather lengthy man with thinning gray hair, and the bushiest eyebrows I'd ever seen. Dressed in a dark coat and gray-striped pants, the man was standing by a staircase. "Charles please take Bucky to Quentin's room, they look about the same size, and lay out some clothes for him. But first find Edith. Please ask her to take care of Miss Van Pelt. Have her draw a bath and maybe some of Ethel's outfits will fit. He smiled at Calliope. "That's some set of clothing you've got on. Rustic. I like that. Now please excuse me. I must return to the officers. See you for lunch."

Quentin's room was smaller than I would've expected. Charles carefully placed a brown suit on the bed and hung a white shirt over a rocking chair.

"I trust they will fit," he said. "You can wash up. There's a basin and pitcher on the table there." He pointed to a table next to a mirror. Over the table was a painting of the Colonel on a galloping horse. He had on his Rough Rider uniform. "When you're ready, come downstairs to the dining room. You can't miss it."

He closed the door and I sat on Quentin's bed, fretting about what would happen to Calliope and me. I went over to the table and studied the painting of the Colonel, a dashing figure on a mighty steed. He wasn't in Cuba, but likely out West somewhere. I washed and changed into Quentin's shirt and suit. The pants were barely long enough. I needed suspenders to hold them up.

I went down the stairs and found the dining room. The first thing I saw was a large moose head on the wall with its big antlers spread out. I spotted on the adjoining wall the head of a mountain goat with tightly curled horns. How many animals did this man kill? The dining room table was set with white linen and dishes and silverware for eight. The chairs around the table had legs with the ends carved like animal hooves. Massively made, they reminded me of thrones you might come across in a medieval knight's castle. I heard a rustling sound behind me. I spun around.

"Sorry to have startled you," said a tall, angular man in an army uniform. He had to be at least six-four. His face was gentle and his eyes a touch a merriment in them, or maybe a touch of devilment. His uniform was spotless and his Sam Browne belt and boots shone brightly. On each side of his collar were two gold crosses. "I'm Father Duffy, the Sixty-ninth's chaplain. I understand you and a pretty colleen will be with us for lunch."

"Yes, Sir. My name is Luther Riley. My Poppa calls me Bucky."

"I've heard all about your Da," Father Duffy said. "TR has told us how he saved his life in the Spanish War."

"He did."

"I was at Montauk when the Rough Riders came back from Cuba. A lot of them were sick with malaria and yellow fever and many died. It was my first work as a chaplain and it broke my heart to see such young men pass out of this world before their time." He stood behind a chair, gripping its back with both hands. There was a strength to him that comforted me, an inner strength I'd never felt in a man before, not even in Poppa. "And now you want to go off to war," he said.

"I do, Sir."

"Young lads like yourself should stay at home, and if fighting and killing and dying must be done, let older men do it then."

"I can't, Sir," I said, knowing at that moment I could tell Father Duffy why I'd come this far to be a soldier like him, that I could tell him anything. "You see, it's my Poppa."

I didn't get a chance to tell him because Colonel Roosevelt entered the dining room with three other soldiers. Two were as tall as Father Duffy, but broader through the shoulders. The third was about the Colonel's height. He had the bluest eyes I'd ever seen, like blue ice, and you sensed right off that here was a man to reckon with.

"Bucky," the Colonel said, "I'd like you to meet Major Bill Donovan and Captain Tom Reilly, both with the Fighting Sixty-ninth, and Lieutenant Hamilton Fish Junior. His cousin, also Hamilton, was one of my Rough Riders along with your father. He was the first of my men to fall to the Spaniards. Now Ham here just graduated from the Plattsburg Officers Camp and is looking for a regiment to call his own. I see you've met the good Father. Gentlemen, this young fellow is Luther Riley, whose father I've just been telling you about."

They greeted me while the Colonel looked around the dining room. "Now, where's Miss Van Pelt?" he asked. "We can't start without her."

He summoned Charles. "Find Edith and see how long she and

our lady guest will be. In the meantime, gentlemen, please take your seats."

It was understood that Calliope and I would be next to the Colonel who, of course, sat at the head of the table in his throne-like chair—Calliope on his right, me on his left. Father Duffy and Major Donovan were to sit next to Edith Roosevelt, who would be at the other end of the table.

"While we're waiting for our other guest, I'd like to boast a little about Bucky's father," the Colonel said as he reached over and patronizingly patted me on the back. "I first met Rough Riley when I was New York City police commissioner. At the time he was a newspaperman for the *Evening Sentinel,* and a splendid one, I might add. He was in my corner when it came to my efforts to clean up corruption. He, Jacob Riis and Lincoln Steffens. Quite a threesome, they were. One reason I took to Rough—that's his nickname because of all his hair-raising adventures—he'd been out West with General Leonard Wood fighting Geronimo and his renegade Apaches. Wood was a captain then. Rough told me stories of those days, how one of the Apaches had sunk a tomahawk into his cheek and it nearly killed him. His stories reminded me of my own time out West. We shared the frontiersmen spirit that made America great. I'm afraid that spirit is vanishing from our country."

While the Colonel rattled on about Poppa, making me feel uncomfortable, I looked across the table at Father Duffy. He'd been looking at me the whole time. As our eyes met I sensed then that he understood about my Poppa and me and why I had to be a soldier. A knowing smile flickered from his lank face.

The Colonel started to go into another of Poppa's exploits

when Mrs. Roosevelt and Calliope made their grand entrance. Well, it was grand to me, especially to see how quickly the officers rose from their chairs, the Colonel as well, when the women came into the dining room. Mrs. Roosevelt was thinner than I'd expected, maybe because of the girth of her husband. Her dark hair showed flecks of gray. She was simply dressed in a white gown becoming a former First Lady. Calliope was similarly dressed. Her copper hair had been washed and tamed by a brush, and then pulled up in the style my sister Louisa often wore. She had on pearl earrings and a blush of rouge on each cheek, and looked fetchingly like a young woman. I think Mrs. Roosevelt had fussed over her quite a bit after the bath and enjoyed every moment of it.

"Delighted you could join us," the Colonel said. I noticed that her beauty had affected him, too. "Let me introduce Calliope Van Pelt," he said. He took Calliope's arm and guided her to the chair on his right. With a hand on each of our shoulders, he announced that we were his special guests. For Calliope's benefit he named each officer. When he got to Hamilton Fish, who sat next to her, she flinched.

"We were once neighbors in Garrison," Lieutenant Fish said. "Do you remember? I'd forgotten your red hair, same as your mother's. But I only remember you as a little girl when we had those dance parties at your home and you'd sit at the top of the stairs and watch us dance the night away. Now look at you—you're all grown up." He had good sense not to mention the divorce.

"I do remember," Calliope said. "I haven't lived there for years. I live with my Mother on Lake George."

There was an icy edge to her voice and Lieutenant Fish knew it was time to take a new tack. To me, he asked, "How did you meet Calliope?"

"They came down the Hudson River together," Colonel Roosevelt answered. "Calliope had been forcibly taken from her Mother, but bravely escaped from the men who had tried to kidnap her. Bucky's a runaway, too. He's run off to join the army. Luck threw them together on a towboat and once they got to New York City they made it here to Sagamore Hill. And Edith and I are most delighted to have them." He leaned forward, placed his hand on Calliope's shoulder and looked challengingly at his wife. "All our children are grown and gone. Our sons are in the army and our daughter is off tending to her husband. I miss the gaiety of young people in this big, empty house. Calliope will stay here until her family problems are sorted out. Don't you agree, Mother?"

"It's a wonderful idea, Teedie," she said. "But we must ask Calliope how she feels about it."

"Oh, Mrs. Roosevelt," Calliope said, and ran from the dining room.

Mrs. Roosevelt excused herself from the table and followed Calliope into the parlor as the startled officers politely jumped to their feet.

"That's settled then," said the Colonel. "Now, Major Donovan, we've another issue to take care of. Bucky. Because you're a battalion commander, I believe you need a striker, a young private to take care of your personal needs. Make sure your uniform is spotless and ready, boots and brass shined, give you a shave and haircut when needed, light cigars for you—all those things that a valet does. I know he's not of age yet to serve, but he's got the size, and I bet the same pluck as his Father. I know you can grant a special dispensation for him. And as your striker he'd be out of harm's way, I'm sure. A smashing good idea, if I may say so myself."

Before answering the Colonel, Major Donovan, who had remained standing after Mrs. Roosevelt had left the table, exchanged glances with Father Duffy. I felt my whole life was about to change. The major, his blue eyes riveted on me, replied, "It's a smashing idea, indeed! As long as the young lad here, while giving me my morning shave, doesn't slit my throat. In fact, Frank and I had been discussing this very thing with Mrs. Roosevelt just now, before she dashed off to comfort the young miss." He shifted his look to Father Duffy. "It was Frank who brought it up at this end of the table."

The Colonel roared, his great teeth dominating his smile. "Great minds think alike, eh, Father Duffy?"

I could definitely see the devilment in the chaplain's eyes as they sought me out. "It seemed to me to be a natural thing to do," he said to Colonel Roosevelt.

It was my lucky day! I knew that Father Duffy and Major Donovan and the Colonel had read the Cap'n's letter and had discussed it among themselves. I thought then that my luckiest day had really been the day I met the one-armed Chauncey Cobb.

"Splendid!" the Colonel said.

Mrs. Roosevelt and Calliope reentered the dining room. Calliope's eyes were red, but it was easy to tell she'd been shedding grateful tears.

"Calliope wants to stay with us very much, Teedie, until we sort things out," Mrs. Roosevelt said. "And you're perfectly right, it will be nice to have a young girl in the house again."

"Well, now that everything's settled let's have lunch," the Colonel said, and we all sat down again.

Chapter Fourteen

After lunch, Major Donovan led me into another of the Colonel's big-game trophy rooms. It was spacious and dark like the rest of the mansion I had chanced to glimpse, with a vaulted ceiling and a great Oriental rug spread on the floor and a bear rug on top of that with the bear's head still intact. Two elk heads with antlers nearly scraping the ceiling guarded each side of an entryway to a study, while a pair of burly buffalo heads flanked a fireplace in which a log fire burned low and warm. On the mantel was a photograph of the Colonel, his son, Kermit, and a bearded hunter named R. J. Cunninghame who had guided the Roosevelts on their 1909 African safari. Nearby, a leopard skin was stretched over a bench and we took seats there, side-by-side. The Major rested his arms along the back of the bench and crossed his legs. His polished boots glistened from the light of the log fire. His mesmerizing blue eyes also glistened from the fire. I later learned that he was called "Billy Blue Eyes" by friends and foes alike.

"I used to hunt up in the Genesee Valley, mostly deer," he said, those blue eyes taking in all the trophies. "I never had any of them stuffed and hung on a wall, though." He ran his hand along the leopard skin and smiled, a forceful smile that put me at ease, maybe because I could feel an honest strength behind it. "Roosevelt seems rather blood-thirsty, don't you think?"

"It looks that way, Sir."

"You know, the other day when it looked like the Colonel was going to get his division I saw a cartoon in the New York Times magazine. The cartoonist showed him in his study with a triumphant grin and all his teeth and behind him the walls adorned with more animal heads than you could shake a stick at. There was even a bearskin rug in the drawing. The Colonel gleefully held a picture of the Kaiser, who looked like some worried wildcat with pointy ears and that upturned mustache of his. The caption read, 'This is the only trophy I need for my collection.' Quite funny now that I've been here to Sagamore Hill."

Major Donovan then shifted his body. "I don't know too much about your Father, just a few of the stories I've heard over the years. A legendary Indian fighter, Rough Rider and reporter, fearless, maybe even reckless." He continued to stroke the leopard skin. "He must be a hard man to live with, I reckon."

Looking into the Major's eyes, my mind drifted back to the time when Poppa caught me in his cloistered study fondling one of his Colt revolvers. I was ten or eleven. I'd taken the pistol from his desk drawer with the thought of playing a Rough Rider. Poppa snatched the pistol out of my hands, his face a knot of darkness and pushed me hard to the floor. "If I ever see you in here again toying with any of my weapons I'll knock the living snot out of you! Now go in the kitchen and play with your goddamn pots and pans!"

"You don't need to answer," Major Donovan said with what I took to be a knowing smile and wondered if somehow he'd read my mind. "I know your old man's the reason you want to be a soldier. I know because my old man was hard to live with, too. He ran the rail yard at Buffalo's main terminal and had to be tough. When his first four children died, brothers and sisters I never had a chance to know or to learn from or to love, he turned tougher, harder, maybe—hard as boilerplate. I was the first child to survive. Growing up wasn't easy, as I suspect it isn't easy for you, with such a demanding father. I came pretty close to giving in to the call of the Catholic Church to become a priest—like you're giving in to the call to be a soldier." The Major continued to smile. "My brother, Vincent, gave in. He's a Dominican priest now. I'm a lawyer instead.

"I read the letter that Captain Cobb wrote. He was very much taken by you and Miss Van Pelt and how you protected her. He wrote that you wanted to be a soldier more than anything in the world, although you're under age. He wrote you'd make a damn good soldier. His words." The Major squeezed my arm. "You're big enough and strong enough, I'll give you that. And if you're as fearless as your Father, and I believe you are, I'd like you to be my striker."

"Yes, Sir" My heart was pounding. "I'd like that very much. I wouldn't shirk my duty, I promise."

The Major nodded. "You need to know that there's a good chance I'll be commanding the Sixty-ninth. The reason I'll likely get command is that the regiment at the moment has no colonel. The acting commander is a Protestant with an English pedigree and the Irish Catholics in the Sixty-ninth don't like him. They're demanding one of their own. Soldiering is more than carrying a rifle. There's a lot goes on behind the scenes and so you'll need to know the politics of it. Can you handle being the striker to the man who'll be leading two or three thousand soldiers? The soldiers, every jack man of them, will ride you unmercifully, and call you the Major's Boy."

"I can, Sir," I said straight into his blue eyes.

"I counted on you saying that. We'll swear you in back at the armory. You'll start as a private attached to the regimental staff.

You'll stay at the armory to start, and that means you'll bunk in with the rest of the enlisted men up in the loft or out in that drafty drill shed. Not much privacy there. But lots of gossipy politics."

Major Donovan stood and I got up with him. He shook my hand.

"I think Father Duffy wants to have a word with you."

As we walked out of the room, skirting the bear rug, he shook his head slowly. "We'll be seeing a lot of death in the days ahead and so steel yourself for it, Bucky, for the dead won't be animals."

Father Duffy's chat was short, too. I sensed in him that same quiet, inner strength that I'd sensed in Major Donovan, the strength that you'd expect from an army chaplain. After all, Major Donovan once wanted to be a priest. Father Duffy asked if I was a Catholic, and I told him no. He wondered if I'd mind serving in a regiment that was nearly all Catholic. I told him I didn't mind at all. He nodded and said, "At least you're of Irish descent." Like Major Donovan, Father Duffy then talked a little about politics. He said that before he had become a chaplain he'd been a teacher at St. Joseph's Seminary in Yonkers and that he'd been kicked out because of his radical views and for the past ten years he'd been a priest in the Bronx. He had a small congregation, but at the Sixty-ninth he had over one thousand in his flock. He said if I ever wanted to talk to him about anything—*anything*—not to be shy. In a fatherly way, he said that I'd better let my Momma know pretty soon where I was and what I was doing. He then welcomed me into the regiment.

"That's what a chaplain's for," he said.

It surprised me that the interviews were brief. I guess they got from me what they needed. I certainly got what I needed from them—a soldier's job.

Major Donovan, Father Duffy and the other officers, including Capt. Fish, Calliope's long-time acquaintance who had seemed to upset her at the dining table, then went back into a meeting with Colonel Roosevelt. I wasn't asked to join them. It was mid-afternoon when the meeting finished. The soldiers got ready to leave and I figured that I would go with them without a chance to say good-bye to Calliope. But in the meeting it had been agreed that I'd stay the night at Sagamore Hill and the next day catch up with Major Donovan at the armory. Morley would take me back to Manhattan on a boat and I'd find my way to the armory on Lexington Avenue. I'd meet the Major there mid-afternoon, get sworn in and begin to learn my duties.

After the officers had gone, Colonel Roosevelt said, "Let's sit on the porch and have some lemonade before the next round of visitors arrive."

We moved to the porch, Mr. and Mrs. Roosevelt and Calliope dressed so beautifully with pearl earrings, and I in Quentin's tight-fitting clothes. The porch faced west and overlooked Long Island Sound. It was so peaceful there on the porch that it was hard to believe we were at war. Sailboats dotted the water. Sea gulls wheeled in the sky over the Bay. And like a family, we sat in big wooden rockers, Calliope and I between the Roosevelts, and sipped lemonade.

"This is my favorite spot on earth," the Colonel said. "I bought Sagamore Hill almost forty years ago and had this house built. Edith and I raised our children here. We had to spend time in the White House, of course, but in the summers we always hightailed out of Washington for this place."

I said, "How was Poppa when he came here?"

The Colonel turned his head in such a way to look at me that I realized he must be blind in his left eye. "Your Poppa was eager for action, even if he was hobbling around on that bum leg of his. He was always like that, whether it was sniffing out dishonest politicians in the wards of New York or shooting Spaniards in the jungles of Cuba. He could never sit still—not then, not now. One call to the *Evening Sentinel* and he was back on the payroll. It was the least I could do. I expect he's headed for Paris at this moment, delighted at last to be on his way."

"You got him his old job back?"

"Indeed I did, and I was happy to do it."

On the other side of me, Calliope and Mrs. Roosevelt were holding their own conversation. Women's talk, I figured.

I said, "I've heard so many stories about him, but I just can't believe they're all true."

"I only know the ones I was part of and, believe me, they're true." The Colonel took out a handkerchief and blew his nose. "Ever since I came back from the Amazon I haven't been able to shake this head cold. Runny nose, congestion, earaches, headaches. It'll be the death of me yet." He put away the hanky. "Thank your blessings you have a Father to impress. Mine died when I was a few years older than you are now. I was nineteen. I miss him still."

I sat there and watched the sailboats and seagulls, my head buzzing. The Sound looked the same size as Lake Champlain, but without the mountains. I don't know why I was thinking of the differences between the lake and the Sound while in the middle of a serious chat with a man who'd been president of the United States."

I said, "My Poppa doesn't think too much of me."

"I don't believe that for one moment." He drank some lemonade and then rocked a little, the chair softly squeaking. I heard Calliope say something to Mrs. Roosevelt about her Poppa, and it made me laugh. Everyone stopped talking at once.

"What's so funny?" Calliope asked.

"We're all talking about our Poppas," I said.

The Colonel snorted and then everyone laughed. The seriousness drained from our conversations after that, and we enjoyed the last of our lemonade and the endless beauty of the Sound. A few moments later, the Roosevelts excused themselves, telling us to enjoy the view for a bit. We watched them enter their home, and when they were out of sight our fingers touched.

"Mrs. Roosevelt likes me," Calliope said. "She said the Colonel's plan that I can stay here as long as I want is a sound one, and that when everything has been worked out, Mother can come and fetch me home." She fingered the pearl earrings. "She said I could keep the earrings, too. Aren't they pretty?"

They were beautiful against her neck. A few wisps of copper hair around the earrings made them even more beautiful. Well, I should say, they made her more beautiful. A great sadness fell over me then. Tomorrow would be the last time I'd see Calliope, perhaps forever. I didn't want to leave her. I took her hand again and she squeezed mine.

The rest of the afternoon lazed by. The Colonel kept himself in his study. Calliope spent time with Mrs. Roosevelt while I poked around the house, studying the heads of so many exotic animals—critters I'd only read about in books. When I went upstairs to Quentin's room to get ready for dinner I found my old clothes, washed and folded on the bed next to my pillowcase. I put them on and looked at myself in the mirror. In the days that I'd run away, I saw a big change. It's not that I looked different. I felt more grown up, I guess, and more worldly. On top of it, I was in love, and I knew that love was returned. That, I hadn't planned on.

Dinner turned out to be a lavish affair because the Roosevelts had more guests. I'm sure they had guests every night. The Colonel still wielded a lot of power, and people wanted his blessings for one thing or another. The guests were two Wall Street bankers, white haired and plump as turkeys. They talked about money and war, and I didn't understand a word of it. One of the bankers, named Lorillard, knew Calliope's Poppa. They'd been part of some deal or two, he said, each had made a killing. The Colonel gave Lorillard a dark glare, as if telling him not to mention Calliope's Poppa again, or at least not use the word "killing." Calliope hadn't shown much emotion, except that she cast me a quick, surprised look that the Colonel caught, and that's when he glowered at the banker. The conversation then returned to money and war. After dinner the three men retired to the Colonel's study.

Mrs. Roosevelt suggested we play a game of whist, and because it was warm and still light enough outside, we moved to the porch. Charles joined us to make up a foursome. He and I teamed up, while Calliope and Mrs. Roosevelt joined forces. We sat around a white wicker table in high-backed wicker chairs, a perfect setting for a summer's evening. Mrs. Roosevelt shuffled the first deck while Calliope, opposite her, shuffled the second. Mrs.

Roosevelt dealt out all the cards. The last card was hers and she turned it face up. It was the nine of spades.

"Spades are trump," she said.

Charles, sitting ramrod straight, his bushy eyebrows hanging like a cataract over his eyes, led off with the four of hearts. Calliope laid down a ten and the light from the lowering sun caught a wisp of red down on her freckled arm and, like an alchemist, turned it into sparkling gold.

"It's your turn, Bucky." Mrs. Roosevelt's voice took my eyes off Calliope's radiant arm. For the rest of the evening the sun's rays never struck her arm again in quite the same way.

Meanwhile, I followed with a five and wished the game were over and Calliope and I could be alone. Our time together was getting short. As we played, Mrs. Roosevelt chatted about the theater and Broadway. She said that "Teedie" hated the theater, but she loved it. He'd rather be out in the woods somewhere bagging a bear, but she preferred the Great White Way.

"There's a marvelous new play by Mr. James Barrie that's opening this week at the Empire Theater," she said, snapping down a seven. *The Twelve Pound Look.* We must go, Calliope. It stars Ethel Barrymore. Have you been to Broadway?"

"No Ma'am." Calliope's ten took the trick. She started the second trick with a deuce of hearts. "I love the flickers. My favorite is the Perils of Pauline with Pearl White."

"The motion pictures are lovely," agreed Mrs. Roosevelt. "Charlie Chaplain, Douglas Fairbanks, Mary Pickford. In fact, Miss Barrymore is in one right now at the Rialto. It's just out. *The Call of Her People,* I think. I still prefer the stage though. But if you prefer, we'll go to the Rialto. Just you and me."

"Oh, no, Mrs. Roosevelt. I'd rather go to the theater," Calliope said. The earrings quivered against her skin. "It would be so exciting."

We played two rounds of whist, and Charles, who never uttered a word the whole time, and I lost by two points. I wasn't much of a card player, anyway—although at home Momma loved to play whist and other such games and so I'd sit around the dining room table with her and my sisters and go through the motions. But I saw in Calliope's eyes that, like Momma, she loved games. When we'd finished our last hand, the Colonel came out on the porch. The bankers had left.

"They want me to go to Wall Street next week and give a pep talk about the war. You know how much I love Wall Street, Edith," he said with a touch of sarcasm. Folding his arms across his barrel chest, he turned his gaze to the west, at the now setting sun. "What a delightful picture. It's the prettiest sunset in the world, don't you think, children?"

Children! We'd both be sixteen in a few months. Old enough to marry. And the sunset was pretty, all right. But it could never hold a candle to the sunsets over Lake Champlain. The land across the Sound was fairly flat. I missed the mountains. I think Calliope missed the mountains, too.

When we didn't answer, the Colonel checked his pocket watch. "Eight o'clock. How about some leftover dessert?"

It was after nine when we finished the leftover dessert, a two-day-old apple pie. We drank milk with it. I watched the Colonel wash down his slice, milk forming a thin, white line over his mustache. He licked the milk off masterfully as a kitten and said,

"Ahhh," and then winking at Calliope, passed his plate to Edith for another slice.

"Teedie!" she said. "One slice is enough."

"Please?" he begged like a naughty boy. He got the extra slice and, again like a naughty boy, sheepishly ate it. The Roosevelts were down-to-earth folks who relished the small, intimate doings of life, and I liked them immensely. Their home would be a good and safe place for Calliope.

That night I slept in Quentin's room. Calliope slept in Ethel's. I dreaded the coming day. But we had the night. At least part of it. It was past midnight when she came to me in one of Ethel's nightgowns. She whispered that she had to wait until she heard the Colonel snoring. The Roosevelt's room was at the top of the stairs, and she had to tiptoe past it, her bare feet soft on the carpet, the creaking of the old floorboards muffled. I'd left the door open a bit and she slipped into the bedroom as quietly as a ghost, and for a moment the moonlight pouring through the open window outlined her taut body, which lay hidden beneath the nightgown's lace and frills. When she snuggled against me in bed, I felt every curve of her as if nothing was between us. I could hardly take a breath—each beat of my heart was like the sound of a kettledrum in my ears. Then she took my hand and placed it against her bare breast and held it there, her nipple hard. "This is so you'll remember me forever," she murmured. And in honor of Cap'n Cobb and that first night we'd slept together, and for that moment when she'd let me see her breasts, she whispered, "Now there's going to be no hanky-panky, soldier boy. But we can kiss," she giggled. And with that her lips touched mine with my hand still on her soft breast, and I melted away.

Morley took his boat out past Centre Island to the open water of the Sound. I was the only passenger aboard. It was a sleek gasoline-powered boat, and he informed me that it was very fast. Before he cranked her up, he pointed with his pipe, smoke curling up from its bowl, back toward Cove Neck.

He said, "Last chance to view Sagamore Hill."

I looked up and saw the great house. On the lawn stood Calliope and with her red hair caught in the morning sunlight. She was waving Stubby's slouch hat. I waved back with both hands over my head.

I don't think I was ever so sad in my life, although I knew another adventure awaited me at the Sixty-ninth Regiment Armory. But that was hardly any consolation. I was already missing her with all my heart. I could still feel her body against mine as well as the silent tears I'd shed when before dawn she'd left me to slip back into her room.

We had promised to write and to let each other know what was happening in our lives—her life as a member of the Roosevelt family—mine as a doughboy with the Fighting Sixth-ninth.

Then, for a moment, I thought of Sheriff Lynch and his threat and felt that I hadn't seen the last of him and wondered if that would be so.

At breakfast we both had been quiet and a bit groggy. The Colonel was grumpy. He dropped the morning edition of the *New York Herald* next to my plate of fried eggs. He opened it to Page 3, revealing a short article by Putt Bigelow about how I'd come all the way from Vermont to join Roosevelt's division only to find out that President Wilson had squashed it. Most of the article was about Poppa and the Colonel, and as I read it I angrily realized that Bigelow didn't like Poppa or the former President. Yet he'd seemed so friendly when we had walked up the hill from the dock. I never figured he had planned to write about me.

"Don't trust newspapermen," the Colonel said. "And that goes for your Father as well, God bless him. If they have nothing good to write about you they will. They'll rake through the muck until they find something. Anything they can use. Best to use newspapers to your advantage. I do it all the time. End of lesson."

His mood then put a damper on the rest of us until Edith slid in front of him the last piece of leftover apple pie from the night before. His mood changed quickly, and he smiled with his great set of teeth.

I left right after breakfast. Charles had given me a real suitcase for my belongings so I wouldn't be embarrassed walking into the armory carrying a pillowcase.

I waved once more to Calliope, feeling her body against mine, again, and then Cove Neck was gone and so was she.

End of Part I

PART TWO
With the Fighting
Irish

Chapter One

"You're on your own now," Morley said as he dropped me off at the South Street pier and then steered me in the direction of the Sixth-ninth's regimental armory over on Lexington Avenue. He told me it would be a long hike, but after hearing about me and Calliope dashing across lower Manhattan, he said it'd be a piece of cake.

On my own, I thought, facing the streets of Gotham this time with a suitcase in hand. The last words from President Roosevelt were, "Good bye and good luck."

On my own. I knew now there was no turning back as I walked along, my heart touched by a bittersweet feeling because I was off on a great adventure while leaving Calliope behind. I didn't have time to dwell on her much, though. There was much to see. The war had turned New York into a frenzy of patriotic fervor and guilt.

On nearly every street corner, recruiters, proud in their fresh uniforms, tried to shame civilians to enlist. I hadn't realized there were so many National Guard regiments even in such a big city, all of them hungry for men. The Seventh, the Twelfth, the Fourteenth, the Seventy-first, I later learned, and a bunch more, including some outfit called Squadron A. All were out hunting down victims of military age, trying to get their regiments up to fighting strength. Whenever one of these potential victims shielded his face with a straw hat or darted across the street, the recruiters hooted after them. "Hey, slacker! Oh, Momma's Boy! What's your sweetheart gonna do when she finds out you're a low-down coward?" They hooted at me, too, even though I was bound for the Sixty-ninth Regiment. "Yoo-hoo, Momma's Boy!" That'd be changing soon.

Posters were everywhere. One pictured a civilian standing by a window while on the other side marched a company of soldiers. "On Which Side of the Window are YOU?" it read. "ENLIST!"

I saw James Montgomery Flagg's famous portrait now turned into a poster of a finger-pointing Uncle Sam that had been on the cover of *Leslie's Monthly* the year before. I'd liked it so much then that I'd clipped it out and hung it in my room. It had been changed. Instead of the words "What Are You Doing for Preparedness?" it now read, "Uncle Sam Wants You!"

As I neared the Sixty-ninth's armory, with the skirling sound of a bagpipe somewhere close by rising louder, I happened upon another poster. It had no pictures of patriotic soldiers, but thrilled me just the same.

ENLIST TO-DAY

IN

THE 69TH INFANTRY

JOIN THE FAMOUS IRISH REGIMENT

THAT FOUGHT IN ALL THE GREAT

BATTLES OF THE CIVIL WAR

FROM BULL RUN TO APPOMATTOX

GO TO THE FRONT

WITH YOUR FRIENDS

DON'T BE DRAFTED INTO SOME REGIMENT

WHERE YOU DON'T KNOW ANYONE

Stephen L. Harris

MEN WANTED FROM 18 TO 40
APPLY AT THE ARMORY
LEXINGTON AVENUE AND 25TH STREET

The life-size poster was plastered against the side of a squat, but a massive limestone structure, three stories high, which took up the entire block between East 25th and 26th streets. A mansard roof slanted down from the top, impressively coated in slate and copper. The entrance was a grand archway of a dozen or so thick granite steps. Sculpted in the center of the archway was a great eagle, its wings spread. Below the great eagle, pacing back and forth was the bagpiper, dressed in a green kilt, playing the enticing, foot-stomping regimental tune, "Garryowen."

I was now in the presence of the Sixty-ninth's armory, barely a decade old. I wasn't alone, staring up at this Manhattan fortress. It looked to me like there were more than a hundred young men, some with girlfriends, wives or mothers, milling about with the same nervous excitement. I knew how the young men felt as they huddled in small family groups, saying their good-byes. At that moment, Calliope filled my heart. Those who were alone paced back and forth like they were figuring out in their own minds if it was the Sixty-ninth they really wanted to join or go to some other outfit. I guess all that pacing meant they were mustering enough courage to march up the steps while the bagpiper urged them on with his stirring music.

For me, there was no milling around. I took as big a breath as I think I've ever taken, because once inside this armory, built solid as Vermont granite, my life would never be the same. I bounded up the steps two at a time. I had to push past several men and skirt the bagpiper to get inside the armory.

A tall, burly soldier, his campaign hat slanted down so his face was partially in shadow, directed everyone to move to the right in a single file where he'd formed a line. I told him I was there to see Major Donovan. He looked me up and down as if he was sizing up a side of beef. The soldier then said with a gruffness in his voice that meant business, "You gotta be Bucky Riley. The major tol' me to keep an eye out for ya." He pointed toward the line of new recruits. "But first a physical. Gotta see if yer fit and, if ya pass, you can then sign up and be a soldier in the glorious Fightin' Sixty-ninth. Otherwise go home to your momma!"

I hadn't expected a physical to see if I was fit. What if I failed? What then? All of a sudden I felt panicky—a lousy time for feeling that way before seeing a military doctor.

He escorted me to the head of the line. "This kid's next, orders of Major Donovan," he said to a lanky, middle-aged soldier. I soon found out it was Major George Lawrence, the Sixth-ninth's chief medical officer. I'd see a lot of him in the months ahead, his apron-covered uniform spattered in blood.

"Donovan, huh?"

"Yes, Sir," I answered. "I'm to be his striker."

"Then you must be that kid everyone at HQ is talking about since the Major and the Chaplain got back from Sagamore Hill. Rough Riley's son."

"I guess so, Sir."

"Okay then," he said. "No physical for you. You're young and look strong." He pointed to a long table near a corner surrounded by civilians signing papers, raising their right hands, swearing oaths and then moving on to get their uniforms. "Head there and sign up and be a soldier in the Fighting Sixty-ninth."

"Yes, Sir," I said, relieved there'd be no physical.

As I walked away, he said so all could hear, "Head of the line for you!"

I signed all the proper papers, and took an oath to serve my country. I'd enlisted, my heart and soul banging inside my body, and my mind not knowing what to make of it all. Then a private threw a brown bundle of clothes at me. Snapped out of my reverie, I caught the bundle against my chest. My own uniform!

"Two pairs of pants, two shirts and one coat. You're big, they'll fit and now get your cap, puttees and boots over there. Make sure they fit, especially the boots 'cause you're gonna march yer arse off, and then move along onto the drill floor."

"Not him," said the officer who had just signed me up. "He's Donovan's new striker."

The private looked me over again with a flashing smirk as did all the recruits standing in line behind me. "Welcome Major boy," he said. "Glad you ain't in my company, boot licker. That it'd be *Company E*. Best of 'em all! Remember it. And remember me, Corporal Post, 'cause I'll be ridin' your butt from here to Tim-buck-two. Now move along."

I stood there not sure where to go.

"I said move along, Major boy!"

Still unsure amid the bustle of the lobby, I went back to the soldier who had first greeted me when I'd entered the armory.

"Go back there through them doors," he said with that same gruffness. "He's out in the drill shed trying to make soldiers out of new recruits, some still in their city clothes and crying for their mommas. You will be soon."

The drill shed was the largest room I'd ever seen with a balcony at one end where you could overlook the entire place. The whole inside of the drill shed was packed with men, most in uniform, some in civilian garb. I guessed about one thousand soldiers, all bunched shoulder to shoulder.

And now I was one of them. But I had no idea where to go or what to do. I stood there, feeling as dumb as a scarecrow on the edge of a cornfield.

"Private Riley, over here!"

Major Donovan's voice, loud and clear above the din, came at me from across the drill shed, and it hit me like the shot from a sniper's rifle. I saw him pacing in front of hundreds of men, all part of the First Battalion I'd been told he commanded. The men were split into groups, companies, I figured. Each had two men in front, a captain or a lieutenant as well as a sergeant. Donovan stopped, turned toward the men and snapped out "Attention!" so all could hear. A shuffling of awkward feet, sounding to me like the shuffling of a giant deck of cards, riffled across the drill floor. The men stood still in various poses of what they thought attention ought to be.

As I walked toward Major Donovan, my uniform and suitcase cradled in my arms, he resumed pacing.

"Gentlemen," he said, his voice again loud and clear. "Here comes the latest member of the First Battalion, Luther Riley. He's my new striker. For you gentlemen who don't know what a striker is, I'll tell you. He keeps me looking good."

I don't know if I heard a laugh or maybe a snicker or two coming from the ranks. I hoped my face wasn't red enough to be seen.

Major Donovan stopped walking back and forth. He cast a dark look over his men. "But don't let that fool any of you."

When I got in front of Major Donovan, his blue eyes drilled into mine. "Put your stuff on the floor," he said. I obeyed. "Now give me twenty push-ups!" I faltered. "Twenty, I said! Twenty push-ups!"

I hit the floor, now really panicky, and, as he counted, I struggled through twenty push-ups. When he finished counting, he turned away from me and back to the battalion. "All of you now, officers included, twenty push-ups!"

Like me, the battalion hit the floor as if it had been mowed down by a farmer's scythe and, like me, the soldiers struggled. I saw that some couldn't even do one push-up. Then the Major said to me so all could hear, "You, too, Private Riley! Another twenty!"

When the push-ups were over and the men back on their feet, Major Donovan barked, "When we reach France, every jack man of you will be in the best physical condition, better than any soldier in General Pershing's army. Count on it!" Then to his captains and lieutenants he told them to resume command of their companies.

To me he said, "Pick up your stuff, Private Riley, and come with me." As he strode off the drill floor, he added over his shoulder in a gruff voice, so unlike his tone back at Sagamore Hill, "If you hadn't given me those twenty push-ups, Bucky, you'd have been on the next train back to Vermont. Rough Riley's son or not."

Chapter Two

The first thing I learned about Major Donovan, he's a man of constant motion. When we entered his small office, he pointed to a bathroom. "Go in there and put on your uniform so you look like a soldier. You can then pack up your civilian clothes and mail them back home. You won't need them until the war's done. By the way, have you informed your family that you're now a soldier, a private in Uncle Sam's army?"

"Yes, Sir."

"Good." He sat down and watched me go into the bathroom. When I came back out, uncomfortable in my stiff uniform, but proud to have it on, collar chafing my neck, boots tight like shackles pressing hard against my ankles, and there was Father Duffy sitting at the desk opposite Major Donovan, legs comfortably crossed.

"Private Riley," he said, and smiled. "I'm told you can do forty push-ups in a heartbeat."

An empty chair was next to Father Duffy, and I wasn't sure if I should sit in it. Instead, I stood, holding my suitcase now filled with all my clothes.

"Put the suitcase in the corner," Major Donovan said. "Then stand at ease. As my striker you need to know your duties, what I expect of you and, perhaps, most important because you and I and Frank here are going to become quite close in the coming days, are the politics that now weigh heavy upon this regiment."

I put my suitcase in the corner and then came back to the desk and stood at ease as I was told.

"Aw," said Father Duffy, without looking at Major Donovan, "take a seat."

The Major nodded. I took the seat.

"First, your duties as a striker," he said the moment I sat. "I'm going to be meeting with my subalterns as well as fellow majors and a bunch of blasted politicians almost round the clock, from the time I'm up in the morning 'til the time I hit the sack."

I didn't know what a subaltern was and felt too nervous to ask, so I just nodded.

Father Duffy cut in with a grin. "Subaltern is a British term for a junior officer. Lieutenant or captain. You see, our Bill has been to England and Germany, last year it was for the John D. Rockefeller Foundation to broker a deal to get food into starving Poland. That meant England would have had to ease up on its naval blockade. England refused, but Bill picked up some British lingo along the way. Sorry to interrupt, Major, with my history lesson."

"Anyway," Major Donovan went on, his blue eyes aimed for a moment at Father Duffy for interrupting, "I'll be too busy to take proper care of personal things. My uniform must be clean and crisp every morning, boots polished to a shine and what few medals I have, I want them shining, too, so shiny as to be seen from afar. Not that I'm vainglorious, but I want people to know who they're dealing with. Each morning, before I put on my uniform, you'll give me a shave. I may be talking to someone or a couple of someones at the time, but you go ahead and slice off my whiskers as close as you can. I want a smooth face—without a single nick, mind you. Also, you'll be running messages for me, many to Frank here and to the regimental commander, regardless of who the hell he may turn out to be. Pardon, Padre. And so keep an ear tuned sharply to any scuttlebutt, any rumors, among the men, officers and, yes, civilians that you run into while making the rounds that you think we, Frank and I, ought to know about. I'm talking about politics here. No nickel and dime gossip. And keep your mouth buttoned up at all times."

I froze. Did they want me to be a snitch? Poppa'd beat the tar out of me if he knew.

Major Donovan shifted in his seat and gave Father Duffy another look, I guess to see if he'd covered anything. Father Duffy then picked up where the Major had left off.

"Here's the politics you need to be aware of and why we need to know who we can trust, the closer we get to the battlefield. Up until this war, the Fighting Sixty-ninth has been strictly an Irish Catholic outfit. God bless our regiment. Last year, during the Mexican troubles when we were down on the Texas border, our commanding officers, Colonels Conley and Phelan, both Irish, both Catholic, were ousted by the War Department because of poor health. We don't believe for one moment it was their health that got them thrown out, but the fact that they were Catholic—too much bias in the army. So, we're still waiting for the War Department to appoint a new commander to replace Conley and we feel very strongly that the government is trying to slip in an outsider who is not one of us to lead the regiment. We won't have it. We must have Bill as our commander."

He paused for a moment before going on, I think in order to let it all sink in. Another history lesson.

"So who can we trust that will side with us when the regiment marches into combat? The acting commander we just had, a chap named Bill Haskell, was alright, but while he was in charge, maybe not realizing what he was doing, he brought in the wrong kind of men to complete our officers' corps, mostly from the snooty Squadron A." Father Duffy looked at Major Donovan. "Our Bill may be from upstate New York, but you can bet that not only is he a strong leader of men, he's Irish and a Catholic through to the core. That's what this regiment always had going back to the Civil War when our soldiers soaked the battlefields of Virginia red with our blood. We need an Irish Catholic commander now to keep alive our Celtic traditions, to keep us strong and ready to fight for the country we love the way we did, starting at Bull Run in 1861. And bless Colonel Michael Corcoran for that."

"But, Sir," I cut in, not knowing for the life of me who Colonel Corcoran was, and now feeling I didn't fit in. "I'm only half Irish, and that's on my Poppa's side, and we're not even Catholic. On my Momma's side we're all Congregationalists."

"Close enough, Bucky," said Father Duffy. A merry twinkle shone in his eyes. "Along with being Bill's striker, you'll double up and serve as my altar boy. That'll fix your not being Catholic. So, in no time you'll fit right in, that's for sure."

"Yes, Sir," I said, wondering what my Momma would think if she knew I was on my way to becoming a Catholic.

"Now," said Major Donovan, rubbing his hand across his chin, "have you ever shaved a man before?"

"No, Sir."

"Well then, let's give it a try."

Chapter Three

Rumors. Everywhere rumors—all about who's going to take over command of the regiment? While that question rang throughout the drill shed, up into the rafters of the armory, spilled out onto Lexington Avenue and was printed and discussed in all New York's newspapers—the *Tribune*, the *Herald*, the *Sun*, the *Evening World* and even Poppa's paper, the *Sentinel*—all I could think about was Calliope. Day in and day out. How was she? Was she still safe at the Roosevelts? I had to know. Of course I had to know about Major Donovan's fate, too. Rumors, even those published in the aforementioned newspapers, claimed that official orders had already been drawn, stating he was the one. Yet there was no proof, although inside the armory it was a given. After all, the Major was Irish and Catholic. But what about the acting boss, Colonel William Haskell, a protestant? Wasn't he returning to lead the regiment to France? Maybe he's the one. No, circulated another rumor, it's the transfer from Squadron A, Charles Lang, again a protestant and politically connected to the powers up in Albany. If either one of them were to take over, the very nature of the Fighting Sixth-ninth would change forever.

And if that wasn't enough to fret about, a completely different rumor swirled through the armory concerning the very fate of the Sixty-ninth. I heard about it one morning while shaving the Major. I'd just draped a towel around his neck, covered his collar and chest, and with soap and hot water lathered up his cheeks and chin. He was in his chair, his head tilted back, his feet up on his desk, the boots I'd proudly shined to a mirrored gloss. Father

Duffy and Captain Mike Kelly, who I was just getting to know, sat facing him, chatting about the future of the regiment. I found Captain Kelly spellbinding. A narrowly built man, he wore a trim mustache that gave him a debonair look. He was far from debonair, though. He carried the nickname "Dynamite Mike" and for good reason. Unlike Major Donovan or Father Duffy, he was a native of Ireland, born in County Clare. And he'd actually been in battle. He'd fought in the Boer War and had been a year in the Burmese jungles, one of the true combat veterans of the Sixty-ninth. Although he'd served in the British army, I discovered he wanted nothing better than to send England reeling out of Ireland, bloody and beaten, and give his homeland its freedom. He was anxious to get back to the battlefield. He commanded Company F. I knew he held the respect of all the men in his company, but even more, the respect of Major Donovan and Father Duffy.

"What about this new National Guard division the War Department's wanting to organize?" Major Donovan said before I put the razor's edge against his check. "It's going to be made up of regiments from all over the country and one from right here in the city."

"Twenty-six states in all," Father Duffy piped in. "I hear it's already been dubbed the Rainbow Division."

"Well, there's a lot of New York regiments to choose from," Captain Kelly said. "It'll probably be the dandy Seventh because of the pull its officers have in Washington." He sounded a bit disappointed.

"I hold the Seventh in high regard," said Father Duffy, always reassuring. "But we deserve it more than any regiment. I'll be sending a lot of prayers heavenward. We'll be the one."

"I hear it'll be the first National Guard division to sail for France," said the Major. "I want us on that ship."

"Whoever gets the nod, it'll be an honor," Father Duffy said. "But I'm counting on the good Lord."

I ran the razor's edge down the Major's cheek, carving a smooth path through the warm white lather. He didn't flinch. I breathed easier.

"What will dominate this division's rainbow when we get in, and we will—the color green." Father Duffy smiled. "The true color of our very own Irish regiment."

The others laughed and I almost nicked Major Donovan's chin.

"Easy," he said.

After I'd shaved the Major, a good job, if I do say so myself, he and Captain Kelly went out on the drill floor to greet their soldiers, so many of them raw recruits like me, struggling into the armory from their homes or places of business for a round of training.

As we left the office, Father Duffy held me back and said, "Bucky, it's time for you to learn the duties of an altar boy. I have two other altar boys-in-training. Both are Catholic, been to mass all their lives and will be able to help you. One's Irish through and through, and the other's Italian." He then sighed. "I believe the ethnic make-up of my beloved regiment is changing and I need to embrace it. We can't turn away any good soldiers, no matter their background."

The boys were not boys. Well, they were older than me by a few years. Maybe eighteen and each about my size. Father Duffy introduced them.

"This is Doogie McDougall from Rockaway Beach, where he's been an altar boy at St. Rose of Lima Church." Rockaway Beach didn't mean anything to me. Doogie was taller than me with black hair and blue eyes and a warm smile. I liked him right off. "This other lad is Tony Margiotta from the West Side" I knew a little about the West Side having run through it with Calliope. "Like you, Bucky, he's learning the ropes, but he's well grounded in the rigamarole of Catholic mass." Tony also had black hair. He was smaller than Doogie, but like him, he had a warm smile. I liked him, too.

We shook hands and when I looked into Tony's eyes there was something familiar about him and I thought for a second I'd met him somewhere before.

"Do I know you?" I asked.

"Don't think so," he said. "Unless you like ragtime music and saw me up in Harlem at the Manhattan Casino where Jim Europe and his band, the Rattlers, play. Love that ragtime."

I let it go at that. "Never been to Harlem, never heard any ragtime music." I felt like the country bumpkin that I guess I was.

"I'll take you up there if we ever get any free time. There's a big concert coming up soon. You'll love the ragtime beat." He then did a little shuffling dance, clapping his hands to some beat only he could hear. "Doogie, you like ragtime?" he asked between claps, his head bobbing.

"Don't know if I do."

Father Duffy cut in. "Okay Lads, we need to get to work."

The first few weeks flew by like they'd never happened, days crowded upon days. I learned the duties of an altar boy. We all did, although Doogie, who'd been an altar boy when he was in his very early teens, had the jump on us. And also doing my primary job, I kept Major Donovan clean-shaven, his uniform wrinkle-free and his boots shined to a high gloss—his medals, too.

All these duties were easy. Learning to be a soldier was not.

While the regiment awaited assignment to a training encampment along with any news about us joining the Rainbow Division, inside the armory Major Donovan drove his First Battalion hard. We learned close-order drills, but mostly physical exercises that brought out the sweat in all of us. Countless push-ups, sit-ups, deep knee bends, jumping jacks and, when they were done, out the back entrance of the armory we double-timed, down Park Avenue South to Union Square, around all the statues there—George Washington mounted on his horse, the Marquis de Lafayette, President Lincoln—then back to the armory, huffing and puffing. A good half hour, if not more. At first, we were dragging, gasping, unable to keep up with the Major's pace. But each day we got better, we got stronger and then we started to sing George M. Cohan's new song "Over There" as we loped along in the street, holding up traffic. The words and tune and the Major's powerful voice leading us on gave me, and I'm sure everyone—even those civilians watching us run in the street—patriotic chills.

Over there, over there,
Send the word, send the word over there
That the Yanks are coming, the Yanks are coming
The drums rum-tumming everywhere.
So prepare, say a prayer,
Send the word, send the word to beware -
We'll be over, we're coming over,
And we won't come back till it's over, over there.

But this physical training was still not enough for the Major. He'd located a bunch of battered boxing gloves. He formed a ring of soldiers. Inside this human circle we battled each other. With the Major and other officers as referees we fought under the Marquess of Queensberry rules. No hitting below the waist, no knees, no gouging or biting. For a number of the soldiers who'd grown up in the tougher neighborhoods of New York like Hell's Kitchen or the Five Points—they had to struggle to fight clean.

Hollered one of them, "How we gonna whip the Hun if we can't kick 'em in the balls?" Shouted back another, "Stick 'em with the bayonet!"

There were even several professional boxers in the Major's battalion. One of them was Richard O'Neill from Harlem who'd won twelve bouts in his interrupted career. He was only five-nine, but could he ever punch and move.

When the newspapers heard of our fisticuffs, a reporter from the *Tribune* came by the armory to interview the Major while I was in the middle of a shave. The Major had me stop. With the reporter ready to take notes, he stated for the record, "Our men are going to learn that it's possible to fight after it begins to hurt. We want every man to be able to stand up and take punishment like a real fighter. And the bouts will do it. These men will be sluggers who will laugh at bruises. They'll be prepared for that day ahead when they'll need every ounce of endurance and courage for the supreme effort."

The next day, the Major read from the pages of the *Tribune* the reporter's article to Father Duffy. Halfway into the article, he paused. Then went on. "Listen to this quote. 'Donovan intends to lead the hard-fisted, hard-hitting battalion into the trenches, that will go over the top like back-fence cats and fight like wild ones.'"

Father Duffy laughed. "Well, I guess that's true."

That afternoon the Major put me inside the ring of soldiers with Tony. We stripped down to the waist. The boxing gloves, clammy inside from earlier bouts, were pulled on and laced up. As the soldiers forming the ring cheered us on, we went at it. I'd never fought before, not even on the playground at school. That was me, Momma's boy. Tony looked like he'd been in a few scrapes. I was bigger. He was faster. We circled each other. We tried a few jabs that fell short. The ring around us jeered.

"Look at them patsies!" someone yelled.

"Yeah, I wouldn't want them in a trench next to me!" another hollered.

"Whattaya want? Them babies are altar boys!"

With that, Tony lowered his head and charged me. I nailed his chin with a short uppercut. He fell back, then lunged forward and grabbed me in a clinch.

"If we wasn't fightin' by the stupid Queensberry rules," Tony whispered, "I'd knee you in the groin right now and the fight'd be over"

He feigned kneeing me, stepped back and caught me high on the cheek with a solid punch. He followed up with a straight jab to the nose. I felt a crunch. Blood spurted out my nose, down my chin and over my chest.

"Jesus!" Tony gasped as Major Donovan's words flashed through my rattled stunned head. *We want every man to be able to stand up and take punishment like a real fighter.*

I came back, hitting Tony square on the left eye. The punch stunned him. I tried to follow up with another to his head. He side stepped my swing and nailed me hard into the ribs.

We clinched again and then the referee stopped our sparring. "Enough for now," he said. "Shake hands."

Someone tossed a towel in my face. I dabbed at the blood seeping from my nose. I saw Tony blinking several times as he rubbed a glove across the eye I'd clocked with the only good punch I'd thrown.

Then the circle around us cheered. The sound made me feel good.

Chapter Four

Inside the elevated railway as it jounced above Ninth Avenue two stories high past darkened offices and sooty apartment windows of the grimy buildings close to the tracks, Tony and I sat next to each other in the last car on our way up to Harlem. Major Donovan and Father Duffy had given us the night off because of our bout. The flesh around Tony's eye I'd socked had turned a greenish purple. My nose did not look much better. Cracked and swollen with cotton balls stuffed up each nostril, and purplish, too, like Captain Cobb's old nose. I had to breathe through my mouth. What a sight we were. We'd laughed at our looks.

Tony had talked me into going with him to the Manhattan Casino to hear the Fifteenth Regimental band known as the Rattlers, led by Lieutenant Jim Reese Europe. It was a special night, he said, one we didn't want to miss.

"If I was a colored guy," he confided, his head bobbing like the first time I'd met him, "I'd've enlisted in the Fifteenth, not the Sixty-ninth. Just to listen to the Rattlers. But the only white guys in the regiment are officers. I ain't officer material, that's for sure, being the son of poor Italian immigrants."

I said, "What's so special about this band?" To me, one regimental band was like all regimental bands.

He stopped bobbing his head. "I can't tell ya. Just listen." He bobbed again to some inner tune only he could hear.

The railway rattled on. Gray buildings swept by. Now and then a blurred body stood by a window staring out, a dim light behind. It spooked me.

I shifted my eyes back to Tony. "So it's a special night?"

"You bet. The Fifteenth got its orders. It's not to be part of the so-called Rainbow Division." Tony smiled. "You know, black's not a color of the rainbow."

"So I heard," I said.

"Well, tomorrow the regiment's off to Camp Whitman, that's someplace upstate. To begin real trainin'. No more of this marchin' around Harlem with broomsticks for rifles. We'll probably be goin' there soon enough, or most likely Camp Mills out there on Long Island. Tonight's performance is a farewell concert. The Manhattan Casino's gonna be packed. Soldiers, civilians, musicians from all over, just to hear Lieutenant Europe and the Rattlers for probably the last time. I don't wanna miss this. Not for the life of me."

Tony was right. It was a special night. The Manhattan Casino was aglow in lights. Cars parked up and down the street. All the entrances packed, people swarming in. Soldiers guarded the doors. I later learned that more than four thousand people had jammed into the place. I felt the excitement and couldn't wait to get inside. I dug into my uniform pocket for fifty cents to purchase a ticket. We pushed in.

It was crowded outside, but it was even more crowded inside. A loud din of voices cascaded through the air. Tables, almost all of them already filled, circled a powdered dance floor, leaving room only for a stage empty, except for musical instruments in their rightful places—bassoons, clarinets, cornets, flutes, saxophones, trombones, drum sets, banjos, too, and many more. There were box seats reserved for high-ranking officers and other dignitaries. I saw a white colonel about to sit down at one of the box seats. He was fussed over by several junior officers—subalterns remembering Father Duffy's definition. I figured the colonel was the Fifteenth's commander, Bill Hayward. I'd heard Major Donovan talk about him. They'd been New York lawyers in civilian life.

An usherette dressed in a nurse's uniform, white with a red cross over her breast, led us through the milling crowd to a round table close to the dance floor. I could tell Tony liked the spot, but we had to share the table with six others—two soldiers and four girls, all black. We nodded at them as they checked out our uniforms.

"Tony Margiotta, Fightin' Sixty-ninth." Tony acted like he fit right in. He glanced at me. "This here's Bucky Riley."

One of the soldiers rose from his seat. I was surprised at how small he seemed, too small, I thought, to be a soldier. He stuck his ebony hand across the table toward Tony. "Henry Johnson," he said. "*Fightin'* Fifteenth."

They clasped hands and shook.

"Looks like you and your partner been fightin' yourselves," Henry Johnson said. "Black eye, busted nose."

"Yeah. Part of our trainin' is punchin' each other black and blue."

Henry smiled. "My fellow soldier is Willie Butler," he said. "We don't know the girls since they were here when we got to the table. But they're cute."

We looked at the girls, all teenagers I was sure. They were cute. They pushed over to make room for us and we sat down next to them.

An awkward moment of silence then followed.

Finally, Willie Butler muttered, "Oh, oh, here comes Captain Fish."

We all followed his eyes. Striding through the crowd straight for us was the very captain I'd met at President Roosevelt's home when he was a lieutenant right out of Plattsburg looking for a regiment, Hamilton Fish Junior. He was a big man who'd been a Walter Camp All-American football star at Harvard and had even killed a player during a game. Broke his neck in a scrum. I remembered that he knew Calliope and she'd been leery of him. He had his eyes fixed on me. My heart jumped up a beat.

When he reached our table we stood, except for the girls.

"As you were, gentlemen," he said. "Private Riley, I need a word with you."

I stepped away from the table. "Yes, Sir," I said.

Out of hearing distance from Tony and the others, he said, "Christ, what happened to you?"

"Training, Sir."

"Of course. I saw in the papers that Major Donovan's using boxing as a method of training. What's the other soldier look like?"

"He's sitting at the table there, Sir."

Captain Hamilton looked over at Tony. "Black eye. Very good."

"Thank you, Sir."

"I'm surprised to see you here, Sixty-ninth soldier at a Fifteenth celebration."

"We're here to listen to the music, Sir."

He nodded. "You don't need to keep calling me sir. When I

saw you, and realized it was you, I wanted to ask about Calliope Van Pelt. Do you mind?"

"No, Sir." I felt more nervous.

"Calliope's family and my family go back a long way. Old New York Dutch, both families. We're neighbors up in Garrison. I watched her as a little girl. My parents had the Van Pelts to our home many times. In fact, for dancing when the Castles, Vernon and Irene, came to teach us all the latest dance steps. Jim Europe and his small group of musicians provided the music." He looked toward the empty stage. "You'll love hearing his regimental band in a few minutes."

He turned back to me. "I can still see little Calliope trying to learn all the new steps. We even danced together. Very awkwardly, I might add. Naturally I was much taller, but everyone clapped when we were out there trying to dance to Jim Europe's syncopated music. I think I was fifteen, sixteen, about your age. She was six, maybe. About ten years ago."

"Yes, Sir," I said. In my mind's eye I saw them dancing together and didn't like what my mind's eye envisioned. I blocked that out, seeing me and Calliope that last night at the Roosevelts. I wondered where Captain Fish was headed.

"During lunch when we were at the Roosevelts, and I'd heard that her father tried to kidnap her and that you got her safely to Sagamore Hill, I couldn't believe it was true. Calliope wouldn't talk to me at the Roosevelts. That upset me some. You see, I know her father. I always liked the man. I guess she sensed that right off. Anyway, I'm friends with her brother, Schuyler. He dropped out of Harvard to join the Seventh. What happened?"

I said, "Ask Schuyler."

"I'm asking you."

"Sir, I don't know. Calliope never talked about her family with me, only to say that on her sixteenth birthday, her Poppa wants to introduce her, his daughter, into society. That's why he had taken her from her Momma in the first place—for that occasion. That's all I know."

I would not tell him about the chauffeur trying to molest her and her Momma, or her Poppa taking her to a rendezvous at some woman's apartment. And the threats she received from the chauffeur and her Poppa. It was none of Captain Fish's business. To me it was nobody's business, but mine.

He gave me a hard look. "That's it?"

"It is, Sir."

"Very well, then. Enjoy the music." He turned sharply away and walked off.

I sat down between Tony and one of the girls. All eyes at the table were on me.

Tony said, "What was that all about?"

"Personal. He wanted to know about my Poppa." I then thought of Calliope—the very image of her. I missed her terribly.

The lights in the Casino dimmed, the din of voices quieted down and a light-skinned Negro stepped onto the stage.

"Oh, it's Noble Sissle," the girl next to me sighed. "He's so pretty."

Noble Sissle raised his hands for more quiet. "Ladies and gentlemen and brave officers and men of the Fighting Fifteenth," his voice loud for all to hear, "for the last time here in good old Harlem, New York, before we depart for camp, here's James

Reese Europe and his legendary Rattlers!"

Nearly everyone jumped to their feet, hooting and hollering and whistling, while a few, almost all white, stood in a dignified manner and clapped. At first, I was the only one at our table not to hop up howling. Tony was the loudest. The girls also carried on as if the very success of the concert depended on their excitement. The Rattlers came on stage, picked up their instruments and faced the audience, at least fifty musicians in all. The hooting and hollering and whistling went on until a broad-shouldered soldier, over six feet tall with glasses over eyes that seemed to pop from his face emerged from behind the band. I picked out the highly polished Sam Brown belt across his thick chest and the first lieutenant's silver bars atop his uniform. It was Jim Europe. His presence quieted everyone.

In a deep voice fitting the size of the man, he declared, "In honor of our colonel, William Hayward, W. C. Handy's 'Memphis Blues'."

Europe turned his back to the audience, then, tapping his foot, raised his baton and brought it down in a grand, sweeping motion. The Rattlers responded in a crescendo of ragtime. Not a beat was missed. I felt the hair on my arms rise and then, without my coaxing, my foot tried to keep time with the music. "Memphis Blues" carried me away.

"That's the Colonel's favorite," Henry Johnson said from across the table, loud enough for us to hear.

"I love it," I heard Tony say, as the dance floor filled, bodies swinging to the jazzy beat. He stood, his head now doing that familiar bob, and grabbed one of the girls' hands. "Let's dance!"

I saw how surprised she was. And so were the other girls as

well as Henry Johnson and Willie Butler. But she got up and, holding hands with Tony, followed him out onto the dance floor. I had no idea what they were doing once they were out there, jumping around. It wasn't the foxtrot or any other dance I knew. A moment later, Johnson and Butler led the other two girls onto the dance floor, leaving me alone with a girl who now had to feel that her friends had deserted her. We looked at each. She had large brown eyes. Her dark skin and tightly curled black hair glistened in the lights overhead. I wondered what she thought of me. I knew she wanted to dance, that she didn't want to be stranded at a table with some shy white soldier from the Fightin' Sixty-ninth. She then looked around, probably hoping someone would come to her rescue.

Another awkward moment.

"Would you like to dance?" My words surprised me. I'd never really danced before, certainly not what I was seeing.

"Yes," she said. She grabbed my hand without a thought. "I'm Linda."

"Bucky," I answered as she led me to the dance floor, probably thinking I was the only chance she had to dance. We weaved through bunched-up people clapping in time with the "Memphis Blues."

Tony saw us coming. "Oh, my God!" he said.

Linda began to shimmy like everyone else. I stood stock-still.

"Don't embarrass us," Tony cracked. "We're the only white guys out here!"

Linda laughed. "Come on soldier boy!" She took my other hand. "Just sway with the beat, like me."

I swayed, slowly at first, trying to find the right rhythm now that I was expected to dance. My face felt suddenly warm from all the blood rushing there on account of my clumsiness. All around us dancers were in constant, fast-paced motion, a blur of bodies.

"Pick it up," she urged, her hands tightening on mine.

I tried.

She pulled me close, our bodies touching. "Sway with me."

With her body against mine, I found the right rhythm. "Good," Linda murmured. "Keep it up."

"Memphis Blues" ended. Linda didn't stop moving against me. I waited, breathing heavily through my mouth because of the damn cotton balls shoved up my nose. I pulled them out and while I stuck them in my pocket Jim Europe announced, "Here's the newest song by composer Sheldon Brooks, the Darktown Strutter's Ball with Drum Major Noble Sissle." The audience roared and the music started again. Noble Sissle's voice was divine.

I'll be down to get you in a taxi honey
You'd better be ready around half past eight
Ah baby don't be late
I want to be there when the band starts honey.

This time I got it. The tempo was slower than "Memphis Blues," but still up beat. Linda's arms were around me. I breathed in the honey smell of her warm body.

"That's my soldier boy," she whispered, her eyes looking up at mine.

Well just remember when we get there honey
Two steps gonna handle them all
Dance with both my shoes when they play the jelly roll blues
Tomorrow night at the darktown strutter's ball

Dance after dance. The music swept by. No break. Sometimes we held each other, sometimes we stepped back. "Clarinet Marmalade." "That's Got 'Em" and then "Jazzola."

Out for a jazzola treat
And she'll love you like she
Never did before—what's more
No need of buying wine!
You'll have a much better time!

We swayed and rocked and her eyes rolled back in pure bliss as Noble Sissle sang in such sweet harmony. I felt the same way. Sweat rolled down my forehead, stung my eyes and dampened my uniform, but I didn't care. What kind of regimental band was this that Jim Europe had put together? And what was I doing out on a powdered dance floor savoring the moment so much, moving in rhythm with a pretty black girl I didn't even know? Damn, I was only fifteen years old.

"My soldier boy," she murmured again.

Chapter Five

The next morning at nine sharp, McDougall roused Tony and me from our cots stuck away in a far nook of the armory's top floor where we all slept. We altar boys had dubbed it, "The Pope's Corner."

"Looks like you guys had a time of it last night, dragging yourselves back here at all hours of the morning. I'm jealous."

Tony ran his fingers through his messy hair. "You should be."

"Yeah? Well, Duffy decided to let you guys sleep in so you've missed the big news."

"What's that?" I asked, trying to shake Linda from my sleepy mind.

"We've got our orders!" He said it with gusto!

Tony and I glanced at each other, his left eye poking out between the discolored skin that surrounded it. The sight of it made me touch my nose. "What orders?" we said in unison.

Doogie straightened up and threw his shoulders back for dramatic effect. "Of all the regiments we're the one's transferrin' to the Forty-second Rainbow Division! We're going over there! We're going to France!"

"When!" We jumped off our cots.

Afraid that I might have missed something important, I threw on my uniform and dashed downstairs to Major Donovan's office. The door was closed. I trotted to the drill shed. Soldiers were in the midst of calisthenics. The Major was not leading them. I hurried over to Father Duffy's office. The door was shut there, too.

It was pressing nine-thirty. I cursed myself for sleeping so late, even though I had permission.

What'll happen to me now that we're in the Rainbow Division?

"Private Riley." I turned toward the voice. It was Major Donovan. "In my office."

Inside, sitting in front of his desk, legs crossed as usual, was Father Duffy alongside Captains Mike Kelly and Jim McKenna. Captain McKenna, a dark-haired, handsome Wall Street lawyer, I hadn't met yet, but I'd heard of the note he'd left on his office door for all his clients to read when he joined the regiment: "I'll be back when we lick the Hun!" He casually rolled a Bull Durham cigarette while I stood by the desk, at attention. They all seemed to be checking me out. It was obvious something was up. It had to be the transfer. Then Major Donovan ran his hand over his smooth chin. I felt a chill. *Who had shaved him? Was that why I'd been summoned to his office? I'd lost my job for sleeping in?* I steeled myself for whatever fate awaited me.

"Shaved myself. Not as smooth a shave as you give me, but no nicks." He winked at the others. "But it'll do."

"Looks clean enough to me," Captain McKenna said, letting a puff of smoke drift away from his handsome face as he lit his cigarette. He rubbed his chin, mimicking the Major.

Father Duffy cut in. "I hear you had a wild night." He winked, too.

I blushed. *Was dancing with a girl pressing her body hard enough against mine, swaying to a sensual musical beat so you felt her every curve a sin?* Did Father Duffy somehow know?

"Well, I'm sure you've heard," the Major said, steering us back to the subject of the meeting. "We're going over to the Rainbow

Division. Just what the doctor ordered. Now we'll be the first Guard unit overseas. I can't wait to get my hands on the Germans."

"Amen to that," said Captain McKenna. I instantly thought of the note he'd posted on his office door.

I was happy for all of us—for I knew then I still hadn't lost my job. At least not yet. But I learned other changes were thrust upon us, and by the sound of their voices I sensed right away they were in a sour mood.

First, we had a new colonel to lead us. It was not Major Donovan. And that bummed us out and broke my heart. But thank goodness it wasn't Lang. The new colonel was Charles Hine. I'd never heard them talk of him.

"A West Pointer," Major Donavan informed us. "Another lawyer as well. He's a veteran of the Spanish War, that's good. General O'Ryan tells me he's a railroad man at heart, started out as brakeman on some railroad in the Midwest."

"At least it isn't Charles Lang," Captain Kelly said, "even though we've got to put up with that bum until we get to Camp Mills."

"Is Hine a Catholic?" asked Father Duffy.

"Don't think so. But we'll give him all the support we can. And we must. He's out at Camp Mills right now awaiting us. It's the damn reason Lang's our acting boss. Our orders are for us to depart the armory within the week. Then we'll be rid of Lang."

The second piece of news was even worse. We lost our numerical designation. Because of the transfer to the Rainbow Division we were now the 165th Infantry Regiment, erasing generations proudly serving under the banner of the Sixty-ninth—going back to our Civil War days when General Lee first called us the "Fighting Sixth-ninth" because of our never-give-up tenacity in battling his Rebels.

"We'll always be the Sixty-ninth," Father Duffy said. "And I pray that someday we'll get our sacred number returned to us."

Then there was another issue that had to be dealt with. The government ordered that the number of men in each infantry regiment be drastically increased from two thousand to thirty-six hundred.

"Holy Jesus smokes!'" Captain McKenna whistled. "That means we have to double the size of the Sixty-ninth."

"Within days, too, if we're going to Camp Mills with a full complement of men," said Major Donovan.

"Where are we going to get sixteen hundred soldiers in such a short time?" chimed in Captain Kelly.

Major Donovan picked up a paper from his desk. He shook his head as he read it. "From the other regiments here in the city. And you can damn well bet no one's going to be happy about this, especially the guys making up the other National Guard outfits— many of them our avowed rivals." He dropped the paper back on his desk. "Each regiment's been ordered to transfer a large number of its own soldiers over to us so we'll be ready to head out. For at least three of our fellow regiments that's up to 350 men— the Seventh, the Twenty-third and the Fourteenth over in Brooklyn. They'll despise this move as much as we do. They could revolt."

Father Duffy shook his head. I could hear in my mind his lament, *The ethnic make-up of my beloved regiment is changing and I need to embrace it*. Now the change that worried him so would come fast and heavy. I wondered, could he truly embrace it—such a large-scale change? Could we all?

We were soon to find out.

A day or so later, the first transfer turned out to be a single soldier from the Seventh Regiment. A good transfer—one we all embraced. Father Duffy had finagled the transfer himself, and he was delighted.

It was Joyce Kilmer, Momma's favorite poet.

Joyce Kilmer had told the Chaplain that after he'd enlisted in the blue-blooded Seventh he realized it was a mistake. He'd always wanted to be in the Sixty-ninth because he was a Catholic and half Irish. One day I heard him tell Father Duffy, "The people I like here are the wild Irish."

"Come on, Joyce," the Father had teased, his eyes full of merriment. The poet was by the door, a tad pudgy with a wisp of a mustache. "You're not half Irish. You know your family were all born and bred English, and you were raised Episcopalian."

I looked over at Kilmer and sheepishly replied, "Well, Padre, I was never good at math."

But he was indeed Catholic. He'd converted when his daughter was on her deathbed, dying of infantile paralysis. His mother had been very upset when she heard he'd converted. I was later told she was an ardent Episcopalian, going so far as to name him after the minister of their church somewhere in New Jersey. I remembered my Momma when she first read his poems thinking Joyce was a woman. She wasn't the only one, me included. Some of the soldiers in the regiment rode him hard because of his name, but he never complained.

Kilmer was soon followed by the rest of the Seventh's quota of soldiers ordered to our regiment—more than 350 men.

How were we going to accept them? Father Duffy stewed over this. Would we resent that many soldiers from another regiment crowding into our armory, taking over our precious space? Then later that day, he burst into Donovan's office just as I was about to hang up the Major's tunic.

"Let's give the Seventh a rousing Irish welcome!" the Chaplain said, slapping his hands together. "Bagpipes, songs, the whole she-bang! That ought to get rid of the resentment any of us might have."

On the afternoon of August 16, up at the Seventh's armory on Park Avenue, the 350 transfers, I bet all of them reluctant, assembled in their great drill shed for the last time. They donned full field jackets and shouldered their rifles. The rest of the regiment who were staying behind, then led the transfers out of the armory with their commander, Colonel Willard Fisk, and the band out in front. From Park Avenue, two thousand marchers swung south toward our armory, the sidewalks jammed with cheering well-wishers. As they neared their destination, those Guardsmen staying with the Seventh peeled off and formed a line on both sides of the Avenue, rifles at present arms. The transfers, with the band in front playing the regimental tune, "Greyjackets," passed gloriously through the line.

Up ahead we were waiting.

Our armory was thick with soldiers, two thousand strong. A number of them pressed against the walls of the drill room or hung from the rafters. Outside, Lexington Avenue was packed with civilians—so many, there must have been ten thousand. I spotted old, grizzled men in faded blue uniforms, sporting Grand Army of the Republic Stetsons, sabers strapped to their sides, their arms raised—a number of them with their sabers waving in their hands, some with their hats stuck on the ends of the blades—shouting out, "Huzzahs!" as they awaited the uptown soldiers. Veterans of the Civil War, I was informed. I remembered a few gray-haired Civil War veterans back home, but here were a bunch of them, all from the Sixty-ninth, donning their uniforms to welcome soldiers from the Seventh. It was these old-timers, fighting at Marye's Heights in the battle of Fredericksburg, that gave us our nickname, "The Fighting Sixty-ninth." Seeing them, medals dangling from their faded uniforms, gave me a sense of the history of New York's regiments and—even though I was a Vermonter—I was now thrilled to be part of it.

Then someone standing on the steps yelled, "Here they come!"

I heard the Seventh's band from where I stood, close to Father Duffy. Our band began to play "Garryowen." It marched out of the armory and down the steps, the rollicking beat of our regimental tune had the Chaplain clapping and stamping his feet, a glow to his face. I knew then without a doubt that he now embraced the transfers into our regiment—Catholic, Irish or whatever. I found myself clapping and swaying to the music—the way I'd clapped and swayed up at the Manhattan Casino to Jim Europe's ragtime beat. Our own men poured outside, and there was a roar louder than any I'd ever heard, drowning out the music. It came from the men of both regiments as they met on the Avenue and from the throng of civilians with family and friends in either the Seventh or the Sixty-ninth.

I looked up at Father Duffy, still stamping his feet, and caught him wiping a patriotic tear from his eye. "Right now, this very moment, something mystical is being born in every breast," he managed to say to me. "Can't you feel it, Bucky? The soul of a regiment!" He slapped me on my back. "Heaven be good to the enemy when these cheering lads go forward together in battle!"

I, too, felt the glory of the moment and was so proud now that Father Duffy had slapped me on the back. My eyes got watery in spite of myself.

The Seventh's transfers, now escorted by hundreds of our own men, mounted the steps and into the armory. Our band switched to a new tune, "Did You Ever Go Into an Irishman's Shanty?" Inside, amid the pandemonium, Charles Lang greeted Colonel Fisk. They saluted, shook hands and the transfer was official.

The roaring went on, nonstop. As the transfers strode by, they could no longer march in step. Military decorum had been scratched by the rousing welcome. I checked out the soldiers of the Seventh as they brushed past me, each company bearing its own flag. As Company K pushed toward the drill room, without warning I felt as if a cold icepick had just pierced my very being. There, among the men in the rush to get inside was none other than Calliope's brother, Schuyler Van Pelt. I clearly remembered that moment back on the Champlain Canal when I saw him for the first time in his Seventh Regiment uniform. And now, here he was.

Once the hullabaloo had died down, the families had left and order had been restored in the armory, the Sixty-ninth—rather, the 165th—went back to business. The transfers from the Seventh seemed to fit right in. I did not seek out Schuyler. I figured I'd run into him soon enough—a meeting that I dreaded.

Our pressing business was to move to Camp Mills where we'd join regiments from other states that were making up the Rainbow Division. In the meantime, we still had not received the transfers from the Fourteenth. As it turned out, the revolt that Major Donovan had feared hit us hard when we got to Long Island. Most of the transfers from the Fourteenth Regiment refused to join us there and were listed as absent without leave—a serious wartime offense.

But one of them did show when we were settling in at Camp Mills. And for me it was another cold icepick to my very soul.

First Schuyler Van Pelt, and now, sporting sergeant's stripes, Sheriff Roscoe Lynch!

It was high time I wrote to Calliope!

Camp Mills, October 6, 1917

My Dear Calliope:

I hope you are well and still staying at the Roosevelts. I'm sorry I haven't written before, but it's been hectic here with the 69th. We're no longer the 69th, but the 165th. Nobody likes the change, and so we still refer to ourselves as the 69th. We're also no longer at the armory, but now are training all day long at Camp Mills out on Long Island.

I had my nose broken during a boxing match with another soldier. It was part of Major Donovan's physical regimen. I not only look like a mug, I think I now look like Captain Cobb. My nose will heal, I'm told. One of my friends is Private Tony Margiotta. I swear I've seen him somewhere before. He doesn't think so. He's the one who bopped me on the nose and broke it.

I shave the Major every morning at six and make sure his boots are shined and his uniform is wrinkle free. Father Duffy made me an altar boy. He hasn't conducted a single mass yet, not even on our last day at the armory when we marched out in grand style, crowds cheering, and took the ferry across the East River and then a long train ride to Camp Mills.

Before we left, the entire regiment went to the Polo Grounds to see the Giants play the Cincinnati Reds. The great Christy Mathewson was there. He now manages the Reds. He tossed baseballs into the stands where we were sitting. I didn't catch one. Later, Martin Sheridan came by the armory and gave a rousing talk about the regiment's Irish heritage. I'd never heard of him, but I found out he'd been an Olympic star and won a bunch of gold medals. He's a New York police detective. He told us the story of the 1908 Olympic Games in London. All the competing nations had to march into the stadium and pass in front of the King and Queen of England and dip their flags in respect. The night before, Martin Sheridan addressed his Olympic teammates, raised our flag and said it dips to no earthly king, especially an English king. The next day, when our country marched past the King and Queen, Ralph Rose, another Irish policeman from New York, a big, burly shot putter, held the flag aloft. Christy Mathewson and Martin Sheridan—it was quite a sendoff.

You hear a lot of singing and fiddle playing at camp after taps. Along almost every company street there seems to be an Irish tenor belting out ballads. There's one singer, named Tom O'Kelly, a lad from Ireland himself, from Company C, who draws a crowd whenever he sings. Such a hush when he steps out of his tent at night. He's been compared to the Irish tenor, John McCormack. I'd never heard of John McCormack. The first thing O'Kelly says, "Here, boys, wind me up. The Lootenant is callin' for his phonograph." He sings the ballads, "The Old Boreen," "Molly, Brannigan," etc. His voice and all the singing reminds me of Stubby when we sang on the towboat. Stubby has a beautiful Irish voice, too.

The other thing we hear and actually see, and even smell, is gasoline from all the aeroplanes flying close by at the field right next to Camp Mills. Men are learning to be aviators and will be sent overseas like us to fight, but only up in the heavens, not in the trenches. I'd never seen an aeroplane before. It's exciting. The aeroplanes do loops and spins and chase each other all over the sky like they were in actual combat. Some of the boys here want to switch over and become pilots.

I'm part of the Headquarters Company's inner circle. It means I stand around and listen to them talk, oftentimes while I'm shaving the Major. I was told not to get too big for my woolen britches and to keep my mouth shut at all times. If anyone wants coffee, I go get it. A couple of the officers, like Captain Kelly, a most interesting character, drink Irish whiskey in the meetings. That's whiskey with an "e." The Irish stuck it in there and I don't know why. The bottle's on the table and they pour their own drinks into their coffee mugs. The only one who doesn't drink is Wild Bill.

I wanted to tell you how very much I miss you, and that I hope to see you one of these days. Since Camp Mills is on Long Island and not that far from Oyster Bay, maybe the Roosevelts could make a visit here and bring you along. I'd really love that.

The big news you need to know, if you haven't already heard, is that your brother, Schuyler, is here in the 69th. He was one of the transfers from the 7th Regiment. I haven't talked to him yet. I thought I'd ask you if I should, and if so what should we talk about. I'm not sure he knows I'm with the 69th. Maybe he doesn't remember me.

The other big news, and it's not good, is that old Sheriff Lynch is another transfer into the 69th. He was with the 14th, a regiment from Brooklyn. A lot of their men didn't want to transfer and went AWOL. They were rounded up and brought here under guard and have not fit in very well like the 7th has. Lynch is a sergeant. I've been avoiding him so far. One of these days we're going to run into each other, and I don't know what will happen. He's got it in for me.

I miss Captain Cobb, Stubby and Thorny and I bet you miss them, too, especially Tripod.

Please WRITE! We get a lot of visitors every day and since you're not far off please VISIT!

Your dearest friend, Bucky!

Chapter Six

Weeks before we headed for Camp Mills, a flat stretch of open land out on Long Island's Hempstead Plains, I guess because it was ideal for training, a detachment of our men went there first and pitched tents—no more sleeping in the armory's drafty rafters up there in Pope's Corner for me, Tony and Doogie. They built a mess hall and other facilities, and then the rest of us followed them. When we got there, crossing the East River and then by train and marching with full packs the rest of the way, I was astonished to see that the Rainbow Division filled up almost every square foot of Camp Mills. Our Sixty-ninth, along with three other infantry regiments, made up the main force of the division—fifteen thousand strong. They came from Alabama, Iowa, Ohio and, of course, New York.

I found out quickly enough that the Alabama boys from the 167th Infantry were rednecks, marching in with a chip on their shoulders. They wanted to fight anybody who was a Yankee, but especially took after us because our 69th had actually fought against their regiment in the Civil War. It got worse when the boys from Harlem showed up. The only black regiment in the whole army and without a division that wanted it. At the camp, the government had squeezed them in right next to the Alabama boys, a stupid decision by Washington's bureaucrats that infuriated Major Donovan and, as you'll see, we came close to a race riot.

I was shaving Wild Bill when he finally erupted over rumors that trouble was stirring in camp. I had to hold back the razor until he finished ranting. He stood up and slammed his fist on his field desk. Papers went flying. I stooped to pick them up.

"Those damn Southerners!" He growled loud enough so anyone outside his tent heard it. "They might have to fight side by side with our black brethren and then they'd want them to have their back in a tight spot. But now, whenever they come across one of them, they beat the tar out him! It's got to stop! Damn it!"

"I was told the other day one of them gouged the eye out of a colored train conductor with his bayonet when they were going into the City," Father Duffy said. "His pals then threw the poor man out of the back of the train onto the tracks. No arrests were made."

Captain Kelly said, "Well, Doug MacArthur, instead of strutting around like a peacock, needs to have a talk with Colonel Whosis over at the 167th."

"Colonel Screws," said Father Duffy.

"That figures."

A movement by the opening to the tent drew my attention. Standing there waiting to be asked in was Captain Hamilton Fish, Junior.

"Major Donovan, Sir," I said, drawing their attention to him, but wondering why he was here in our part of Camp Mills when he should have been with his Harlem soldiers. "Captain Fish is here."

We all looked toward the Captain, his imposing size almost filling the open tent flap.

"Major Donovan, Sir," Captain Fish said, "may I have a moment?"

"You may."

"I need ammunition and I was told the 165th has bullets."

All our eyes went to the .45 holstered on his hip.

"Is that weapon loaded?" the Major asked.

"It is, Sir, and for good reason." Captain Fish entered the tent. "There's trouble stirring again. This time it could get out of hand. The Alabama boys are planning a raid tonight on my regiment, the Fifteenth, in their words, to teach the uppity Yankee Negroes to respect Southern rebels. As I think you know, when our weapons were issued our men were not allowed ammunition for the damn reason they're colored. We're defenseless without bullets. I won't stand for American boys firing on American boys because of their color. We're supposed to be fighting Germans, for God's sake, not each other."

"So you want to slaughter white boys?"

"No, Sir. I want my men to be able to defend themselves. We already had trouble at Camp Wadsworth when we were down in South Carolina, and that's why we're up here, ironically, to be out of harm's way. As soon as there's a troopship ready we'll be on our way to France."

Major Donovan nodded. "When is this raid supposed to take place?"

"Midnight, Sir. I believe New York soldiers, black and white, must stand united."

"Then let's stop this raid before it gets started. Frank and Mike here and I will go with you. You bring Colonel Hayward and one of your black officers and we'll face down Colonel Screws, or any of his boys who step in our way."

I said, "I want to go, too."

Now all eyes were on me.

"Private Riley?" Hamilton Fish seemed to take notice of me for the first time.

"We're going armed, Bucky," the Major said. "You're not allowed a weapon."

"I have one, Sir," I said. And wielded my razor, still dripping with creamy foam.

It was almost midnight when we crossed over into the 167th's sector of Camp Mills. The Major, Captain Kelly, Father Duffy, who like me carried no weapon, but clasped a Bible, Captain Fish, Colonel Hayward and Lieutenant Jim Reese Europe, the sole black officer. I was astonished to see him. He was a bandleader, I thought, not a real soldier, but a musician. He was big enough, though, not a guy you'd want to tangle with. He had those big eyes, too, almost popping out of their sockets. He looked fierce. We were quite a posse, I thought.

We walked in silence, a determined group. I was last. I don't know how fast their hearts were beating. Mine was racing. Captain Fish had his .45 out, and it held behind his back. No one else had their revolvers out. My razor was back in the Major's tent. I was not allowed to bring it along.

Although Colonel Hayward was the ranking officer, it seemed to me that the Major had taken charge. We were headed straight for the headquarters of Colonel William Preston Screws. All we'd heard about him was that he'd made a name for himself in the Philippines during and after the war with Spain. Was he a bigot? We didn't know. But his men were—at least a number of them.

When we got to the company square we found it filling up with armed soldiers. Both Major Donovan and Colonel Hayward raised their hands for us to stop.

The major said, "Do you see any officers there?"

"Two captains for sure," Captain Fish said. "Let me talk to them."

"Okay," said Colonel Hayward. "Bring Jim with you. We have you covered."

Captain Fish and Lieutenant Europe moved toward the crowd. I saw the Captain still holding his .45 behind his back. Lieutenant Europe's .45 remained in its holster, but he'd unsnapped the flap for a quick draw.

I thought of the time on the towboat when Captain Cobb and Stubby stared down Sheriff Lynch. Would it be the same? Who'd flinch first? This time there wasn't a sheriff and two deputies, but thirty or forty soldiers with rifles. The dark night, flickering camp lights, shadows of men standing about and two men of size—Captain Fish and Lieutenant Europe—closing in with long strides made the scene surreal—something out of an adventure novel.

As they crossed under a lamppost near the company square, the light caught their faces—one white, one black.

"Look!" someone shouted. "A nigger!"

"What the hell is that black bastard doin' here!"

The Alabamians moved forward, and I wished I'd brought my razor. Colonel Hayward, Major Donovan and Captain Kelly pulled out their .45s and along with Father Duffy, they hurried after Captain Fish and Lieutenant Europe. I was right behind them.

A gunshot resounded in the dark. Everyone stopped. Where had it come from? Father Duffy was looking toward a tent at the edge of the company square. Standing there was a man ramrod straight, his tunic unbuttoned, his strong face as hard as steel, his hand holding a .45 pointed at the ground. I saw a wisp of smoke rising from the revolver.

"Enough!" he roared. "Everyone back to your tents or by God I'll court martial the lot of you!" Then he stared at us. "And what the hell are you men doing in my sector?"

I heard Father Duffy whisper to us, "Colonel Screws."

"To see you, Colonel Screws. I'm Colonel Hayward of the Fifteenth and with me are two of my officers as well as Major Donovan, Captain Kelly and Chaplain Duffy of the 165th."

"Then come into my headquarters." Turning to one of his officers, he snapped loud enough for everyone to hear, "Captain Jordan, I ordered you to take care of this! Now get those troublemakers settled down. I've got enough to worry about than a bunch of Goddamn darkies. I'm sick of it!"

We headed for Colonel Screws' tent.

"You stand outside, Bucky," Major Donovan ordered.

He and the rest of our posse followed the Alabama colonel inside his tent. I was surprised Lieutenant Europe went in.

As the mob of soldiers began to break up, several walked up to me.

One hissed, "Damn Yankee!"

"Leave him be," I heard Captain Jordan snap.

"Yes, Sir," he answered, his face close to mine. I could tell by the scars pocking his cheeks that he'd had chickenpox as a kid and his teeth were bad. He most likely came from the hills where no doctors were around. Already a number of the Alabama boys had succumbed to the diseases that hit the camp, their weak immune system unable to save their lives. I felt sorry for him.

"Ya'll call us boll weevils," he hissed some more, "yet ya'll ain't nuthin' but Yankee white trash."

He spit in my face, spun round and swaggered into the night. I wiped the spittle off, and still felt sorry for him.

Lieutenant Europe came out of Colonel Screws' tent. He put his hands on his hips. "To think I was born in Alabama," he said with a voice of sadness. He carefully watched the rest of the Alabama soldiers disperse.

"Yes, Sir." I didn't know what else to say.

"Looks like this little brouhaha is over—for now." Then he smiled, but it was not a smile caused by joy. "We almost had a real riot when we were down in South Carolina. Not with any soldiers because all of them were New Yorkers. The good old Twenty-seventh Empire Division, which we should be a part of. It was townspeople. Whenever our men were in town they were pushed around, knocked into gutters. My drum major, Noble Sissle, was assaulted in a hotel lobby. That was the last straw. Our men had to be restrained from shooting up Spartanburg like what happened a couple of months ago in Houston with the Buffalo Soldiers. You can bet those poor black bastards who did the shooting are going to get hanged."

I'd read about the Houston riot. Black soldiers stationed there finally had blown their tops because of the way they were mistreated. They marched into town and shot to death a bunch of citizens. It came on the heels of another race riot in East St. Louis where in July more than one hundred colored folks had been butchered. A sudden sadness then fell over me, a rube Yankee from Vermont, so much so that I wanted to cry. *Why was it so?*

The Lieutenant shrugged, as if that was the way life would always be for him and for all blacks. Yet here they were willing to fight for Democracy. At that moment, standing next to him, I sensed an inner strength in the man, a strength I'd never detected in my Poppa, and I knew right then how remarkable he was. As I looked at him in a different way, he asked, "Weren't you dancing at the Manhattan Casino at the farewell concert? You and another soldier?"

"That was me, Sir." I was taken aback by his question.

"Looked like you were having a good time with that girl."

I felt heat rush into my face. How'd he know? Eerie—like Father Duffy.

"The reason I remember is you were dancing with Linda Wright, the niece of one of my drummers, Herbie Wright. She goes to every concert, she and her girlfriends, and dances her little heart out. I keep an eye on her because of her uncle. He can come unglued at times. Got to watch him, too. Linda has a thing for Noble Sissle. She loves his voice as well as his looks. The way you two were dancing it looked to me like she had a thing for you, too. Maybe it's the other way around, huh?"

"Yes, Sir," I said, still not knowing what to say, my face burning. I could feel Linda's body pushing against mine.

Lieutenant Europe chuckled. "Hayward made me an officer because he wanted me to raise a regimental band solely for recruitment. I told him I would do it if afterward I could be a gun-toting officer. He agreed and now I'm the Fifteenth's machine-gun officer."

Why was he telling me all this? I was a kid, basically. Big for my size, but still a kid.

"Funny thing, we haven't any machine guns. I wouldn't know how to fire one even if I had to. Sorry commentary for the United States Army in wartime. And now in a few days we're off to France—the baby National Guard regiment of New York, no armory, no military experience, just a bunch of much made over boys under the leadership of a politician colonel." He seemed to sigh. "The Man has kicked us right to France."

Colonel Hayward, accompanied by Major Donovan, Captain Kelly and Father Duffy came out of Colonel Screws' tent.

"Well, that's settled," said one of them.

"Come along, Jim," said Colonel Hayward. "Sorry that Screws asked you to leave." Lieutenant Europe shrugged one more time, and then I saw his sad smile.

As we hiked back to our company sectors, Colonel Hayward said loud enough for all of us to hear as we went our own ways, "In two days we ship out for France. Only a few of my men have ever fired a rifle. When we go into the trenches it'll be a slaughter. God help us."

Sagamore Hill, October 10, 1917

My Most Dearest Buck-eroo!

I read your sweet letter over and over again. I kiss it every night and keep it tucked under my pillow. I miss you so much. Please write again soon because I've heard the regiment is going overseas any day now and it will break my heart to see you go. Teddy—I call him Teddy now because I'm part of the family—has promised a trip to Camp Mills. He wants to address the regiment, all the regiments at the Camp, before they depart for France. Buck 'em up, he said. Instill the same fighting spirit he instilled in his Rough Riders during the last war. He's all worked up about it. But more than that he wants to say good-bye to Quentin who is at the airfield field next to your camp learning to fly an aeroplane.

Sagamore Hill bustles everyday with visitors. Just this week a delegation from Belgium showed up, wanting to hear what the former Presi-

dent had to say. I was allowed to be in the room with them. The Colonel said there will be no peace unless it is a just peace, and Germany must pay for its war crimes. They roundly applauded him. Also, more than 100 giggling girls seemed to barge in, all students from Columbia University. The Colonel was overwhelmed and chatted with them about bird life and all his stuffed animals. They went wild over the leopard skin on the bench and couldn't keep their hands off it. And then a gray-haired Texas Ranger hobbled in, spurs ajangling, a cowboy hat in his hand, but no chaps, and a big old mustache almost as bushy as Captain Bingham's. He begged to join the regiment. Said he came all the way from the banks of the Pecos River. Teddy was "delighted" to see him, but sadly told him there was no regiment because of Wilson. I thought the Texas Ranger was ready to cry. I think he knew it was his last chance to fight the Germans. When he left, I dashed to the window to see if he'd ridden up the hill on a horse. Spurs and all. No such luck. He rode off in an automobile.

Teddy himself wants so much to be involved during this great moment in our country's history and it dashes his spirit when he entertains college girls and thus plays second fiddle to the President, a man he cannot abide. Sometimes during an evening he mopes around Sagamore Hill or sits on the porch staring out at Long Island Sound, and I hear him sigh.

Without me here, the big house would be so empty and I don't believe the Roosevelts can stand being alone. They need young people around, their children have all grown and are away because of the war. Ethel and her husband are down south with the Roosevelts' grandson. Their other children—the boys—are all off somewhere in the army. You know how the Colonel loves little children. I know it'll be hard for them to give me up once things are settled between my parents. A resolution is still a ways off. And mother still hasn't left our place on Lake George. It's a long trip from there all the way down here. I think she's afraid to make the journey, afraid she'll have to face father. I don't blame her one bit, but I truly miss her—the way I miss you.

Please talk with Schuyler. It might help clear some things up. I love him still. He is my only brother. Be watchful of Sheriff Lynch. He's a no good person. I can't believe he got transferred into the 69th. The Colonel said the 14th was full of ungrateful men.

How is your nose? I wonder if you really look like Captain Cobb! Ha!

Yes, I miss the crew onboard the old Frank White and, like you wrote to me, especially Tripod. But I miss other moments of our trip most of all. You better remember them. I hope to see you soon.

With lots of love, Calliope.

Chapter Eight

Two days after our showdown with the Alabama regiment, the Fifteenth marched out of Camp Mills. It was quite a sendoff.

"Let's do something special like we did with the Seventh," Father Duffy had urged. "Really special for our black brethren when they depart this camp."

We decided to repeat what the Seventh had done down in South Carolina when the Fifteenth had left Camp Wadsworth. We knew the route the black soldiers had to take to reach the gates of the camp on their march to the train station where they'd then travel to the East River, be ferried around Manhattan to Hoboken and to a troopship waiting there to take them to France. We were all envious of them, the first soldiers from New York to head for the Western Front.

On the morning of departure, Colonel Hine, readily following the Chaplain's farewell plan, had our regiment line up like a gauntlet along both sides of the path the Fifteenth would come down. We had our rifles at present-arms. Well, I didn't have a rifle, but I stood there just the same. As the sun rose above us, sending the warmth of its October rays upon us, the Fifteenth came into sight, the crunch of their booted feet on Long Island's sandy soil. Drum Major Noble Sissle, brandishing his baton, was out in front with the regimental band, high stepping for all he was worth. He sure seemed to like the attention, and I could sure see why Linda Wright had a thing for him. Next came Colonel Hayward and his staff, and then each company, officers and men. Lieutenant Europe was back with his Machine Gun Company, that's where he wanted to be—not with the band. It was easy for me to spot Henry Johnson. He was the smallest soldier marching. For a rag-tag bunch who had mostly trained on the streets of Harlem I thought they looked as polished as any crack outfit in Uncle Sam's army.

The moment they strode into our line, Noble Sissle raised his baton high over his head like he was trying to touch the sky. Before he could bring it down, our entire regiment, 3,000 strong, opened up with "Over There," the song our battalion belted out while we'd jogged the streets around the armory.

Send the word, send the word over there
That the Yanks are coming, the Yanks are coming
The drums rum-tumming everywhere.
So prepare, say a prayer,
Send the word, send the word to beware -
We'll be over, we're coming over,
And we won't come back till it's over, over there.

As we sang, Noble Sissle finally brought his baton down with his usual flourish and the Fifteenth's band joined in with its rag-time version of "Over There." We picked up the beat while the black soldiers sang along. Every soldier, every visitor in the camp, even people outside the gates, had to hear such a rousing rendition of the song. We sang until the last of the troops disappeared from Camp Mills. As the music faded away, we heard the band switch to Colonel Hayward's favorite, "Memphis Blues." The tune brought to my mind's eye that time at the Manhattan Casino when I first heard ragtime music and awkwardly danced the night away with Linda.

That was the last I saw of the Fifteenth New York, the "orphan" regiment with not much military training.

The day after our rousing send off, Father Duffy held his first regimental Mass since our war with Germany had been declared. He'd always held Mass at his small parish up in the Bronx almost every Sunday, but none while at the armory. He worried much about the parishioners that he'd been tending at his church for many years and was afraid to leave them. At Camp Mills he decided to open up his Mass to all in the Rainbow Division and their visitors, and that included the boys from Alabama. Tony and I felt we'd been put in a spot because we'd not yet taken part in a Mass. Doogie told us not to worry. He'd lead us through. And he did.

It was also the morning I finally ran into Sheriff Lynch.

Father Duffy worried there might be rain on Sunday morning, but vowed Mass would take place rain or shine. "You know how the Irish like their religion," he said, with the usual merriment in his eyes, "with just a little touch of hardship."

There had been no reason to worry. The sun rose against blue skies. We erected an altar of sorts just inside the opening of his tent. The flaps had been pulled far enough back to make the opening bigger to reveal our altar, a simple table set on wooden planks where we'd put a large brass cross on top. We placed candles around. We added a chalice and an open Bible. When we were ready, Tony, Doogie and myself stood off to the side, Father Duffy at the front.

The soldiers, some with families or friends, started trooping in at nine o'clock and gathered in front of the tent. Soon the crowd had grown to well over several thousand. Major Donovan was there among them as well as Captains Mike Kelly and Jim McKenna—good Catholics all. When Father Duffy thought everyone was ready and that he had their attention, he raised his hands. There wasn't a sound among the soldiers, many of them kneeling.

"I come to you in soldiers' togs, with a message from the Church," the Chaplain began in a voice that carried to the farthest reaches of the crowd. "I want to be your friend, whatever your religion may be."

For the first time I felt the true strength of the man, the same strength that I'd felt in Jim Reese Europe, a quiet strength that spread outward toward everyone assembled. I almost knelt myself.

"I know many of you are leaving families behind you and will have many worries. Come to me with them and you will find me ready with a wise word and a merry one. God grant you through this gruesome business of war."

He looked over at Major Donovan. "Whatever the faults this old regiment ever had, it never yet lacked faith and courage." Then to all the soldiers, "The sun has never been too hot, the rain too strong to drive us from the field when Mass was being celebrated. We will be hearing Mass before the war is over on ships where our lives will be none too safe; by the smiling streams and the sunny fields of France, in the shattered cathedrals of the Old World, in the trenches and over the very graves of our own men. May God be with us through all the days ahead. I know how you'll fight, men. I have an infinite faith in every one of you. You'll wage your glorious battles like the archangels of God who pressed the demons down into hell."

At the end of the sermon, we had no wine or wafers for communion, but soldiers still came up to our crude altar and knelt while Father Duffy traced the sign of the cross on their foreheads with his thumb.

Afterward, we altar boys put the tent back to the way it was before Mass, and we worked our way toward our own tent, one row back from the parade ground. Coming toward us was a sergeant—I could tell by the three strips on his sleeve.

"Private Riley!"

I knew the voice right away! Sheriff Lynch! My stomach knotted up. There was no time to get away.

"You wait right there! You, alone!"

I froze.

He came over, Fourteenth Regiment insignia still pinned to his uniform like he didn't want to quit protesting his transfer. I took a deep breath, my eyes going to his teeth. The gap was still there. I felt better.

"I saw you up there on that makeshift altar. Whattaya doing in the Sixty-ninth? They ain't looking for sissies like you who hit men when they can't defend themselves." Lynch's tongue poked through the gap. He smiled, a wicked curve to his lips. Tony and Doogie moved to the side, but didn't walk away.

"I'm Major Donovan's striker."

"Donovan, huh?" That took some of the bluster out of Lynch. "He's leavin' soon. Didn't get the big promotion. I heard he's off to a desk job in Washington. When he's gone I'll be seein' you. Count on it."

He turned and strode off.

Tony said, "What's that all about?"

"Yeah," Doogie said. "He don't like you."

"Long story," I said, watching Lynch head down one of the company streets. "He's a sheriff who'd tried to kidnap a friend of mine. The kidnap had been ordered by the father of my friend after a messy divorce. It failed and the sheriff blamed that on me. He's still bitter."

"What happened to the friend?"

"She's now living with President Roosevelt and his wife until the divorce gets sorted out."

"The Roosevelts!" Tony and Doogie exclaimed in unison.

"Yep!"

"You're kiddin' us? How'd she wind up there?" Tony asked. "With the President of all people?"

I shrugged. "Luck, I guess."

"Is she your girlfriend?" Doogie asked.

"I think so?" It was more a question than a statement of fact.

Tony clasped his arm around my shoulder and laughed. "What about that colored girl at the Manhattan Casino?"

"She wanted to dance, so we danced."

"Hot stuff." He winked at Doogie. "See what you missed, Doogie Boy."

"Well, that's because I didn't get a black eye or a broken nose and was not allowed out of the armory. I shoulda punched myself in the face so I'd look like you two bums."

I said, "You don't need to whack your puss to look like us."

We all laughed and then headed toward our tent. But now I was worried that Major Donovan would be transferred. Then what would happen to me?

The next morning, after shaving Major Donovan, as I held his tunic open and he slipped his arms through the sleeves, I asked if he was being transferred out of the regiment to the nation's capital because he hadn't been promoted to colonel.

"Where'd you hear that rumor?"

"From a sheriff over at the Fourteenth."

"Sheriff?"

"Well, he was a sheriff. Now he's a sergeant."

"That isn't the character who tried to kidnap Miss Van Pelt?"

"It is."

"Sounds like he's got it in for you."

"I think so, Sir."

"If you run into him again, tell him Major Donovan's going nowhere, but up!"

"Yes, Sir." I hoped I didn't sound too smug. Yet I knew Lynch would be lurking about somewhere, biding his time.

Chapter Nine

On October 28, orders for our regiment to ship out finally came.

Father Duffy jumped out of his chair. "At last!" he exclaimed, and hurried over to Major Donovan's desk so he could read the orders over his shoulder. After a quick glance, he slapped the Major on the back. "Hot damn!"—a rare expletive from the good chaplain.

"About time, too," piped up Captain Kelly, clapping his hands. He'd been reading the *New York Times*. "It's irked me that some of the other Rainbow Division units have left already, letting us hold down the camp against those hillbillies from Alabama."

I could see then that Wild Bill was miffed about something. All of a sudden, he jumped out of his chair and held up the orders for all to see. "This is insane!" he snapped. "A featherbrained decision by the War Department."

We stared at him. What bothered him about our orders? What made them insane?

"The damn bureaucrats down in Washington are splitting up our regiment so we now ship out of two ports—five-hundred-damn-miles apart! And in the dead of night, too, so no German spies will notice. Like the Boche are that dumb. One troopship out of Hoboken, the other far to the north out of Montreal, Canada—of all places!"

"Montreal?" Captain Kelly said. Disappointment sounded in his Irish voice. "A long way off."

The Major slammed the orders back on his desk. "Yeah. Like I said, another featherbrained decision by bureaucrats. And as luck would have it, guess whose Battalion has been selected to leave from Montreal? Ours, damn it. Sure as hell we'll travel north by slow train to get there. How many hours is that sitting idly on our butts?"

"Canada," I whispered, mostly to myself.

"I'll have my men in the aisles doing push-ups, that's for certain. It'll be too dark for them to while away the hours looking out windows."

Father Duffy said, "We're on our way and that's what counts!"

The Major sat back down and rubbed his eyes. It was an order nobody liked, except me. The train had to pass through Burlington on its way to Canada. I might see my hometown and maybe for the last time, my Momma and sisters. Didn't the train have to stop there so it could pick up passengers? Then again, maybe it didn't because it'd be a troop train, seats all crammed with soldiers. If there were any civilians picked up, they might be suspected spies.

Father Duffy shot me a quick look. He knew my thoughts right then. He always did. It was uncanny. "You can wave to your family through the window," he said. His eyes sparkled again, filled with that merriment I was getting to know so well. "You can bet Miss Van Pelt is still out at Sagamore Hill keeping the Roosevelts company and I think you'll be seeing her soon."

What did he mean by that?

The night we were to leave, I found out.

Colonel Hine had planned a farewell ball for the officers and their wives or girlfriends at the Garden City Hotel. Word came down that the Roosevelts would be in attendance. The former President felt it important to show support for the soldiers on the eve of their departure.

After I'd gotten the news of the farewell dance, an awful gloom settled over me because I'd lost my last chance to say good-bye to Calliope. Would I ever see her again? The trip down the Hudson was always fresh in my mind, and, more than anything, that last night at the Roosevelts.

Major Donovan drew his arm across my shoulders. "Perk up, Bucky."

"Why?"

"Well, look at me. Ruth, my dear wife, is way up in Buffalo and we won't be able to say our proper good-byes to each other. Only God knows if we'll ever see each other again. How do you think I feel?"

"Badly," I said. "If you feel like me."

"I do. But for you, Bucky, I've got some news that'll perk you up. As you've heard, the Roosevelts are coming. And I'll be dog-goned—they'll be accompanied by a young colleen, name of Miss Van Pelt! And, oh, the Colonel has given you permission to come to the ball."

Thank God for the Roosevelts!

The day before the ball two things happened—one good, the other bad.

Tony got leave time to visit his parents.

"You gotta come with me," he urged. "Mom and Dad would love to meet you and I want you to meet them. They're from the old country. They run a small store on the West Side. Lotsa Italians there. Great food!" He kissed the end of his fingers with a flourish to show me how good the food tasted.

"I'd love to come. I'll see if the Major will give me time off."

"Aw, Donovan's a good sport. You know he will."

I got the afternoon off. We took the train and the ferry to Manhattan and then walked fast over to the West Side in our uniforms, getting a warm reception along the way from the pedestrians we passed by on the crowded sidewalks. His parents lived on Canal Street and when we got there the neighborhood seemed familiar. I was sure I'd been there before. He led me down some steps and under a stoop. With a great smile on his face, he banged on a door.

"Mom! Mom! It's me, Anthony. I'm home!"

The door opened. "Anthony!" His Momma stood there, tears welling up in her eyes. "My dear son!" She rushed into his arms. "Oh, Anthony!"

The voice. The face. Then looking into the one-room apartment, the strong aroma of food cooking everywhere, it registered in my mind why Tony had reminded me of someone. It was obvious, he was son of the couple who'd befriended Calliope and me during our escape from Sheriff Lynch so many months ago.

"Mrs. Margiotta!" I couldn't help but cry. "Remember me?"

Tony jerked his head around. "What?"

"Tony," I said. "The first time we met I said I thought I knew you?"

"Yeah, yeah. I remember."

"It's because you look a lot like your Momma, and it was your Momma and Poppa who saved Calliope and me from Sergeant

Lynch, the guy I told you about, when he was chasing us across Manhattan, the very same guy who'd come up to us after Mass. We hid beneath the stoop out there and then snuck into your folks' place so he couldn't find us."

"Darn," he said, his eyes darting back and forth between me and his Momma. "It's a small world."

Mrs. Margiotta released Tony and gave me the once over. "Momma mia! It's you!" She clasped me in a bear hug and kissed me on the left cheek. She stepped back. "Anthony, go get your Father. He's out back in the store."

I recognized Tony's Poppa the moment he walked into the apartment. In my mind's eye I saw him still in his bed, holding a pistol and saying "My son a bad man. He be home soon."

Tony a bad man? I couldn't help but smile.

"Whattaya smiling at?" Tony asked.

"You," I said, and let it go at that.

The homecoming, as brief as it was, proved to be so warm that I found myself missing my own family back in Vermont. Mrs. Margiotta had been working all day on Tony's favorite food.

With each heaping spoonful, she announced to me, who'd never had a home-cooked Italian meal before, what was piled high on my plate. "Antipasti," she said. "Caprese. That's mozzarella cheese, tomatoes and basil. Look at the color. Red, white and green—the Italian flag." She announced everything, a proud smile on her face. "Sliced salami, prosciutto with roasted peppers. Lasagna with sausage, meatballs and braciole. Later, you get my home-made cannolis."

Of course, the cannolis turned out to be scrumptious!

All through the meal I drank wine for the first time, washing down every bite with a delicious Chianti until I felt flush, a nice warmth to my face. I even sipped a glass of anisette, too, and drank my fill of espresso.

When I was through I thought my stomach was about to burst. Tony kept eating while in between every mouthful he and his parents talked on and on.

How'd he keep his body so trim, chomping down all that food?

Right after the grand meal we had to dash back to camp. It was getting dark and we had to catch the ferry across the East River and then the train back to camp. It was such a tearful departure between Tony and his parents that I found myself caught up in this loving family's good-bye that I had to brush a tear from my eye, too.

As we were leaving, Mrs. Margiotta tugged at the cuff of my uniform. Still wiping her eyes, she handed me a bag full of leftover cannolis. "You take care of my Anthony," she begged.

We made it to the ferry and grabbed the last train to Garden City.

"Time for one drink," Tony said as we stepped off the train.

Next to the station, beckoning to all soldiers returning to camp, stood Bat's Shanty, a seedy saloon always crammed with thirsty soldiers. I'd never been in a saloon before and wasn't sure I wanted to start.

Tony said, "Come on, one little drink."

"What'll I do with the cannolis?"

"Shove that wop food up your ass where it belongs, Private Riley!"

There, standing aslant against the frame of the door to Bat's Shanty, was my nemesis, Sergeant Lynch.

"Let's go," I said to Tony.

"Hey, Sarge." Tony stepped up to the saloon door. "We're leavin' in a day or two. I'd sure like a drink for the road."

"I'm so sorry." He blocked the door. "I'm closing the saloon to all privates with ass-kissin' jobs."

I noticed other soldiers had gotten off the train and were now close behind us.

"We ain't ass-kissers," one of them shouted. "Clear the way. We're comin' in!"

They brushed past us, about five or six of them, and up the steps. Sergeant Lynch moved aside. To my surprise, Tony trailed them into the saloon. Looking over his shoulder once, he shouted, "Hurry up, Bucky."

Sergeant Lynch let Tony go, but not me. "You and me got a score to settle." He pointed at the gap in his row of teeth. "Like the Bible says, a tooth for a tooth."

"I think it's an eye for an eye," I said, wondering what to do with the cannolis.

"Then I'll take your eye, too."

He came off the steps swinging. A wild roundhouse alerted me that he was drunk. I ducked and stepped away, still holding the cannolis."

"Put that wop food down and fight like a man."

"I'm only fifteen." I stepped away again.

"You're big enough so stop moving."

I wasn't going to run, but I wasn't going to let him hit me either. I quickly moved to the side. "How come you treated Mrs. Van Pelt and Calliope so badly?"

"What?" He put his fists down, but then brought them back up and lurched forward. "Come on. Fight."

"I'm not fighting with you. I want to know why you were mean to Mrs. Van Pelt and her daughter. You didn't have any authority to kidnap that girl."

He took a swing and missed again. I heard his heavy panting and even from a distance of three or four feet I smelled his whisky-fouled breath.

"What's it to you?" He made another lurch in my direction.

I said, "You're gonna need help getting back to camp."

"Old man Van Pelt paid me to bring his daughter back to the City. I did my damn job until you and that one-armed pirate came along. Cost me a bundle. Now stand still, damn it."

"No. When Tony comes out we're heading back to camp."

Sergeant Lynch sat down on the ground. "The hell with it," he said. "I'll settle with you later."

I waited until Tony came out, about fifteen minutes later. Sergeant Lynch and I had never said another word to each other during that time.

"Let's go," I said.

Tony looked down at Sergeant Lynch. "Can't handle your booze?"

"Shut up." Then to me, "Here give me a goddamned hand up." He held out his hand.

"Don't do it," warned Tony.

"We can't leave him sitting here."

"He's drunk."

I grabbed Sergeant Lynch's hand and hoisted him up. I should have heeded Tony's warning. A sudden, hard right caught me on the bridge of the nose and square between my eyes. A streak of light, like lightning, flashed in my eyes. The blow didn't knock me down, but sent me staggering backward until Tony caught me. The cannolis went flying.

"See, I told you," he said. "Never trust a drunk."

"I think he re-broke my nose."

"Watch it!" Tony cried out.

Sergeant Lynch was coming at me, fists up. "Gotcha now!"

I was still trying to shake off the pain that throbbed between my eyes and so I hadn't seen him moving in, crouched over like a Vermont catamount ready to spring on its prey. The next punch was a sweeping uppercut. It missed the chin, but slashed against my cheekbone with razor-like results—opening up a gash.

"Now a tooth for a tooth!" he grunted.

He cocked his arm, ready for the coup de grace.

By now Tony had circled behind him. Before Sergeant Lynch could launch his fist, my friend grabbed him around the neck. He jerked him backward, flinging him back to the ground.

"Damn you, you damn wop!"

"Let's get going," Tony said. "Before the MPs show up."

I wiped the blood on my cheek. "Okay. But what about the cannolis?"

"Leave em be. We gotta scoot."

And scoot we did, back into camp, blood dripping down my cheek, my nose aching and me thinking what a sight I'd be for Calliope to feast her eyes on.

The last thing I heard came from Sergeant Lynch as we headed off, "We ain't finished yet, Private Riley!"

Chapter Nine

A sight for sore eyes, that was me. Two shiners, a cut across my cheek and a swollen nose. And each one still hurt like the blue blazes.

Major Donovan was livid when he first saw me. Father Duffy couldn't help himself. He laughed. "Miss Van Pelt will wonder what we do around here," he said. "Training must be hard on lowly privates."

He and the Major then talked about what to do with Sheriff Lynch, a sergeant striking a private. Court martial they felt was too extreme. Strip him of his rank down to private.

"What do you think, Bucky?" the Major asked. "You didn't fight back and now you look like his personal punching bag."

"Leave him be, Sir," I pleaded. "It'll make it worse. He'll see me as an ass-kisser to the battalion commander, a privileged private who seeks revenge and gets what he wants because of who he reports to."

Father Duffy's eyebrows shot up when he heard "ass-kisser."

"Nobody kisses my butt around here and gets away with it," said Major Donovan. "And that means you, too, Private Riley." He rubbed his face and finally smiled. "The worst thing you do is give my chin a nice nick now and then."

"I'm still learning, Sir."

"Well, you haven't slit my throat yet."

"Tomorrow night's the ball," Father Duffy purposely cut in to change the subject. "Then we're on our way."

"Any sermons planned for the troops before we depart?" asked the Major.

"On the ship over."

"We're going over on two ships. How are you going to pull that off?"

"I guess we need another chaplain. I've put in a request for at least one."

"Catholic or Protestant?"

"I'll take a rabbi if one could be assigned to the regiment."

"Not many Jews in the Sixty-ninth."

"There's Sergeant Blaustein," I said. "Transfer from the Fourteenth."

"I've met him," said Father Duffy. "Good soldier. He got a raw deal when he

transferred in, though. Our guys paid him a corporal's wages even though he's a sergeant. I heard he'd quipped to the paymaster, 'You not only transfer me into this Mick outfit but make me pay two dollars for the privilege.' I've heard he's been called a Jew bastard by some of our own men. I need to address that in my next sermon."

Father Duffy and the Major were quiet for a while.

I finally said, "I wonder if I'll run into my Poppa over there."

"Did you read the latest issue of the *Sentinel?*" Major Donovan asked.

"No, Sir."

"He's on the front lines. Quite an article he wrote about American soldiers making our country's first raid into no-man's land. I can see why your old man's got the reputation he has. The paper's in the trash. Dig it out and read the article. You should read it, too, Frank."

"I will. Usually I don't read the *Sentinel.*"

I retrieved the newspaper from the trash and was about to hand it to Father Duffy. He held up his hand. "You read it, Bucky."

I moved to my chair, which I kept in the corner to be out of the way at all times because the Major's tent, like his office back at the armory, was always abustle with officers and politicians coming and going. When he wasn't out drilling his men, organizing boxing bouts or leading them on cross-country runs, sometimes to Long Island Sound for a swim, it was a never-ending stream—and some of them were indeed ass-kissers.

"Read it aloud," Father Duffy ordered.

It was so odd looking at my Poppa's byline. I sat down and gulped.

Led by French Soldiers, Americans Go Over the Top For the First Time

By Special Correspondent Luther "Rough" Riley

WITH THE AMERICAN ARMY IN FRANCE, Oct. 29—Under the cover of darkness last night, American soldiers braved enemy machine gun fire and for the first time in the war crept into No Man's Land in search for prisoners. Led by veteran French troops, a patrol of General Pershing's intrepid men, with rain beating down, slipped through barbed wire and slithered over muddy, gas-infested shell holes to hunt down their prey. Twelve soldiers, all volunteers, armed with grenades, revolvers and trench knives, climbed scaling ladders and crawled into an empty stretch of earth where not a living creature survives for very long.

When the company captain had asked for volunteers, every man stepped forward. Those not chosen were sorely disappointed not to be part of American history. For censorship reasons, the names of the heroes who went over the top are known only to General Pershing, his staff, the tight-lipped soldiers of the regiment and a handful of bureaucrats in Washington.

After several nights of training, the Franco-American patrol made its move in the sodden dark night of October 28th. First a French lieutenant eased himself out of the trench, then an American. Like Indian scouts of old, the soldiers silently made their way across No Man's Land toward an unsuspecting enemy.

I stopped reading. I plainly saw my Poppa somehow down in the trench with the mud-caked soldiers, seeing their eyes wide with fearful anticipation, their hearts pounding while Poppa hoped for guns to go off and bullets to zing past them. *Pop! Pop! Pop!* Blood and guts! He was now back in the action he'd so terribly missed, making himself the center of it all. I crumpled up the newspaper and crammed it back into the trash.

"Don't you want to know what happened?" Father Duffy asked, a puzzled look on his face.

"No, Sir," I said.

"Well, I do." He pulled the newspaper from the trash, smoothed it out, scanned Poppa's article and began to read where I'd left off.

Chapter Ten

For the farewell dance, every room in the elegant Garden City Hotel was lit up like there'd be no tomorrow. And I sensed there'd be no tomorrow for many of the couples—the husbands and wives, the mothers and sons, the fathers and daughters, and all the sweethearts. In the middle of the night our regiment would be off to war.

I saw the lights glowing from afar, lighting up the edges of the golf course as the motorcar I was in with Father Duffy and, with Tony driving, swung through the gate and along the gravel drive leading to the hotel entrance. People were crowding through the doors. I felt my heart quicken. Was Calliope among them?

Reading my mind right on cue, Father Duffy tapped me on the shoulder and said, "She's here, Bucky."

He'd gotten the motorcar for us or otherwise I would've walked or jumped a ride from some unknown civilian character. Then who knew when I'd get to the hotel.

Earlier, back at Camp Mills, after the Roosevelts had come down from Oyster Bay and the Colonel was getting ready to address the troops in an open field, I looked for Calliope. I didn't see her. Nor did I see Mrs. Roosevelt. That's when I feared maybe they hadn't come after all. Maybe I wouldn't ever see Calliope again! I'd been forced to listen to the Colonel. It was the first time I'd heard him speak before such a crowd. He shouted, that high voice of his carrying over the heads of the soldiers: "To you is given the supreme privilege of meeting the call of your country, as the men of Washington's time met the call of their day, as those of Lincoln met the call of their generation."

He closed with words that surprised me and made Father Duffy chuckle. "By George, boys, I'm more pleased than I can say and I'll bet on you against any sauerkrauters that ever were born!"

Sauerkrauters?

Still, there was no Calliope to be seen.

Inside the hotel, music floated out from the grand ballroom. It came from our regimental band—good, but not in the same class as the Rattlers. I'm sure no one knew the difference except Tony, and now me as well. The dance floor was already filled. Couples swayed to the music. Others stood along the outer edge of the dance floor. No Calliope! I was having a fit.

An officer then called for everyone's attention, even as the ballroom continued to fill. The band stopped playing.

"We leave you, our friends," he said, "with a smile on our faces and joy in our hearts. Make it as happy as you can for us, and always remember the last dance—*Send Me Away With A Smile*. It is time for rejoicing—not sorrow. We are happy in the thought that before long we have done our duty, licked the Kaiser—and then you can welcome us home with a dance. On with the dance! Strike up the band! It's our last good-bye!"

The band started up again. And there was Calliope! In the middle of the dance floor in the arms of a soldier! I knew it was her—the red hair falling on the shoulders of her dance partner. She saw me. Holding the soldier's hand, she came toward me.

"Oh, Bucky," she said. Her voice, how I missed it.

She let go of the soldier's hand. It was her brother, Schuyler.

"Calliope!" said I, so happy to see her that when I smiled my nose hurt from where it'd been broken and then rebroken. I touched it. What a sight I must be.

She smiled back, almost laughing. "Boy, are you a sight for sore eyes. And your nose looks worse than old Captain Cobb's nose." Then she rushed into my arms. "Oh, Bucky, ain't I glad to see you! Nose and all!" Her hold was so tight—as if every being in her body wanted to be one with mine. I squeezed her just as hard. She then pulled back. She nodded toward her brother, "you remember Schuyler?"

"Yes." I reached out my hand, noticing he wore the stripes of a corporal. He refused to shake hands.

"Private Riley," his tone letting me know that he outranked me, not only militarily, but socially, "the last time we met was not pleasant. Up on the Hudson River. Remember? You tried to keep my sister from me."

No, she was using me as a shield.

"Please, Schuyler," Calliope cut in. "Tonight's a time for loving good-byes."

The band struck up "Memphis Blues." I recognized the tune from the Manhattan Casino as Calliope took my hand. "Come on, let's dance." Without looking back at her brother, she led me out onto the dance floor, suddenly reminding me of the way Linda had led me on to a dance floor. The beat of "Memphis Blues" made the memory more crystal clear. When we touched I felt guilty. I couldn't help but think for a moment of Linda.

"Are you okay, Bucky?" Calliope asked, her hand on my shoulder. "Don't give my brother another thought. He still sides with father—thinks I belong with them. But he doesn't know the full story. He never will. It'd break his heart."

Linda then faded from my mind.

"Let's go out on the veranda," she said. We hadn't danced a step.

Other couples were on the veranda, the autumn moonlight magically turning their last embraces into a romantic setting I'd never forget. We left the veranda for the damp grass stretching away to the golf course. And then Calliope and I were kissing. Her lips pushed against mine.

Why was I going overseas when this was all mine? I was too young! Damn you, Poppa!

I said, "I'll miss you so much."

She pulled back. "Didn't you miss me already?"

"All the time."

"I'll be so old when you come back. I'll be sixteen next week."

"We'll be gone for only a few months. They say the war will be over by Christmas. Doogie McDougall, he's an alter boy like me, goes around saying, 'Heaven, Hell or Hoboken by Christmas.' Then when I come back we'll celebrate your birthday and mine, too."

She said, "Don't bet on it. Maybe *next* Christmas you'll be coming home." She kissed me again, more earnestly this time. In my ear she whispered, "No hanky-panky."

It was then I saw movement on the veranda. Instead of embracing couples, a man paced back and forth, then stopped and placed both hands on the railing around the veranda. He looked toward us. The way he stood reminded me of the first time I saw Calliope's Poppa at the dock in Burlington staring out at Lake Champlain while waiting for permission to board *The Frank White*. It made my back crawl then, it made my back crawl again.

"What?" said Calliope, opening her eyes. She turned toward the veranda. "Oh my God, it's father! He must be here to see Schuyler off. I don't think he knows I'm here. Unless Schuyler told him. And I bet he did, the rat!"

I saw her brother then, standing behind her Poppa.

Calliope clutched my hand. "Let's go!" She started running away, farther into the dark. She pulled me along. I wasn't sure if her Poppa or brother saw us as we tried to run from the far-reaching glow of the lights. She stopped, apparently thinking we were far enough away. Breathing heavily and trembling, she said, "I can't face father. Take me away."

Knowing there was no chance I could take her away, I said, "Let's find the Roosevelts."

"Yes," she said. "I know where they are." Still trembling, she added, "They're in the hotel."

I said, "There's got to be a side door."

Before we took another step we heard "Taps" coming from inside the ballroom.

Calliope squeezed my hand. "What now?"

"I have to go. I must report. There'll be one more dance and then we're off!"

"Off?"

"Yes," I said. "We're being called to arms."

I wanted so much to stay out on the grass. Instead, as the couples on the veranda began to break up and move reluctantly into the ballroom, I steered us toward the bright lights of the hotel and to where Calliope's Poppa waited. I had to figure out a way to slip by him and Schuyler.

We didn't make it. "What are you doing here with him?" her Poppa said. I remembered him so well when we'd first met on the towboat. His hair was still parted in the middle and slicked down. His magnificently waxed and tapered mustache still twirled upward in grandiloquent flourishes. And he still looked like one of those villains in the Saturday matinee flickers.

"To say goodbye," Calliope said in a cold voice, trying to brush past her Poppa.

"Well, you've said it. Now you're coming home with me." He blocked her way. Schuyler didn't move, but stood silently off to the side. I tried to get by. Her Poppa grabbed my arm. "You some kind of snot-nosed kid?"

"No sir."

Calliope used that moment to slip under her Poppa's arm and make it to the entrance to the ballroom. "Come on, Bucky, they're playing *Send me Away With A Smile.*"

Both her Poppa and now Schuyler moved between Calliope and me. I was hemmed in. I was afraid to start a fight. It'd spoil everybody's good-byes.

"Oh, Bucky, hurry before the music stops!"

I felt then I'd never get a chance to say my good-bye to Calliope. The hell with it! I made up my mind to push past them.

"Hold on there, Private Riley."

Turning, I saw Father Duffy striding toward us.

Calliope's Poppa let go of my arm. "Who are you?"

"Father Frank Duffy, chaplain of the Sixty-ninth. You must be Miss Van Pelt's father." He nodded toward me. I took that as a signal to follow Calliope into the ballroom, sure Father Duffy could handle her Poppa in a way that would quiet everything down.

On the dance floor, wrapping my arms around her, I said, "I wanted our farewell to be something special."

"Isn't this special? You, me and father." She laughed. "That's the way it's always gonna be."

I didn't want to let that remark pass by, but before I could reply someone started singing.

Send me away with a smile, little girl,
Brush the tears from eyes of brown.
It's all for the best
And I'm off with the rest
Of the boys from my own hometown.

"That's us," Calliope said. "I'll send you away with a smile." When she smiled tears filled her eyes. "Will I ever see you again?"

I felt my eyes welling up, too. "I'll come back," I said. "Then we'll go look for Captain Cobb, Stubby, Thorny, the whole crew, especially Tripod."

"My dear, Bucky." She reached up to kiss me just as the last words of the song faded away and the new commander of our regiment, Colonel Hine, strode to the center of the ballroom.

"It's time, gentlemen," he said. "Report to your units. We leave in two hours."

At that moment, all the women on the dance floor gently pulled off their scented gloves and handed them to their husbands or boyfriends, a keepsake to carry into battle.

"I don't have any gloves," Calliope dabbed at her eyes with her bare hand. "Goodness me," she sighed. "But I do have this." It was her hankie. "Remember, no hanky, no panky." She tried to smile. "Now you have my hanky."

Those were the last words I remember.

End of Part II

PART THREE

Over There

Chapter One

As Major Donovan's striker, I went with him and his battalion to Montreal by train where we were then loaded onto a liner bound for Liverpool, England. Father Duffy and my fellow altar boys, Tony and Doogie, went instead with the rest of the regiment to Brest, France, aboard a troopship that steamed out of Hoboken. I'm sure that on my train, the Major and the Chaplain had earlier arranged for it to stop in Burlington, that somehow they'd gotten word to my mother to be at the station for a last good-bye. They never told me they'd done it. A big surprise.

Nearing Burlington in the early morning light, unaware of what was in store for me, I kept my face pressed against the window. It'd been half a year since I'd lit out for Oyster Bay and the Roosevelts' home atop Sagamore Hill. Now I was passing through my hometown, but only for a look-see through a train window.

Union Train Station is down by Lake Champlain. The tracks run between the station and the lake. I'd positioned myself so that I was facing the lake, not the city. The reason: when the train chugged into Burlington, I hoped to see *The Frank White* docked along the waterfront, spot Captain Chauncey Cobb or Stubby or Thorny or maybe even Tripod patrolling the deck. I'd bang on the window to get their attention and then wave. Of course they weren't there. Once we passed that part of the waterfront, I moved to the other side of the car and looked out at the city it-self—wanting so much to see my hometown for maybe the last time. Take in the white steeple at the end of Church Street so familiar to me or the hill where I lived that swept up toward the University. I most wanted to see my Momma and sisters.

I felt the train shudder to a stop. The door to the car opened and Major Donovan poked his head inside. Almost all the soldiers in Headquarters Company scrambled to their feet, except those who'd dozed off.

"As you were," he said. Then, "Bucky, you got five minutes."

Standing on the waiting platform were Momma and my sisters.

He said, "Move it, now!"

I quickly climbed down from the train, my heart filled with happiness. Momma rushed up to me. She touched my broken nose and then hugged me for all she was worth.

"Luther, you naughty boy. How could you run off like that? Go to war?" Her face was wet with tears.

My sisters, Clara, Anna and dear Louisa crowded in, their arms wrapped around Momma and me.

Louisa whispered in my ear. "See, you could do it. I told you so."

Then I heard a pounding on the window of the train. A number of the boys were waving and whistling and throwing kisses at my sisters. Anna heartily waved back and even tossed a kiss. That brought on more pounding and whistling and more kisses. Next came Major Donovan's voice. "Let's go, soldier!"

"Oh, no," Momma cried. "Don't go, Luther. You're much too young! Oh, dear me! Write often."

"I'll be fine. I'll be safe. The Major and the Chaplain are watching over me."

"Now Private!"

"See," I said.

Momma wiped a tear and kissed me once more. The last thing she said was, "Your Father knows you're coming. Watch for him in Paris."

Louisa tugged at my sleeve as I turned to leave. "Love you, Bucky." She reached up and kissed me on the mouth.

More banging on the windows.

I climbed back into the car—Momma's last embrace, still warm. Looking back I saw her sitting on a bench, her face buried in her hands. My sisters were trying to comfort her. At that moment I felt uncertain—uneasy was more like it—as to why I'd left my family in the first place to go chase after Poppa and upset Momma. What was I thinking?

Inside the car, the boys still hooted and whistled. "You lucky bastard!" one of them hollered over the din. "I wanna get off and kiss one of those pretty gals!" another yelped. "Brother, do I ever!"

The train lurched forward. I looked out the window. Momma looked up from the bench and then she and my sisters waved for the last time.

Then I heard a snide shout, "Ain't it great to be the Major's boy."

A lot of changes took place once we landed in France. The liner we sailed on, the *Tunisian*, had civilians on board. Even so, Major Donovan had us up on deck every day, running and sweating over calisthenics to stay in shape. We hit a storm halfway across the Atlantic. The *Tunisian* rolled and tossed and spray spilled over the deck like the mighty Niagara. All of us, it seemed, the Major included, couldn't keep anything down. The boys were throwing up in almost every corner of the liner. Me, too. Once we got close to Europe, British warships escorted us the rest of the way across in case German U-boats prowled under the water.

We finally made it to Liverpool. From there we took a train to the English coast without a chance to enjoy the strange countryside, green like much of Vermont except hardly any trees. Well, not what I'd describe as trees. We were next ferried across the English Channel to the sprawling port of Le Havre.

On deck, the Major had the Battalion line up by company, with Headquarters Company assembled at the rear. We then stepped down the gangplank onto the harbor's cobbled streets. The French were waiting for us. I have never seen such a reception. They lined the way or stood in doorways or leaned out windows—many of them waving American and French flags—and cheered. I saw they were mostly women and children. Hardly any men at all, except those who were old, bent and gray-haired. A lot of the women wore black mourning dresses. Children danced alongside us as we marched through the city. We were there to win the war.

"Hello, boys!" sang out a little girl with eyes as bright and hopeful as a Vermont harvest moon.

I heard others singing, "Hail, hail, the gang's all here! What the hell do we care! What the hell do we care, now!"

Up ahead a boy marched with us playing "Yankee Doodle" on a flute.

Then another boy, no more than nine or ten tugged at the sleeve of my uniform with one hand while the other, close to his lips, mimicked holding a cigarette. "Cigaret pour Papa?"

I shrugged. He raised his eyebrows in a "you just don't get it way," quickly moved on to another soldier, grabbed his sleeve and looked up full of hope.

At the Le Havre train station, freight cars for hauling farm animals were lined up to carry us toward the frontlines. On the side of each car was written "40 Hommes, 8 Cheaveaux."

"What the hell does that mean?" several soldiers asked.

"Forty men, eight horses" came the answer from one of us who knew French, a private named Frank Bean, who I'd seen around the armory a lot. He was fairly short and heavy with a big head and was always trailing after a lieutenant. He'd lived in Paris for a few years, I soon learned, studying art. He was even a friend of Calliope's brother, Schuyler.

"Get on!" ordered the sergeants.

We were packed in. The last in remarked loud enough for all to hear, "Forty men and eight horses, my Noo Yawk ass. Smells like the horses are still in here."

The questions everyone wondered, "Where are we headed?" and "When we gonna meet up with the rest of the regiment?" All we knew for sure was that we were headed to the front to train with French soldiers who'd been killing Germans for years and knew all about the treachery of trench warfare.

"Paris," said Frank Bean, squeezing in next to me. "I know this railroad route, Le Havre to Rouen to Paris. Traveled it many times back when I was studying in Gay Paree. We're off to Paris. First stop! Guaranteed!"

"Paris!" a soldier said. "I hear the women there are loose. You know whatta mean."

Paris, I thought, as the train rattled on. "Poppa!"

Chapter Two

How we got almost the entire Headquarters Company into that one freight car—fifty boys with rifles and packs and a few of them pretty much overweight—was a marvel. The moment we were all squashed in, with a lot of cussing and pushing and hunting for a place to squat, the heavy door rolled shut. At least it wasn't locked. But we were in the dark until our eyes got used to it. Then we were off to Paris.

As the train rattled eastward, I thought of Poppa.

I saw him limping around the house on his bum knee, relying on his gold-knobbed cane for balance, cursing his misfortune. How Momma had put up with it I don't know. Well, he was back doing what he loved best—telling the world what was going on in his own personal style that had made him a household name before and after he'd saved President Roosevelt's life up on San Juan Hill. He'd written about that adventure, too, a first-person account syndicated in almost every newspaper across America. Even the President had written about it. Then Poppa's byline began appearing daily on the front pages of the *New York Morning Sentinel* as well other newspapers. He loved it. A celebrity. Then his knee acted up, got in the way, and he was confined to the city desk editing copy written by hack reporters, first in New York, then Burlington—a step down for him. No byline. No celebrity. Just bitterness. He took that bitterness out on everyone, but mostly on me.

The train crept along, the sound of its metal wheels clacking over the tracks. I wanted to see outside, take in the French countryside. Although there were cracks in the sidewalls, there was not enough space between them to make out anything but a blur.

"Hey," came a voice close by. "I hear you're Rough Riley's son. That right?"

Turning, I saw through the dim light Frank Bean and remembered him dropping down next to me.

"Yes," I said.

"Thought so. Hey, I'm Frank. I know the Van Pelts. Schuyler is a friend. We call him Van for short. You know he's a corporal over in E Company, Second Battalion."

I nodded, then realized he probably couldn't see me very well in the dark. "I only met Schuyler a couple of times," I said, remembering West Point and then the Garden City Hotel. Unpleasant recollections. "How'd you know about me and the Van Pelts?"

"Van told me just before we left Camp Mills. Said you and I were in the same battalion."

Not knowing what else to say, I asked, "You know the Van Pelt family long?"

"Since I was kid."

"Are you from Garrison?"

"That's right. How'd you know?"

"Well, that's where the Van Pelts live."

"Hey, you're right, although they got a place on Fifth Avenue." I felt him try to get more comfortable in the close quarters we were all clumped together in. Once settled, he said, "I never got to know Van's sister very well. By the time I came into the picture, she was gone. I think somewhere in upstate New York."

Not sure where Frank Bean was going with our conversation, I muttered "Uh huh."

"Sorry. Just asking."

"So you've been to Paris?"

"Oh, yes. Went to school there, Ecole Beaux Arts to study architecture. Then in 1914 the war came along and I had to hurry home. Now here I'm heading back to Paris, not as a student, but as a soldier. Ironic, huh?"

"Is Paris as beautiful and wild as I hear it is?"

"Beautiful and wild doesn't do it justice. Tell me about Calliope"

I said, "My Poppa's in Paris."

"Hey, I read the *Sentinel.* Come on, tell me about Calliope. What kind of girl is she?"

The train stopped. The door slid open. A sergeant hollered, "Pee call! Climb out and do your thing, then hop back on. No dillydallying! This ain't no sightseeing tour!"

Out we staggered onto an empty field. Frank Bean stayed close to me. "She's cute, isn't she? Calliope?"

I said, "She's only fifteen."

"You know, she's turning sixteen in a few weeks."

How'd he know that? "Me, too," I grumbled. I was beginning to not care for him. He sealed his fate with the next question. "Hey, those girls waiting at the train station back in Vermont must be your sisters? Really cute. Any of 'em have boyfriends?"

"All of them," I said. I buttoned up my pants and got back into the freight car. I wiggled to a dark corner. He found me.

"You got a thing for Calliope? Van says you have. And he doesn't like it."

"What's with all the questions?"

"Just asking, you know. I'm curious about the Van Pelts. They got a lot of money, more than my folks, live high off the hog they do."

I didn't think Calliope and her Momma, the former scullery maid, lived high off the hog. Maybe they did because of the divorce. "Well, you know more about them than I do so let's talk about something else."

"How about your sisters?"

Then some angry soldier, fed up that he was cramped inside the freight car, kicked open the door. Light poured in. "There, goddamn it," he yelled. "Now we can see and breathe and get some of that stink outta here!"

A cheer roared around the freight car.

"Don't anyone fall out," came a shout.

"It'd be better than sittin' on our ass!"

Another cheer.

I was happy with the excitement. For the moment, at least, it had made Frank Bean shut up.

Looking out the doorway I saw we were passing through a village. Alongside the track, people cheered, waving American flags. No doubt in their minds we were coming to save them.

"We'll be in Rouen soon," Frank Bean said. "Then Paris. I wonder if we'll be let off the train, get a chance to stroll around?"

Paris again made me think of Poppa. If he knew when the train was coming into Paris maybe he'd be at the train station. More likely he'd be out somewhere with our First Division writing about the war. Well, so be it.

The train clattered on. Frank Bean stopped asking questions. He lit a cigarette. Time passed. Village after village, field after field. Everywhere along the tracks were ecstatic French women and children and gray-haired men with medals from the Franco-

Prussian War pinned to their coats. Our soldiers crowded around the open door and yelled to them our appreciation. Some of the soldiers tossed out cigarettes. When the train slowed going through a village, young girls ran alongside, reaching out with flowers. We took them, held them to our hearts or over our heads.

"This is something!" I said.

"Yeah," said Frank Bean. "They're so happy that American boys are ready to die to save their sorry asses."

I had nothing to say. I'd be rid of him once we got to Paris.

Chapter Three

Night fell, stars twinkled and the train went on.

"Close the damn door!" someone hollered. "I'm freezin'!"

"Me, too!"

The door rolled shut. We were thrown into darkness. All I could see were the lit ends of cigarettes.

"Looks like we aren't stopping in Paris after all," Frank Bean said, a cigarette dangling from his mouth. "Should've been there by now."

No Paris. No Poppa.

I breathed out a sigh and, feeling a cramp ready to grab my calf muscle, I tried to get up. I realized I hadn't stood for hours. How long were we going to be bottled up inside the smelly freight car? If we weren't going to Paris where were we headed? Unsteadily, I got to my feet. I swayed and caught my balance.

"Where you going?" Frank Bean stubbed out his cigarette.

"To Paris," I said.

"What?"

Then I surprised myself by stepping over slumped bodies of sleeping soldiers, avoiding arms and legs and packs and rifles as I worked my way to another corner of the car.

"Hey," I heard a few grumbles. "Watch it! I'm trying to sleep here!"

I made it, squeezed down and hugged my knees. Frank Bean hadn't followed me. I let out another sigh. Closing my eyes, I tried to sleep, but I knew sleep wouldn't come. No Paris. No Poppa, I thought.

And on went the train through the night.

Finally, we reached our destination. Two nights, three days cramped together. The nearer we got—and we had no idea where we were going—the more destruction we saw. The worst was French soldiers trudging along chalky white roads, rifles slung over shoulders, heads down, a sorry lot with the slump of defeat in every step. We kept quiet. What were we getting into if French soldiers, poilu they were called, the hairy ones, looked so downcast?

The train stopped. The screech of locked wheels on metal tracks meant we'd come to the end of our journey. A sergeant showed up in front of the door.

"Every one of you sorry bastards out and fall in!"

Stiff in every joint of our bodies, we grumbled and slid out of the freight car, blinking in the daylight and shivering in the crisp November cold. I looked up and down the length of the train. Hundreds of soldiers were climbing down, finding their footing on the ground and struggling to form up by company. I took my place in line. Frank Bean stood next to me.

"Well, we made it," he said.

"Attention!" yelled the sergeant.

We brought our feet together, straightened ourselves up as best we could after so long a train ride and stared straight ahead. Except for me, rifles were slung over shoulders. Because of my age a rifle still hadn't been assigned to me. Not yet, anyway. Maybe I'd get one in another eight days, on my birthday.

A lieutenant stepped next to the sergeant. "Men," he said, "welcome to Vaucouleurs, once the home of Joan of Arc. Well, this berg is not the end of the line. We're gonna march to our new location, a bunch of miles to the east. Then we'll settle down for more training. We're in the Meuse area of France. The German border is about 100 miles from here. Not too far to the north is Verdun. Bar-le-Duc is close by, too, and that's where most of the French army in this battle zone is encamped. You'll be hearing a lot of artillery fire from now on, especially when we get closer to the border. You'll all be happy to know that the rest of the regiment is here, at our new training ground. It arrived two days ago."

I felt better.

"There'll be no barracks, no tents," the lieutenant went on. "We'll all be sleeping in barns, sheds or in houses owned by the residents in the villages we'll be located in. When we get there, treat them as you would your own home, your own family. Anyone of you who don't will be in a world of trouble. Understand?"

There was a loud chorus of "Yes sir!"

"Understand?"

"Yes sir!"

"There's a mess set up here in the village square. Once you've all had something to eat, we'll head out. The sergeant will now lead you to a hot meal. Take 'em away, Sergeant."

"Follow me, men," the sergeant ordered.

As we fell out, from out of nowhere Tony Margiotta ran up to me. "Bucky! Hey, we beat you here."

"Tony!" It was great to see him.

"Bucky, there's been a change in orders. You're now a full-time altar boy with me and Doogie, reporting directly to Father Duffy. Donovan's been sent to Paris. No telling when he'll be back. That's the reason you're with us. But when he does return you'll go back to being his striker. Come along now, my friend, I'm to take you right away to our new location, about fifteen miles from here in a village called Grand. We're bunking in a barn with three guys from E Company."

"From E Company? How come?"

Tony shrugged. "The Chaplain wanted 'em. Said we better all get together"

I wondered why. No boys from First Battalion or Headquarters Company. How odd, I thought.

"You'll see this barn ain't as swell as Pope's Corner," Tony went on. "But it's okay if you can stand the cow stink and chickens and a big white duck the family calls On-Ree or something like that. I think it's a pet."

"You sure it's not a goose?"

"Goose? Duck?" Tony laughed. "How would I know the difference? I'm from the City. All I know is the frogs build their barns in town, not out in the fields like normal farmers. So we gotta put up with the stink. Our barn is at the edge of town. Father Duffy's staying in the farmhouse. It's a block from an old church he's taken a liking to. He wants to hold a big mass there. The farmhouse belongs to a war widow. She lives there along with her father and three daughters. So come along."

The barn was made of stone, and Tony was right, it did stink. A dozen chickens were pecking in the backyard. I didn't see On-Ree. I followed Tony up the ladder to the loft to stow my stuff. The floor was strewn with straw and the packs from the E Company boys.

"Over in the corner," Tony said. "Toss your pack there. Doogie should be back soon. He and Father Duffy are checking out the church. Then we'll eat."

I said, "There's mess being served in the village square."

"Not for us. We eat here in the farmhouse. The lady who owns the place cooks our meals. She loves doin' it. Well, she's cooked up great meals yesterday and the day when we first got here. A lot of potatoes with thick cream and other stuff, but no chicken yet. Ain't we lucky?"

"How'd you and Doogie find this place?"

"Our platoon commander, Sergeant Murray. He's in charge of billeting our company. Father Duffy told Murray what he wanted, a place close to the church, and we got first dibs. Speaking of being lucky, wait'll you see the daughters."

"You said the mother's a war widow? How's she holding out?" I couldn't imagine losing a husband or any family member.

"All I know was her old man was killed at Verdun and she has a son fighting somewhere. So she's always on edge. She speaks a little English. Let's go."

The war widow's name was Jeanne. A tall woman with dark, graying hair, pulled back in a bun and a pretty face etched with lines of sorrow. Her dress was mourning black, the same black that most French women seemed to be wearing. War widows all. She smiled when I stooped through the front door into the living room. I held out my hand for a shake. Instead of taking it, she grasped me by the shoulders, leaned forward and kissed me on both cheeks.

"Ahh, Private Bucky," she said, then stood back to size me up.

Private Bucky, I thought—curious how she knew. "Yes, Ma'am," I said. I took off my helmet.

"Madame," she corrected. "Madame Jeanne."

"Yes, Madame Jeanne." I should have known growing up close to the Quebec border where French was Burlington's second language.

"Welcome to my home." She smiled. I could still see the sadness in her eyes. I guess that sadness would be there for the rest of her life. I was sure that she now prayed every night for God to keep your only son safe.

I heard voices coming from the kitchen. Two girls walked into the living room. They each had their mother's pretty face, but without the lines of sorrow, and hair as black as the darkest night. One was maybe ten, the other eighteen or so. They saw me, they curtsied. I thought how quaint. I didn't know whether to bow or just stand there. So I stood.

"Private Bucky," Madame Jeanne said. "Mon filles, my daughters, Marie, the eldest, and Poppy, the youngest. My third daughter, Sienna, the middle one, is at the market. She'll be home soon."

"Hello," I said.

"My son, Victor Marie, is at the front with the Thirtieth Division." She crossed herself.

Two Maries? I'd find out that the son had been named after the writer Victor Marie Hugo, and so had been the eldest daughter.

The front door opened up and in stepped Father Duffy, followed by Doogie. The Chaplain nodded to Madame Jeanne. When she looked at Father Duffy I glimpsed a sudden glow of warmth in her cheeks because a priest had entered her home, blessing her and her family.

Turning to me, Father Duffy said, "Glad you finally made it, Bucky. Your nose looks a lot better. Major Donovan's in Paris to learn about our mission and what's expected of us from here on out. He's due back in about a month. I'm praying he'll get that promotion to command the regiment. Hine's okay, but no Donovan. In the meantime, you've been permanently assigned to me. Hope you like your new digs, cows, chickens and Henri."

"Henri?"

"Yes. The pet goose."

I shot a glance at Tony.

He shrugged.

"If we're still here at Christmastime, don't expect a goose for dinner. Henri's part of the family."

The front door opened again. The third daughter, Sienna, carrying a parcel filled with goods from the market, passed over the threshold. She had hair as dark as her sisters. We shyly looked at each other. We were about the same age. It then occurred to me that this family was like my family, three daughters and a son. The only difference was their son was the eldest while in my family I was the youngest.

"Sienna," her mother said, "this is Private Bucky."

Like her sisters, she curtsied. This time I bowed, a bit awkwardly, all the while thinking of Calliope, her red hair and oh how I missed her.

The whole time Father Duffy took it all in, letting that amused smile of his show. Did anyone else notice that smile?

He looked at me and said, "How was your trip across?"

"Pretty rough," I said. "Most of us got sick. Even the Major." I was glad to take my eyes off Sienna.

"It is dinner time," Madame Jeanne cut in.

She led us into the kitchen where a huge table was set for all of us, Father Duffy, Tony, Doogie and me, the three sisters, the mother and a place at the head of the table for the man of the house. I hadn't yet seen any trace of him. We sat, our host family on one side and us Americans on the other. Madame Jeanne made Father Duffy sit at the head of one end of the table, fussing over him as a mother would a child. I sat across from Sienna, Tony from Marie. He had pushed Doogie away so he could face the eldest sister.

A side door opened and in came the man of the house. He had a messy mat of thick white hair, eyebrows that almost covered his eyes, a mustache that drooped over his mouth and a glare that showed he was not pleased with the new housing arrangement. The men rose. The women stayed in their seats, except Madame Jeanne. She pulled out his chair and when he sat down kissed the top of his head. He kept his glare.

To me she said, "Mon beau père. My father-in-law."

Father Duffy nodded toward the old man. "Monsieur Moreau," he said.

Madame Jeanne took her seat and nodded to Father Duffy.

"Grace," he said. He held out his hands. We joined our hands, except Monsieur Moreau. We bowed our heads. Monsieur Moreau glared ahead, across the table at Father Duffy. Closing his eyes, Father Duffy recited grace. "Bless us, O Lord, and these, Thy gifts, which we are about to receive from Thy bounty. Through Christ, our Lord. Amen."

We crossed ourselves. I was still not comfortable doing it. Back home, we never crossed ourselves. Well, we never said grace. Tears filled Madame Jeanne's eyes. She ran her fingers down her cheeks. The daughters then got up and began to serve our meal. Monsieur Moreau's glare softened a bit watching his grandchildren. I later learned that not only had his son been killed at Verdun, but his younger brother and two nephews. No wonder he'd glared at Father Duffy during grace. To him there was no God.

After the meal, Father Duffy said he was going over to check on the soldiers in the regiment, to see if any of them needed a good word or two. He believed it was his blessed duty to walk among the boys, offering whatever cheer or strength his presence might provide.

The day was coming when his presence would be sorely needed by all of us.

Chapter Four

That night I found out why Father Duffy had three boys from E Company, Second Battalion, bunk in with us in our loft that we'd decided to nickname the Bishop's Corner because it was not as plush as the Pope's Corner. One of the E Company boys was Corporal Schuyler Van Pelt.

It was quite a jolt for us both.

"Well, if it isn't my little sister's boyfriend," he said, a touch of sarcasm in his voice. "What's the Chaplain scheming this time?"

I had no idea how to respond.

"You guys know each other?" one of the other boys from E Company asked. He was a three striper, a buck sergeant.

"Slightly," Schuyler answered.

I still had no idea how to respond. Sleeping up in the loft would now be like lying down in a bed of poison oak. Maybe worse.

Tony thought it was funny. He knew the story, or at least some of it. "My parents know your sister," he said.

That caught Schuyler off guard. "What do you mean?"

"You know. When that sheriff was chasing her all over the place. Wanted to arrest her. Haul her off to jail or something worse."

I cringed.

"Where'd you hear that?"

I think Tony realized he'd gone too far, maybe got the story mixed up. A quick look toward me and he shrugged. "My parents told me."

I cringed more.

Now Schuyler looked at me. "You spreading rumors about my family?"

I was dumb struck.

"I'm asking you! Private Riley!" He took a menacing step toward me.

"There'll be no fighting, Corporal Van Pelt." It was the buck sergeant. "And that goes for you, too, private! We'll have plenty of fighting on our hands soon enough!"

I wasn't about to fight Schuyler anyway.

"I still want to know why you're spreading rumors about my family."

Finally I said, "You know Sergeant Lynch? I think he's in your battalion."

"Lynch? You mean Sheriff Lynch?"

"I do."

"Well, what about him?"

"He tried to pick a fight with me back at Camp Mills," I said, wondering if I should keep going. I pointed at my nose. "Tony here saved me. He knows all about Lynch. Neither one of us are spreading rumors."

Schuyler seemed to relax. "The Chaplain must have put us together for a reason. He broke us apart at the Garden City Hotel, but now he has us rooming together. He's up to something."

"I don't like this any better than you do," I said. "Best we make the most of it."

"Yeah. But first I want to know about you and Calliope. She's still staying at the Roosevelts, and they won't let her go. Like she's in prison. My father can't even get to see her."

"What about your mother?" Why didn't I keep my mouth shut.

"Leave my mother out of this." Schuyler again took a step toward me.

"Corporal, watch it!" the sergeant warned.

"This is family business."

The punch landed square on my nose. Lights went on. I reeled back. Tony caught me before I hit the floor. The sergeant stepped between us, me and Schuyler.

"I'll have your stripes, Van Pelt." He said, pushing him away from me.

Blood seeped from my nose. Getting whacked on the sniffer was becoming a regular occurrence.

"Stay out of it, Sarge! It's my family he's insulting! I won't stand for it!"

"I didn't hear any insults," Tony cut in. "He saved your sister."

"How'd he do that? My father wanted her back for a special occasion, her coming out party, and this snot-nosed bastard kept her from him!"

Snot-nosed? My sorry nose was taking too much abuse. Wiping away the blood, I now got angry. "When was the last time you saw your Momma, the last time you talked to her?"

"I told you to leave my mother out of this!"

"When was the last time, Schuyler? Tell me!"

"None of your damn business!'

"Come on, tell me!"

Schuyler dropped his fists.

"A year? Two years? Tell me!"

"Five, damn you! Five!" Schuyler raised his left hand. I stepped back, expecting another punch to crash into my nose. Instead, he touched his eyes. "Damn you!" I then saw he was fighting back a tear. "Five, damn you!"

I figured the last time he saw his Momma he was only sixteen. My age soon. When I last saw my Momma I felt sad. She was weeping, and that was only three or four weeks ago.

"Schuyler," I said, "I'm sorry."

Tony grabbed the sergeant's arm. "Let's go," he said to him.

The sergeant nodded and the two of them backed down the ladder, leaving Schuyler and me alone up in the loft

When they were gone, Schuyler closed his eyes. "Damn you," he said again. His shoulders shook for a moment. He took a deep breath. "Damn the divorce. Damn father." He wiped his eyes and sat on a hay bale. I stood, not knowing what to do or say.

After a bit, he said, "I'm okay."

I said, "It's been hard on Calliope as well." On my nose, too.

Schuyler didn't say anything. He stared straight away. I sat down next to him and pinched my nose. We were quiet for a few minutes.

"Gotcha good, didn't I?" he said.

"Yeah." It'd stopped bleeding.

Then we were both laughing.

After a moment, Schuyler said, "You know, I've kept that divorce hidden from my mind all these years. Families aren't supposed to get divorces, not families like mine. There's like a rule, you're not supposed to marry down like my father. Of all the women in the world, an Irish maid." He took a deep breath. "I love my mother, and I hardly know her."

I said, "I guess Calliope was the fortunate one."

Schuyler shot me a hard look. I could see in his face the same features I saw in Calliope's face. Brother and sister.

He said, "I suppose you're right."

"She didn't want to leave her Momma, I can tell you that for sure."

"Why? A home on the Hudson, a home on Fifth Avenue, an old New York family and tons of money?"

"You answered that question when you agreed with me that she'd been the fortunate one."

Schuyler was silent for a long time. Then, "What's she like now?"

"Didn't you talk with her about all this when you saw us on the Hudson?"

"I did. But I guess I wasn't listening. More like not believing."

"I can say for certain, Calliope's got a mind of her own. Feisty. And plenty of courage. How she got away from Lynch and snuck onboard our tow boat without getting caught, well, I still marvel at that."

"What about that one-armed pirate?"

"Captain Cobb? Great man. Stubby, too."

"Stubby? The short guy?"

"Yep. He was on the USS Maine when she blew."

"Really?"

"Yep. And Captain Cobb lost his arm in the Philippines."

"You don't know this, but my father wants him arrested for kidnapping. Got a warrant still out, but nobody can find him."

"Kidnapping?"

"I'm afraid so."

"The only kidnapping was by Lynch, I can tell you that. He came close, too."

Schuyler ran his hand across his face. "I wish I could sit down with Calliope now, spend a day with her. You know, get to know her again like back when we were little kids together. When we get back, if we ever do, I'll make it a point to spend more time with her." He paused for a moment. "And mother, too. That, I must do."

From down below came a shout. It was Tony. "Hey, can we come up now? It's gettin' late, and we need to hit the sack."

"Come on up," Schuyler shot back.

We stood and Schuyler put out his hands. "No hard feelings?"

"No hard feelings," I said.

Later, I thought, *Father Duffy knew what he was doing.*

Chapter Five

My sixteenth birthday came and went.

The Moreaus surprised me with a chocolate cake adorned with sixteen candles, a wartime extravagance. But they insisted. Even Old Man Moreau came out of his room to enjoy the cake. For a moment the glare was gone. I was glad to see that. Before blowing out the candles, I touched in my breast pocket the hanky Calliope had given me back at the hotel, and then wished I might see her someday soon, very soon, but I knew it wouldn't be possible. I envisioned her as I first saw her, though, scrunched up in the corner of the bunk of *The Frank White* with her knees up under her chin, eyes wide, tangled hair and the gold crucifix at her throat. When I extinguished the flames on all the candles in a single breath, Sienna and her kid sister, Poppy, clapped with delight. By the sudden glow of joy in their pretty faces you'd hardly know their Poppa had recently been killed, and their brother now off fighting, his life in constant peril. Sienna and Poppy each gave me a hug, with Sienna calling me "Booky." Then it was back to work.

Being an altar boy wasn't much of a job. Mostly Tony and I tagged along with Father Duffy as he went among the boys in what he rightfully called his "Parish," bucking them up and lending an ear. He was trying hard to learn the name and home address of each and every soldier so that every time he ran into one of them he could call them by name and ask how they were doing and if they'd heard any news from home. Tony and I passed out cigarettes and, of course, helped out during mass. I was disappointed that Doogie was no longer with us. He'd been sent over to A Company as a clerk. The E Company boys, Schuyler included, went back to their unit. So only Tony and I slept in the loft. Now and then, as the weather turned colder, Henri, the goose, flew up in the loft to nestle in the hay, stay warm and be with us.

The days dragged on. When the wind was right we heard the big guns firing at each other miles away. French soldiers, back from the battlefields, trudged through the village, a number of them bandaged. Each time, Madame Jeanne stood by the front door, searching for her son. Only then did the war seem so close.

Every day now our regiment awaited orders to move up. None came. It was only a matter of time.

Sienna got to calling me Booky. She began to follow me around. She could hardly speak any English and kept asking me about certain words. I knew a little French, well, actually a very little French Canadian growing up close to Quebec. I soon discovered it wasn't the same as French French. In the backyard with chickens pecking about our feet, Sienna picked up one and pointed to it.

"Le poulet," she said.

Knowing what she wanted, I answered, "Chicken."

"Chicken," she echoed back. "Chicken."

I nodded. She pointed to Henri.

"Goose."

"Goose," she repeated. Then she took my hand and squeezed my thumb. "Le pouce."

"Le pouce?" I laughed.

Sienna laughed, too. She kept hold of my thumb. "Le pouce."

"Thumb."

"Thumb." She was still laughing when she dropped my thumb and reached up to touch my mangled nose. "Le nez."

I had to smile. "Nose."

"Ooh, nose." She stopped her laugh and made a sad face. "Ooh Booky, pauvre nez. Nose. Pauvre nose."

"Ooh, my broken nose."

"Broken nose." She took her hand from my nose and placed it over her heart. "Coeur," she said. "Le coeur."

"Heart," I said.

Then she took my hand and brought it up against her cheek. The softness and warmth of her skin was unsettling. Smiling now, she said, "Joue."

I didn't answer. She kept my hand on her cheek and looked straight into my eyes. "Joue, Booky, joue."

"Cheek."

"Ooh, cheek." She kept my hand pressed lightly against her face, so soft. She seemed to want to keep it there, her eyes still looking straight into mine. "Booky," she said.

And then it dawned on me why she was—I don't know—trying to seduce me. She was fifteen, maybe sixteen, a time when girls and boys were drawn together in ways other than innocent childhood friendships. She wanted a romantic relationship, but there were no boys in her village to flirt with or, maybe, something more. They were all off fighting. Or dead. So many would never return. Sienna's older sister, Marie, must have felt the same way—a loss of one of life's great joys, taken away cold-bloodedly by the war.

I let her hold my hand against her cheek. For a moment I felt a tear wanting to seep from my eye. I wouldn't let it fall.

"Mon Booky," she said.

"Sienna!" It was Madame Jeanne calling from the house. "Feed On-Ree and the chickens." At least that's what I thought she was yelling for her to do now that I knew poulet was the word for chicken.

At the dinner table that evening, Sienna looked over to me, smiling. She ran her hand along the side of her cheek and then touched her heart.

Our regiment's stay in the foothills of the Vosges ran into December. By mid-month, even though we heard the constant roar of artillery, every soldier grumbled about when we'd get into the war. Were we destined to sit it out? The French soldier looked beaten, from where we heard and saw him. Maybe the war was already lost and we, the Americans, had arrived too late. Father Duffy assured us that was not so.

"Our time to put in our licks will come soon enough," he told us.

Major Donovan was still in Paris. There was no word about when he might return and if he'd come back as commander of the Sixty-ninth. We still referred to the regiment as the old Fighting Sixty-ninth, never the 165th—unless it had to be official.

We trained and trained. At last I was given a rifle because I was sixteen. It was the standard Springfield rifle. Before learning to fire it, I had to learn how to take it apart, clean it and then re-assemble it. I kept at it until I had it down pat. I slept with it, too. Next, I marched out to the firing range a mile away on the outskirts of Vaucouleurs. There I blasted at a target 100 yards distant with other soldiers. I couldn't hit the target at first. But I had to keep at it until my face, sore from the rifle's kick each time I fired, looked like I'd been struck so many times by Jess Willard, the so-called Pottawatomie Giant—the world's boxing champ. I caught a lot of ribbing because of the way I looked—red, puffed out cheek and smashed nose. Ears ringing, too. I didn't care. My Poppa, I'm sure, would've been proud—maybe not the sharpshooter he'd once been back chasing Geronimo with Capt. Leonard Wood, but I could now hit what I was aiming at 100 yards distant.

If only Calliope could take a gander at me now, I thought, a beat-up rifleman ready to take on the Kaiser's army. Ha!

Christmas was a week away and Father Duffy was planning a grand midnight mass for the entire regiment and for any soldiers in our Eighty-third Brigade—the Ohio boys from the 166th Infantry and the Wisconsin boys from the 150th Machine Gun Company.

"If there's one day in all the year that wanderers far from home cannot afford to forget it is Christmas," he said. "Let's give them a religious ceremony they'll remember for many a year."

The poet, Joyce Kilmer, a sergeant in the Intelligence Section, who had converted to Catholicism when his daughter was dying, asked if he could pitch in. The Chaplain liked him a lot for his intellect and said it was fine with him if it was okay with his boss, Capt. Basil Elmer. A Colgate man whose parents were both professors of English literature, Elmer had no problem. He, too, enjoyed the poet's intellect. Kilmer joined us and it was such a thrill that I wrote my Momma and Calliope, too, all about him.

Meanwhile, Sienna wanted another English lesson. She chose the barn. She was not interested to learn about the chickens or the pet goose or the three cows that had to be milked every morning before they were let out into the fields at the edge of the village.

Touching the ladder that went up to the loft, she said "Echelle."

I was no fool. I knew what Sienna was leading up to. I found myself in a bind. Do I put an end to her game right away or do I play along? Maybe one more move.

"Ladder," I said. "Ladder."

From above came Tony's voice. "Don't come up!"

Sienna looked at me with her eyes wide. "Marie!" she whispered. "Marie!"

She ran out of the barn. I followed her. Then she stopped so sudden, as if she'd banged into a stonewall. "Oh!" she gasped! Her eyes were focused on three men approaching her house—two French soldiers, the other a priest.

"Victor!" she cried! "Oh Victor Marie!"

She bolted for the house. I went after her, but stopped. I hurried back to the barn. "Tony," I hollered. "Marie must go to her house right now. Something's happening and she needs to be there. Hurry, Tony!"

I left the barn and went toward the house. Before I opened the backdoor, I heard the anguished wail of Madame Jeanne.

And then Sienna.

Chapter Six

Midnight mass was to be a joyous moment for us all, but Tony and I had no such feeling. I wondered about Father Duffy.

The Moreau household was in total despair. Madame Jeanne clung to the Chaplin every time he came into her home. He did his best to comfort her and the girls. He could not hide the sorrow he felt. And neither could we, Tony and I. For the rest of the days we lived with the family there were no more English lessons for Sienna. She stayed mostly in her room. How could you ever get over the loss of your father and then your brother? Both killed—one at Verdun, the other up in the Vosges Mountains so close to home in a slice of woodland in the Forêt de Parroy called Rouge Bouquet? It would be with them forever. It would stay with me, too, all my days.

Yet there was one thing our regiment could now look forward to. Orders had arrived at last from Chaumont, General Pershing's Headquarters. The Rainbow Division—25,000 strong—was to move closer to the front, into those foreboding mountains, the Vosges, to train in the trenches with French veterans. There'd be no train ride to get there. It was close enough that we were to march to our new location, stepping out on the 26th of December, the day after Christmas.

Midnight Mass, then, might be the last time many of us would ever celebrate at Christmas. Father Duffy knew this and was determined to make it a mass to remember for all the boys far from home. In a letter to the Archbishop of New York, Cardinal John Farley, he promised a "great celebration."

I'd never been in a place so old—a seven-hundred-year-old church. It had a watchtower made of thick stone. The inside was cool and dark, lit with just enough candlelight to give off a reverential hush to the whole interior. I imagined Joan of Arc there, sitting in one of the pews. The Chaplain had me place the regimental flags around the chancel with the French tricolor and Old Glory at each end. Our band took a place close to the altar. To help with Confession and the Holy Communion, he recruited the chaplain of the 150th Machine Gun Battalion as well as the priest from Grand, the same one who I'd seen carrying the news to the Moreau family about Victor Marie. The priest did not speak a lick of English, but our boys were to confess their sins to him anyway.

Father Duffy asked Tony how he'd feel about giving his confession to a priest who did not know English. I laughed at Tony's answer. Father Duffy did, too.

"Fine, Father," Tony said. "All he'll do is give me a penance, but you'll give me hell."

On Christmas Eve it began to snow, reminding me of all the Christmas Eves back in Vermont. Always white, and my Poppa outside shoveling the walkway until it was my turn to take over that endless chore.

"Looks like a good old-fashioned Christmas," one of the boys said as he entered the church and brushed the snow off his shoulders.

As midnight approached, the church filled up with so many soldiers that many of them had no place to sit. They stood packed along the aisles and against the walls or were huddled outside by the entrance, hands thrust deep in their coat pockets. I spotted Schuyler, who nodded, and then Lynch, stone-faced like some playground bully—a sergeant now in Major McKenna's Third Battalion.

General Mike Lenihan, the commander of the Rainbow Division, and our regimental commander, Colonel Hine, like myself a non-Catholic, but starting to feel more Catholic everyday, took the front rows in the sanctuary. Next to them, Father Duffy had set aside a place for the Moreau family—Monsieur Moreau, his daughter and his granddaughters. They came and took their seats, all but Monsieur Moreau. He no longer had faith in God. During the entire ceremony, Sienna kept her eyes on me.

Father Duffy later wrote to Cardinal Farley, "The church was so full that a cat could have gone from door to altar from head to head without touching the floor."

I could tell those assembled, sitting or standing, were moved deeply by the Chaplain's sermon.

Afterward, everyone sang "Oh Little Town of Bethlehem" and "Come All Ye Faithful." Holy Communion was then received. I never saw so many line up in front of our three priests and wait to receive what they truly believed was the very body and blood, the divine soul, of Jesus Christ. It wasn't until two in the morning that the last soldier left the church, stepping out into the falling snow.

"Exiles though we are," Father Duffy said to Joyce Kilmer after we had finished, "we celebrated the old feast in high and holy fashion."

The poet bowed his head and I wondered then if he was thinking of his poor daughter somewhere in the cold ground and his wife alone in their home in a New York suburb.

Outside, as we left the church, stood Sienna, looking so forlorn. Snow covered her head and shoulders. She'd been crying. As

I came up to her, she took one step toward us and then flung her arms around me.

"Booky," she cried, "je suis si triste."

As Father Duffy and Joyce Kilmer walked by, the Chaplain gently touched my shoulder and then they moved on.

Sienna still held tight, crying. After a bit she let go and, through the falling snow, we walked hand-in-hand back to her home.

Chapter Seven

I've seen it snow in Burlington, especially when the wind blows across Lake Champlain after it freezes over so that the flakes skitter wildly across the ice like drunken fairies. Snow shuts down streets and piles up in drifts so high sometimes you can't get out on the stoop to shovel. But I'd never seen snow the way it came down on the day after Christmas, the day the entire regiment marched off to the village of Longeau, its new location in the snow-capped Vosges Mountains—in the best of conditions, a one-day hike.

Father Duffy wisely hitched a ride on one of the supply wagons. Tony and I had to march. I wouldn't describe forcing one foot in front of the other through the deep snow marching. My hobnail boots were snug, though, and I was glad. When we first stepped out, I looked up and down the street at all the soldiers coming out of the barns and sheds and homes they'd been staying in. They fell in by company and then by platoon and, I was certain, shivering almost to a man in the snow-swept wind. With many of the villagers looking out of their houses to see us off, I felt the regiment was in for an epic trek.

Tony said, "I've never seen anything like this."

"Me neither." It was Frank Bean, standing behind us. He'd come out of nowhere. I hadn't seen him since we'd gotten off the train. Now he was back.

"Look at those supply wagons, look at the one the Father just got on," Tony said. "The mules can't get their footing. Maybe we won't either once we get going."

The mules were indeed having a hard time. The wagoners got off and slipped chains around the wheels. By digging into the icy road with the chains on, maybe the wheels would make the wagons roll easier and be less of a burden for the struggling mules. It seemed to work. The mules got going and with a lot of effort the supply wagons crunched over the snow. Father Duffy optimistically waved and was off.

"It'll be a long walk," Tony said, burrowing his head deeper into his great coat and his bare hands into his pockets. "And all uphill every foot of the way."

Our platoon commander, Sergeant Colin Murray, a fascinating soldier because he was an exile from Ireland where he'd been a foot soldier in the Irish Republican Army, acted like he was oblivious to miserable weather. He yelled out orders and off we went.

"Jezuss, it's cold!" Tony shivered.

"Never been this cold in New York," piped up Frank Bean, rubbing his hands to try to keep them warm. "But you, Bucky, must be used to this damn weather, being from Vermont and all."

Yes, I thought, I was used to this weather—most of the time when I had gloves or mittens. Today, however, turning my body into the wind with snow whipping into my face, I wondered if I could survive. I'm sure all the soldiers felt the same way.

One step at a time, that's all we could hope to do.

The road wasn't a good road in the best of weather. It'd been torn up by the many military vehicles, either mule drawn, horse drawn or motorized, that had for three years passed up into the mountains and down again. Exploding artillery shells had done their destructive work as well. The snow now hid ruts and small shell holes that the French soldiers, those too old or too infirm to fight, were assigned to fill in. They hadn't done their job well. Stepping into those snow-covered holes sent many of our soldiers stumbling, swearing and even falling down.

The first to stumble, hardly one hundred yards into our march, was Frank Bean. Dropping to his knees, he grumbled, "I'm so God damned uncoordinated, like a circus clown." Tony and I picked him up.

"So sorry," he said.

Ahead of us another soldier fell. He rolled to the side of the road and just sat there. "No human should be out in weather like this," he complained. "So I ain't movin' another step!"

"Oh yes you are!" Sergeant Murray grabbed him by the lapels of his great coat and yanked him to his feet. He shoved him back onto the road. "Now get your sorry ass moving or you'll know what real misery's like!"

The soldier didn't say another word, but trudged on.

"I better not fall again," said Frank Bean.

Then Tony stumbled. "Jezuss!" He grabbed my arm to keep from falling.

Several soldiers tripped and fell and got back up, but mostly we kept a slow, steady pace for a mile or so. Then off to the side a supply wagon had skidded into a ditch. Thankfully, it wasn't the wagon Father Duffy had hitched a ride on. One of the mules struggled to stand, but kept slipping.

"Can't one of you damn boys help me!" the wagoner shouted through the snow. "I can't get him up."

"Let's go," Tony said.

About seven or eight soldiers, Tony, Frank and myself included, went to help. As we circled the fallen mule, the wagoner warned us that the mule might kick, so watch out. The wagoner's warning caused several soldiers to back off. Tony went to the mule, got his hands around its neck and whispered into its ear, "Easy now." The mule's eyes, wide with terror, rolled around until they locked on to Tony. "Come on, easy now!"

"Wait! Don't let him up yet!" said the wagoner. "Keep him there. I wanna wrap cloth around his feet."

Tony continued to hug the mule, whispering gently into its ear. The wagoner tied rags round each hoof.

"There," he said. "Let him up."

We all eased the mule to its feet. It shook the snow off and then seemed to settle down.

"Thanks, guys. Let's get the wagon back on the road."

We led the mule and the wagon to the middle of the road. The wagoner climbed on board, tipped his hat, snapped his whip and, with the mule stepping lively in its new hoof wear, was off.

"Where'd you learn to talk mule?" Frank Bean asked, staring at Tony in amazement.

"In the old country," Tony said, and then to me, smiling, "I ain't never been to the old country, but I sure felt like it."

"What old country is that?" Frank Bean said.

"Ireland. You might think I'm Italian, but now that I've been in the Fightin' Sixty-ninth all these months, I'm Irish."

"Me, too," I said.

"Well, you're only half Irish."

"Yeah. Me and Joyce Kilmer."

All day the regiment slogged on. The going was slow and it looked like we weren't going to make our night's destination. As the road wound its way up into the foothills, the mules had a devil of a time pulling the wagons. As many as ten or twenty soldiers on foot had to push the wagons up every rise, easing the mules' burden. The snow kept piling up.

Frank Bean dropped back and then was off to the side of the road, bent over like he was about to throw up. He huffed and puffed, his hand on his chest.

"I don't think he's going to make it," Tony said.

I said, "We can't leave him there."

"Why? He's a burden to us. To the platoon." Tony then shrugged "Aw, shit. Let's go help the poor bastard."

We went to Frank Bean. Tony wrapped his arm around him the way he'd done with the scared mule. "Easy now, Frank. Easy now."

"I can't breathe!"

"Sure you can. Deep breath. Really deep." Then to me, "Grab his other arm."

We held Frank Bean, letting him catch his breath. I felt him shaking from the cold.

"I'm so fat," he said.

"You ain't that fat," Tony said. "Look at Private Erb over there." He cocked his head toward the heaviest soldier in the platoon. "And he's making out just fine. Easy now. You can do it, too, Frankie. Easy now."

Frankie?

"I can't. I just want to die here. Bury me in the snow."

"Okay. Bucky, dig a hole and I'll stick Frankie in it, cover him up and let the ice worms eat his eyes out."

"Ice worms?"

"Yeah. You know, those long, silvery worms?" He laughed in a sing-song like way. "Whenever you see a hearse go by, you know someday you're gonna die. The ice worms crawl in, the ice worms crawl out, the ice worms play pinochle on your snout."

I had to laugh. And so did Frankie. "Okay, okay," he said. "Help me out onto the road."

"Just keep your eyes on Private Erb over there. Don't let him show you up. If that bastard can do it, so can you."

Frankie took two steps forward. "I can do it!"

And off we went again.

A mile more and some soldier shouted out, "Look at my damn hobnails!"

As if on command, we all looked down at our boots. Mine were soggy, like wet sponges. No wonder they felt heavy. Then I noticed the front part of my sole was flapping loose. My toes were sticking out.

"My boots are falling apart!" I said to Tony.

"Mine, too!"

"Oh, no!" Frankie bent over and touched his torn boots. "My toes are frozen solid!"

Everyone in Headquarters started to curse and moan. "Cheap hobnails!"

Sergeant Murray walked among us, checking our boots one-by-one. His expression said it all. He'd seen a lot in Dublin fighting for the IRA, but now he didn't know what to do. We'd never make it to Longeau barefoot. We didn't even have gloves or scarves to wrap around our feet, like the Revolutionary War soldiers had done at Valley Forge.

"Do the best you can, men!" Sergeant Murray said. He went back to the front of the platoon. "Move out!"

After a few steps I saw blood spotting the snow. A number of the boys began to limp. Each painful step drew more blood, marking a trail of red across the white snow.

What more could happen? I thought. We'd been on our hike for hours and with more hours to go.

I shouldn't have had that thought. I saw chunky Private Erb just as he looked down at his feet, then looked skyward, took one more step with his eyes rolling up into his head and pitched face down in the middle of the road. He didn't move.

"He's dead!" Frankie blurted out. "I know it! He's dead! We're all going to die if we keep this up!"

"Sarge," Tony shouted. He hobbled over to Erb. "Man down!"

I followed Tony. He bent over Erb, rolled him onto his back and brushed the snow off his face.

"He's not dead yet," Tony said. He took off his great coat and placed it over Erb. "We gotta keep the poor bastard warm. Give me your coat."

I took it off and handed it to Tony. He laid it on the ground like a blanket. "Here, help me lift Erb onto the coat." He was damn heavy, but we got him off the snow and onto my coat. Tony began to rub his face. "Darn hands are so cold, I don't know if this'll work." He kept rubbing as Sergeant Murray came up.

"What's this? Another slacker?"

"No, Sarge. Private Erb's in poor shape. Don't know if he'll make it."

The platoon had stopped. "Keep marching!" Sergeant Murray stooped next to Tony. He pressed his hand on Erb's throat. "He's still breathing." Sergeant Murray looked around. "We need to get him inside somewhere. Might be a farmhouse nearby." He kept looking around. "Private Riley scout ahead for a farmhouse. Hurry!"

I took off, trying to run in the snow with my hobnails split open. Each step was more painful than the other. I'd gone maybe a half-mile when up ahead I made out through the snow a farmhouse. I rushed back, breathing in cold air so hard that my lungs hurt.

"There's a farmhouse about a couple hundred yards up the road," I said.

"Good," Sergeant Murray said. "You, Tony and two other men carry him to the farmhouse. I'll go on ahead and make the farmhouse ready for him. We'll most likely have to use the barn." He looked at Frankie.

"Not him," Tony said. "Pick two other guys."

Sergeant Murray jumped to his feet. He tapped two privates, jerked his head toward us and then was off down the road, disappearing into the snow. Each of the four us took a corner of my coat and hefted it up. Private Erb, his bulky body as still as death, turned out to be heavier than I figured. I feared his weight might rip my coat down the middle as we lugged him. Thank goodness it held. Frankie trailed behind us, wringing his hands—either because of the cold or he was scared he was looking down at a dead soldier.

"Do your thing, Tony!" he cried. "Do your thing!"

We ignored Frankie.

We soon saw the farmhouse. Sergeant Murray was out front. "In the barn," he said. "Follow me." Obeying him, we slogged around the back of the farmhouse and into the barn. "Put him here." We placed Private Erb on a pile of hay that he'd made into a crude bed. "We're stayin' the night here. The whole damn platoon. I'll tell 'em. You get this poor private's blood going' by rubbing his face, hands and feet. Maybe we can still save him."

Tony took on Private Erb's face. I pulled off what was left of the hobnails and massaged his bloody feet. Frankie, who hadn't let us get out of his sight when we went into the barn, worked on the hands.

"Do your thing, Tony," Frankie said.

"What thing is that?"

"You know, 'Easy now, easy now.'"

I caught Tony's eyes. He rolled them. Then he put his mouth close to Private Erb's ear. "Come on, easy now. Easy now, Erb. Easy now."

Like the mule, Erb's eyes opened and looked into Tony's eyes.

"My God," I said. "The magic touch."

"See," Frankie said. "I told you!"

It looked like Erb smiled. He closed his eyes.

"Don't stop rubbing!"

Meanwhile, the platoon entered the barn, about twenty-five of us. Everyone plopped onto the floor. Boots were taken off and examined. Feet checked.

Sergeant Murray came in last with First Lieutenant Tom Fleming. I didn't know much about Lieutenant Fleming, a rough character, except that he'd come up through the ranks. At thirty-seven, he was the oldest lieutenant in the regiment. He held our respect.

"We'll be here for the night," he told us. "That means no mess.

So suck it up men. We'll get our grub tomorrow when we meet up with the rest of the regiment somewhere near Longeau."

The lieutenant found us among the now huddled men of the platoon.

"How's the trooper doing?"

"I think he's exhausted, Sir," Tony said. "He needs to rest and warm up, but I don't think he'll make it any further. Look at his feet. Any wagons coming up behind us?"

"Yeah, another caravan of supplies. How are your feet, trooper?"

Tony looked at his feet. Then we all did. None of us had bothered to worry about them while lugging Private Erb up to the barn. My toes were numb. On closer examination I saw they'd turned bluish white.

"Get those feet warm, wrap 'em in something warm. Your coat. All of you. I've got to see to the other troopers. Maybe we can start a fire, warm this place up."

"You heard the Lieutenant. Take care of your feet."

"Yes, Sarge," said Tony. "But what about these damn boots. Look at 'em. There's hardly anything left of the soles and our toes stick out."

"Must've been made in London," Sergeant Murray said.

"London?"

"Damn right. Now take care of your feet."

"What about Erb here?"

"Keep him warm."

Sergeant Murray left to look after the other boys in the platoon. A few of them were doing jumping jacks to warm up. I sat down, took off what was left of my boots, wiped the blood off and started kneading my toes and the soles of my feet to get the blood still in my veins circulating. I glanced down at Private Erb. He was still flat on his back, eyes closed. But he was breathing. Tony and Frankie had their boots off, too, and were tending to their feet.

Then Tony laughed. "What is this? A massage parlor?"

We slept during the night hugging our hobnails. In the morning, many of us jammed straw into our boots or paper, if any were found in the barn. Outside, three supply wagons waited in the falling snow to pick up the boys who could no longer walk. Tony and I were able to lift up Private Erb and get him onto one of the wagons.

"Thanks," he muttered and tried to smile. "I owe you guys."

"Just stay alive," Tony said.

Sergeant Murray snapped out orders. "All right you sorry sums bitches who've survived yesterday, the hell with the snow, let's head out!"

Another day of trekking along a road we couldn't see. A few more soldiers fell by the wayside and were later picked up by the next caravan of wagons coming up behind us. Rumors floated back to us that that several soldiers had dropped dead and the only thing showing through the snow that blanketed their bodies was torn boots and bloody toes.

There were dead mules, though. They weren't cut out to haul wagons up a slippery mountain road in weather so cold the inside of their nostrils froze solid.

On we plodded. Another day, another night asleep in a cold barn hugging our boots.

By noon on the third day the snow stopped. Then a mile ahead, a church spire was spotted. Our destination was near. Closer to the village, Sergeant Murray told us to halt.

"Men, we're going to march into Longeau. In step, shoulders back, chests out! The Lieutenant and me don't want to see any slackers among us. We're soldiers true! We're the Fighting Sixty-ninth!"

Straightening up, we made our bloody entry down the main street of Longeau. And we were singing at the top of our voices.

With the birds and the trees'es
And sweet scented breezes
The good old summertime
When your day's work is over
Then you are in clover
And life is one beautiful rhyme
No trouble annoying
Each one is enjoying
The good old summertime
In the good old summertime
In the good old summertime

Somewhere In France, February 20, 1918

My Dearest Calliope:
 HAPPY BIRTHDAY!
 I'm sorry I haven't written for a long time. Please forgive me. How are you? Are you still at the Roosevelts? I can't believe we're now both 16. The family we were living with before coming here to bake me a birthday cake. It was so sad. Their son was killed.

You'll be glad to know that Schuyler and I are now friends, sort of. He wants to spend time with you once the war is over.

Major Donovan is back with us. He was in Paris for a long time. He's not the XXXXXXXXXX. We got a new commander, a Colonel Barker. He's a West Point man. He fought in Cuba and the Philippines, got wounded, suffered from Yellow Fever and was already over here in France when General Pershing first arrived. He was there to greet him in Paris. Father Duffy likes him, I think, even if he isn't a Catholic or has not an ounce of Irish blood in him. I think he likes him because he believes our new Colonel is a true warrior.

Our hike from XXXXXXXXX to XXXXXXXXX was an adventure. More snow than I've ever seen, more than in Vermont. We are now up XXXXXXXXXX. I'm back being Major Donovan's striker now that he's with us again, but I serve as an altar boy for the Chaplain, as well. That's good because I get to spend time with Tony. He's my best friend. He's got a mystical way about him when dealing with people who are having a hard time. I don't know how he does it. He can even talk to animals. I saw him do it with a mule. Spooky. What's more spooky, I told you it was his Momma and Poppa that saved us from Sheriff Lynch.

About Sheriff Lynch. I've seen him once since we got to our new loca-

tion. I saw him when we were moving up. He pointed at his missing tooth, then pointed at me and shook his fist. We're going to have our moment of reckoning one of these days, I'm sure. I don't look forward to it.

The regiment is about to go into the trenches for more training with the French. It's in a place called the XXXXXXXX. That's where the family we were billeted with lost their son. We're to go in for a few weeks at a time, each of our battalions, see what it's like and how to fight in such confined situations. Major Donovan won't let me go in, though. I'm to stay behind at Battalion Headquarters. He and Father Duffy still look after me. Too much, I think. But I now carry a rifle and learned how to be a marksman. Bang, bang I can hit a target, maybe not the bull's eye, but at least the target. I hope I never have to shoot a German, though.

That's it from over here. Boy, do I ever miss you! And HAPPY BIRTHDAY again!

Love, Bucky

Sagamore Hill, March 1, 1918

Bucky, My Beloved:

I'm still here with the Roosevelts. Busy as ever. You'd think he was still President. The house is never empty. Some people still want him to raise another division of Rough Riders, but it won't happen with President Wilson ruling the roost. Mrs. Roosevelt and I have become fast friends. She misses her children, even if they are all grown. She worries a lot about Teddy Junior and especially Quentin who she tells me has a devil-may-care way about him that will get him in danger. She believes it's because he's flying those flimsy airplanes and that he's always been reckless, always looking for trouble.

The real news is that I met with Father. Colonel Roosevelt allowed him to come to Sagamore Hill to see me three days ago. He'd promised Father he could when we had that fiasco at the Garden City Hotel. Remember? Father and I sat on the porch for privacy. Here's what happened.

The first thing he did was apologize for everything, from the divorce to hiring that creep Lynch to kidnap me. He assured me it was not a kidnap. Ha, ha! Just said it was to make sure I got to the canal landing safe and sound. I told him what really happened. How that creep pushed mother around and hauled me off like I was a felon wanted for murder. That set Father aback. He didn't know what to say, only that everything would change if I came back to live with him, and as soon as Schuyler was home from the war it would be so different. We'd be a family again.

Ha, ha! I said what about Mother? Would she come home, too? That shut him up. He touched my hand and said he wanted to hold me, to say again how sorry he was. I said it was time for him to go. He surely didn't want to, so I folded my arms across my chest, stared out at Long Island Sound and uttered not another word. He said, "Calliope, please." I was silent as a mouse. Finally, he got up and left. I wonder if I'll ever see him again.

Mrs. Roosevelt came out to the porch and put her arms around me. I didn't know what to do. I cried, Bucky. I cried.

That's all the joyful news from Sagamore Hill. What about your Poppa, as you call him? Have your trails crossed yet? I'm so anxious to hear.

Love you to pieces, my dear soldier boy. Do you still have my hanky?
Calliope

Chapter Eight

I certainly had kept Calliope's hanky—keeping it safe and, naturally, romantically in the pocket over my heart. And just seeing her handwriting and touching the page on which she had written thrilled me, too. How I missed her.

As for Poppa, our trails hadn't yet crossed. I had followed him to France. Did I now want to find him?

Momma sent me a care package, and in it she included a copy of the *Sentinel*. It was a couple of weeks old by the time I got it, but it carried one of Poppa's stories on the front page. He was with an American engineer regiment from Brooklyn that was putting down train tracks for some British army near the Belgium border. The engineers came under fire, but they were able to hold the line against a German raiding party, using sledge hammers and shovels and rifles they'd pick up from dead British soldiers to drive them off. Poppa wrote in his usual "you are there" style. So he wasn't in Paris after all. Maybe our trails wouldn't cross.

Spring was a month away, the terrible blizzard we'd hiked through was now a fading memory and the Rainbow Division was mixed in with the French, getting lessons in trench warfare from hardened soldiers who'd seen it all. The Sixty-ninth, most of us still called it that and always would, had been assigned a meandering stretch of trenches in a hilly place in the Forêt de Parroy known as Rouge Bouquet.

I found it eerie because it was here only months before that Victor Marie Moreau had been killed. Was this some kind of bad omen for us, moving into these woods the regiment had code-named "Camp New York" where so many French and German soldiers had been slaughtered over the years? Wooden crosses marked the spot where they'd fallen. Now and then a bony arm or leg or a skull poked above the torn-up ground where a shell had hit and exploded. The stench of rotting flesh seemed to float over the battleground like a sinister mist.

I wondered if the ghosts of the dead haunted the place? Was Victor Marie's decomposing body out there somewhere in the wood they called Rouge Bouquet? Such an image made me shiver.

Forêt de Parroy was now considered a quiet zone and that's the reason we were there to train. Not much of a chance of getting blown away. No one from the regiment had been down to the trenches yet and Major Donovan, always thinking ahead, wanted to scout them out before any of his men set foot there. Our battalion had the honor to go in first, to taste what it was like to be a mud rat in a hole in the ground, especially with the snow mostly melted. It was like a mire, sloppy and hard to walk in.

"You want to come long, Bucky?" he asked, completely surprising me.

We were at his crude headquarters, a dugout on the reverse side of a wooded hill so it was protected somewhat from artillery fire, but still gave us a good view of the trench system zigzagging this way and that below us.

We shared the dugout with a French officer, Captain Louis Cristo, who was our guide, and his aide, also Louis. To differentiate between the two, we called the Captain, Count Monte Cristo, and the aide, Louie 2. To our surprise, the Count was actually a real count. He liked that we called him the Count. He constantly puffed on a much chewed-on pipe, and I wondered if it was to keep him from smelling the stench of death. I wanted to ask the Count if he'd ever known Victor Marie, but I dared not. I didn't want to stir up any ghosts.

As we were leaving the dugout, the Count looked me over. He shook his head and said something in French to Louie 2. The Major picked up on it. "He thinks you better be careful in the trench because of your height. He wants to make sure your head doesn't stick up and get shot at. He's already seen several of his taller men who'd forgotten to duck down and got picked off. So keep low."

I was just over six feet tall, probably taller than my Poppa now that I'd turned sixteen, but still growing. I knew my Poppa was over six feet.

When we came down the hill and entered a narrow slit in the earth that wound its way to the front-line trenches, the Major said, "Duck down, Bucky. This may be a quiet zone, but the Count says there are German snipers in the trees a few hundred yards off. As he said, they're ready to shoot at anything that pops up. They're looking for heads to plug, so be extra careful."

I had to smile at the Major. He was short enough that he didn't have to worry about ducking down.

The bottom of the trench was sloppy with mud and water. Duckboards had been laid down so that soldiers wouldn't sink to their knees. Mud still oozed up between the wooden slats. I'd been warned about trench foot, and I saw then how easy it would be to suffer from such a terrible ailment that ravaged soldiers holed up for months on end in a place only a pig could love. It was the duckboards that made my head stick up above the rim of the trench. I kept low, like a hunchback.

Atop the trench were sandbags and rolls of barbed wire. We literally oozed past soldiers standing guard. They looked through peepholes into no-man's land.

The Count talked to the Major in a mixture of French and English. I picked up some of it. He told him what to expect and to always be watchful for raiding parties. Both sides liked to sneak off into no-man's land, capture a soldier or two, haul them back and then interrogate them. They used trench knives, he said, and pulled his out of its sheath and waved it menacingly around. It was a slender blade with a handle much ike a sword's hilt. He laughed and slipped it back into the sheath and said something.

"Knuckle duster," translated the Major.

After walking through the trench, the Count took us down into a hole marked as Dugout One. It was a dank room big enough to hold a platoon of thirty men. Bunks lined the earthen walls, a table was set in the middle and, to my surprise, the dugout had electric lights. Major Donovan, after looking all around and up at the timbered ceiling, said to me, "This place doesn't look too sturdy to me, but I guess it'll have to do."

We hiked back out and up the hill and over to Camp New York, our headquarters, which now, after seeing the inside of the dugout, seemed quite plush to me.

A few days later, after a first-aid station had been set up and Major Donovan and Colonel Barker had conferred, First Battalion got set to enter the trenches for its two-week stint in the frontlines. The Major sent a memorandum to all his captains and top non-commissioned officers. He warned them that they were to conduct themselves and their men quietly and with discipline because they were in the presence of the enemy. They were to follow the strict orders he had outlined. One of the orders called for platoon commanders to make sure that their men changed their socks at least once a day and to make sure they bathed and rubbed their feet daily.

It was near the end of February when the battalion filed into the trenches. I stayed back, of course, and so did the Major, counting on his subalterns to do the right thing. The Germans had to know what was happening. As if on cue, there was a whistling shriek sounding to me like a banshee of Irish myth wailing the loss of a loved one. It was an artillery shell hurtling toward the trenches. It struck close to our dugout with a most jarring whomp that shook the ground.

"Go back to Camp New York right now!" the Major said. "Report to Frank! Move it, Bucky!"

I was out the back of the dugout and on my way as another shell came flying through the air with that banshee shriek. And then the terrifying whomp!

The Major was watching over me like he'd promised President Roosevelt—keeping me out of harm's way.

I scurried back. When I reached Father Duffy's shelter at Camp New York, Tony came out.

"Did you hear those explosions?" he said. "Wow!" Then, "Whatta you doing back here? You're with Donovan now."

"He sent me back here for safety reasons. Yeah, I heard them. One artillery shell almost struck our dugout. That's why I'm here."

"The Father's up on the hill there," he said, jerking his head in that direction, "watching the fireworks. He told me to stay down here."

"I guess it's just you and me stayin' out of trouble." We ducked back into the shelter just in case.

For two weeks it was the same, day after day. Artillery shells flew back and forth, but caused no real damage. Two soldiers got wounded from shrapnel, the first blood drawn by the regiment. Tony and I were able to stay out of danger. When its stint was over, Major Donovan led his First Battalion back to Camp New York while Second Battalion went in for its turn.

"It was rather quiet," he said. "For the most part the worst the boys dealt with in the trenches were rats, flies and cooties."

What happened next will haunt me the rest of my life.

I wasn't there to see what happened at first. I heard the stories and then I became part of it.

The tough guys from New York, Hell's Kitchen especially, had been warned about the snipers, but that didn't stop them from taunting an enemy they couldn't see. Foolishly and less disciplined than the boys from our battalion, they climbed atop the parapet and dared the Germans to come out from behind the trees and fight them man-to-man.

A German, who spoke perfect English, yelled, "Hey, dandy Yankee, pull out your doodle so we can shoot it off!"

A moment later, one of our boys toppled over, the crack from the rifle echoing from the far woods. The parapet was cleared in a flash. Next came that banshee shriek of an artillery shell. It exploded in front of the trench, but it brought enough chaos for the commander of the Second Battalion to send his troops down into the dugouts in a hurry. Moments later another shell struck the top of one of the dugouts where a platoon from E Company had taken refuge. The roof caved in, burying them all—at least thirty of our boys. A few were able to crawl out. The rest were trapped beneath tons of dirt and timber.

When word of the disaster got back to Camp New York, Major Donovan began to pace. It wasn't his battalion out there, but he knew he couldn't sit still. He had to act—to save those boys—even if it went against direct orders from Colonel Barker to stay away. Father Duffy tried to calm him down.

"Easy, Bill," he said. "It's not your battalion. They'll be dug out soon enough."

"I don't think so, Frank. We've got to go there—help out. We can't let those poor boys suffocate. I was in those dugouts. They're old and poorly shored up with rotten timbers. I'm surprised they didn't collapse under their own weight. They sure didn't need an artillery shell to do the dirty work."

The Major won his argument and he and the Chaplain headed back to the trenches.

"Come on," I said to Tony. "Let's go. We can help out, too."

"I'm not going," he said.

"Yes you are. Let's go!"

I ran out and took off after the Major and the Chaplain. I looked back. Tony was following me. Neither Major Donovan nor Father Duffy was pleased to see me.

"Go on back," Father Duffy ordered.

"No, Sir. I can help"

Neither one objected. Tony caught up with us as we climbed

down into the trenches. We hurried over the duckboards, the Major leading the way. Soon we heard shouts.

"Dig! Dig!"

"Dear God," said Father Duffy.

Crawling on top of the collapsed dugout, now a massive mound of dirt, a dozen or so of the boys were digging furiously, using their helmets as shovels. Some of them had formed a bucket brigade the way firemen did when no hoses were available, passing up helmets filled with dirt, tossing out the dirt and then sending the empty helmets back down. In charge of the helmet brigade was Abe Blaustein, the Jewish sergeant from Brooklyn. He was at the bottom of a pit, shoveling dirt into a helmet and handing it off.

"Sergeant! What can we do?"

Abe didn't look up. "Start your own line next to ours and dig with everything you got!"

The Major slid in next to Abe. "Sorry, Sir," Abe said, without stopping.

"Just keep doing what you're doing, Sergeant!"

I slid down next to the Major, Tony behind me and then a few boys joined us as we formed our own helmet brigade. The Major scooped up a helmet filled with dirt, handed it off to me and I quickly shoved it up to Tony as he gave me an empty helmet. I passed it to the Major.

"Nonstop, men! We gotta keep going!"

Finally, a small hole opened up. A helmet banged on the top of a head.

"Get us out! God, please, get us out!"

Between Abe and the Major they dug away the dirt that pinned the soldier into the hole so we could see his head and then his shoulders. Abe reached under the soldier's arms and he and the Major lifted him out of the hole.

The moment he was free, the soldier scrambled up, sputtering, "Thank God, thank God! Save the others!"

I knew him. It was Corporal Post, the first soldier I'd met when I'd entered the Sixty-ninth armory. We exchanged glances, his eyes wet with tears, mud streaking his cheeks. I wondered if he remembered me.

Two other soldiers were freed along with several rats. One of the soldiers saw the Major. He spat out a mouthful of dirt. "I think Lieutenant Norman's dead, Sir."

After a quick look at the soldier, the Major yelled down into the hole. "We will get you out! Stay calm. We'll get you all out!"

We'd been digging for hours so fast and so hard we'd paid little attention to the swarms of flies, and the constant shelling that thankfully missed the front-line trenches, but thudded behind us and sent up cascades of dirt. Soldiers came out of the other dugouts and were firing into the far woods to keep German snipers from shooting back or sneaking across no-man's land to take prisoners.

We pulled up another of the boys spitting out dirt.

Without thinking, I blurted, "Is Corporal Van Pelt down there?" I knew he was in E Company.

"Yeah. He's trying to save Norman, but I think the Lieutenant's a goner." Coughing, he crawled away.

Schuyler! I must save Schuyler! The urgency to get him out overwhelmed me.

I prayed that if we could haul them up one by one, there'd be a chance we might save the whole platoon. Schuyler, too! Loose dirt kept sliding back into the hole and it was a constant battle not to let the small opening fill up.

"Stay calm!" the Major shouted down into the opening.

Then, without warning, what was left of the roof of the dugout completely collapsed. All of us on the top went down with the roof. None of us were buried, but all our work was gone in a thick shower of dirt and debris.

The Major was stunned. "Don't stop digging!" His order sounded hollow. I felt then that his heart wasn't in it. I knew then it was no use. I looked at Abe. He'd quit, too. I wouldn't quit, though. I had to get Schuyler out! I slammed my helmet into the damn dirt and dug and dug. I began to sob. Mud-streaked tears blurred my eyes. Still I dug. *Oh, Calliope, dear Calliope!*

I then felt a hand gently squeeze my shoulder. It was Father Duffy. He'd climbed down into the pit we'd carved out of the dirt.

"We did our best, Bucky," he said. "We did our best."

"No," I cried. "I know we can save them! We must!" I dug on. With my fingers shredded, I threw dirt over my shoulders as fast as I could. But the stubborn dirt rolled back into the pit time and again. I couldn't stop crying. "Calliope's brother's down there! We must save him!"

"I know." Father Duffy tried to comfort me, his hand still on my shoulder. "And so are a number of other brave souls. Let this be their tomb, Bucky. Their lasting memorial."

"Oh, Father, why? Why?"

"Come, soldier," he said and lifted me up. With his arm around me he led me out of the pit. On the other side of me was Sergeant Blaustein. I could see he'd been crying, too.

"A rotten way to go," he muttered. "My Brooklyn friends. Ah, but soldiers everyone."

"We will honor them," the Chaplain said. "We will honor them."

I got back to Major Donovan's headquarters, the tears drying up. He was at his field table writing a letter to his wife, Ruth. His head was bent and I could tell he was upset. His hands were dirty from the dirt he'd shoveled out of the pit, his face streaked with mud. He mumbled as he wrote, but I understood every word.

"Today in a little promontory in a Lorraine forest, a lieutenant and his men are done with the war. For my part, I think, it is a fine thing for the regiment to have them meet so honorable a death."

An honorable death, I thought. How could it be so honorable? They never had a chance.

He wrote about revenge, and closed with, "It is only that they have gotten a little sooner, what each of us always expects."

He folded the letter and glanced my way. "This is just the beginning, Bucky. More death-filled days lie ahead."

It was St. Patrick's Day that Father Duffy had chosen to honor the entombed boys from E Company. The first mass he held was for the Third Battalion, now in the trenches. Next, he had Tony and me help set up an altar tucked away in a grove of birch trees near Camp New York. He donned his colorful vestments, and when he was ready, he had the bugler from the regimental band sound "church call."

From the trenches and hillsides surrounding Camp New York, the boys came. Some with shamrocks pinned to their uniforms or stuck to their helmets. They gathered round the Chaplain.

Later, I heard one of the boys, a recent immigrant from Ireland, describe him at that moment as the "apostle of the Sixty-ninth."

I was standing behind Father Duffy. I saw how erect he stood and how he looked out at his soldier congregation with love in his face. Ironically, artillery fire rumbled in the distance.

"Top o' the morning, boys!" he said in an Irish brogue.

He told us that we'd been called upon to "fight for human liberty and the rights of small nations, and if we rallied to that noble cause we would establish a claim on our own country and on humanity in favor of our dear land from which so many of us had sprung, and which all of us loved."

His words meant a lot to those from Ireland or with strong Irish roots. I felt then I was full-blooded Irish, and it was a good thing to feel on St. Patrick's Day.

Far away, the guns roared. Father Duffy pointed to the east. "You will uphold on that front the name and reputation of the Sixty-ninth of which I am proud to be chaplain."

He next slipped a piece of paper from under his garment. "Our poet, our regimental poet, Joyce Kilmer, a few days ago penned this poem in honor of the dear souls we just lost. It's entitled, 'In the Wood They Call Rouge Bouquet'." He then began to read.

> In a wood they call the Rouge Bouquet
> There is a new-made grave to-day,
> Built by never a spade nor pick
> Yet covered with earth ten metres thick.
> There lie many fighting men,
> Dead in their youthful prime,
> Never to laugh nor love again
> Nor taste the Summertime.

I doubt I was the only one fighting back a tear. *Rouge Bouquet.* It was here that Victor Marie Moreau had died and now our own boys. I knew the place was a bad omen. Closing my eyes, I listened to our Chaplain.

For death came flying through the air
And stopped his flight at the dugout stair,
Touched his prey and left them there,
Clay to clay.
He hid their bodies stealthily
In the soil of the land they fought to free
And fled away.
Now over the grave abrupt and clear
Three volleys ring:
And perhaps their brave young spirits hear
The bugle sing:
"Go to sleep!
Go to sleep!
Slumber well where the shell screamed and fell.
Let your rifles rest on the muddy floor,
You will not need them anymore.
Danger's past;
Now at last,
Go to sleep!"

I saw them, the boys from E Company and Schuyler, not sleeping, but still trying to claw their way out. Had we quit too soon? It was too late now.

St. Michael's sword darts through the air
And touches the aureole on his hair
As he sees them standing saluting there,
His stalwart sons;
And Patrick, Brigid, Columkill
Rejoice that in veins of warriors still
The Gael's blood runs.
And up to heaven's doorway floats,
A delicate cloud of buglenotes
That softly say
"Farewell!
Farewell!
Comrades true, born anew, peace to you!
Your souls shall be where the heroes are
And your memory shine like the morning star.
Brave and dear
Shield us here.
Farewell!"

A solemn quiet fell across the assembled soldiers of the Sixty-ninth. Father Duffy nodded to the band. The bandmaster brought his arms up and then swung them down and a rollicking Irish tune resounded throughout the encampment. Some of the soldiers jumped up, hooked elbows and danced an Irish jig.

All I could think about was Calliope. How could I write to her now? Father Duffy suggested I not write to her until sometime after he'd sent a letter to President Roosevelt about the death of Schuyler Van Pelt. I bowed my head. What could I ever say anyway?

My dear Calliope . . .

Somewhere In France, March 27, 1918

My Dearest Calliope:

My hand is trembling as I try to put words on paper. You can tell by the shakiness of my handwriting. It's been three weeks since tragedy struck our regiment and the toll has been heavy on all of us. Yet I can't imagine the toll it has taken on you and your parents. I know that Father Duffy has explained what happened. I am so, so sorry. . . .

I put the letter aside and didn't get back to it for another week. I wanted to hear from Calliope first. No letter arrived in the daily mail sack. I went back to my letter.

. . . The Chaplin told us that there was no better memorial to the soldiers who died at Rouge Bouquet than where they now rest in peace. As you can see, I've put into the envelope a poem by Sergeant Joyce Kilmer. It was read to the boys on St. Patrick's Day. The last few lines say it all, I think

"Comrades true, born anew, peace to you! Your souls shall be where the heroes are and your memory shine like the morning star."

Like the morning star. My dearest Calliope, you are my morning star. So be brave and I will follow my morning star back to you.

Love, Bucky

Chapter Nine

After our heartbreak at Rouge Bouquet, with its pain still lingering, a pain I'd never get over, we got a new commander. The Sixty-ninth's never-ending revolving brass door was how Father Duffy described it. Colonel Barker, who I sensed had never fit in, was sent to Washington and in burst Colonel Frank Ross McCoy. Another West Pointer fresh from General Pershing's staff in Chaumont and, again, much to Father Duffy's chagrin, neither Irish nor Catholic. He was Scottish. Well, close enough. He had Scotch-Irish blood, and that was good. When he strode into camp with a bull terrier named after the black comedian, Bert Williams, tugging on a leash, he said to both the Major and the Chaplain, "I guess you'll want me to change overnight from a canny Scot to a bold Irishman." He looked them in the eyes. "I won't fail you, and you can count on it, by heck."

We learned that not only was 'by heck' the worst swear word he'd use and use often, but during the Spanish War, he'd been wounded at San Juan Hill as a young lieutenant fighting with the Tenth Cavalry. I remembered Poppa taking me out to Fort Ethan Allen where he told me about the Tenth Cavalry, a regiment of buffalo soldiers that he'd gotten to follow in his early newspaper days out in the old West. In Cuba, he said they'd actually beaten the Rough Riders to the top of the hill and should have gotten credit for knocking back the Spaniards. They were Negroes, Poppa said, and so much for history, Poppa said. Pershing was one of the regiment's captains, the reason he was called "Black Jack," and that's where Colonel McCoy and he became fast friends. Even though the Tenth was a cavalry outfit, it had no horses in the charge up San Juan Hill—another thing Poppa told me. But then neither did the Rough Riders have any mounts, except for Colonel Roosevelt, a chestnut gelding, Little Texas, that was my Poppa, as you now know, had recklessly jumped on to save the future President's life.

The Chaplain liked our new commander right off. What I liked best about him was that he'd been an aide to President Roosevelt. They were very close. So close, in fact, he knew all about me. So it should have come as no surprise that after he'd met with all the officers of the Sixty-ninth, figured out who he could rely on in a tight spot and who he had to keep a careful eye on, he called in the Major and the Chaplain—and me—for a last bit of business.

"Gentlemen," he said, petting Bert Williams snuggled in his lap. "You know I used to be an aide to Roosevelt back when he was President. He and I have kept in close touch ever since. I've been out to Sagamore Hill a number of times. When he found out I was to command the Sixty-ninth he made a number of requests. One is to bring Private Riley here on to my staff as . . ." He paused and shrugged. "How the heck do I know?" He laughed. "I'll keep him busy, though. Maybe have the lad take care of old Bert Williams here when I can't. Or be my striker. Sorry, Bill. Any problems?"

I saw the look on the faces of the Major and the Chaplain. I wondered what my expression looked like. We were all startled. Didn't we already have an agreement with President Roosevelt? I meant Major Donovan and Father Duffy had the agreement? They were to look after me. Right?

"But," cut in the Chaplain

"No buts, Frank. Orders from the President himself. Bucky will still serve as one of your altar boys, however." He scratched Bert Williams' ears. "You like dogs?" he asked me.

"Yes, sir." Back in Burlington where we lived close to downtown I didn't see many dogs. Bert Williams was ugly, all black with a long snout that looked unnatural. He was no Tripod. I guessed I'd better get along with him.

"Here." Colonel McCoy lifted Bert off his lap and handed him to me to see if that strange-looking animal and I could, indeed, get along. I took Bert, let him settle on my lap while I scratched the top of his head. He seemed comfortable. "Old Bert likes people, and it seems he likes you, Bucky."

"What's his rank?" Father Duffy asked with that twinkle in his eyes.

Colonel McCoy let out a loud laugh. "By heck, that's a good one." He was quiet for a moment. Then, "I'll promote him to private. Yes. That means I'll have to promote you, Bucky, to private first class. You need to outrank Old Bert so you can keep him in line." Colonel McCoy laughed again and soon we were all laughing.

By the middle of June, the Forty-Second Division had finally finished its training with the French. We were off again, headed somewhere along the Marne Valley. The Sixty-ninth piled into mule-drawn wagons or struck out on foot, shod in new hobnail boots—this time in warm, almost balmy, late spring weather. A far cry from our last march in a blizzard we'd forever remember as our "Valley Forge." We left Camp New York in the middle of the night, as Father Duffy said, "On our hunt for new trouble."

I marched along with the Regimental Headquarters Company, sporting new PFC stripes on my sleeves. Bert Williams was up front in a Cadillac motor car with Colonel McCoy and his driver. I only tended to the dog when we were settled in camp, and who knew how long that would be on this march.

Yet another, more pressing thing, was on my mind. It'd kept me awake many a night. There'd been no letter from Calliope in a very long time. Not since before her brother had died at the Rouge Bouquet cave-in. Well, I hadn't written to her, but once. It was that awkward letter and I didn't want to write again until I'd heard back from her. Had she left the Roosevelts? Was she with her Poppa now and couldn't write knowing how he didn't like me? Had I said something wrong? Or maybe she had a new friend?

"You're quiet there, Bucky." It was Tony. We were together on the march, as we always were. He'd been promoted to private first class, too. I didn't say anything. "Well, it ain't snowin'."

A full moon lit up the road and it was turning out so far to be an easy hike. We soon heard shouts coming from the front of the line.

"What's that about?" Tony said.

Someone up ahead hollered back to us. "The Seventh-seventh Division is coming toward us! And will be passing by soon!"

"Them scaredy-cat lads who were afraid to volunteer?" another voice hollered out.

The Seventy-seventh was a division of draftees, all right, picked off the streets of New York. They called themselves "New York's Own." I sensed right away our boys didn't like that one bit.

Taunts were thrown against each other as we passed by in the night. Big Mike Donaldson, one of our sergeants and a former boxer, bellowed in answer to an insult flung at us, "What are you givin' us? We was over here killin' Dutchmen before they pulled your names out of a hat!"

Came a sharp reply, "Well, thank God we didn't have to get drunk to join the army!"

So the reputation that the Irish are drunkards came back to haunt us.

Moments later, the first boys of the Seventy-seventh started to march past me and Tony and the rest of the regimental head-quarters company.

"Hey," Tony yelled, "any of you guys from Canal or Walker Streets on the West Side? Know Margiotta's Smoke Shop?"

"Hey, I do! Julius Gibertie here!"

"Jesus Christ, Jules. It's Tony!"

"Tony! Tony Margiotta?"

"Goddamn right!"

Both boys broke ranks and dashed into the middle of the road. They slapped each other and then hugged. What is this, I thought? Tony's some kind of mystical guy. Too many coincidences! Then I saw up and down the line of march, soldiers breaking ranks and running to greet each other. Boys from the same neighborhoods. Even brothers. It was wonderful. And then we were all singing, our voices rising above the cadence of our hobnail boots as we went our separate ways.

East side, West, side,
All round the town,

The tots sang ring-a-rosie,
London Bridge is falling down.
Boys and girls together,
Me and Mamie O'Rourke,
We tripped the light fantastic
On the sidewalks of New York.

When we finally reached our next destination, in the Champagne sector along the Suippes River, we Rainbows were attached to the French Fourth Army. The general in charge was a one-armed, one-legged, red-bearded character called the "Lion of Africa," Henri Gouraud. Colonel McCoy, after meeting with him and with the commander of the Forty-second, Major General Charles Menoher and his top aide, Colonel Douglas MacArthur; his staff and all the division's brigade and regimental commanders, came away impressed.

"Gouraud is every bit the hero," he informed his own staff as well as his own battalion and company leaders. His voice beat with excitement. 'Well, gentlemen, our marching days are over for now. We dig in to await orders to meet the enemy. The General's plan—it came down from Generalissimo Foch, the supreme allied commander—is to hold our front along the river with a token force, let the Hun attack, thinking he's overrun us, and then we counterattack, hit him with everything we've got. If it works, and I believe it will, the war will have reached a turning point. The Hun will be on the run. Heck, that rhymes. I like it. Hun on the run."

Our regiment was to hold the division's left flank. As ordered by General Menoher, Colonel McCoy posted his Second Battalion, led by Major Alexander Anderson, barely twenty-nine years old, on the front line with Major Donovan's and Major McKenna's First and Third Battalions in support. He set up his command post close to General Gouraud's headquarters and called it Camp Bois de la Lyre. It was thirty feet underground, hopefully better protected from artillery than the dugouts at Rouge Bouquet. It had bunks and a slop bucket to pee in. Our rifles were placed next to our bunks, easy to grab in case the Germans tried to overrun us. Telephone wires snaked from Colonel McCoy's camp table, running out to battalion headquarters.

"I think you'll be safe here, Bucky," he said. 'You stay in here no matter what happens. You understand?"

"Yes, Sir."

"And make sure you don't trip over the telephone lines."

Inside the deep dugout, it was just me and three runners to carry messages if the telephone lines got destroyed by artillery. All were privates, and I didn't know a single one of them. Also, there were two aides to the Colonel—a Captain O'Toole and 2nd Lieutenant Page. Of course, Father Duffy was there, too, but seemed quite antsy.

"I'm going up front to be with Anderson's battalion," he said. "I want to be there before the battle begins."

Colonel McCoy seemed to be taken aback by the Chaplain. So was I. Major Anderson's command post was a hole in the ground, fortified by sandbags and a corrugated-iron roof and barely room enough for two men. I'd seen the hole when Colonel McCoy and his staff had walked the very ground we were to defend. I'd been allowed to tag along. I don't think the Colonel wanted the Chaplain to be out on the front line.

"It should be all quiet here until Bastille Day," he said. "You know that's when the shooting match is to start. Not 'til then"

"It makes no difference when the guns will go off," Father Duffy replied. "The boys need me now, and I intend to be there."

"By heck you're right," the Colonel admitted. "Keep your head down. There're snipers out there."

When Father Duffy left, tossing his trademark smile at me, I felt lonely, even with the others in the dugout. Colonel McCoy's pup, Bert, had been taken away, to be out of the sound of artillery fire. Tony was with Headquarters Company. I didn't like being separated from him. He was now the best friend I ever had. I worried about him.

Generalissimo Foch and the Allied forces, bunched up from Château-Thierry to the Argonne forest to the cathedral city of Rheims, knew exactly when the Germans planned to open their attack. Ten minutes after midnight on July 15. The battle plan, coded named the Peace Assault, including detailed maps, had been miraculously discovered on a captured officer only days before it was to be launched. Now that Foch knew what was coming—and when—his plan was to beat the Germans to the punch, strike at exactly midnight.

With almost a million men ready to die for the Fatherland, the Germans had an overwhelming force that dwarfed the Rainbows and the other American divisions in the Champagne Sector and along the Suippes River where we all waited for the opening salvo. The goal of the Germans in our sector was for them to cross the river, and by noon the next day, enter the streets of Châlons and then march on to Paris.

Just before midnight, Colonel McCoy checked his watch. There was a brightness in his eyes I hadn't noticed before. The old warrior was in his element. His staff crowded round the table where he sat. I stayed on the edge of my bunk, my heart in my throat.

"Gentlemen," he said. "Five more minutes!"

The roar of artillery sounded as if the end of the world had come! The night exploded into flashes of orange and red and blinding white and noise so terrible eardrums were punctured and the ground shook and split open. The roar carried all the way back to Paris.

Our dugout trembled. Earth fell from the ceiling like a brown blizzard. My bunk shook. I clutched the sides to keep from tumbling off. A runner, Private Tommy O'Rourke, clapped his hands against his head and squeezed his eyes shut. Captain O'Toole grabbed the back of a chair as if he was about to stumble and turned toward the entrance to the dugout. I turned, too. Dirt was billowing in beneath the canvas flap we used for a door. The flap kept snapping like a sail caught in a hurricane-force wind. Outside the big guns continued to fire nonstop—so loud I thought my own eardrums would burst.

"By Heck!" exclaimed Colonel McCoy.

Somehow his excitement made us feel secure even if hell was all around us.

The Colonel was on the telephone immediately, trying to reach Major Anderson. For days, with his majors and staff by his side, he'd walked over the entire ground where all the men were now burrowed in their shelters, knew every inch of it, every stone, every pebble, every bush and tree, and told them where best to place their men. He had them dig reverse trenches, facing away from where the attack would come because they'd be more protected from artillery fire. Now he had to know how Major Anderson and his battalion were holding up under the endless onslaught of shells.

"Oh, heck! I can't get through," he grumbled as the dugout shook and earth kept tumbling from the ceiling.

Looking up, I cringed, thinking of Rouge Bouquet.

Minutes later the canvas flap flipped open all the way and a soldier rushed in, breathing as if he'd run a marathon. He had no helmet. His uniform was coated in dirt. To my utter surprise it was Frank Bean. I hadn't seen Frankie in weeks. He rushed up to Colonel McCoy and, still panting, passed a paper to him.

"Sir, a message from Major Anderson!" Frankie shouted over the sound of the great guns. "Our telephone is torn up! Useless! There was an explosion so close it knocked us all down. Father Duffy was sent sprawling. Head over heels. But he's okay."

The Colonel took the message, read it and said, "Our boys are holding on. The Germans haven't attacked yet, but right now there's a rolling barrage that's sweeping across our front and that means Hun soldiers should be charging right behind it."

That moment, as if on cue, the enemy barrage rolled over our command post. The ground shook as if an earthquake had struck—worse than before. More clumps of dirt tore loose from the ceiling and showered down on us.

Thank God the roof held. No Rouge Bouquet yet!

The Colonel scribbled on a piece of paper and then gave it to Frankie. "Here, get this back to Anderson on the double. When the Germans attack across our front, he's to pull back most of his men. Donovan and McKenna will back him up." He handed the paper to Frankie.

"Where's your helmet, soldier?"

"Blown off, Sir!"

"Okay. Bucky, give him your helmet." Looking helplessly at Frankie, our eyes briefly holding perhaps some secret message, I did as I was told. "Now Private Bean, get your ass outta here!"

Frankie took the message, stuck it in a pouch belted to his waist and ran through the doorway, pushing aside the canvas flap. For a moment our eyes met and then he was gone, into the wild night.

A shell struck close, the boom so loud it blew back the canvas door.

"Christ, you better check outside," Colonel McCoy ordered Captain O'Toole in a voice so urgent that it carried a dire warning. It was the only time I ever heard him use a cuss word.

"Yes, Sir."

Captain O'Toole went through the opening and up the wooden stairs, but was back in a heartbeat, his face as white as a ghost. "He's gone, Sir. There's nothing left but his legs. Jesus, one bloody toe sticking out of a boot." The Captain gulped. "That's all I could see. There was no head, no nothing, but the stumps of his legs."

Frankie! I felt my insides churn. I knew I was going to throw up. The vision of Frank blown up, his body gone forever, except for his booted legs. I tried to stop the bile from coming up, but I couldn't. Whatever I had in my stomach—a yellowish green fluid—sloshed up and onto the floor. No one said a word.

"We can't mourn over Private Bean until after the battle." Colonel McCoy wrote out another message. "O'Rourke! Take this message to Anderson's command post! Now! And watch yourself!"

"Sir!" O'Rourke slipped the message into his pouch and without a thought was out the door and into the dark hole of death.

"Brave soul," the Colonel muttered. "You okay, Bucky?"

"Yes, Sir." I wiped the vomit off my mouth. "Yes, Sir"

There was another loud boom close by. The Captain rushed outside. When he came back his face wasn't as white as before. "Looks like he made it."

"Thank God for that."

The Colonel picked up the telephone, held it to his ear. "Donovan!" There was a crackling noise. The Major's lines had held. "The Hun should attack at any moment. Cover Anderson's men when they pull back. I'm ordering McKenna to do the same. Good luck and God bless!"

He then reached Major McKenna and gave him the same orders. "Now we wait," he said. "May the Lord save our souls."

The bombardment lasted for six hours. Then the Germans attacked, sweeping across the Suippes River. On the opposite bank, a token force of Major Anderson's battalion, and other battalions of the Forty-Second Division, lightly resisted and then retreated. On the ground now empty of American soldiers, the Germans kept coming, sure they had us on the run. On cue, another barrage, this time from our own artillery, rained down on the Hun where our boys had just been. When it eased up, we attacked in force—Major Donovan's and Major McKenna's boys, mixed in with Major Anderson's, crashed into the stunned Huns, yelling and screaming, blasting them to pieces with their Springfield rifles and then slashing and stabbing them with their bayonets. A bloody sight.

Colonel McCoy went outside in the midst of the fight. Captain O'Toole and Lieutenant Page followed him. The other private, Bobby Hughes, shrugged and went with them. Although the Colonel had told me to stay put no matter what, I got up and, with no helmet on, trailed after them.

I should have stayed inside.

Private Hughes was throwing up. "Don't look," he gagged.

I couldn't help myself. The stump of poor Frankie's legs, still encased in his boots, was all that was left of the poor soul. There was no body, no head. Obliterated. Close by I saw my helmet. For some God forsaken reason I didn't barf, although my stomach felt queasy. All I remembered was how annoying Frankie had been, and now I regretted feeling that way about him. I thought back to Tony, and the mule lying on its side in the snow, and its eyes looking at Tony, and then an astonished Frankie saying, "Where'd you learn to talk mule?" It was one of the last words I remembered him saying.

The continued rattle of rifle fire, the clash of bayonets and the yells of men in a death struggle took my eyes away from poor Frankie's legs. Horses and men were dead on the ground or terribly wounded, some trying so desperately to rise up, but couldn't. Medics were bent over some of them. Stretcher-bearers carted others away to a dressing station beyond the fighting. With all the wounded scattered about, I thought there weren't enough stretcher-bearers to go around. Aeroplanes darted overhead like angry bees, swooping down with machine guns ablaze. The sky was red.

Then, out on the battlefield amid the chaos, walking among the wounded, stooping to comfort them, holding their hands, blessing them with the sign of the cross or giving them their last rites, was Father Duffy. Neither bullet nor hand grenade nor thrust from a bayonet caused him to falter. He moved with a calmness and an undaunted courage I'll envision for the rest of my life. I knew then I'd never look at my Chaplain again in the same happy-go-lucky way.

"Get your ass back inside," bellowed Colonel McCoy. After what I'd just seen he still wanted to treat me like a child.

"No, Sir." I shouted back.

Without thinking, or maybe I *was* thinking, I scooped up my helmet, put it on and ran toward Father Duffy. *I can help. I know I can help.*

I heard the Colonel bellow one more time, "Bucky!"

As I neared Father Duffy, a shell went off near him. He refused to duck down. I dove to the ground, my arms over my head. My helmet rolled away. I then saw its inside, coated in blood along with a reddish, gray glob of something that had to be bits of Frankie's brain. Not wanting to come across as a coward, I jumped up, picked up my helmet and made it to him, stepping over a mangled, dead doughboy. Unlike poor Frankie, there was at least a body to bury.

"Go back, Bucky," growled the Chaplain. "This isn't a place for you."

"I must help, Father Duffy. Please tell me what to do."

He bent down over a wounded soldier and reached for his hand. He cupped it in both his hands and then gently said, "Through this holy anointing may the Lord in his love and mercy help you with the grace of the Holy Spirit." He traced a cross on the soldier's forehead. The soldier's eyes stayed on Father Duffy. I soon saw the light in the soldier's eyes go out, and I knew then he had died.

Dabbing at his eyes, Father Duffy said to me, "You need to go back, Bucky."

"No, Father."

"Then put your helmet on and go back and get a blanket. Maybe we can carry some of the wounded to the nearest dressing station. Hurry!"

Without putting on my helmet, I ran back to the command post, down the steps and, once inside, grabbed two blankets. I was off and running again, aware of the fighting all around me. I heard bullets zing and whine and pop and then thud when they struck a body.

"Over here!" Father Duffy shouted. He was leaning over another soldier. Blood covered the soldier's chest and ran from his mouth and nose. His eyes were glazed. "Lay the blanket on the ground next to him."

I spread the blanket out. Father Duffy and I lifted the soldier onto the blanket.

"Now put on your damn helmet and let's go!" he said. I closed my eyes and settled the helmet atop my head. We each lifted an end.

Crouching, we made our way to the dressing station, a hundred yards or so back from the most intense fighting. The dressing station was a corrugated hut. Sandbags, piled as high as a man, surrounded the hut. Several machine gunners guarded the dressing station. Model T ambulances, red crosses painted on their sides, were idling on the far side of the hut. Now and then one took off down a dirt road. Inside, medics worked furiously. Outside, the wounded were lined up, some sitting and smoking, grimfaced; others stretched on the ground hardly moving. Each awaited their turn to be treated. For some, it was too long a wait. One look and I could tell they were gone.

"You better get used to this, Bucky."

Kneeling among the living, the Chaplain tried to talk to each one. Now and then he reached into his pocket and took out a cigarette. He placed it between a wounded boy's lips, lit it and then patted him on the shoulder.

"Father," one boy murmured. "Please hear my confession."

"Bucky, go inside the station and see if you can help. I need to hear this confession."

I'd learned that a confession was only between a priest and a member of his congregation. All the soldiers of the Sixty-ninth were his clergy. It was impossible for him to hear all the confessions. We needed another chaplain.

I went in as ordered. Wounded boys were sprawled on a dozen blood-soaked cots. Medics worked over them, moving from one to another.

"This poor lad needs to go to the hospital right away," a medic said in a desperate voice. He spotted me hovering around. "If you're not hurt, help Elliott here get this lad into an ambulance." I hurried to the cot. "Sure you're not hurt?" the medic asked. "There's blood dripping from your helmet down on your forehead."

"I'm okay. I'm okay."

Elliott and I carried the wounded soldier out of the rear of the dressing station to an idling ambulance. It was filled with five soldiers, groaning on bunks. The capacity was six. There was one bunk left and we gently placed him on it. Two other wounded soldiers sat on the floor.

"I need one of you guys to ride with me," the driver said. "Help unload these poor souls back at the hospital. My sidekick's been wounded himself and is being treated at the hospital. Who's goin?"

"I can't," shot back Elliott as he leaped from the ambulance and ran into the dressing station.

"That leaves you, soldier," the driver snapped at me. His stripes showed he was a sergeant. "Let's go!"

And we were off. The road was filled with traffic. Soldiers on foot, coming from or going toward the battle. Mixed in with the soldiers were mule-drawn wagons. Both clogged the road and we had to swing around them, bouncing over ruts, almost hitting our heads on the ceiling of the ambulance as we jounced along.

"You'll get used to it," the driver said. "I try to avoid as many bumps as I can because of the poor guys in back. It's impossible. I feel sorry for them. By the way, I'm Charlie FitzPatrick, been driving ambulances since early in the war, back in 1915. Driving as a civilian volunteer for the American Ambulance Field Service, first in Belgium, but mostly at Verdun. I hauled French soldiers out of that burning city, or what was left of it, anyway, down the *Voie Sacrée*, the Sacred Way, to the village of Bar le Duc. The death and destruction there was much worse than here, I can tell you. What about you?"

"Bucky Riley," I said. "I'm from Burlington, Vermont. I've been with the Sixty-ninth, well, the 165th, since about the time we declared war on Germany."

Sergeant FitzPatrick swung around another wagon. "Vermont, huh? Nothing but trees up there and I bet lotsa snow."

"You can say that."

"What made you join the Irish regiment?"

"Luck, I guess. I was in the right place at the right time."

"And where was that?"

I felt it was none of his business. "New York."

"Well, I dropped out of Harvard my sophomore year to volunteer—do anything to save my beloved second country—France. Sailed off to Paris and started driving ambulances. Driving, I met some interesting characters. A famous jockey, a great white hunter who'd led President Roosevelt on his famous African safari."

"Cunninghame," I said, remembering the photograph on the mantel over the fireplace in the Colonel's trophy room.

"Cunninghame? Medivu the natives called him. The master with the beard. How'd you know that?"

"I guess I read it in the newspapers."

"What? That had to be ten years ago." He checked me out. "What are you, sixteen? Seventeen? You reading newspapers when you were six?"

"All my life," I said. "My Poppa's a newspaperman."

In the back of the ambulance a wounded soldier screamed. "Shoot me! Please, God, someone shoot me! I can't take the pain!"

I spun around in my seat. The soldier was writhing on the bunk. He'd been tied in so he wouldn't fall off. "What do we do?"

"Not much we can do," Sergeant FitzPatrick said. "Besides we're almost to Base Hospital Number One on the outskirts of Vichy. Another mile."

The soldier kept screaming. Sergeant FitzPatrick had the ambulance going as fast as it could. He steered around one more wagon and into the courtyard of a massive building of stone and turrets, two red cross flags flying above its roof. There were several other buildings, also with red cross flags over their roofs. The buildings had once been hotels, but had been converted into hospitals since the start of the war. Other ambulances were lined up at the front entrance to the main building, unloading the wounded or already empty of bloody passengers, driving out of the circular entrance to head back to the front line.

"We got ambulances coming in from all fronts that the Forty-second's holding down, not just your regiment," Sergeant Fitz-Patrick said. "This is the division's major hospital. The real serious cases will be carted back to Paris by train."

We pulled up behind an ambulance. Before we'd stopped, soldiers assigned to the hospital were pulling open our doors and jumping in to take the wounded out. The soldier who'd been screaming was silent now.

"I think he's passed," Sergeant FitzPatrick said. "Happens all the time." He hopped out of the driver's side. "Gotta see how my sidekick's doing."

I felt useless sitting in the ambulance. I slipped out and followed Sergeant Fitzpatrick into the hospital. Cots filled almost every space of the entryway and spilled over into a large room that led to a terrace behind the building. Each cot held a wounded soldier. This time there were real doctors and nurses at work, keeping up a frantic pace. Their footsteps clattered on the floor. Calm voices called to each other—for this or for that.

To see women so young jarred me. Many of them were in their uniforms with red crosses and splotches of blood over their breasts. *Women and war*. In my small world they didn't fit. But then, of course, they did. There was a grace about the nurses I don't think I'd ever seen in a woman before—not in my mother or in my sisters. And I noticed they brought out the best in the wounded men they tended to, their bravery, their grit and an astonishing humbleness, I think, only the suffering can show. Somehow these nurses pulled the boys through such a ghastly moment they now had to endure.

I stood dumbfounded.

"Get out of the way, soldier!"

I jumped to the side. I'd been in the doorway, blocking it. Three more badly wounded boys were hustled in. The soldiers carrying them looked frantically for empty cots. Because I'd been standing around I knew where there were two empty cots.

"Follow me," I said. I led them across the room. As they placed the wounded on the cots and one on a blanket on the floor, two nurses moved in. The nurse nearest me said, "You have to move."

Here I was in the way again.

"First, help me with their boots," she said. She began unlacing a boot of one of the boys on a cot. "The man on the floor."

I took her to be about twenty, maybe a year or two more. She wore her brown hair up in a bun. Her eyes were blue. She had a touch of rouge on her checks. After the loss of Frankie Bean and others—all that death—she was refreshing to see. I knew then why they were called angels.

Slipping off both boots, and trying not to think of the stumps of Frankie's legs encased in his hobnails, I thought I'd better find a way to get back to Colonel McCoy's command post. Hitch a ride on one of the ambulances. I looked for Sergeant FitzPatrick.

He wasn't anywhere to be seen. I started to get up.

"Take off his shirt and pants," the nurse said. She was working fast and had already stripped her soldier of his uniform. I began to unbutton my soldier's blouse. I fumbled. "Here, let me do it." She was close enough to me now that I felt her warm breath on my face. Deftly, she unbuttoned the blouse and then quickly, gently and hardly moving his body took it off him. She reached into her nurse's uniform and took out a pair of scissors. She cut away his under shirt, revealing a bullet hole in his chest, blood oozing from it. "There," she said. "Now can you take off his pants?"

"Yes, Ma'am." I unbuckled his belts and slid his pants off.

"We need to find a place for him." She stood and looked around the busy, crowded room. "Over there. Help me carry him."

I took the soldier by the shoulders and the nurse held his feet. With her backing up, she led the way to an empty cot. We placed him there. From a bucket beneath the cot, she found a blood-soaked cloth and used it to wash the soldier's chest. Not the greatest in hygiene, I thought.

"A doctor will be here as soon as he can," she said. "Thanks for the help." She looked at me. "What happened to you? Are you okay."

I didn't know what she was talking about.

"There's dried blood on your face. Your nose is crooked. Here, take off your helmet."

I did as told, remembering the gore inside my helmet. "It's not my blood," I said. "A friend's. He . . ." I shut my eyes and saw Frankie's legs and my helmet. I fought back a tear.

The nurse washed off my face. "There, you look better. Sorry, I couldn't straighten out your nose. Thanks again, soldier." Then she was gone, weaving back into the chaotic mishmash of cots, groans, blood and that one ray of hope to find another sole to save.

I needed to find Sergeant FitzPatrick and get a ride back to Colonel McCoy's command post. He and Father Duffy had to be wondering what had happened to me. Scanning the room, I failed to see him anywhere. Maybe he was out on the terrace. He wasn't there—only the wounded who'd already been tended to. They were either sitting in chairs or stretched out on more cots. For the first time, I noticed amputees. There were boys missing arms and legs. Some had bandages over their eyes. How many were still out on the battleground who had lost everything, like Frankie? Never to be found? All of Frankie that could be buried were his feet.

I felt faint. I leaned against the doorframe and shut my eyes. I should've stayed at home, I thought. *Home.*

"We need to get through!"

Again, in the way. I stepped aside. Two men carried a soldier through the door and out to the terrace. The soldier's face, drained of all color, was in a tight grip of pain. His left leg just below the knee was missing. Turning quickly, I went back into the main room and then into the entryway and back outside. Ambulances were coming and going. More wounded were being unloaded and taken inside. There was no Sergeant FitzPatrick. I sat down on the stone steps, but far enough away from the front door so as not to be in the way again. From the distance, you could hear the battle as it raged on.

I had to get back to my regiment. I had to find a ride.

The ambulances ready to head to the front that I'd first begged for a ride on were not going to the Sixty-ninth's front. There had to be at least one going my way. No such luck.

A sudden tiredness swept over me. Rubbing my eyes, I realized I hadn't slept for twenty-four hours, maybe longer. I'd been up all night, throughout the artillery barrage and then the attack and the start of the counterattack. I closed my eyes.

"Hey soldier."

I felt someone nudge me. My eyes flickered open. Had I fallen asleep? Sitting next to me was the nurse. She was with two other nurses, on their break, I guess. One was smoking a Bull Durham cigarette.

"You look like you could use a cigarette," the one smoking said. "You want one?"

"No, Ma'am. I don't smoke."

"You sure?" She wasn't as pretty as the other two.

The nurse I'd helped smiled. "I think he's too young to smoke. You look like you're sixteen? How old are you?"

"Sixteen."

"What are you doing here?"

"Trying to get a ride back to my regiment," I said.

"No, no. How'd you come to be in the army?"

"Looking for my Poppa," I said and quickly regretted it.

"Your Poppa?"

"It's a long story." I looked at a new ambulance pulling up to the front door. Maybe it'd be heading back to my regiment.

"What's your name, soldier?"

"Luther Riley. My Poppa calls me Bucky." Why was I talking

about myself to this nurse? It was none of her business. But there was something about her that made it seem all right.

"Bucky. Why does he call you that?"

"After one of his Rough Rider friends, Bucky O'Neill."

"Your Father was a rough rider? With Teddy Roosevelt?"

"Yes, Ma'am."

"Oh, don't call me Ma'am. I'm Louisa. Louisa Kelley."

Louisa! I couldn't believe it. "I have a sister, Louisa."

"No kidding?"

"Yes, Ma'am. I'm not kidding."

"Louisa, please. My two nurses are Greta and Sally. Greta's the smoker. We all joined Base Hospital One in New York City when it was formed at Bellevue Hospital last year. We joined at the same time from our hometown. We're not from the City, but from Westport, Connecticut. It's a small town on Long Island Sound."

"I'm from New England, too. Burlington, Vermont. It's on Lake Champlain."

"I know Lake Champlain. My family summers there on the other side, in Westport, New York, oddly enough."

I didn't say anything for a bit. Then, "How come you all became nurses?"

"We have to do something to save the world for democracy," Greta said. "Isn't that what President Wilson told us to do? Save the world for democracy?"

I nodded. I didn't remember him saying that, but I guess he did.

"Where's your Father, I mean your Poppa, now?" asked Louisa. "Do you know?"

"Somewhere over here. He's a war correspondent for the *New York Morning Sentinel.* The last I knew he was in Belgium."

"Why do you want to find him?"

"I don't know. Just that I have to."

"We have to go," said Greta. "Break's over." She dropped her cigarette on the steps and stood. She flattened the butt with her shoe. "Let's go."

Louisa and Sally got up. Louisa touched my shoulder with her hand. "Well, I hope you get back to your regiment, and I hope you find your Poppa."

"Thank you," I said.

She squeezed my shoulder. "Good luck and stay out of harm's way. I don't want to see you coming back here on a stretcher." Then she went back to work.

Chapter Eleven

I had been reported as missing in action.

It took me two days to finally return to the Sixty-ninth. During that time, Colonel McCoy had submitted to General Pershing's headquarters in Chaumont his list of casualties for the battle—the killed, the wounded and the missing in action. I was on that list. He and Father Duffy had no idea where or when I'd disappeared. The last time the Chaplain had seen me was at the dressing station.

And after what had happened to Frankie, well, maybe they thought there was nothing left of me to find.

Another name on the casualty list—not the Colonel's list, but the list sent in by the Army Air Service's 95th Aero Squadron—was Lieutenant Quentin Roosevelt. I learned that he'd been in an aerial fight, struck in the head by machine-gun fire and crashed near the village of Chamery. According to Father Duffy, the Germans had buried him with full battlefield honors. Since the plane had gone down so near the front lines, the Hun soldiers, in respect for his Poppa, bound two pieces of basswood saplings together with wire from Quentin's Nieuport aeroplane, fashioning a cross that they then placed over his grave. When Father Duffy heard about it, he was keen on making a pilgrimage to Chamery to bless the gravesite.

Back in Oyster Bay, the Roosevelt household received two telegrams that concerned the missing—Quentin and me. A few days later a third message arrived in person by high-ranking military officers. It confirmed that Quentin had been killed. My body still had not been found.

Colonel Roosevelt had to have taken the death of his son hard. I remembered my quick stay at Oyster Bay when I'd worn Quentin's clothes while I was there. The thought gave me the shivers.

But now I fretted so much about how Calliope was taking the news that I was missing in action? First Schuyler was killed and now, maybe, me. I was at a loss as to what to do.

Somewhere In France, August 25, 1918

My Dearest Calliope:

I am not missing. I've been helping out the wounded by bringing them to a hospital and then working inside the hospital. But only for a very short time. Father Duffy had no idea where I was and put me down as missing. I am okay.

Are you still with the Roosevelts? I have not heard from you in such a long time. I am worried. Please write to me.

The Roosevelts must be devastated about Quentin. How are they taking it?

This must be a short letter. We are getting ready for a major counter attack. I can't tell you about it, except it might bring the Germans to their knees. I'm sure you'll read it about in the newspapers pretty soon.

PLEASE WRITE!

Love you, Bucky

The day after I went missing an ambulance drove up to the hospital where I'd been stuck. Behind the steering wheel was Sergeant FitzPatrick. After his wounded were unloaded, he saw me. "Well if it isn't old what's his name. You need a ride back?"

"Yes, Sergeant."

"Your outfit's on the move. The Forty-second's been transferred from the French Fourth Army to the French Sixth Army. It's headed for another river. The Ourcq, I think it's called. I'll take you there. The best news—the Germans are on the run."

On the run! Like me? Did the Colonel and the Father think that maybe I was on the run since I'd up and vanished? I found out two hours later.

"Where the heck have you been, PFC Riley!" Colonel McCoy snapped in his best I'm-in-command voice.

"At the hospital, Sir."

"Hospital? Are you wounded?" He looked me over. "Hmmm. What the heck happened then?"

"Well, Sir, I helped Father Duffy carry a wounded soldier to the dressing station. He sent me inside so he could hear the soldier's confession in private and the next thing I knew I was ordered to ride in an ambulance to the hospital back behind the frontlines. It took me some time to find a ride back."

"Glad you're okay. That's the most important thing. But you will not disobey my orders again. Understood?" His voice was stern. "When I tell you to stay put, you better by heck stay put. Got it?"

"Yes, Sir."

"Isn't that right, Captain O'Toole?"

The Captain had been standing behind me. "That's right, Colonel," he said in a voice just as stern.

Then turning gentle, the Colonel said, "Get close to me,

Bucky." I did and he clutched my upper arm, held it. "I have a big job for you, and only you. I believe you can do it."

"Whatever it is, Sir, I'll do it."

"We'll see." He kept clutching my arm. "Since you've been gone these past two days several things have taken place. The first, we're with the French Sixth Army led by General Jean Degoutte, and he's pushing us hard to overtake and whip the Hun. We'll see how that goes. The second, we got ourselves a new chaplain, Father Jim Hanley, from Cleveland. He'll be a tremendous help. He's a second generation Irishman. But here's the rub. I'm more worried about Frank—Father Duffy. He's never been in combat before. Most of our men haven't, for that matter. Rouge Bouquet hit the Chaplain hard as it hit all of you hard. But there were no dead or suffering to see. They were all buried, all out of sight. No mangled bodies out in the open. I've seen men suffer and die in Cuba and the Philippines. You never get used to it.

"I know, Sir."

He gave me a quizzical look. "Yes, of course." He let go of my arm. "Our recent fighting in the Champagne touched Frank to the point where, I think, he's been overcome by so much death and suffering. The boys out there—the dead, the dying and those blown to bits—he knows them. He's tried to know them all, to learn some personal thing about each one. He calls them by name, asks about them, how they're holding up, about their families, about any news from home. He encourages them, pats them on the back, passes out cigarettes and, perhaps most of all, blesses them and prays over them."

"Yes, Sir," I said, not knowing what else to say, but understanding exactly what the Colonel meant.

"Our next engagement will take the Forty-Second across the Ourcq River. We now know the Hun has stopped its withdrawal from the Marne salient and is now well entrenched on the other side of the Ourcq. Germany's not retreating anymore. This is her last stand. If she stops us here then who knows what'll happen next. It's going to be a bloody mess out there, although Degoutte doesn't think so. He believes the Germans will hightail it once we cross the river. If I know anything about war, there will be more dead and dying. More body parts, more wounded. It'll be hard on everyone, Bucky. Everyone."

"Yes, Sir."

"It'll be hardest on Frank. He'll be out there, walking the battleground to do what he can. He's a man of God, and he'll be praying according to his Church, hearing confessions, and giving last rites, but all the while he'll have to watch those poor souls die—as if there was no God at all. His faith will be tested to its limit. Can the good Chaplain hold up?"

"I don't know, Sir."

"Well, I don't know either. I sure as heck don't want to lose him. He's the heart and soul of the Fighting Sixty-ninth. So here's what I want you to do, Bucky."

I straightened up and wondered if maybe I couldn't do whatever it was he wanted me to do.

"Just stay with Frank every step of the way. He likes you. I believe he thinks of you as the son he'll never have. If you're with him, helping him, being by his side, having him know you're there at all times, he just might pull through mentally. When you went missing I thought possibly that Private Margiotta could handle it. He may be Frank's altar boy, but he isn't as close to the Chaplain as you, nor is he mature enough. Well, can you do it?"

"I'll try, Sir."

"I know you will, Bucky. It'll be dangerous, that's for sure. Carrying a rifle will be a nuisance, especially since I'm going to have you and Tony be stretcher-bearers. So I'm authorizing you to carry a sidearm, a forty-five. Frank does not carry a weapon and you'll certainly need one, and you'll certainly need to use it to protect our Chaplain, and maybe yourself."

"But I don't know . . ."

Colonel McCoy held up his hand to shush me. "Captain Tim O'Toole here will show you how to use a forty-five. The Captain knows all about the forty-five. There's a place where you can learn all about taking it apart, reassembling it and firing it. He'll give you five clips. That ought to be enough. O'Toole also knows all about your new assignment."

I nodded.

Chapter Twelve

The Germans were ready—and we didn't know it.

Chasing them for the past week had been an easy go. They hadn't stood and fought, but rather, ran. General Degoutte, an old-school soldier who believed in glory over death, assured Pershing and the Americans under his command that the enemy would keep on running, and when we caught them we'd beat them hands down, using only bayonets.

What we didn't know then was that the Germans had quit withdrawing and taken up strong positions on the north bank of the Ourcq River, a shallow tributary of the Marne that ran near the deserted village of Villers-sur-Fère that had been wasted by three years of war. The Ourcq wasn't much of a river when compared to the Hudson. It was eighteen feet across and four feet at its deepest. I chuckled when I heard that the Irish in the regiment called it the O'Rourke. Its north bank rose up gradually. It was covered in wheat fields, tangled underbrush, apple orchards and a farmhouse at the crest of the hill called Meurcy Farm, and beyond, another wasted village called, Sergy. Machine-gun pits, barricaded with sandbags and timbered roofs, had been dug in throughout the hillside and around Meurcy Farm, many hidden in the tall wheat. Minenwerfer pits had also been dug. The minenwerfers were a short-range mortar cannon, deadly at close range. We had no idea how fortified the farm might be or Sergy, but guessed that both were loaded with the enemy. On the far side of the hill, artillery cannons had been set up.

The Germans planned to hold fast at all costs.

For the Sixty-ninth, taking Meurcy Farm, the hilltop and then Sergy meant, for the first time, that we had to charge head-on into a well-fortified foe. We'd find out that defending a river was one thing—crossing it was another.

Assigned to lead our regiment over the Ourcq was Major Donovan's First Battalion, shoulder-to-shoulder with the Alabama boys of the 167th Infantry on our left flank, and Major McKenna's Third—the Shamrock Battalion, he'd nicknamed it—shoulder-to-shoulder with the Ohio boys of the 166th Infantry on our right flank. With the 168th Infantry from Iowa also poised to attack, the Forty-second Division had four regiments in a virtual straight line facing the north bank of the river.

I suddenly thought that when our First and Third Battalions crossed the river together and battled through the wheat fields and orchards there was a good chance the boys would get mixed up and that out there somewhere I'd run into Sheriff Lynch. He was a platoon sergeant in Major McKenna's K Company. That thought troubled me, but I couldn't worry about it much.

Colonel McCoy found an abandoned stone farmhouse hidden in one of the apple orchards just outside Villers-sur-Fère. Looking it over, and seeing how it would give him a commanding view of the Ourcq and its northern slope, he made it his headquarters. Inside the village, Major George Lawrence, our chief surgeon, took over a dozen houses to be used as field hospitals.

With a keen eye for history, and after studying all the battles of the war, Colonel McCoy said to those assembled inside the farmhouse for the last time before the battle—his brigade commanders and staff as well as Father Duffy and our new chaplain, Father Hanley, "Men, when we attack across the river it'll be the first time since the beginning of this war a battle will be fought on open ground—not in the trenches. It'll be a fight of movement and I believe it's to our advantage."

He paused, "Aw, heck," he went on. "As we know, our orders from General Degoutte are to attack without artillery support and to use the bayonet. He keeps telling us the Germans won't stand and fight. They'll run the first chance they get. If that's true, and we catch the Hun by surprise then we'll carry the day. And we will. But if they don't run we'll be put at a slight disadvantage and the bayonet will be pretty much useless. So use your own judgment, gentlemen."

Looking at Father Duffy, I saw a cloud of doubt cross his eyes. Wheat, no matter how tall, and apple trees, no matter how thick the trunks, offered little protection from the Hun machine gun or the Hun mortar shell. I think we all realized that, and I didn't think a single one of our boys would rely on the bayonet.

"Have your men fix their bayonets," the Colonel said, almost with a shrug. "We will attack before dawn tomorrow." He ran his hand across the top of his head. "God bless everyone of you and God bless our troops."

After the meeting, Father Duffy came up to me. "What's with the pistol?"

"The Colonel thinks that if I'm going to be out there helping to carry the wounded, or do whatever you want me to do, then carrying a rifle might be too cumbersome. He thinks a pistol is better."

"You know how to use that thing?" The Chaplain did not look pleased.

"Yes, Sir. Captain O'Toole gave me a few lessons."

Father Duffy's eyebrows went up in astonishment. "Really?" He shot a quick look at the Captain. "Does Tony have a pistol, too?"

"I don't think so. I haven't seen him in a while." I knew he didn't have one. The Colonel had picked me to watch over the Chaplain, not Tony. I prayed I wouldn't have to use it.

Father Duffy shrugged. "Okay then, stay with me." We'd taken a few steps when he said, "I hope you're not lying, and that you really know how to fire that forty-five." He touched the cross on his uniform. "Weapons are not part of my trade."

If the Germans were going to turn and run they didn't show it throughout the night. For every artillery shell the French Sixth Army fired across the Ourcq, they answered with a heavy barrage of their own. The roll of thunder was worse than what I'd heard on the banks of the Suippes River, but we were far enough away from the shells raining endlessly down.

Waiting for the hour just before dawn, Tony and I were finally together again, scrunched inside a foxhole that was far enough back from the Ourcq and relatively safe for the moment. Our stretcher we'd placed in front of the foxhole, offering a little more protection. But not much.

"I feel like I'm Buster Brown and you're my dog, Tige," Tony said in between the roar of the big guns and our flinching each time they went off. "Instead of living in a shoe here, we are in an earthen hole in this god forsaken shaky ground. The only difference between you and Tige is you have a forty-five." It was obvious Tony was jealous that I had a sidearm and he did not.

"If I remind you of Tige in the Funnies," I said, "then you remind me of the Yellow Kid 'cause where you come from is just like Hogan's Alley."

"Hogan's Alley? The West Side?"

"Wherever."

We then laughed. *Kaboom*! And recoiled at the same time. "All this pounding sounds like a ragtime beat. Old Jim Europe. Miss it." *Kaboom*!

Father Duffy was up front in Major Donovan's command post, maybe fifty yards from us. The new chaplain, Father Hanley, was with Major McKenna.

"We're sticking with Father Duffy," I said. "Where he goes we go."

The Forty-second launched its attack at four in the morning. It was supposed to be a surprise, but the Germans knew we were coming. They relentlessly continued their deadly artillery barrage that landed in our midst. The Ohio boys of the 166th stalled. We pressed on toward the banks of the Ourcq as trees crashed down around us.

"We're not going to make it across that damn river!" Tony cried when we jumped out of our foxhole to follow Major Donovan's battalion.

He picked up the stretcher. I needed to have my hands free. A few soldiers in front of us had fallen. Medics were working on them. Thankfully some stretcher-bearers were close by. We ran past them to the river's edge. It was then I heard the first round of machine-gun fire coming from the enemy.

Bullets whined and whistled past us. The wheat bent like in a heavy wind. Trees split apart, the crack of their trunks and limbs like thunder. The screams of the boys, some in anger, others in excruciating pain, rose up in front of us. And we hadn't even crossed the river. Now it seemed as if there was no way the Forty-second could get to the other side. The regiments flanking us stopped altogether. The Fighting Sixty-ninth, as if in Civil War days of old, plunged ahead. Into the river, boiling with exploding mortar shells, we went.

It was a wonder how Tony and I were able to keep up. But we did. Drenched from the waist down, we rolled onto the north embankment, tossing our stretcher in front of us.

"Christ, I'm soaked. Whatta we do now?" Tony yelled over the roar of battle.

"Find Duffy," I yelled back.

We got to our feet, bullets digging up clods of dirt all around us. We dashed ahead. Boys fell on either side of us. How we weren't shot down was a miracle.

"God is my sole savior!" Tony screamed! "I'm not ready to die!"

We kept on.

Then, at last, we caught up with Father Duffy. He was rendering last rites to a dying soldier. One of the Chaplain's hands was on the poor boy's forehead, the other held his hand. I gave them room. When the boy passed, Father Duffy looked around, searching for another wounded lad to comfort.

But how was I to comfort him?

"Over here, Father Duffy!" someone hollered. A medic was

working on a soldier who was sitting up. Blood gushed from his mouth. The front of his tunic was crimson. His eyes were rolled back. Father Duffy rushed to him. I was right behind. I recognized the boy. And so did the Chaplain. It was Corporal Post from E Company, the first soldier from the Sixty-ninth I'd met when I joined up, and the first one we pulled from the Rouge Bouquet cave-in. I could still see him as we hauled him up into the daylight, globs of dirt glued to his face from the tears he'd shed, his mouth open to breathe in fresh air and eyes wide with relief. Now his eyes were rolled back in terror. He had to realize he was dying. I remembered how proud he'd been inside the armory that first day, telling me not to forget he was a soldier in E Company, and that I was the Major's Boy.

"Jimmy, me lad," Father Duffy said to him, his face close to Corporal Post. "You're lookin' like you could use a shot of good old Irish whiskey."

Through all the blood, Corporal Post focused his eyes on Father Duffy. A look of pure love shone from those eyes.

"Father," he said. "Dear Father." His eyes rolled back into his head. "Hear my confession, Father. Hurry."

"Not yet, Jimmy. You got more life in you. We're going to pray first so you can go home and see your mother, Jean, one more time"

"I don't think so, Father."

"Remember when we got you out of Rouge Bouquet? You weren't a goner then. You aren't a goner now. So let's pray."

"Yes, Father."

Father Duffy wiped some blood from Corporal Post's face. "Be with me, Jimmy." Then, keeping the palm of his hand on Corporal Post's cheek, he prayed. "Almighty and Everlasting God, the eternal salvation of those who believe in You, hear us on behalf of Your servants who are sick, for whom we humbly beg the help of your mercy, so that, being restored to health, they may render thanks to you in your Church. Through Christ our Lord. Amen"

Wiping away more blood, Father Duffy moved his hand to Corporal Post's forehead. He made the sign of the cross. "He's gone," he said. It was a moment before he spoke again, his voice choked with sorrow. "He was a good lad, and I couldn't save him. I failed to hear his confession."

"There're so many to save, Father," I said. "So many."

"Yes," he said in a hush that was hard to hear.

Another soldier was calling out his name.

I shadowed Father Duffy, sticking close to him every hunched-over-step of the way. Yet I had to keep leaving him to help Tony carry the wounded back to Major Lawrence's field hospital across the river in Villers-sur-Fère. We weren't gone long, but long enough, I thought, that something bad might happen. Each time I ran back, Father Duffy was busy tending to another one of our boys. He was covered in gore. Blood dripped from his hands. A smile was always on his face, but never showed in his eyes.

It looked like our boys were now closing in on Meurcy Farm. On our right, the Alabama boys, with their Rebel yells, were working their way up the hill, too. It was still a bloody mess all around.

Father Duffy seemed in a daze. Too many wounded and many more dead. Bullets had torn into his tunic, but not one had miraculously touched his body. He never hesitated to move among the boys who cried out to him.

"God bless, you Father," I said and reached out and touched his arm.

Tony and I dropped our stretcher next to a soldier. He looked dead to me.

"We can forget this one," Tony said.

We searched out another wounded to carry back to the field hospital.

"Take this one," Father Duffy pointed out. "He'll make it if you hurry."

We placed the wounded boy on the stretcher, his left arm dangling over the side and, half running, headed for the river, past other fallen soldiers.

Then Tony grunted. "Ooh!" Dropping his end of the stretcher, he plopped down at the river's edge, his hand over his chest. The boy we were carrying rolled into the river. I pulled him out and left him on the bank.

"Ooh!" Tony again moaned. Blood oozed between his fingers. He fell back. "Bucky, I'm dead!"

I jumped to his side and cradled his head in my arms. "No you're not."

"Oh, yes."

"Let me get Father Duffy."

"Too late."

"No it's not!" I scrambled up and went in search of the Chaplain. I was wasting precious time. I had to get Tony to Major Lawrence fast. Back I ran. I tried to lift him by grabbing him under the arms. "The last thing your Momma told me, she said

'You take care of my Anthony.' So I'm taking care of you, Anthony!"

Tony said nothing. He looked at me, a vacant look that I was getting to see a lot of, trailing after the Chaplain. It meant one thing. I slung him over my shoulder and waded into the Ourcq. The heaviness of the water around my waist made it hard to carry Tony. Making it to the bank, I stumbled. Tony fell on the ground. Behind us Father Duffy came charging toward the river. I huddled over my friend.

"We gotta get back and hear old Jim Europe again," I begged. "You know, dance once more with those girls." I clicked my fingers a couple of times to get the beat. "Ragtime."

"Ragtime," Tony sighed.

It was the last thing he said. I whispered in his ear, "Come on, easy now. Easy now," remembering how he'd said the same to the mule and to poor Frankie, both fallen on the roadside during our Valley Forge march. "Come on, Tony. Easy now. Come back to me."

Father Duffy came up to me. Dripping river water, he stooped down and felt Tony's throat. "Through this holy anointing may the Lord in his love and mercy help you with the grace of the Holy Spirit."

"No," I said, tears in my eyes. "It's not fair, Father. Everyone I know is dead." I hugged Tony. "Come on. Easy now. Easy now."

Then I was sobbing, mostly because I was too angry to feel any sorrow.

Father Duffy got up. "Come on Bucky, we've got to get the other boy to the hospital. Let's go." He started back across the river. "Let's go!"

I didn't want to leave Tony. I had to, though. Wiping my eyes, I reluctantly followed the Chaplain, taking one last look at Tony.

When we got to the soldier I'd left on the bank, we flipped him onto the stretcher. He groaned, and tried to lift his head, but it fell back.

"Thank God, he's still alive," Father Duffy said. "Let's go."

Inside the field hospital, a raucous place of surgeons and medics doing their best to save lives, we dumped our boy just inside the front door with others waiting to be tended to. Would he make it, I wondered?

"You stay here, Bucky. I need to get back across the river."

Father Duffy went outside. I was right behind him. "I told you to stay here."

"I can't, Sir. Colonel's orders."

"Well, I'm countermanding his order. You're not to leave this place. Back inside. Make yourself useful."

He turned and sprinted toward the Ourcq and the fighting on the other side. I stood there unsure of what to do. I watched as he splashed across the Ourcq and up the north bank, heading closer to action as it moved doggedly through the wheat field and up the hill to Meurcy Farm.

Make myself useful, he'd demanded.

Colonel McCoy's orders then rang through my head. *I have a big job for you. Just stay with Frank every step of the way. He likes you. I believe he thinks of you as the son he'll never have. If you're with him, helping him, being by his side, having him know you're there at all times, he just might pull through mentally. Can you do it?*

Oh, damn, I said. I then sprinted after my Chaplain.

Chapter Thirteen

What would my Poppa think now? Momma's boy still?

Shoving that thought from my mind—so rattled by what I was seeing, hearing and feeling—I waded into the Ourcq. Around me, bodies bobbed in the water that had turned pinkish from so much blood. More bodies littered the north bank and the hillside. And still more bodies had matted down much of the wheat. Mortar shells continued to hit the ground, exploding and gouging out holes and ripping off limbs of so many.

It was the pitiful groans of the wounded that tormented me the most. Fearing that I might soon join them, I hurried on. The zing of the bullets didn't bother me as much as the thump and whump of the mortar shells and the chunks of earth that showered down. I expected something bad to happen.

Skirting shell holes and hopping over the sorry dead, I pictured myself charging up San Juan Hill alongside my Poppa. Spaniards were up on top firing away, not Germans. Would my Poppa be proud? I finally caught up with Father Duffy halfway to Meurcy Farm. He was on the ground holding the hands of two boys. I heard the words I was getting to know so well. "Through this holy anointing may the Lord in his love and mercy help you, Ted and Doogie, with the grace of the Holy Spirit. May the Lord, Ted and Doogie, who frees you, from sin save you both and raise you both up."

Doogie!

Father Duffy saw my shattered expression. "Doogie died a brave soldier," he said. "I saw him fall. His last words as he charged toward the farm were 'Heaven, Hell or Hoboken by Christmas.' We'll miss him."

As the Chaplain rose, he grabbed my arm. "Now, what are you doing here? I told you to stay on the other side of the river and make yourself useful there." I could see his cheeks wet with tears.

"Following   orders,   Sir."
"Not my orders! Now get back there!"

With bullets flying, we both ducked down.

"I can't, Sir. The Colonel wants me with you at all times. Since he outranks you I'm doing what he's told me to do."

Father Duffy didn't say anything for a long time. He only stared at me, I think in disbelief. "Well then follow me and stay close. My work out here amid this death and destruction is too precious. So the good Lord won't let anything happen to me. But you're another thing."

We went from one wounded soldier to another. The two battalions, First and Third, had intermingled. Even some of the Alabama boys from the 167th Regiment had crossed over into our sector. Father Duffy comforted and blessed all soldiers. I think my presence helped him do the Lord's work—mostly because of the added worry of looking out for me.

And somewhere on the battlefield, Father Hanley was doing the same dangerous thing. Did he have someone like me to be with him at all times?

Meanwhile, the Germans had put up a stout defense. Our boys had stalled.

We were close enough to Major Donovan to hear him bellowing out orders to troops around him. I was surprised to see Sergeant Joyce Kilmer by his side. The two of them kept inching through the wheat as bullets whined overhead. Then Sergeant Kilmer crawled on ahead by himself. Suicidal, I thought.

At the crest of the hill, directly in front of us, a machine gun, barricaded in a bunker, fired endlessly into the midst of our boys.

"Sergeant O'Neill!" the Major yelled, "Take your platoon and shut down that damn machine gun that's got us all pinned down!"

"Yes Sir!" O'Neill stood, signaled his platoon to follow him and raced up the hill. Transfixed, I watched him push through the wheat, alone. His platoon had not followed him. He jumped into the machine-gun bunker like a crazy man, disappearing. He had to have been killed. But then moments later he jumped back out. The machine gun had been silenced. He took a single step, and then a bullet hit him. He fell and started rolling down the hill. German riflemen fired at him at will. He must have been hit a dozen times.

"Let's get over there," Father Duffy said.

Sergeant O'Neill had stopped his free fall when we got to him. His wounds looked desperate. "Let's carry him back."

We got him on to the stretcher, lifted him up and sprinted toward a dressing station close by.

Because Sergeant O'Neill had shut down the machine-gunners, Major Donovan's battalion once again moved up toward Meurcy Farm. Leaving Sergeant O'Neill in the good hands of the medics, Father Duffy and I followed.

Over the crest of the hill, a half-dozen Germans with their strange spiked helmets on top appeared out of the heavy haze of gun smoke. Their hands were over their heads, holding their rifles with bayonets so we could see them. They shouted "Kamerad! Kamerad!"

"They're surrendering," Father Duffy said as they came down toward us. "Good sign."

"What do we do?" I asked.

"Our boys will round them up. I'm praying more of them will give up. End this damned thing."

It was freaky seeing them in the midst of a fight walking right up to us, arms raised, yelling "Kamerad!"

"Shoot 'em!" one of our boys screamed. "Don't let the bastards live. They'll kill us sure!"

"Don't!" Father Duffy was up in a flash, coming between the Germans and our boys. "We're Christians! God's on our side!"

The Germans continued to yell, "Kamerad!" Bayoneted rifles still over their heads.

Our boys motioned for the Germans to drop their weapons. They did, tossing their rifles in front of them, barrels and bayonets pointed toward us. As they stood behind their weapons, our boys seemed to relax.

Now what?

The Germans saw our boys waver. In a flash, they dropped to the ground, scooped up their rifles and swung them to their shoulders. Before we could react, they took aim at us. Our boys got to the ground just as quickly.

Father Duffy was in the midst of them all. Without another thought, I dove into the Chaplain. I had to. We crashed to the ground, the clash of rifle fire so close to us. One of the Huns sprang to his feet and charged, his bayonet pointed our way. None of our boys shot him. They were too engaged in the intense firefight with his treacherous comrades.

Again, there was no time to think. I unsnapped the flap to my holster and yanked out the .45. The Hun was so close I could hear him panting and see the wildness in his eyes. My sister Anna's words came back to me a rush, "I don't think you could ever shoot a German." I prayed. Had I slid a bullet into the pistol's chamber?

"Oh, Father," I cried, shaking and trying to take aim at the enemy, his bayonet thrust a foot away from us. "I'm so sorry."

I pulled the trigger!

The report of the .45 jarred me and rang like a cannon in my ears. My arm, unsteady as it was, flew up. My finger remained on the trigger and I fired off another round, the bullet sailing away. But even with my ears constantly ringing, I heard the first bullet smash into the Hun, heard him grunt and then, in a perfect New York dialect, "Christ, he got me!"

The impact of the bullet stopped him inches away from Father Duffy, the bayonet practically at the Chaplain's throat. The Hun fell backward. He tried to get up. I fired a third shot directly into his head. The bone covering his forehead splintered like broken glass. Instead of scattering outward, it stabbed into his brain. Blood splattered like paint down his face and onto his tunic. His body convulsively twitched. I watched, trembling in horror, until the body stopped twitching. I still had my .45 pointed at him, even though I knew he was dead.

Father Duffy and I were struck dumb, neither one of us wanting to utter a word.

Next to us the firefight was over, although the rest of the hillside was still ablaze with soldiers battling each other in the wheat and orchard. All the Germans in front of us were either dead or dying. Only one of our boys got hit. He was sitting up and seemed to be fine.

"Those dirty, sneaky bastards! Those low-down, Goddamn Bosche!" he yelled, holding his arm. "We showed 'em, didn't we boys?"

Finally, Father Duffy got up and, although visibly shaking, went over to the soldier. "Are you all right, son?"

"Yes, Father. Just a nick." He rubbed his arm. "What a low-down trick."

Father Duffy nodded.

The soldier looked at him. "Are you okay, Father?"

"It was close," he replied. "But, yes, I'm okay." He then turned back toward me.

Like him, I was shaking. He came back and knelt on his haunches. He took my chin in his quivering hands and looked me square in the eye. For a moment he said nothing. His eyes then welled up. Finally, "You and I didn't sign up to kill people, but this is war and the business of war is to kill. Whether we want to or not."

"I killed him," I said. My eyes filled up, too.

He stroked my cheek. "You're so young, but God will watch over you and you will come through."

We were quiet again, just our eyes, maybe, looking into each other's souls. He then wiped away my tears.

"I think I told you I was out on Montauk Point back in '98 when the Rough Riders came home from Cuba," he said. "It was my first time among the wounded and sick. I was barely twenty-eight and had been a priest for only a year. I remember some of the Rough Riders talking about your father and how he'd saved Colonel Roosevelt and took a bullet in the leg. I never told you this, but I saw him there and prayed for him, and he was receptive to my prayers. It was a nasty wound and I wondered then if he'd ever walk again. He thanked me. Yet it was the sick that were carried off the ship that hurt me more. The soldiers burning up with Yellow Fever and dying the second they hit American soil, so far from the battle they'd just fought and won. For them, it wasn't supposed to end that way. They'd fought and lived through it and believed in their hearts that they'd survived and were now home, heroes to their nation and family. But the fever got them in the end. Not a Spaniard's bullet. A dirty trick."

He had stopped shaking, and so had I while listening to his story. My Poppa receptive to a prayer? And from Father Duffy—of all priests.

"Back to comforting the living," he said. He slapped me on the shoulder. "Let's go."

And go we did.

At last, the Fighting Irish, anyway, what was left of them, broke into Meurcy Farm and drove out the Hun.

I didn't get to see it.

And neither did Joyce Kilmer, the author of my Momma's favorite poem, "Trees." He'd made it to the crest of the hill and was crawling over it when a bullet struck him dead. I had to bring his body back to the edge of the Ourcq and leave it there. He was later buried on the banks of the river.

I went back up, dodging my way once again over and through the carnage. I had a hard time finding Father Duffy. Then I spotted him entering the courtyard of Meurcy Farm with our boys. They slipped in cautiously, bent over, their rifles at the ready. Racing up the hill to catch up to the Chaplain, I'd thrown all care to the wind. I felt like Father Duffy—God would watch over me. But he hadn't watched over Calliope's brother, Schuyler, buried at Rouge Bouquet. Or Tony, shot through the chest. Or Doogie shot dead, too. Poor Frankie Bean blown to bits, only his booted feet ever found. And now Joyce Kilmer had fallen. Where was God then?

I never felt the bullets that got me.

The first, ironically, struck me just above the knee, most likely saving my life. The impact, while knocking me sideways, also spun me around. The second bullet slammed into the back of my shoulder, broke my collarbone and came out in gush of blood. If I'd been still facing up the hill, the second bullet certainly would've punctured my heart. Instead, it sent me into a somersault—almost like I'd done a double twist off a diving board. Instead of water, I slammed head first into the hard, chalky French soil. The landing opened a gash on my forehead, but worse, broke my nose. It was the first thing I felt. The crunch of my nose. Then I hurt all over—a pain so intense I fainted.

I might have bled to death if I'd been left out on the battlefield. But someone had seen me fall. He'd come running down the hill in a shower of bullets, I was told. He fell to his knees when he got to me. A bullet had grazed his cheek. Using the strap to his rifle, he tied a tourniquet above my knee, cutting off the blood flow. He pulled me into a sitting position and then wrestled me onto his shoulder. My head banged against his back. The first steps were shaky going downhill until he got his balance. Then he was running fast. Faster. Almost stumbling. Almost losing his balance.

That's when I came to. As my eyes opened and focused, I saw a swathe of blood on the soldier's back. My blood. He'd sensed I'd come to.

"Hold on, Riley!" he sang out, breathing hard.

The voice! I knew it. It wasn't Father Duffy. Then who?

"Almost there! Another twenty-five yards!"

Seconds later, at a dressing station, I was rolled off his shoulder onto a stretcher. A medic began to tend to my shoulder wound. Because of the medic, I couldn't see who'd brought me down off the hill. Then he reached down and took my hand.

"Let bygones be bygones, Riley," he said.

I jerked.

"Easy," ordered the medic.

I nodded. Not at the medic, but the soldier who'd just saved my life. The soldier smiled, showing off a tarnished gold tooth. My Lord, it was Sheriff Roscoe Lynch and the gold tooth had replaced the one I'd knocked out months before on the sidewalks of New York. I tried to smile back.

"Been keeping an eye on you ever since I saw you following that priest," he said. "Well, gotta go now and kill some more Germans." He flashed another golden-toothed smile and then was gone, back into the fight.

Chapter Fourteen

The stretcher-bearers lugged me back across the Ourcq to Major Lawrence's field hospital. It seemed like hours before I was carried inside and placed on a table and worked on. It was all a blur. A fuzzy blur—everything was out of focus, cloudy's more like it. Then, sinking into this dark haze, I could feel I was on the move again, carted out and strapped inside an ambulance with other soldiers, some worse off than me. I felt the Tin Lizzie bounce along the road. I don't remember anything after a mile or so. I'm sure I'd passed out. When I opened my eyes again and the haze began to slip away, I was in for a surprise. I was on a cot in Base Hospital One.

"How're you feeling, Bucky? You've been out for a bit. Lost a lot of blood. The leg looks like you won't be up and about for some time."

I looked into the blue eyes of Nurse Louisa Kelley. Her brown hair was still up in a bun and a touch of rouge still on her checks. I wanted to say, "Hi," but all I could do was smile.

She smiled back, the smile, I guess, only a nurse can give—a smile that seemed to say everything will turn out all right. "You don't need to say anything. I know how you're feeling. It's all in your eyes." She fussed over me. As she turned to leave, she said, "I need to tend to others. An awful lot of the wounded are coming in from the fight all along the Ourcq River. But I'll keep special watch over you."

I closed my eyes and for some eerie reason I saw in my mind Sheriff Lynch's tarnished tooth like a gold nugget in need of polishing. It would stand out better against his other teeth, all yellow, if it'd been buffed up. *Let bygones be bygones.* I laughed thinking about it. A pain racked my shattered collarbone. I couldn't help it. I cried out.

Nurse Kelley was by my side in an instant. She put her soft finger against my lips. "No laughing," she said. "You're to keep still." She leaned close to my ear. "I know you've been wounded in the leg, too," she whispered. "The boy next to you, in the other cot, was also wounded in the leg, almost in the same spot. Yesterday, the doctor had to take the leg off just above the knee. You're going to keep your leg, Bucky, so be grateful."

She was gone this time for an hour or so. Then she was back. "I need to clean your wounds and change your bandages. It might sting for a little bit." As she carefully removed the bandages, she continued to talk, mostly to distract me from the sting. "Nothing I can do for your nose. It looks more crooked than the last time I saw you. Actually it makes you quite handsome."

Handsome?

She saw the odd expression that I showed.

"Yes, handsome. And by the way, I found this in your breast pocket." She held up Calliope's hanky. During all the hellfire, I'd forgotten I'd put it there. "Belongs to your girlfriend, I bet."

I smiled and saw Calliope's beguiling smile and heard her words, "No hanky-panky, Bucky."

"Here, let me tie it around your forehead." She tied Calliope's hanky firmly around my head. "There you go. What is her name?"

"Calliope Van Pelt," I said.

"I bet you miss her."

She didn't say another word until she was done, and I'd gotten clean bandages. The hanky was a joy around my head. Then Nurse

Louisa surprised me. "I've news for you, Bucky. Tomorrow you're going by hospital train to Paris." She saw my surprise. "To the American Hospital in the suburb of Neuilly. The hospital's been around since the beginning of the war. It was started by the Vanderbilts. Very modern. That's where I wanted to be assigned when I volunteered to be a nurse. But now I like being close to the front lines. Our care here is more urgent."

Finally I spoke, "Why Paris?"

"Shhh. Special orders just for you. I've been told a priest made the request."

"How'd did Father Duffy make that request so fast?"

"Shhh, I said. Yes, Father Duffy. He said to tell you that he was doing well and if he got the chance he'd come to visit you in Paris and thank you for saving his life. Well, Bucky, you've been here for three days. Passed out most of the time. The battle's over and the Germans are back on the run." There's talk the war will be over soon. They say one more push is all we need."

I hated to go, hated to say good-bye to Nurse Louisa and the special way she'd taken care of me. Of course, I knew she did that to all the wounded—caring for them in a way that gave them all hope. She kissed me on the cheek and then sent me on my way with that smile I'd always remember. I bet every soldier under her care hated to say good-bye.

The ride to Paris in a Tin Lizzie, no hospital train for me, rattling along the road, was never ending. *It soon startled me that the road was a long, dirt highway in Vermont. I'd been on it numerous times— from Montpelier to Burlington—that followed close to the banks of the Winooski River and was always flooded and filled with tire ruts. It sure wasn't the road to Paris. I discovered I was propped up in the front seat next to the driver. It wasn't Charlie FitzPatrick. It was my Poppa!*

"We'll turn down here and take this road," Poppa said. "It's a faster way home."

The road turned out to be a dead end at the banks of the river. We had to turn around and get back on the main road.

"Up ahead, there's a shorter way. Your Momma hasn't slept in the year you've been away. She's been pacing the floor every night in her night gown worried if she'd ever see you again. Your sisters worry, too."

Off the main road we went again, down into a gulley with no way out. Another turn-a-round.

"Damn! Damn! Damn! I'll get you home!"

We bounced back on to the main road. The ruts got deeper. It was like dropping down into a gulley that rose above the big old Cadillac Poppa's was driving, not the Model T ambulance that we'd started in. It was the same Cadillac that Colonel McCoy drove from battleground to battleground. We couldn't see over the top of the gulley. It bent over the Cadillac like it wanted to gobble us up. Poppa backed up in a hurry and got out of the menacing gulley that wanted to keep us from home. He steered the Cadillac into a farmer's field, past cows and a few horses.

"There," he said.

The herd of cows doubled, then tripled and then were all around us so we couldn't move. Poppa hobbled out the Cadillac, slamming the door. He grabbed his hat, and if it wasn't identical to the hat Colonel Roosevelt wore on his famous charge up San Juan Hill. Poppa limped among the cows, yelling and waving the hat in the air.

"Git, you sorry sons of bitches!"

The cows just looked at him. He swatted a few on their rumps. That got them going. He swung back into the Cadillac and drove back out onto the main road.

"Now I'll get you home to Momma."

The road abruptly ended. There was nowhere to go. Waving us to slow down and stop was my dear sister Louisa and the German I'd shot in the head, his face still a bloody mess. I squeezed my eyes shut, forcing out a tear.

"Damn, I will get you home!" Poppa said.

The American Hospital in Neuilly was in a building of brick and stone, built around a courtyard filled with ambulances. The rooms were large because the hospital had originally been built as a school before our country took it over. All the rooms were large and well lit. I found out there were even dormitories for the nurses as well as dining rooms for the great staff of doctors, nurses, orderlies and ambulance drivers.

My first day there, after I'd been roused from a dark sleep, I was rolled into a room that overlooked the courtyard. I think I shared the room with fifty wounded soldiers, at least. It surprised me that they weren't all Americans, but French, British, Australian, Moroccan and even German. There was no turning away any of the wounded, no matter what side they'd fought for. A life was still a life and it had to be saved.

My first afternoon there an orderly came to my bed. He was holding an envelope. "Private First Class Riley," he read from the address on the envelope. "A well-traveled letter, from Oyster Bay, New York, to Forty-second Division headquarters to the One-Hundred-Sixty-Fifth Infantry Headquarters Company to here. It took more than a month. Kinda crumpled." He handed me the envelope.

At long last, a letter from Calliope.

Sagamore Hill, August 22, 1918

My Beloved Bucky:

Schuyler's death is such a sad blow to everyone, my mother especially. When she got word she came directly here to see me and comfort me, but, I suspect, mostly to comfort herself. She has no other family, but me. The Roosevelts, even in their own grief with the loss of Quentin, welcomed her. She wants to come to France to where Schuyler's buried, to bless that hallowed place. But she has to wait until the war is over, whenever that will be. I will come with her. And so will Father. We will all be together for the first time in years. I'm afraid I don't know how that will all work out. There's still too many bad feelings in our family.

How is your friend, Tony? I bet his mother's so proud of him. I can't wait to meet him when the 69th comes home, if it ever does.

I have not heard from you in some time, and I've been negligent in my letter writing, too. So sorry. I miss you. Oh, how I miss you! WRITE!

Love you to pieces, Calliope

I held the letter over my heart. And, oh, how I missed her, too.

I had to write back right away. What was I to say, though? And how was I to write? My wound had knocked my writing hand out of action. It would be impossible for me to put pencil to paper. When a nurse in her Red Cross uniform walked past me, I called out, "Ma'am!"

"Yes, soldier?"

When she stopped by my bed, at first I didn't think she had the loving tenderness of Nurse Louisa. She was pretty enough with black hair, up in a bun like all nurses. "I need to write a letter, but I can't," I said.

She sat on the edge of my bed. "I'll write it for you. Tell me what you want to say, and I'll put it down. Is that fine with you? I've taken dictation hundreds of times since I've been here."

I nodded.

"Good. I'll go get some writing material."

When she returned she again sat on the edge of the bed. "My name's Andrea. Everyone here calls me Nurse Andy. I'm from Boston. And you're from?"

"Vermont."

"Oh, I love Vermont in the fall."

I didn't want to chat. In my head, I was trying to compose a letter to Calliope, with words I'd now have to share with Nurse Andy, and maybe she'd share with some of the other nurses. I wasn't keen on that. I needed to write to Momma, too, and my sisters. I had no idea where my Poppa was. Off on some battlefield, pursuing a story that'd keep his name on the front page of the *Sentinel*.

"Shall we start?" Nurse Andy asked, pencil poised above a sheet of YMCA paper.

I suddenly didn't know what to say in front of Nurse Andy. If I had her put down what I really wanted to say to Calliope, well, I'd be embarrassed.

"Dear Calliope," I said. Not my dearest. Just dear. It felt hollow.

"Is Calliope your girlfriend?"

I nodded.

"Now, is that bandana around your head hers?

I nodded again.

She touched the hanky in a very tender way. "Well, I'm writing down 'My Dearest Calliope.' Is that okay with you?"

I nodded again.

"That's how I wrote to my boyfriend when he was back in Boston before he was drafted. 'My Dearest Johnny'."

I felt a bit more comfortable.

"He was a first lieutenant in the Yankee Division."

I was now uncomfortable again with her use of the past tense. "My Dearest Calliope," I dictated. "I miss you like heck." *Colonel McCoy's preferred expletive.* I looked at Nurse Andy as she wrote down my words. "What happened to Johnny?" My question caught her off guard.

"Johnny," she sighed. "Let's get back to Calliope." She repeated my words. "I miss you like heck." She stood. "Please excuse me." She left the pen and paper on my bed and walked away, her back to me. But I could see she was crying. She left the room. She was gone for maybe five minutes. When she came back and sat back down on my bed her eyes were bloodshot from the tears she'd wiped away.

"Johnny was wounded leading his platoon across the Marne River," she said. "He died at Base Hospital One. I wish I'd have been there to take care of my Johnny. Such a sweet boy. Now let's continue." She picked the pen and paper.' "I miss you like heck . . ."

"Yes, I do miss her like heck. We met on a canal in upstate New York. She was running away from her Poppa. We fell in love. I don't want to tell her what I've been through over here. I don't want anybody to know. I just want to see her again, her red hair and freckles and that stubborn, stout personality of hers that keeps her strong."

"I can tell you're not ready to write to her. Not just yet. I'll be back."

I knew then I'd always have Calliope.

When Nurse Andy had left, almost on a cue I heard music coming from out in the courtyard and I recognized it right away. Ragtime jazz! The same ragtime jazz I'd first heard up in Harlem that night with Tony. The music brought a sadness that swept over me. Calliope's letter had much to do with it, too. The sadness.

"Nurse Andy!" I cried out before she'd gotten too far away.

She hurried back to my bed. "Yes?"

"Please, can you get me over to the window? I want to see the band out there."

"Of course. I'll get a wheelchair."

Other soldiers, mostly those who could walk, were already looking out the windows. They made room for me. One was bobbing his head the way Tony had done so often. *Tony. That night up in Harlem.*

"That's the Three-Sixty-ninth," Nurse Andy told me.

"I know," I said, looking down at Jim Reese Europe and his regimental band that I'd last seen at Camp Mills when the regiment was then the 15th New York.

"They come here every afternoon about this time and play for an hour or so. Keep everyone's spirits up. Even my own. I understand they've been in combat. The band."

I was surprised.

"Yeah," cut in a soldier next to me. A thick bandage was wrapped around his head, covering one eye. The other eye was clear and he was able to look down onto the courtyard. I almost felt embarrassed to have my forehead wrapped in a loving hanky, not a bandage. His hands were wrapped in bandages, too. "Check out their instruments. That tuba player. See the dents in it? From bullets no less."

Nurse Andy and I looked. Sure enough, it seemed like a number of the instruments had been struck by bullets—or something. Jim Europe led the band, his back turned from us. I could see in my mind the time we stood together back at Camp Mills after the run-in with the Alabama boys. Here we were together again, well, sort of, in Paris, far from New York.

"I've met him," I said. "Jim Reese Europe."

The soldier gave me a startled one-eyed look as Nurse Andy left to go back to helping other soldiers. "You're kiddin'?"

Before I could answer I felt a hand on my good shoulder. "Bucky!"

It was a voice I knew so well. Turning around and looking up, I saw my Poppa standing there, holding on to his gold-knobbed cane.

"How's my boy?" he said.

"Poppa!"

"Your Chaplain got word to me that you'd be here," he said, his hand still on my good shoulder. "Good thing I'm in between assignments or I might have been somewhere chasing down a story. Your division's off to St. Mihiel. Did yeoman's work on the Ourcq, I'm told." He took his hand away. "Your fighting days are over, Bucky. Now you can come home. And me, too."

His eyes were as they always were. Dark and steady. Worldly wise. Always looking about to see what was going on, what he might be missing, might be something he ought to be part of. Even now. He couldn't keep them on me.

"Great band out there," he said, tapping his cane on the window. "Buck up the troops."

"Poppa, did you ever lose a friend in battle?" I had to ask.

"Huh?"

"Did a friend of yours ever get himself killed?"

"Yes, of course," he said. He tried to smile, his mind probably going back to his days as a Rough Rider. "Your name sake. The nickname I gave you—Bucky O'Neill, the cowboy from Arizona. He was my friend before we rode with Teddy Roosevelt. We were out in the west when I was reporting for the old *Kansas City Times,* chasing Geronimo. We shared some hard times drinking lousy coffee, sleeping on hard ground under starry skies and shaking off scorpions. Never a compliant."

"How'd he die, Poppa?"

"Why, son?"

"I need to know."

"Well, before we charged up the hill, he stood up, shook a fist at the Spaniards and hollered there wasn't an enemy bullet that could kill him. On cue, a bullet smashed into his forehead and down old Bucky went."

"What did you do, Poppa?"

"What did I do? There was nothing I could do. We'd already lost Ham Fish in the jungle and then Bucky." Poppa's face softened and then he ran a finger across his eyes. "So I wept," he said. "I guess that was all I could do."

I'd never seen Poppa seem so sad. "Did you ever kill someone?" I had to know that, too.

He blinked and this time he looked me squarely in the eye and held that look. He had to be searching my soul, his look so strong.

"No, son. I never fired a shot running up San Juan Hill. You know my claim to fame was doing something almost as insane as Bucky O'Neill daring the Spaniards to shoot him. Jumping on Teddy's horse, Little Texas, the only horse there, and putting myself between him and the enemy lined up on the ridge of the hill. Teddy was pissed, I can tell you that. Then I got shot and that changed everything. His life. My life. But you already know that. No, Bucky, I never killed anyone."

"Oh, Poppa. I saw a lot of the boys die. So many. My best friend, Poppa. I promised his Momma I'd take care of him, but I didn't. Oh, I tried, but I couldn't"

Poppa's eyes had not left mine.

"I killed a man, Poppa." I shut my eyes and saw the German's body twitching, blood gushing from the bullet I'd fired into his brain. "He spoke English like an American."

Poppa turned away. He looked out the window at Jim Europe and his band. Ragtime music. For the first time I felt close to him. I even felt his equal.

Then, leaning close, he kissed me and, in a cracked voice, said, "Poppa's boy!"

THE END

About the Author

Stephen L. Harris is the author of the award-winning trilogy about New York City's National Guard regiments in World War One, including *Duffy's War*, named by the World War One Historical Association as one of the best books ever written about America's participation in the war. The other books in the trilogy are *Duty, Honor, Privilege* and *Harlem's Hell Fighters*, praised by documentary film producer Ken Burns. He also wrote *Rock of the Marne: The American Soldiers Who Turned the Tide Against the Kaiser in World War I*. His latest book, *No Excuses*, is a young adult novel inspired by his son, Mark.

Steve served in the US Army from 1966 through 1968. After his service, he edited the *Pilot*, a weekly newspaper in Redding, Connecticut; was a political reporter for the Burlington (Vermont) *Free Press*; the first morning news anchor for Burlington's WCAX-TV Channel 3; and then communications director for Champlain College, also in Burlington.

Steve left Champlain in 1979 to edit General Electric's corporate magazine, *Monogram*. In 1996, Steve wrote *100 Golden Olympians* for the U.S. Olympic Committee that honored America's greatest living gold medalists as part of the Modern Olympic Games' 100th anniversary. He was the senior writer on a CD-ROM history of the Olympics, *Olympic Gold*, produced by SEA Multimedia of Tel Aviv, Israel. *Olympic Gold* won the 1996 Cannes Film Festival's "Oscar," the Gold Milia d'Or, for world's best reference title. He also edited the *Journal of Olympic History*, the official publication of the International Society of Olympic Historians. The Society awarded its prestigious 2016 Vikelas Plaque to Steve for his many contributions to Olympic history.

Steve lives in Middlebury, Vermont, with his wife, Sue.